A BIG
ENOUGH
LIE

A BIG ENOUGH LIE

A Novel

Eric Bennett

TRIQUARTERLY BOOKS
NORTHWESTERN UNIVERSITY PRESS
EVANSTON, ILLINOIS

TriQuarterly Books
Northwestern University Press
www.nupress.northwestern.edu

Printed in the United States of America

10 9 8 7 6 5 4 3 2 1

Library of Congress Cataloging-in-Publication Data

Bennett, Eric, 1975– author.
  A big enough lie : a novel / Eric Bennett.
      pages cm
      ISBN 978-0-8101-3121-7 (pbk. : alk. paper) — ISBN 978-0-8101-3122-4
  (ebook)
      1. Truthfulness and falsehood—Fiction. 2. Iraq War, 2003–2011—Personal
  narratives, American—Fiction. I. Title.
      PS3602.E4686B54 2015
      813'.6—dc23
                                                                    2015006071

For A.

I thought about Tolstoy and about what a great advantage an experience of war was to a writer. It was one of the major subjects and certainly one of the hardest to write truly of, and those writers who had not seen it were always very jealous and tried to make it seem unimportant, or abnormal, or a disease as a subject, while, really, it was just something quite irreplaceable that they had missed.

—ERNEST HEMINGWAY, *GREEN HILLS OF AFRICA*

mundus vult decipi ergo decipiatur
—PETRONIUS

A BIG
ENOUGH
LIE

THE WINNIE WILSON SHOW

Rocking and sweating on secondhand crutches, John Townley could almost say to himself that the long, strange game was over, could almost admit that his defeat would arrive this afternoon as the final entertainment for eight million people who only half-cared anyway, if half. But from way back he had a talent for wagering against the obvious. Since childhood he had hoped and in fact dreamed against it. Six months ago the credulous public reception of his memoir convinced him that its unconventional truth could live forever, or, if not forever, then at least until it faded as every media sensation faded. It would become increasingly harmless, decreasingly recalled, eventually obliterated, finally inert, gone for good, until some trend of nostalgia revived it as a throwback to everybody's college years, those good old days of 2007. But what he envisioned now, in lieu of exposure, who knew? This was his second appearance on the *Winnie Wilson Show*. Even in the depths of denial, he sensed it would be his last.

By the laws of his body he might have thrown the crutches to the floor, but by the laws of his mind there was no way in hell, they were part of him. He could as soon have flown away as departed on healthy legs. His perfectly healthy legs had grown weak with the injuries he'd faked since long before the words had been pressed to handsome pages and wrapped in jackets of gold. Rocking, willing the future away, he studied the cheap stuff of the greenroom floor. It had been scuffed last time, too. He remembered it all from before, from the filming of that episode six months ago when praise for *Petting the Burning Dog* showered down from Winnie Wilson like a cascade of rose petals. He had ascended to the ranks of a world of imperial bogusness.

Before you appear on TV, TV is a glistening utopia, the skin of its stars glowing in tan defiance of blemish and anemia, its armchairs and sofas filling each set as props of godly comfort. Seraphim themselves iron the shirts of the hosts and anchors. No longer a schoolyard liability, eyeglasses are an empyrean ornament. Yet here, twenty yards from the soundstage, an arm's length from America, dinginess and flimsiness pressed hard on John's mind. The lightest breeze of reckoning would knock it all down for good.

Even his own face was not what it would look like in the eye of the camera. A makeup artist, whose clothing and lisp drifted on the high waters of stereotype, had made him up incredibly. In the greenroom mirror he caught sight of a beast, a lion, a monster from a school play. His eyes were dark, his skin garish. He was fat and hairy, having let the buzz cut grow in and a beard grow out, having gorged for weeks on donuts and freedom fries in order to become unrecognizable even to those who loved him, and there were no longer so many who loved him. The ones he most wanted to love him did not.

Emily White did not love him. Heather Kloppenberg did not love him. His parents: who knew? But even as an unloved monster from a school play he would look angelic on the screen. The tapes of the first interview, from six months ago, astonished him, and he had watched them endlessly on a shuddering VCR, basking in the praise from Winnie Wilson and in his own telegenic splendor.

He was not stupid. She would invite him back only to bust him, to bring him down. Even in the depths of denial, he knew it. All that remained was to discover who had come forward—who had called the hoax. But "hoax" sounded wrong to him. He could not have done what he did as a hoax. He was about to be shamed for the truest gesture of his life.

In the mirror on the wall he watched himself rock. On television you wore clothing you never wore in life. The producers made suggestions. Yesterday an intern named Samantha took him to Nordstrom and cheerfully saved him from his habitual superstitions of dress, his self-sabotage. Six months ago an intern named Charlotte had taken him to Bloomingdale's. The Bloomingdale's outfit hung in the closet in the Florida cabin that he rented as a hideout. It hung there like the baseball uniform of somebody's beloved son tragically struck dead at seventeen. He was twenty-seven, aggressively obese, and shaggy all over.

He had met Winnie Wilson these two times only, six months ago and yesterday. But he did not feel he'd ever met her. He'd watched her all his life as her empire expanded and expanded more, as she changed her hair and her theme song and her themes, as she launched a magazine and gave America its last fleeting interest in books. He felt like he knew her form and her spirit, that she belonged to his experiences in the same way certain teachers did. But yesterday during rehearsal, as she sat across from him, he encountered that second Winnie Wilson, smaller than the first, the actual one, with skin less hermetic, with eyes less perfectly glossy and wise, with an unexpected scent like coriander.

Just as before, during the first rehearsal, she asked him questions he found difficult to answer and kept asking them until the answers improved. She insisted always on a mediated process. Ms. Wilson (said the woman with the clipboard) did not speak to guests off script. "I remember," John said. He was not to address her except in the formal course of rehearsal. So they ran the script four times. Each time he felt more familiar with it and more baffled. Each time Winnie smiled at something other than him as she spoke. The questions were practically the same as before. Between each session they adjourned, she disappeared through a door, and a slab-cheeked, red-skinned man came out, sat in her chair, and spoke to John as if in confidence.

"Winnie loves your answers," he said. "She likes it when you smile when you answer. You've got a great smile. She likes your answers when you really just come out and say it. You've got your point—it's clear you've got your point you want to make—and when you make it Winnie loves it for sure. You don't have to talk around your answer. Everybody's ready to hear what you've got to say for sure. It's there on your tongue for sure. She likes it there for sure."

Throughout the rehearsal Winnie pretended still to believe that John Townley was Henry Fleming. She pretended nothing had changed. But he was being set up, his bones told him, his heart did, his intense brain did. If he averted his gaze from the obvious, it was merely on faith that the worst that could happen was not even bad. The final revelation had been the point all along. The whole thing depended on the whole thing unraveling. He counted on its not lasting, its not lasting would be the final stage of its success. Its failure would be its success. It was complicated, and he could not always keep track of his own arguments. He had gone farther than he meant to go, and the details drifted in and out of focus. He supposed he believed the words on the page were exempt from the codes of morality that would brand them as lies. He had proven something true. Every piece of theater, every costume and pseudonym, affect and fib, each fabrication, even this ugly fat and this hideous hair on his body had proven something. He had reached the point he had dreamed of reaching and waited with a now almost cheerful sense of perplexity for everything to fracture and fall. The only question was who blew the whistle?

He rocked on the crutches and stared at the Styrofoam cups. Seconds counted down to the live take. He fidgeted and rocked. The room smelled like stale coffee. The ruddy man in the suit who coached him yesterday appeared at the threshold, smiled, and gestured for John to come. Artificial cheer. A wire connected his ear to a box on his belt. John followed him down a short hallway to a door beyond which the soundstage glowed like a stadium floor. He stared at the wire connecting the ear to the box. Then the faceless audience was roaring with applause. Winnie Wilson, in her purple pantsuit, had risen but was not clapping.

Before the cameras John felt the frantic frictionlessness of time and the weirdness of his hands and feet. He was distant from himself and just as nervous as six months ago. His substance as a person contracted to nerve endings firing in a strange present. It took work to cross the stage on crutches. The black cables connecting the cameras to the national audience stretched with dark heft between the stage and the studio audience. Was music playing? He felt the chair against his body and remarked to himself on Winnie's petiteness as she sat smiling on the sofa across from him. Then came a silence like the whine of a bulb.

A well-dressed stagehand invisibly took away the crutches. The applause: endless, eternal. The smiling faces beyond the lights: abstract and hostile. He imagined stuttering when he spoke. Sometimes he stuttered. The clothing on his body was new and strange on his skin. He pictured the beast in the mirror on the wall and did not know himself.

"Welcome," Winnie said, the applause dying obediently, cued by lights. "Welcome, welcome back." She did not address him by name. She did not call him Henry Fleming. She turned to the blinking camera and said, "My guest today joined me last November to talk about his book about the war in Iraq, *Petting the Burning Dog.*"

She said book, not memoir. It was a memoir. It was no longer a memoir. John wanted to blurt it out before she did. But she controlled the show like a car in which he was a child passenger. "We have a second guest today," she said to the camera, then turned to John. "Somebody I think you shouldn't be surprised to see here."

Beyond the soundstage a field of women in their forties waited, their husbands sitting next to them and wincing, trying to be good sports. In the anticipatory lull John longed to break the silence and say, "It's only where it began, it's not where it ended, things never end where you thought they would when you were beginning them. Look at the war itself." He wanted to say, "What if there are truths we can absorb only through hypothesis and imagination? What if there are powers of sympathy exercised only by exposure to the untrue?"

He was not here to say these things. The rhetorical questions themselves were hypocritical. He deserved this. He was petty. He had written the memoir out of private passion, out of two private passions, out of three, max. It had nothing to do with a cause. He was a fraud who loved idiotically, who loved with such violent narcissism that sometimes he couldn't breathe. Sometimes he couldn't breathe, and always the objects of his love retreated. His mind was too much for this world. Yet none of this mattered. He was here to ride passively in the car Winnie Wilson drove. He was here to watch the whistle get blown.

But by whom?

Antoine Greep, the one survivor? Stang? Emily? Donald Rumsfeld?

A whining silence like a flashbulb. He swept his gaze across the faces of the audience. The crowd appeared fixed on a spectacle far different from the mere sight of him. He squinted at the wings. Stang or Emily or Rumsfeld would emerge from the darkness. They would point a finger at him and say, "His name is John, and he's a liar."

Even these were only the minor scenarios, imagination's foreplay.

For it would be Heather Kloppenberg—she herself, the woman closest to the hoax—not a hoax—the person who annealed with him in the crucible of sex and conversation, of crippled love, the very premise of the thing. For ten days his imaginings had climaxed in this scenario. It was, frankly, what he wanted. He pictured her emerging from the darkness and pointing the finger and consigning to limbo the rest of the scene as she emerged—obliterating from his mind Winnie Wilson, the audience, the cameras. With a gait deferential to the phantoms of anxiety, which haunted her always, she would patter across the stage. She would enter a field of privacy expanding from John's eyes. The moment would cease to be about television and would be instead about the tragic past and gathering future of their love.

7

Heather Kloppenberg was the girl he'd done it for or perhaps better to say the woman whose presence had caused him to forge on instead of crawl back. She was the lover whose anger, the night she left him, pushed him past the dull flatlands of composition and onward to the abyss of celebrity. She was the person for whom he had turned an abstract idea into two hundred pages impossible to construe in any simple way.

In the fantasy she was all curls, Heather Kloppenberg was always all curls, and her curls would catch the stage lights gorgeously, auburn and loose and luminous. She was all eyes, and the wide, blue beautiful things would drift across the space with unfocused wonder. Above the neckline she would be her old self, her young self, her winsome nervous gorgeous self—but she, like he, would have undergone a transformation at the hands of Samantha in Nordstrom—would be wearing, against her own habits, elegant layers of black. In Arden, Indiana, where they met, she had worn jeans and skirts and T-shirts and sneakers, always sneakers, or cheap sandals, or what she happily called her slutty wedges. Now she would be a stranger in handsome black pumps and a shock to the eyes.

When they had made love long ago it had been always on the pretense that his legs were no good. This would occur to him as the audience roared at this incoming guest. He had lain beneath her as a cripple on a futon in Indiana. Watching her move he would regret for the hundred thousandth time that he had never taken her using the full strength of his legs. They had only ever made imperfect love and would now never make any kind of love at all.

She would not look at him, and when he realized this, he would rise from his chair—crutchless, forgetful, no longer caring, standing on legs officially useless, exposing himself fatally.

"Henry?" Winnie would say, astonished at the sight.

He would die if Heather didn't look at him. He had finished writing the book only by drawing on the anguish she had caused him. She could at least turn to him now and see this on his face. He had published the thing as a letter to her, a cry, a plaint. She had never responded, not until now—and now she would refuse to respond with her eyes, with any glance in his direction. His legs would be shaking beneath him.

Standing on the revelation of healthy legs he would almost yell, "You knew. You knew long ago. And you practically promised. We had a pact of silence. This was practically your idea. I became what you wanted. Isn't this what you wanted?" Breaking the rules, he would bark twice—once over loud applause, once over sudden silence—"You practically promised."

Imperious professional consternation would flash in Winnie's eyes. John had been briefed and lectured and had signed the forms. The audience would wait in a state of shocked curiosity. Heather would stop before she reached the furniture. Without looking at him she would say in a nervous voice barely loud enough to hear, "It was not my idea. It was never my idea."

As clearly as he could picture her entrance, her anger—her curls and eyes and clothing—he could not invent to his satisfaction the words she would speak. They had made love many times and talked long into the night, yet she remained mysterious to him. She had always been opaque to him, incapable of being fully known. Since their last violent night together, since the last day he ever saw her, she had grown into a force in his life, immense and even more inscrutable in imagination than in life.

"Please welcome Antoine Greep," Winnie said.

So it was, in fact, the obvious. From the wings, in reality, appeared the handsome figure known to everybody from CNN and TEX News, the face John had made himself famous by slandering, the man he had never met: tall, handsome, black, winning, aloof. The real Antoine Greep—an avenging angel from the heaven of truth—gazed past Winnie at John. He showed in his eyes, not a look of anger, vindictiveness, or righteous crusade, but the saddest, most disconcerting look of peace.

"Antoine," Winnie said over dying applause, "is this Henry Fleming as you remember him?"

How long did the silence last?

John held onto it, felt it slow and freeze. In the frozen moment he returned to himself, to a long distant old self, to the tedious nobody whom, through hard research and endless revision, he had transformed into this fat, bearded nobody. He had gone further than he ever believed possible. He would go no further now. That, at least, was what he thought. But he was wrong.

"It's Henry Fleming all right," Greep said. "I'd know Hank anywhere, beard or no beard, fat or no fat. Howdy, Hank. How's it been?"

Part One

I.

For two years after college, muddling through in America, far from the army, I tried to write books, fictional ones, wrote pages and pages about cities in little danger of getting blown up and about people the furthest thing from soldiers. I polished those pages and sent them to agents, and nobody would listen, because who was I but some white guy with a pretentious vocabulary and a typical childhood in Massachusetts, somebody neither obnoxiously rich nor heartbreakingly poor, somebody with no boon nor boom nor bane nor bust worth writing about, just tricks with words, like that one. I went to Boston University, did classical studies there, thinking the old myths would give me a good grounding in storytelling, a stupid idea. I graduated in 2000, and after graduation kept the accounts for my dad's construction business based out of Waltham. He was more contemptuous than grateful, because why wasn't I hanging Sheetrock?

I wasn't hanging Sheetrock because I was bookish, a milquetoast in his eyes, not that he ever used that word—"pussy" would have been more in his register—and, in this upside-down world, I joined the army and became a second lieutenant and went to war because I was deficient in this way. War seemed like a cool solution, or at least the obvious one. Henry Fleming, yours truly, was just too cautious and normal otherwise to mess his life up in a newsworthy way. Any writer worth his salt has got to draw close to the flame of chaos, and if he can't do it through his personality, he can do it through the Department of Defense. You'll notice Ernest Hemingway didn't spend his late adolescence hanging out in Kansas.

My enlistment was a strange thing insofar as it looked like bravery. I never demonstrated anything resembling bravery in my day-to-day life. On streets and sidewalks I made way for hotheads, apologized randomly to rude strangers in a hurry, and let myself be honked at. At home I allowed my father's low-grade bullying to soak in like harmless drizzle, unless it secretly got to me on some level, which it probably did. I was brave almost only in the realm of ideas, but there at least I was Genghis Khan.

The attacks of 9/11 made enlisting easier, not because I shared the spirit of all the delusional mavericks vowing revenge, nor because it gave new significance and respectability to serving one's country, but because it crystallized the image I had in my head of coming to matter to history. Go figure. If my father was not won over by the gesture, he at least understood it or thought he did. I have no doubt it baffled him, coming from his milquetoast pussy of a son. Soon enough it would baffle me, too, or really just make me miserable—once the sleep deprivation and push-ups and spittle-flinging screams at Fort Benning began. But in the privacy of my vast imagination, ahead of time in Massachusetts, the solution, as I say, looked cool, or right, or OK.

So that's one version: I enlist because my life is boring, I want to write books, and I have no subject matter. Another version: I enlist because of unresolved issues with my dad. Or I enlist to defy my undiagnosed obsessive-compulsive disorder. Or because the girl I'm sleeping with fills me with such potent, electric, erotic misery that I want to kill myself.

That last one is probably the best. But I don't actually want to kill myself, I just want to do something as drastic as killing myself that I nevertheless get to stick around and watch the consequences of. I enlist because I'm too in lust to be in love, and will die without controlling the love I want to be in. I enlist because Hillary Dollenmaier drives me crazy.

Hillary Dollenmaier was the girl in the back row on the first day of Introduction to Sociology my freshman year at BU, and her eyes never landed on a boy in the classroom. She fixed her gaze on the blackboard with an unflinching gorgeous haughtiness as if she were trying to seduce those statistics in chalk. She did not look otherwise seductive, dressing in opposition to her looks, not outrageously, but taunting them indifferently with blue jeans and a polo shirt. She smoked on the way out of class, admitting a cigarette to her lips as if nothing else could touch them. She was the girl whose hair you noticed first, its auburn fullness—strawberry blondeness, in September—its curls and luster. Once I got to know her she confessed she believed it always looked messed up from sex, which, in the time since then, I've come to learn is a kind of trope among women, but which, at the time, I'd never heard before, so, in my mind, it still belongs to her. She was the girl people took a long time to talk about or dare to approach, so sufficient was the radius of disdain that she radiantly enforced.

My attraction grew from the sense that she knew, despite this radius, that I was there. Somehow I wasn't surprised when two weeks into college an acquaintance, a friend of hers, came up to me and said, "You should talk to Hillary."

I talked to her, and she made clear that she wanted to go on a date. I proposed a date. She accepted. I have a vivid memory of picking out something to wear that night. My favorite shirt, the only one in which I reliably felt comfortable and confident, I had been wearing when I asked her out. Everything else in my closet touched me with disgust. I couldn't look at myself in the mirror. My face seemed too round, and my hair too lank. I was sure that odors beyond my perception drifted from me. With great reluctance I pulled on jeans and a polo shirt.

On our first date we talked about de Sade, whom I pretended I'd read. On our second date we walked by the neighborhood porn shop, and she asked me sweetly whether I ever went in there. I did, and told her so with burning cheeks. She told me she was a poet and loved the poetry of Neil Dubuque and would never in her life read enough true crime to satisfy her so help her God. On our third date she told me that she could tell from the beginning that I was the kind of boy who liked to do bad things. Was I the kind of boy who liked to do bad things? I had never done a bad thing in my life. I said I was.

Hillary was wild in her way, but it was a cautious kind of wild that could not come into being without the presence of a countervailing mildness, and that's what I provided. We were opposites who attracted. Her impulses concealed themselves behind her radius of disdain and depended for their existence on the presumption of their nonexistence. If I had gone looking for them they would not have been there to find. She was never wild with wild boys, felt a deep antipathy toward perfumed jerks preying on freshman girls, hated players, and had decided on me as suitably awestruck, awkward, and humble.

She introduced me to marijuana and taboo acts. She got me to smoke cigarettes and drink more. She enticed me into learning to override my aversion to chaos, which I longed to do. Under her influence I leavened the classics I studied with the culture of the populace—with pop culture. We got on mostly alone: left the college parties early, lounged in our dorm rooms and later our apartments, explored Boston as a pair, had a daily ménage à trois with the glow of the television and a biweekly one with the equally anesthetizing glow of substances.

I knew throughout college that I loved her too much. I feared that her wildness would expand beyond me, and this fear guaranteed a kind of amorous intensity that I could neither give up nor really enjoy. It was not, exactly, that I did not trust her. But she maintained, even in the depths of our intimacy, the illusion—or the truth—that her inner life involved more than I would ever know. She was remote, even in her closeness. She radiated secrecy, secrecy that I always partly but never completely got to share. The remainder, the secrecy that hovered darkly at the edges of our confidence, almost made me lash out. My jealousy sustained the passion it corrupted. But I am not a violent person and was not ever violent.

Version four, of the story of my enlistment, leads back to version three, the obsessive-compulsive one. My jealousy was profoundly related to impulses that long preceded it. From the dawn of memory I harbored a crippling aversion to uncontrolled and imperfect states. In another family I would have been sent in and diagnosed for it, but my father lent credence to gushing blood and scorching thermometers and practically no other index of unwellness. So I was fine. OK. I was fine. But I was only as fine as a little kid who cries when the neighbor makes footprints in the fresh snow in the backyard. My mattress had to be centered on my box springs before I could even entertain the idea of sleep. I had sought out and found every last asymmetry in my body—lymph nodes, testicles, teeth—and regarded each, in panicked succession, as proof of leukemia or scrofula or perdition. Patterns and rituals inoculated life against fatal diseases, uncertainty, and flux—I hoped. I hoped, and hoped, and cried when it snowed. I was nutty.

What in elementary school was meteorological or mechanical or hypochondriacal became in high school social. Virginity, meaning its absence, tormented me worse than the worst skewed mattress or crooked uvula. Later, forcing myself into a kind of feminism, wanting to force myself into it, I would be tormented by the lingering fact that virginity tormented me. At the time, in high school, the torment was unselfconscious and all consuming. When my girlfriend, Daphne Fritz, told me she'd had sex with her first boyfriend, I felt like I'd found a third tonsil on the bottom of my tongue. It had less to do with sexism than with a kind of megalomania so intense that I feared it would kill me. The world should star Henry Fleming and Henry Fleming only. So I dated Hillary Dollenmaier to defy myself, to let go of the mattresses and sidewalk rituals and snow fantasies and to know a woman with a past.

In college it worked, and I thought I was cured, or at least not sick enough to call myself sick any longer. I had outgrown my obsessions and compulsions, broken their fussiness with the hammer of my girlfriend, let loose. But during those four years I underestimated, I now see, the soothing power of the implicit structures: semesters, classes, dorm rooms, class years. The safety of college, its artificiality, freed me up to experiment, to abide disorder. After we graduated, things did not revert immediately, but slowly gave way. By September I was feeling the turbulent pull of the forces that caused my earlier self to cry at trampled snow. It was as though an agoraphobic person had suddenly noticed the walls were gone.

My breakdown took the form of jealousy—the old jealousy amplified into a power that distorted not only my perceptions of the world but the world's perception of me. "You're being ridiculous," Hillary said, at first with laughter, then, after my outbursts had lasted too long, with strained, loving patience, then with intense irritation. "I'm not interested in him," she said of whomever it was that week. "I don't know why he texted me," she said. "Fine," she finally said. "I met him for a drink, but only because you're acting like a psycho."

In January of 2002 I signed my name on the dotted line and headed off to Officer Candidate School at Fort Benning, Georgia, and fourteen weeks later emerged as a second lieutenant in an armored division of the U.S. Army. The gesture dispelled my jealousy like a fever breaking. Suddenly I was free again from clinging with creepy vigilance to the minutest changes in Hillary's movements and inflections. In the short time before I left, our sex felt like it used to, and she couldn't find it in herself to say "no" when I asked her if she wanted to get engaged. Once I was gone she missed me terribly, I truly believe she did, and it felt wonderful. The orderliness of the army felt OK too. It was college in spades. The mattresses were square, the boots shined, the steps regular. If ever order fortified itself against chaos, it was here.

Afghanistan was already up and running that winter, so I thought I knew what I was in for, but of course a year later the drums were booming on the path to Iraq, so Iraq's where I found myself in the spring of 2003.

Until now, the public hasn't known any of this. My name is a household name shrouded in fog. Until now, people have known only where things ended: I went to war and died as the most shadowy member of the Babylon Seven. The tape of my murder was missing, and my body was missing. In this way I differed from J'Million, Duckworth, Schwartz, Eccles, and Frank, all of whom appeared in skittering footage that filled computer screens in American suburbs for countless hours in early summer 2004. I differed, too, from the one soldier everybody knew survived, Antoine Greep.

Beginning in June 2004, after my supposed death, the talking heads talked far and away more about Greep than the rest of us. What they had to say about me was what you have to say about any enigma. He's enigmatic. My mother was long gone, and my siblings nonexistent. My father, dead himself by then—of cardiac arrest at an ice cream stand in the autumn of 2003—could provide nothing. Nobody at Waltham High School or Boston University remembered much about me. "He was quiet," teachers said on news shows; true enough. "He did his work on time, and did it well"; thanks for that. At Fort Benning I had stayed low on everybody's radar: competent, never obtrusive, obedient, sufficient for leadership, bland. Only Hillary Dollenmaier might have filled in the blanks. She was out there and aware, through my letters, of everything except the final moments of my "life." She must have known the truth about Greep. But Hillary let the talking heads talk.

Even the millions of Americans who ignore all but the most explosive headlines will know the name of Antoine Greep, son of the famous American League pitcher Bobby Greep. As the presumed sole survivor of the Babylon Seven, he nodded and smiled and cried throughout the interviews of 2004, putting a face to an ordeal beyond imagining. Through soft words on flashing screens he transformed unwitnessed crimes into a Medal of Honor.

I had enlisted to gather textures for fiction—to place myself in situations where my life took on interest. I had enlisted to come to terms with my father. I had enlisted to rein in disorder. I had enlisted to kill myself without dying, to commit a nonfatal suicide, inspired by the black flood of lust and love and jealous rage. Whichever version you believe, you should know that I had no intention of emerging from the dead to write something like the following. If war teaches you anything, though, it's that fate isn't great at honoring intentions.

For a year in Baghdad we were what we were. Then things started to change in April, and shortly before the transfer Breitbart called me into the FOB, I remember it distinctly, to ride his twin moral hobby horses, Antoine Greep and hardcore porn. Greep and porn formed a package tied with the bow of my failures as an officer, and Breitbart loved ripping the wrapping off. That afternoon he was waiting at the TOC with his hands on his hips, and I had trouble not feeling embarrassed for him. He was my commanding officer, the captain of the company, and an outcast and a freak. War movies echoed in his skull and blasted out his mouth. "WHAT IS THIS?" He clenched pages of magazines and shook them at me. "WHAT IN DOG'S NAME?"

"It's the graphic depiction of sex acts, sir."

"YOU BEING SMART?"

"No, sir."

"YOU A PATENT NITWIT?"

"No sir."

"YOU EVER HEARD OF GENERAL ORDER 1A?"

Every last E1 had heard of General Order 1A, the street urchins of Tikrit had, the washwomen of Fallujah had. It prohibited booze, porn, pets, and looting. But that was officially, because practically speaking it prohibited only booze. Asking an army to kill without jacking off was like asking Catholics to confer without drinking. But Breitbart had a thing about porn that derived from his thing about Jesus. He was a Christian whose contempt for sex surpassed his fear of roadside bombs.

I told him I had heard of General Order 1A. "YOU REMEMBER WHAT I SAID ABOUT IT?"

"You said no exceptions, sir."

"Bitchery and abomination." He lowered his voice for the sake of drama, the pages for the sake of decency. "I can't even look at these."

The stuff was standard issue ridiculousness, positions reserved for the professionals or for a new generation of American teenagers imitating the professionals. He had pulled the pages from the bunks of the tents we used when we weren't at the bunker. "I can't bear to have my fingers on them. I can't stand to have them in my hand."

He walked to a burn barrel and swatted them in. I watched him trudge out and back. In the last hour I had drunk four liters of water and would not piss again until 1500. It was a hundred and ten degrees. But as he returned his forehead seemed to drip only with fury, not even heat. He was past forty and had lived all his adult years in the army. He was slender and bald with white gristly stubble from ear to ear round the back of his skull. Skin hung loose at the tendons in his neck and down from his jaw as if his jaw had once been squarer than it was, as if his face had been pressed narrow and the excess skin never cut away. He squinted for the benefit of a nonexistent audience of millions. "It's Greep. Don't doubt that I know that. You better think hard about continuing to do nothing about that thug. I find one more page of smut in that bunker, it's curtains for both of you."

Curtains? Really?

I thought about that on my drive back. I had come for the mail and left with the mail plus the deafening echo of a cartoon tirade in my head. Camp Triumph, where Breitbart did his barking, filled an island on the Tigris where, until last year, an amusement park had entertained Ba'ath Party members and their children. Three months ago Iraqi mortars knocked the Ferris wheel flat on its side, crushing an E2. I had been there. Concrete cartoon mice, twice as large as men, grinned at the dead soldier.

My platoon slept on the island half the time and at an outpost deep in the hectic terror of the city half the time. I had special dispensation to take mail from the FOB and deliver it to our bunker. In the mailbag today were letters for Eccles, and a package for me from Hillary, the thought of which, even more than Breitbart's echoing tirades, distracted me from the streets I needed to stay focused on.

A specialist named Kirk Frank (later, one of the Babylon Seven) drove the Humvee. Everybody called Kirk Frank "Kirk Frank," both names. It was a good example of a Greepism, a phrase bored into our brains through repetition and charisma. Usually they were longer. *That's when the shit hits the fanny. That's where the buckwheat meets the corn. Bob's your Uncle Remus.*

When we weren't doing mail runs, Kirk Frank was the driver for the tank I commanded. No matter what he drove, he drove it well. He basically didn't talk unless he was telling jokes. The jokes he told were stupid and weird. He transformed corny riddles into spooky utterances. He was mysterious and doggedly quiet. He had froggy eyes, intelligent ones, and limp, dank, dark hair that grew in like seaweed on the hull of a boat. It was always a relief when he got a fresh buzz cut. He took pride in things done with silent competence and was one of my favorites.

"How was Saddam like Little Miss Muffet?"

We were part of a convoy, three up-armor Humvees, one ahead, one behind, and it would have taken four more to dispel the mood of hari-kari. We also should have had a third man between us to watch the overpasses while I scanned the traffic and the storefronts. Abandoned Toyotas, charred and skeletal, lined the streets, the blood of enemies and friends blackening patches of ground every seventy-five yards, the power lines drooping and dangling and crackling and buzzing above the heads of feral children. We passed a modern high-rise with massive concrete flutes dotted with satellite disks like fungi on industrial logs. The shops surrounding lay in ruins. I studied heads in passing cars. Boom. That's what you were always thinking. Boom. At intersections during the last few months the kids had stopped waving and smiling; the men had never waved or smiled. Boom. The shit from Iraqi bodies and the trash from Iraqi kitchens clotted in the street and baked in the dust. On every inhalation the smell rankled near your brain, the stench of something you'd be hard pressed to believe democracy could grow from.

If there was anything good about being in Iraq, which there wasn't, it was that it obliterated my obsessions and compulsions. The pressing specter of profound danger changed my relationship to how my mattress was squared, to how white the snow was. Leukemia no longer haunted my teeth. Virginity became a trifle. Yet perversely the force of the obsessions and compulsions still, even here, shaped itself into the old violent jealousy. After the relief of the heady days of my enlistment, my longing for Hillary had curdled again. It was a funny thing to worry about, her secret world.

"How was Saddam like Little Miss Muffet?" I said.

"Both had Kurds in their way."

I honored the joke with a moment of silence. Then: "Brietbart went apeshit."

"I could hear him," Kirk Frank said. "They could hear him in Iran."

What made it more perverse was that I was with Breitbart regarding the porn. In addition to spreading democracy, the army was papering the Middle East with reams of depravity.

The convoy left us at the bunker gate. Stepping into the bitch of a sun I pulled the duffle with the mail from the backseat as Kirk Frank waited at the wheel for the concertina wire to be dragged clear. Eccles and Schwartz were standing guard, and it's best to introduce them this way, because they went together, like R2-D2 and C-3PO or Rosencrantz and Guildenstern. Eccles and Schwartz had been partners in crime since basic training, or really since birth. They were both named Brent. Two Brents, but two who could not, even in their abject whiteness, have looked less alike. It was a boot camp joke. The sergeant pretended they were indistinguishable, fat Schwartz and skinny Eccles, pushy Schwartz and Eccles the pushover. Schwartz looked like a fat southern cop. He burned bright red and blistered and peeled. His mouth hung open in a default position of brute disgruntlement. I hated him.

"He get something from her?" He nodded at the mailbag.

"What do you care?"

He spit evasively.

"Eccles's mail is Eccles's business," I said.

"He makes it my business. He makes it everybody's business. Hallelujah the day he don't." The hole of Schwartz's mouth disgusted me, the outraged portal in his fat cheeks. Eccles watched like a kicked dog. "Every day something sets him off," Schwartz said. "She's a whore."

"She ain't either," Eccles said.

"Listen to him," Schwartz said to me.

"She's none of your business," I said.

"Tell *him* that," Schwartz said. "He makes it my business."

Eccles stared at the bag. He was tanned like a dream, resembling a tawny Ichabod Crane. His fiancée in Fayetteville, a plump pale partier named Pat Mapp, rivaled Schwartz in corpulence. She wrote Eccles twice a week to break up with him. She squeezed a lot of love and panic and money out of him through semiweekly breakup letters. Schwartz was right that it was annoying. But I hated Schwartz.

"Your letters'll be inside," I told Eccles.

Home sweet home. Concrete walls topped with barbed wire. A u-shaped plot of dust. A cracked bunker. There had once been a gate, but all metal in Baghdad had long since gotten stolen and melted down and recast as mortar shells. The American unit here before us replaced the gate with a coil of concertina wire to be dragged back and forth. Plastic bags fluttered in the blades.

The bunker faced a guardhouse where an Iraqi family lived. By American standards it was too small to kennel a dog in. It housed five Sunnis whom the departing officer vouched for. Around us sprawled a middle-class neighborhood filled with grudging Saddam loyalists who had no real passion for the Ba'ath Party and too many tortured uncles to mind the overthrow but who also knew their Shiite neighbors were waiting for an easy kill. You think Baghdad is a city, but really it's a million little city-states, neighborhoods filled with tribes who hate the other tribes. To stay alive the family in the guardhouse depended on us, a dependence that made me queasy. It drove them to incessant acts of cheerful craven helpfulness. They were always underfoot. The father had a paunch and a moustache and skinny arms he waved at his son as if the son were backing up a trailer instead of dragging concertina wire. Ayad, a boy of eight, trotted back and forth on dirty little legs, wearing army-issue work gloves ten sizes too large for him and keeping the gate.

Ayad and his father were bit players for me in this tragicomedy, the war. Ayad's sister, Shamhat, was something else. Most mornings she sat next to her grandmother in the shade of the house on a green plastic chair. Her dark eyes were gorgeous, her skin buttery and screaming for love. When you studied her for a minute you realized the skin and the eyes and too-short shorts blinded you at first to the mannish features she inherited from her father. I'm not convinced that all the men in the platoon got around to studying her for that long. Shamhat and the grandmother would sit facing our bunker all day, staring and being stared at.

Early in the war some American had given Shamhat a Cabbage Patch Kid, a white-skinned, red-yarn-haired doll. The doll belonged in the arms of an eight-year-old abiding in a land of white people. Shamhat must have been thirteen. Clutching it, holding it to her chest, glowing with joy, Shamhat had hurried over to me one morning and forced me to admire it. I held the doll and studied the girl—not only her brown eyes and buttery skin and crooked mouth and mannish nose but also her movements. The smiling and the fidgeting were childish. The set of her body was womanly. I felt like I suddenly understood rites of passage. You simply could not get by without bat mitzvahs, coming out parties, graduations ceremonies, etc., because children do not cease being children in a blink. The spectral shift is nauseating. I had handed the doll back, and ever after we smiled at each other as if we shared a storied friendship. But we never spoke much. Her brother Ayad, on the other hand, I got plenty of.

"Salaam alaikum," I said to him now.

"Alaikum salaam," he said. "Pen?"

"Not today."

"Mister? Pen today?"

"Not today."

Then he held his fist up for Rock Scissors Paper. Each week we played approximately seven thousand rounds of it. He was always at my heels, and from his father and from other soldiers he was accustomed to far meaner treatment than he got from me. He was cheerful in the face of kindness and equally cheerful in the face of cruelty, so I was never sure why I even bothered. Now, across the courtyard, a tableau distracted me from his hovering fist.

Greep, J'Million, and Duckworth were standing in the shade of the wall. Greep wore an expression of mock solemnity. J'Million was grinning. Duckworth looked morose. It could not be good. I strode over.

"The puppies," Duckworth said to me, almost in tears.

Duckworth was our eldest, ancient by army standards, maybe thirty-five and the lowest ranked and the least intellectual is the merciful way of putting it. A dim bulb. He had bell-pepper ears and a nose the size and shape of a drinker's nose but without the pores and veins. High on his head grew light blond hair rendered basically invisible by the buzz cut, worthy of a baby. His shoulders hung from his frame as a burden. In his size and slowness and sweetness you pictured him mopping floors and humming ditties in an old folks' home. He often looked perplexed and culpable, as if to blame even for catastrophes that lay beyond his comprehension. Was the war itself his fault? it seemed to say. He was a hog farmer who had spilled his coffee on the floor of the Louvre.

"Stop with the puppies already," I said. "We already settled it."

For days now he had been obsessed with dogs we befriended out at a traffic checkpoint. From the moment he laid eyes on them he was worrying about leaving them behind.

"We aren't taking them with us when we go, but we aren't going yet, so don't think about it."

A mantra for this entire ordeal: don't think about it.

The mangy, handsome mother dog kept her litter of puppies in a box in an alley two klicks west. The creatures were the only things for blocks that stood a remote chance of making you smile. Duckworth cupped the puppies in his hands every chance he got. He gazed at them stupidly, tacked Polaroids of them over his cot. Grown dogs in Iraq skimmed through alleys and trash heaps like jackals, like specters from bad dreams, like evil. But not these.

"But it's not . . ." Duckworth glanced at Greep. Greep kept up a steady smirk.

"What did you tell him?" I said.

Greep once convinced Duckworth that Iraqis peed purple, so who knew what was up. The smirk broke to an ingratiating grin. My anger relented. It's hard to resist Greep's smile. You know this yourself if you watch any TV at all. Greep, duh, was smarter and better looking and far more white than the other black guys in the platoon—far more white-acting, whatever that means. He was the least white-looking, though, and the blackness of his skin threw into relief the intensity of his smile. He understood perfectly well the power of the intensity of that smile. It was like the cracking open of a pod of charm. "Just something I heard," Greep said.

"Which was?"

He shrugged. Tears rimmed Duckworth's dumb eyes. Greep was a cat with a bird in its mouth. I turned to J'Million.

"Something about a transfer," J'Million said.

J'Million you also know from TEX News. He was the one whose laughter brought out the strangeness of his face. It looked like his eyes and teeth had been spread wide with a turnkey, like his face had been expanded down the center line. You could imagine him dandling his sister's baby and then going out, finding the motherfucker who owed his cousin money, and shooting him in the face. He was an amazing gunner, was the gunner on Greep's tank, and there wasn't a man in the platoon who didn't like riding with him. He chronically neglected to respect my command.

"Brietbart didn't say anything about a transfer," I said. "I saw him an hour ago."

Deafening silence.

"Which reminds me," I said, anger rising, "burn the darn porn. All of it. Now!"

Smirks.

"You've got half an hour to clean up"—my voice rising—"or the porn hounds will be drinking crotch water." I could hear myself. I sounded like Breitbart. Curtains. Bitchery and Abomination. Porn hounds and crotch water. I hated the sound of myself. "Burn the porn!"

Duckworth made for the bunker, I guessed to root out porn, which he never looked at. Greep and J'Million lingered, going only after making clear to me that they considered my orders forever optional. Then I was alone in the courtyard with Ayad. He had been kicking dirt. He looked up. "Pen?"

"Not today."

He held up a fist.

"One game," I said.

Our fists bounced. Mine became scissors, and his remained a stone.

Practically every significant command in the army comes twice, takes two forms, first as rumor, a beast as winged and strange as its apotheosis in Virgil, flapping through the ranks, stirring confusion, blurring its own form. I won't make a habit of invoking Virgil, but it comes to mind and seems right for this scene, the image of Fama, or Rumor, from the *Aeneid*. She's a weird winged monster with a million feathers with an eye on each one. Things really hadn't changed. E-mail from home alluded to orders you hadn't received, CNN getting ahead of the troops on the ground. Sometimes you half-believed that CENTCOM was in Atlanta and that Nielsen dictated tactics. Today for once I sensed I was hearing the truth in whatever Greep had told Duckworth. Iraqis peed as yellow as anybody, but a transfer hung in the air like a possible storm.

The stairs to the second floor jutted from the outside of the bunker's west wall, throwing blue squares of shadow on the concrete. I ascended, feeling the circular throb of the anger in my patterns of thought. As the commanding officer I used the two rooms upstairs to sleep in and work from. The elevation was dangerous, more exposed to mortar shells and rounds from snipers, but more private, and I traded the safety for the privacy. In a moment I was sitting on my cot in the heat, feeding the fire of my mood on the phrases I had failed to think of in time to yell.

I pulled Hillary's package from the mailbag, so happy something had come. I stroked the brown paper her fingers had taped, then tore it open.

The box held a new video camera.

The one I brought with me a year ago had gotten trashed early on. The note read, "Watch before you tape." I hit power and pressed play and saw Hillary's face for the first time since leave in October. How can any man convey the profundity of the superficial? What I loved most about her was how she looked. Or what I loved most about her was what she contained, was the way her looks fused with what she contained. I could never distinguish the anxious gorgeous electricity of her large blue eyes from her fearsome aversion to rodents from her love of having her nipples sucked from her unshakable observance of old points of etiquette, like sending thank-you notes through the mail. I could never distinguish the mania of her strawberry blonde curls from her depressive taste in indie rock from her erotic consumption of true crime novels. Her mouth was her anger and her love; her hips her patience and ecstasy. You see, it gets maudlin. I ached, just ached, at the sight of her.

She held up a cat.

She hated cats. Since the beginning of our relationship she had hated them; since infancy. Throughout college and after graduation she had savored hating them in my presence, since I loved them. But now she held up a black one, a rescue from a shelter in Pawtucket, Rhode Island, where she was living in an apartment with three women I didn't trust not to bring home eligible womanizers. "I'm not getting soft," she said. "I just thought you'd like him when you got home. I named him Chittenango."

Joy flooded through me. It might have lasted hours, except then the radio crackled. "Formation at 1800, over."

"Thanks for the advance notice, over."

Silence from the FOB.

"This about the extension and transfer, over?" I said.

"No details, over."

"My men seem to have plenty of details, over."

"So ask your men, over."

I returned to the cot and picked up the camera. So it was true. Fuck. I did not want an extended tour. I did not want a transfer. I did not want to spend three more months in fatal conditions with insubordinate subordinates. I did not want to fear for three more months for the lives of the men I loved. I thought of Duckworth's huge hands and Kirk Frank's kelpish hair and corny riddles. I had been counting down the days since the days began. I had been imagining how it would feel to leave, how simple it was, how impossible. It was bad karma to redeploy, we had been in Baghdad from the beginning and had memorized the runs and absorbed the rhythms. We knew the corners we went to, and I had learned some Arabic and used it for the cars we stopped. A lot of the drivers I recognized, and the ones I didn't recognize I had instincts about. I knew when to take precautions and when to let go. We were all bored as hell, tense daily, but you made a faith out of the routine. We had believed we could count down the days in confidence, steadily, superstitiously. A new town meant new runs, rhythms, corners, faces, and necessary instincts.

I left the camera on the cot. In the courtyard Duckworth squatted in the shade playing with pebbles, his huge fingers sifting the dust. He studied me with his watery eyes as I descended. Ten yards away Ayad was whacking the wall with a black fragment of tire. From the chairs in the shade of the guardhouse, Shamhat and her grandmother stared at me, the girl's eyes forming a point of beauty almost monstrous, a single point of beauty, two points, and her thighs too, her thighs unreal. She wore emerald shorts, and the skin of her legs was like flowers blooming in shit. She held the Cabbage Patch Kid on her lap.

"What do Baghdad and Hiroshima have in common?"
    "Remind me," I said.
    "Nothing, yet," Kirk Frank said.

Twenty minutes later half my platoon was standing with two hundred others near the FOB on the island out in the worst of the sun. The statues of cartoon mice grinned at the hubris and futility that formed an invisible cloud above our heads. Lieutenant Colonel Akana, the battalion commander, paced before us with his hands behind his back. He was earnest, Hawaiian, grim and short, known to be rocketing through the ranks. Three line companies and the HQ company stood at attention, and he addressed the crowd in a voice far larger than his body.

"Look," squinting his eyes, pausing for emphasis, "I know you want to go home." Behind the rows we stood in, the chaos heaved just out of sight, beyond the river, across the walls. Mortars could fall at any time. We simulated order under terrific heat, light, and duress while the air smelled like burnt aliens. In the distance I saw a line of palm trees like frayed scraps of black bone. I felt like I was burping up Burger King, but it had been six months since I had eaten Burger King.

"You're going home. You're going home *soon*. But first they need your help in Karbala."

The Internet had made clear to everybody that Karbala was a shit show waiting to happen. "It'll be for a month. I need you to do this, and I know you can do this." From the force of his final words, hearts were sinking around me, you could almost feel the emotional movement displacing the dry air. By maybe it didn't matter, Karbala or Baghdad. The capital was festering, preparing to blow, and Sadr City had just blown. You saw fatal tensions everywhere—in the faces, in the patterns and movements of passing cars, in the duration of honking, in the sounds of crowds at markets, in the fervor of mosque calls. A guy I knew from our time at Fort Benning was using his computer to calculate his chances of dying each day. He punched in indices:

when and where people died, what they were doing, how long they had been on the ground. Since March his chances had gone from one in five hundred to one in three hundred. He offered to run my numbers too. I asked him if he could feed me spoonfuls of glass while he was at it.

The formation dispersed like a crumbling heart. Breitbart strode over and studied me in his half-cocked, crazy-ass, Bible-thumping way.

"They're cleaning the place up," I said.

"You're soft on Greep because you're soft."

"I gave Greep hell."

"His uniform is a mess," he said. "He needs a new blouse."

"I'll tell him."

"You can't read the name on his blouse."

"Is that all?"

"Akana wants to see you." It clearly pained him to say it. What did command want with me? It couldn't be bad, or it wouldn't pain Breitbart. If I were in trouble, he'd look thrilled.

Inside the FOB the temperature plunged forty degrees. The AC gave you a savage urge to piss. I squeezed my legs together until an assistant called me in to the office. Akana was a small man behind a large desk, who said, "You studied classics at BU."

It was about the last thing I expected. His face gave nothing up.

"Yes sir."

"I studied classics there," he revealed. "Greek with Wilson?"

"Wilson was there but on his way out. Two semesters with Clyde. I did more Latin."

"I don't know Clyde."

"New, a little trendy, but first rate."

"Isn't Latin always a little trendy?" Akana said.

"If you have tragedies for me to translate," I said, trying to be funny, "my hands are full. The men demand tutorials in demotic pretty much every evening."

"You wouldn't think a PR mission would have anything to do with classics," Akana said, "would you?"

"Karbala is a PR mission?"

He thought this was funny. "How's your Akkadian?"

"I've read half of *Gilgamesh*."

"Perfect."

"In English."

"You're our man. We need some American faces with the Italians at Babylon on archaeology patrol. The Shiite militias have been looting sites and destroying statues because they think they're obscene. It's a kind of archaeological censorship campaign. Conveniently, the other relics are worth something on the black market. They're selling the stuff to buy guns. Do you know what a tell is?"

"Why I lose at poker, sir?"

A wincing smile I admit I deserved. "It's a pile of dirt. You see it and know there's ten thousand years of history there. Tribes build on the ruins of tribes, other tribes build on top of that. Then the wind erases everything, and what's left is a big heap of treasures. It's an owl pellet for Indiana Jones. There's hundreds here. The archaeologists take them apart layer by layer. The insurgents use bulldozers. We need a unit in Camp Babylon to drive out to the nearby sites—show up and make the looters scatter. There's sure to be television crews, and we want somebody who can say smart things on camera. The looting last year was bad news. Right now the cameras show an army not very interested in ancient history. I have orders to find good news. I want a soldier who can hold up a chunk of cuneiform and not sound like a moron."

"Thank you, sir."

"The Italians out of Nasiriyah have been working with the museum director down there. They'll send a unit up to meet you on the road to Karbala. You'll go with the convoy halfway. Let me know if you have questions. Prepare your men as if you were preparing to go to Karbala."

Walking out of Akana's office I thought our lives had been spared. His orders brought almost as much relief and happiness as the footage of Hillary. I shouldn't have been so eager to jump ship on real sorties. But who could even distinguish should from shouldn't? If you think the suburbs make you feel ghostly and meaningless, if you think your failure to grasp how the work you do each day at the office helps anybody, if your mind boggles at where your money comes from, if you wonder why the system goes, or why anybody even cares if it goes, if you search your soul for signs that your life is gathering toward meaning, try going to war. You break through to the far side and find yourself faced not with the heart's consummation but with less than nothing. Behave heroically all you want, but, in this landscape, in this century, the Scud missiles and tanks dwarfed you, the shells and bullets outpaced you, the malfunctioning hardware re-

30

duced your intellect to a random flash of uselessness. In return, what? Every dream of heroism ended in animosity, feeble cheers, burnt cars, trashed houses, black sewage, and putrid plumes from the burning trash of three generations of people who hated you and couldn't read.

The name Babylon reminded me of where I was, not in weeks and months, not in tactics and strategies, but in centuries and millennia. Akana's orders cheered me up. The irony of that I'd see soon enough.

II.

Four years before his first appearance on Winnie Wilson, John Townley picked up his best friend from the airport in Tallahassee, Florida. Marshall Franklin Stang went off to fight in Iraq in March 2003 and returned five months later having never written home about the war and barely having called. John drove to meet him as a high-pressure system was doing its best to suffocate everything sentient and insentient on the Florida panhandle. August in northern Florida was like the hell season in hell. Dogs and palms looked miserable, pedestrians delirious, roads wavering and viscous and pitchy. Debbie Duncan, Stang's mom, didn't go to the airport to fetch her son because she couldn't get the hours off that day from greeting people at the box store she worked at.

John Townley, hardly a soldier, savored the duty of driving to the airport. He had met Stang when they were both eleven, and in the years since then John's mind had grown like a tree around the fence post of Stang's existence. Yet unlike Stang, who would always be a Florida boy, John believed he was destined to move to New York and make something of himself. It just hadn't happened yet in the five years since high school.

In the airport terminal the air conditioning all but froze the sweat on his back. From the floor of the baggage claim he spotted on the escalator a brown face above faded, pixilated fatigues. The soldier held crutches in one hand and a massive duffle in the other hand and after reaching the lower level was hobbling athletically toward John. The soldier stopped short and pulled from a pocket a disposable camera and photographed John, propped awkwardly on the crutch and smiling. John had recognized Stang already, but only at the sight of this smile did he truly believe it. Across the familiar features, the freckles made such a dense, dark pattern that there was almost no background skin. The blue eyes flitted weirdly behind the checkered mask.

"I should be the one taking the pictures for once," John said.

"Of me looking the best I've looked."

"You look great."

"Don't sweat it," Stang said. "They'll find it."

"Find what?"

Stang disengaged from the hug and shook a terminal pant leg. The foot was gone. "So stop feeling sorry for yourself about your pinkie," Stang said.

John had lost a finger when he was fifteen, more or less Stang's fault.

As a horn blatted and a belt groaned into motion, John fell silent, studying the space below the calf. This set Stang to yelling, "You over-serious son of a bitch," addressing everybody, nobody, the baggage claim area as a whole, "you overserious son of a goddamn bitch," the faces around them heavy with patriotism, discomfort, annoyance, uncomfortable solemnity. "It was covered in dog piss and Iraqi turds, who wants a foot like that?" He was grinning and asking the world at large.

Fetching his other bag and leaving the terminal, Stang moved on the crutches as if playing a game, allowing a handicap to throw into relief his haleness. He was still plenty hale and could no doubt win bar brawls even now. The town still remembered him breaking records at a track meet sophomore year wearing a giant arm cast, speeding around the track ahead of everybody despite the extra weight.

"Ask me about the war," he said.

"Tell me about the war," John said.

"Total blast," Stang said. He laughed with raw laughter, weird laughter. In a moment they were waiting for shuttles to pass, then entering the crosswalk as Stang watched over his shoulder at the travelers on the curb. His arm swept awkwardly from the crutch. "A total blast!" he yelled. "Thanks for asking!"

"God bless," somebody called.

"God bless America," Stang yelled. Then to John: "Keep staring at me with them big sad eyes I'll rip your dick off with a donut." Then: "What the—!"

"Good gas mileage," John said quietly.

"Exactly one kind of mileage," Stang said, looking over the car they had stopped at. "Pussy ass driver mileage, humiliating mileage, you should wear a pink skirt and hum Jewel through a bullhorn if you've gone this far. Christ, I keep it together four months in a war zone and you lose it in northern Florida." They climbed in. "Good thing I need less legroom."

As they drove in silence, John's mind raced speculatively to see everything as it might look to a soldier back from Baghdad and Germany and Walter Reed. He felt sudden vicarious contempt for the fast food restaurants and pristine vehicles, the landscaped freeway, the staggered palms, the warless viridity of the middle distance. He felt contempt for himself that here lay the scope of his existence.

"What do Baghdad and Hiroshima have in common?" Stang said.

"Sorry?"

"Nothing, yet. What's the five-day forecast for Baghdad?"

"What?"

"Two days. Those ones are of historical interest. I know you're interested in history. How was Saddam like Little Miss Muffet?"

"How was Saddam like Little Miss Muffet?"

"Both had Kurds in their way."

"Curds in their whey."

"Didn't know a Kurd from my asshole when this whole thing started. You know about Kurds?"

"Not so much," John said.

"What happened around town while Marshall Franklin Stang was off to war?"

"Nothing," John said.

"How's your epistolary romance?"

"Fuck you once and for all," John said.

"Your words, right? Epistolary romance?"

They were John's words from ten years ago. He had said them once in romantic effluence, and Stang had said them four thousand times in mockery. John had been referring to his written correspondence with his cousin by marriage and had never lived it down. John's epistolary romance was not a romance but a dream of one. When he was thirteen, Emily White had visited for the weekend. She came with John's Uncle Marion and Uncle Marion's new wife Sallie. Emily was fourteen then, beautiful, dauntless, cultured, and self-possessed. After that weekend John wrote a letter a week, more or less, for a decade, and never saw her again, except in the form of tight, gorgeous handwriting on blue stationery. If he had been two years younger, the Internet would have prevented such a relationship from developing.

"She got a new job in New York," John said, "at a publishing house."

"Cool," Stang said. "She can write my memoirs for me."

Later Stang's remark would make John feel even sicker in light of things to come. All the more, because John would remember saying: "That's not how it works I don't think."

At first, Stang seemed like Stang even without his foot. But ten minutes shy of their exit Stang ordered John to pull to the side of the freeway. Then, as John waited behind the wheel, Stang was crouching in weeds and grinning at the sun with his pants down, apparently crapping. He groaned and whooped while he was at it, bent and flapped his arms like chicken wings. Still it could have been normal. But then he stood without wiping or pulling up the pants. The pale skin of his upper thighs belonged to one race, the brown freckled mask of his face to another. For an interval he gazed at the highway. Even with only one foot and without crutches he didn't teeter. John listened to the engine tick without really hearing it. He pretended only for an instant to be in Iraq. "Stang," he yelled. Something was wrong.

In a welter of charisma and audacity, for the twelve longest years of their lives, Stang had been always prudish about his body, it was the only thing he was prudish about, which made it sickening to John that in a moment the returning soldier, standing dazed by the roadside, was aiming an erection at the freeway.

Until he went away, Stang lived in a house a half mile up the road in the bad direction, and always had. Whenever he emerged from that house he emerged with a lightness of spirit that, from the first day of their acquaintance, John hated himself for not sharing. Everything that makes your face burn as a teenage boy made Stang's mouth crack to a wide grin. He feared no gods and obeyed no authorities except unpredictable internal ones. For reasons beyond fathoming, they inclined him to be polite to certain grown-ups, including Frank and Mary Townley, John's folks. Stang understood manners, possessed charm, and had the capacity to make adults with advantages believe in the inherent nobility of people without advantages. He had no advantages besides his charm, manners, and mercenary intelligence. Before elementary school wrapped up he was already doing the shop-

35

ping for his mother using the food stamps her income entitled them to. He kept an eye out the screen door for a father no longer welcome at the house, a sadistic and pusillanimous son of a bitch. Once upon a time a fourteen-year-old Stang had driven off Marsh Stang with his fists. About this encounter, as about everything else in his narrow, difficult life, Stang was facetious and cavalier. Such stories bore him through childhood as the crutches bore him home from the airport, a challenge to mock by proving the irrelevance of.

John had advantages. They allowed him to teach Stang words like "sadistic" and "pusillanimous." Stang could fairly have picked on John because of the nature of the advantages. John's father and mother had distinguished themselves as undergraduates at Emory, where they had fallen in love. They read books and talked about them and treated movies as things to analyze. His father had started a PhD in English literature but quit to go to seminary and now preached to a venerable congregation of Presbyterians. Venerable, as in hemorrhaging members to the Bible Church. The Bible Church had lots of tambourines, Frank Townley said, and no theology. Theology by osmosis was the greatest advantage John enjoyed over other youth in Apalachicola. Theology by any means was not in high demand at Apalachicola High School.

Stang entered John's life on the second day of sixth grade. This was the year the United States had driven Iraqi forces out of Kuwait, which the boys in sixth grade knew about only as a source of awesome T-shirts and interesting television. On the day John met him Stang was wearing a T-shirt with eagles and flags and letters stenciled in triumphant menacing martial epic grandeur. The new school year took John to a new school to which four elementary schools funneled. It was immense and frightening. When the year began, John had no way of knowing that he should arrive each day only as the first bell was ringing, not earlier. Arriving earlier amounted to inviting Tim Erwin and Joe Schultz to pummel you spontaneously. In fifth grade, the year before, nobody pummeled you like that, because adults still stood in for gods, and fights resembled games. But on the second day of sixth grade John's mother's taillights were still visible when a force from nowhere struck his back terrifically.

He lost his breath and fell to the ground. There was laughter and insults incomprehensible in their pitch and weirdness. He scrambled and tried to see. Then Tim Erwin was sitting on him, smelling not so good. Joe Schultz with open mouth bent over his face and let a string of spit descend to touch John's forehead. Three years ago these boys had played pirates in the Popeye pageant as fifth graders when John was a third grader back at Davis Elementary, so John knew their names and faces, although their faces had changed. Even as an eighth grader Joe Schultz retained his creamy baby fat, but now with pimples ravaging its surface. Tim Erwin, skinny and smelly, pinned John down with his bony ass.

Then more violence and confusion.

Suddenly Joe Schultz was lying on the ground, whimpering, sort of. A tall, blond boy wearing an awesome T-shirt had kicked his face. Now the same boy was shoving Tim Erwin off John's chest. Tim Erwin's skinny palms skidded on the pavement and in a moment were shedding blood. The unexpected avenger moved easily and happily, as if stomping on bubble wrap. "Nobody messes with this guy. You know who this guy's dad is? Fucking nimrods." Joe and Tim hastened a fat and skinny retreat.

John had already learned the f-word but only as something you whisper. He had never heard it delivered so effortlessly by another eleven-year-old boy. The boy offered him a hand, pulled John to his feet, and led him toward the school without looking back. John's frame rippled with intense gratitude. "You know my dad?"

"Not from Nimrod."

"You know me?"

"Not from Nimrod."

They walked in silence for a moment. The boy owned the silence and broke it only to show John that he owned it. "You live down the road. I see you riding that banana seat bike everywhere, the grampa Schwinn, you need to raise the back of the seat, it's totally sagging, it looks like a big black boner, the front of that banana seat sticking up. Don't you want a dirt bike? I'm going to get a Mongoose. You got a niggercock bike, that's all I know about you or your dad from Nimrod."

John asked him his name. "Marshall Franklin Stang." Even at that age Stang gave every syllable its due. "Pleased to meet you, niggercock John."

"John Townley."

"John Townley of the Niggercock."

The n-word in the Townley household was worse than anything else you could say. John's parents had heard Martin Luther King Jr. speak in Dallas in 1962 and invoked it as a touchstone of their lives.

Both Frank and Mary had been born before the baby boom, in the early 1940s, and embarked as parents only as Ronald Reagan ascended and middle age set in. "You turned out better, as an accident, than most of our intentional decisions," his father once said. In the future John would understand that his parents were liberals from the 1950s and not liberals from the 1960s. All his life they seemed ancient to him. They had never done drugs or grown their hair long, but they had read Reinhold Niebuhr and had had their hearts lifted by the sit-ins and boycotts and civil rights legislation. They instilled in John a feeling that uttering the n-word was tantamount to murder. So when eleven-year-old Stang appeared at the screen door the next Saturday, and Mary Townley said, "Oh, hi, I know you're Marshall, I'm John's mother, would you like to join us for lunch?" the prospect of the n-word threatened John's thoughts like a rabid bat.

At lunch Stang said "please" and "thank you" unremittingly. His manners were as stilted as French phrases learned from an audio tape. He called Frank Townley "Reverend" maybe fourteen times. He wore a freshly washed Desert Storm T-shirt and did not use any racial epithets.

"*What* was *that?*" his father said when he left.

"That's Debbie Duncan's boy," his mother said.

"Debbie Stang? Marsh's wife?" his father said. "They don't have a teenager, just the toddler."

"That was the toddler," her mother said. "And it's Duncan now, Debbie Duncan. Frank, you remember all this."

The next day, John rode his bike to Stang's house, four doors away, but on this county road that meant half a mile. It was a place long known about and always vaguely feared, a house you took note of as a kid as so creepily different from yours that its insides could not be imagined. Trees had grown up around it and softened the horizontal lines of the ranch structure. The walls looked sunken six inches in the earth. Tar paper covered patches of wall, and piles of clutter and scraps of blanched cloth blocked the windows. Stang appeared at the door as if knowing John was coming. When John entered there was a smell more complex and living than that of a person: humid, dense, warm, sour, baked. On top of it, the stench of cigarettes.

Standing in the foyer, John could see Ms. Duncan smoking at the kitchen table. His parents so firmly laid down the law about cigarettes that cigarettes smelled like moral chaos. Ms. Duncan did not rise to greet him. That was another huge difference. Nobody entered

John's house without Frank and Mary greeting that person at the door. Nor would Frank and Mary have created clutter like this, or allowed a guest to see it. There were stacks of catalogs and neglected dishes, ashes in ashtrays, a television displaying to nobody a skittering golf tournament, and piles of unfolded laundry in which cats dozed and shed abundantly.

Stang led him down the hallway without saying anything. Against all expectations the room he led him to was as clean and austere as a barracks. It was swept and scoured, squared and minimal, a bedroom barely large enough for its desk, bed, and bookshelf. A poster of a comic book vigilante wielding guns hung on the walls perfectly square between the windows. On the shelves a dozen books formed a wedge from tallest to shortest. G.I. Joe figures stood arranged by color. In the closet on a bookshelf Stang had also sorted his T-shirts by color. As John was almost gawking, Stang handed him a stack of photographs of grown-ups he didn't recognize. "Is this your family?" John asked.

"People at the mall," Stang said.

"That you know?"

"No."

"That you don't know? You just took pictures of them?"

"They didn't notice," Stang said. Then he produced from the closet, from underneath the shirts, a stack of magazines. John's blood went funny at the sight. It blew his mind that Stang could have these. At his house it would have been easier to hide a live chicken. Stang encouraged him to look and laughed at his nervousness. "Does your mom know—?" John whispered.

"Mom don't care." Stang never said "my mom" but always "Mom." He didn't lower his voice.

John knew the word "vagina" but had never pictured a vagina as a line or seam or a thing of folds. The penises defied known scale and defied the sense of smoothness and meekness derived from the evidence at hand. It almost sickened him he was so excited. Stang held up a picture of a black woman. "Picture THAT on your niggercock." Then: "Let's get a snack."

"Mm," Ms. Duncan said in the kitchen. Her eyes were elsewhere. Standing before her, John felt the images of the naked bodies pressing so hard on his brain that he thought they might appear on his face. Surely they had corrupted his eyes or shone from them. But Ms. Duncan smiled faintly and smoked robustly and sipped diet soda. Her fat pressed against the edge of the table and hung from her arms with ponderous sway. John could not see the resemblance between mother and son. He was offered Doritos. His mother and father made of nutrition a virtue next to godliness. The house astonished him in every detail and respect.

Back home John said nothing about where he had been. A day or two later his mother came out to him in the backyard and said, "Marshall can come over here to play. But I'm asking you not to go over there." She went back in the house. John could tell she had been preparing to say this and had had to work herself up to it and did not enjoy it. But how did she know?

You didn't have to listen to town voices very long before you heard things about Stang. As a fifth grader he had brought sneezing powder to school and given it to a first grader who distributed it to a class of first graders who sneezed all day. This startled the powers that be as it resembled pushing drugs. Also in fifth grade, Stang and Rick Force were caught stomping ketchup packets in the stands at a football game, quietly spattering the backs of the pant legs of the spectators sitting in front of them. In sixth grade word went around that Stang had been caught driving a car down by the water. Throughout sixth grade he disappeared from school for full weeks and always returned cheerfully and in great health. John learned about Stang from sources his parents had no access to, so there must have been many sources, since his parents learned things too.

When John was in seventh grade, his mother said: "His father is a convicted criminal. You're twelve and almost an adult so I'm going to speak to you like one. The man spent five years in prison for making drugs. He used to sell drugs out of that house. Debbie and your friend Marshall have been through hell. I feel sorry for them, and I wish the best for Marshall. He is welcome here anytime. But it's dangerous for you to go to that house, and I forbid you from going there." It was true that John had disobeyed her first command. Nor did he obey this second one.

Stang never ripped the wings from flies or lodged firecrackers in the asses of cats. He swept his room and helped his mother grocery shop. He had saved John from Joe Schultz and Tim Erwin. That bond was stronger than anything. John appeared to his parents as a mostly obedient son because his conscience and good sense usually conformed with their desires and opinions. But his conscience and good sense kept their own counsel and led him unhesitatingly to Stang's house, even when he was grounded for going there, which happened four times before Mary simply gave up.

The summer after seventh grade the action that counted went down at the freshwater sinkholes. At the edges of the sinkholes, the forests became jungles, and alligators lurked invisibly as a remote fatality that heightened the energy with which boys played and fought. Deep shadows in the vegetation and harsh patches of sun pulled off tricks on the eyes. As you approached a sinkhole the shouts said everything, whether war or play was afoot; when you arrived, the faces did. Play turned into war all the time. One afternoon John peeled off his shirt as he approached their favorite sinkhole but could tell that swimming was not going on. He arrived to find a crowd of boys standing naked around an almost naked Jimmy Kendrick.

Jimmy Kendrick, by any ranking other than size, ranked last. He was larger than everybody, his arms hanging like the arms of a grown man from broad shoulders already stooped from being different from everybody else's. Until kindergarten he had had tubes in his ears and had not been able to hear well as he was learning to talk. It made him seem retarded. He was not retarded; John's mom had explained it to John long ago. But, even now, everything Jimmy Kendrick heard he listened to for just a moment too long, as if English were not his first language. English was his only language, and he spoke all the more clumsily when he was being picked on.

At the sinkhole Jimmy always made a bad situation worse by swimming in white briefs when the other boys swam without clothes, even prudish Stang. Jimmy also made a bad situation worse by beating everybody to puberty. His penis pressed against the wet white fabric like a field mouse in the full, dense, dark tuft of hair also wet against the fabric between his legs. It was too much hair for a boy their age to have.

"Just drink it," Stang was saying to him. Rick Force stood next to Stang and yelled, "Drink it!"

Rick Force terrified John. He had too many moles and a face squashed between a heavy brow and chin. Whenever Rick did the delinquent things that Stang did, he made them seem criminal and frightening instead of funny and righteous.

"Give it back," Jimmy said.

"Drink it and he'll give it back," Stang said.

"Do it," Rick said.

On the smooth rock shelf that broke off above the water and formed a place to dive from, the boys stood like a pack, brown, handsome, simian. The bullying had been going on long enough that the last of the wet footprints had evaporated and the heads of hair were ceasing to drip. John could not remember, a decade later, who else was there, probably Tom Monk and Joe Schultz and Tim Erwin. But what would remain in his memory was the image of Rick Force goading poor hairy huge Jimmy Kendrick. "Drink it and he'll give it back." What would remain in memory above all was Stang squinting through the viewfinder of a disposable camera and snapping pictures of Jimmy being bullied.

"Don't take pictures," Jimmy said.

"It's fine," Rick said. "You're wearing underwear."

"Give it back," Jimmy said.

"It" was a pencil, *the* pencil, John saw. They had stolen Jimmy's lucky pencil. Jimmy was known and mocked and hated above all for his lucky pencil. "Why do you always have that," people would ask him. "It's my lucky pencil," he always said. He wore it behind his ear. The pencil was embossed with the word Challenger and with a tiny image of a space shuttle, although the paint had worn away over time, so John knew the graphic only from memory. It was years since Jimmy had written anything with the long scuffed nub. It rested year after year on a faulty ear. His mistake was carrying it over from elementary to middle school.

Rick was gripping the pencil in one hand and in the other a coffee can full of water, some kind of water, or some kind of liquid. He waved both things at Jimmy, the coffee can within reach, the pencil out of reach. Stang photographed convivially.

"Drink it," the chorus shouted, "Drink it."

"Give it back," Jimmy said.

"He'll give it back if you drink it," Stang said, clicking and winding.

Jimmy eyed the coffee can miserably and asked what was in it.

"It's good for you," Rick said.

Jimmy took the coffee can. The splashing contents did not look clear like water. He stared into the can and asked again what it was.

"Drink it!" everybody yelled. He drank some of it and dropped the can and the rest spilled out on the rocks.

"You asshole," Rick said, and threw the pencil in the sinkhole.

The pencil fell to the surface. Jimmy trotted in his drying briefs down the path to the easiest ledge to enter from. Before he could scramble into the water Rick cannonballed in. Then Stang did, then the rest except John. Jimmy splashed around the now choppy water, groping and searching for the purple pencil. John, watching from above, caught sight of it. From down in the water Stang saw this and asked where it was. John pointed and Stang found it and swam it over to Jimmy. The sight of the gesture lifted a tremendous weight from John's chest. "Why'd you give it to him!" Rick Force yelled, sneering. Jimmy climbed from the pool gripping the pencil in his hand. He dressed using one hand, pulling the dry clothes over his wet body, still gripping the pencil. He did not look back as he cut into the forest heading home.

It did not matter. It made things terribly hard for John but did not change things for him. He saw how it was, but could not turn on Stang. There were rules and feelings deeper than anything you could think or reason out. It looked so very different when you were on the strong side. It transformed it from a mortal horror to a rough but basically innocuous game. John did not think this was right, but he could not escape it.

By the time the boys started at Apalachicola High School in 1994, John knew his parents hated Stang, or, claiming as Christians to hate nobody, hated Stang's place in John's life. His charm, very real, stopped working for him and in fact worked against him. In general the responsible adults of Apalachicola were not huge fans. Principal Wiffin, who presided over the halls of the high school with the eyes of a hawk and the pursed lips of a embittered Lutheran, had been bracing himself. Months or years ago the scuttlebutt had warned him that a troublemaker named Marshall Franklin Stang was heading his way. Wiffin viewed himself as the man who nipped delinquency in the bud, and got out the nippers.

Freshman year, when Stang meandered in late on the third day of school, Wiffin caught him and called him to the office. "No game for you Friday," he said. During tryouts in August Stang had made the varsity football team, but only as a benchwarmer, so he wasn't seeing game time yet. "But it's the principle of the thing," Stang said later that day.

"No pun intended," John said.

"But what Nimrod doesn't know is he can't keep me out."

Stang had already come up with a plan. On Friday, John watched from the stands as it unfolded. Stang arrived unrecognizable in the costume of the school mascot, a plush snapper, a furry fish suit. The appointed mascot, Tom Monk, had agreed to let Stang borrow the costume. Tom Monk was a weird, skittish kid whom Stang never called "Tom" or "Monk" but always "Tom Monk." Stang pushed him around in a way that seemed affectionate to everybody including Tom Monk. For three quarters of the game, Stang, incognito, turned cartwheels and thrashed plush arms at the huge crowd, including at Principal Wiffin. At one point he charged the stands and threw the plush arms around the principal in a warm hug as the crowd roared.

In the last quarter of the game he took off the headpiece and grinned. His hair lay flat with sweat and his face was red. He grinned at Wiffin until Wiffin noticed. It did not take Wiffin long. Suddenly red himself, the principal charged down to the field and dragged Stang off it. Stang waved at a crowd roaring with delight. "LET—HIM—GO," people started chanting.

After that, Stang was banned from games entirely.

Principal Wiffin was not obese but had the triple chin of an obese man, and the folds of flesh formed a cushion on which his first chin rested, never touching the chest it was contemptuously tilted toward. He meant for his few strands of black hair to be combed over his bald patch, but they waved instead to the side of his head, expressing the exasperation, the befrazzlement, caused him by nipping delinquency in the bud. He was a tyrant and a fool. Stang thought so, John thought so, and even Frank Townley did. John's father's opinion of Wiffin lent credence to the idea that there was something truly transcendent and righteous about Stang, which there seemed to be.

As the years went on, John and Stang started playing pranks, few of which had to do with Apalachicola High School. Sophomore spring, they discovered in the shallows of a sinkhole a piece of limestone that Stang got in his head looked like a meteor. "You mean meteorite," John said.

"Nimrod," Stang said.

"Plus, this just looks like a rock," John said.

It took five boys to lift it from the floor of the sinkhole to the ledge. It took seven, with a sling rigged up by Stang, to carry it to Rick Force's truck. It took seven again to heft it, late one night, from the back of the truck onto the roof of Stang's father's 1987 Lincoln Town Car, which they found parked outside Honeys, a strip club eighty miles from Apalachicola. Before crushing the roof, Stang had ransacked the car and found in the trunk a clunky video camera. "Dad won't mind if I borrow this for a couple of years," he said. So he captured the evening on tape.

Which meant that he captured the big moment of John's year. The prank was a hilarious affair until its climax. During the panicked scampering hefting, the rock dropped onto John's pinkie. For a moment nobody knew it, and it lay there on top of the finger as pain blinded John. "Off!" he yelled in the darkness at the blinking red light of the video camera. Then he fainted.

"You'll be fine," Stang said, after the stone had demolished the roof and John had revived. Stang wrapped John's hand up in dirty rags. The gang left John at the emergency room at a hospital in Tatsberg, sixty miles from home.

"What were you doing out here?" his father asked without wanting to know, driving him home in the small hours. His mother asked him the same question the next day, expecting an answer. But John refused to give details, which was incriminating, but so were the facts, and so was lying. "It was stupid," he said. "It was the stupidest thing I've ever done. I got what I deserved."

Frank and Mary thought their son got far more than he deserved, and if Stang had severed the pinkie with a hatchet before their eyes, they couldn't have been more sure of his culpability. In many respects John's adolescence, so his life itself, divided into those two phases: before and after the loss of his pinkie, before and after Stang's probationary period in the Townley household. Probation was over, but not the friendship.

Seven years later, John was sensitive and symbolical and literary enough to see the dramatic irony in the loss of Stang's foot. His parents were sensitive and symbolical and literary. It certainly would resonate. So when John returned from the airport, he anticipated with irritation and something close to anger the conversation at dinner. It went about how he imagined it would. "How is Marshall?" His mother posed the question in a solemn tone that begged the question.

"Stang's Stang," John said.

Clanking and chewing.

"He lost a foot."

"He lost his foot?" Frank Townley said.

"Oh, dear," Mary Townley said. "Debbie didn't say anything about it."

"I don't think she knew yet," John said.

"I'm so—" Mary said.

For seven years they had sought to expel Stang from the bounds of acceptability and never quite found the means. They trusted their instincts; he was a dangerous kid. His enlisting in the army had constituted a significant piece of evidence that they had been right all along. The loss of a foot was a major piece of evidence, however irrational this was. John had prepared himself to be angry. "You're so *what*?" John said.

"I'm so sorry!" Mary said.

"I believe you're sorry," John said.

"Why are you taking this tone with your mother?"

"She's sorry, sure thing, but she's also confirmed, right? You're both confirmed? Doesn't this just confirm it? Didn't he get what he was headed for?"

"John," his father warned.

"No disrespect intended." He was speaking with untypical force. "I apologize, I'm just saying what's true."

"I don't recognize it as true," his father said.

His parents studied him, trying to make sense of him. By the standards of the family this was extreme behavior. When Stang aimed his erection at the highway John had thought, *This is what they wanted.* It had flashed in his head and given him no place to go. "You've always hated him," John heard himself saying. "This is what you were hoping for, here's your proof, treat this like your proof!"

"John," his father said.

"Treat this *as* our proof," his mother corrected. "You mean as."

"Take a minute to get a hold of yourself," his father said. "We'll be here when you're ready to eat with us."

John rose from the table and went down the hallway. He should have left home when it was time to leave home. He had planned to move to New York after graduation. Why was he still living here? In his room he sat at his desk with a hot face, incapable of hooking his thoughts on something to anchor him amidst the flood of feeling. Then he took out paper and started writing.

He wrote a letter to his cousin Emily in New York. He described his day and slowly regained control of himself.

He went back to the dining room and apologized.

Ten days later he received a letter from Emily asking if she could come to Florida and write a book about Stang. John had wanted to see her again for the whole of his adult life and had never imagined it would happen for a reason like this. He thought back to what Stang had said in the car on the way home from the airport: "Cool. She can write my memoirs for me."

III.

In zones of unremitting low-grade fatal terror your blood does your work for you, your skin does it, your nose or your ESP does it, the reptilian part of you, some primordial core of atavistic sensitivity responding before the laggard brain, encumbered by reasoning, straggles onto the scene. So I knew it was a bad crowd at first glance. Postures, faces, barely heard snatches of speech: I knew.

My men had gathered in the courtyard and circled something, were circling. Kirk Frank standing silently at the fringe. A rare cheerfulness on Schwartz's fat face. J'Million looming and leering, fixing his gaze on the action, his eyes too far apart, his teeth gapped and roomy, that face on which insubordination and reliability were perversely one. Hornbuckle and Kingdinger on the outer ring. Corez and Malik. At the center?

Eccles?

I was striding toward them, ready to scream, in possession of nothing but the spasming of my nerves. Only then, from a bent position, did Duckworth rise into view. They were raping Duckworth. They were not. His helmet, cupped in his massive hands, obscured his upturned face. Towering above the circle he made even J'Million's thuggish mass look slight. His hands cupped the helmet like a chalice, the bilge spraddling his jaw, his eyes on nothing, on a sky empty of the God that justified this war only in the minds of sons of bitches.

He was drinking crotch water, the sudsy bilge of an impromptu bath from a canteen and a helmet, how we bathed out here. The men were standing and watching, and it was in fact Eccles who was bullying, Eccles at the center of the crowd, slender and tawny, craven and goofy. "Drink it, Duckwad!" he shouted. "Drink!"

"Duckwad" was a Greepism. There were no Ecclesisms.

At the sound of my screaming the circle dispersed, leaving victim and culprit to be dealt with, Duckworth soggy and teary, standing alone, gripping the helmet, training on me eyes doleful, confused, and despairing. I yelled at him to dump the water. There was not much left to dump. I took in the faces, waiting to see if I was worth being scared of. Only as the circle broke apart did I catch sight of Greep on the far side. He lowered the video camera as soon as he saw me.

"I found it sitting out," Greep said. "It's yours?"

I had moved at him as if to hit him, but I would never hit him.

"Eccles was just obeying orders, boss," Schwartz said at my elbow.

"I found the porn on his cot," Eccles said.

"Of course it's mine!" I yelled. "You know it's mine!"

"The porn's yours?" Eccles said.

"The camera's mine," I yelled at Greep.

"What about Duckworth's load of porn?" Schwartz said.

Duckworth had no porn. Duckworth was staring at his boots. No gesture occurred to me. Rage short-circuits you, rage with two sources. I looked from Duckworth to Eccles to Greep. "Did you just use the tape that was in it?"

"It wasn't blank?" Greep said.

In the bunker Duckworth's cot was heaped with tattered pages. Duckworth hadn't looked at a *Playboy* in his life. The others had done this to him. People were clearing out, everybody suddenly a casual bystander, guiltless. I fixed on Greep. He shrugged and grinned. "I just came up when you did. I can't be everywhere at once."

"That's exactly where you seem to be," I said.

"Crotch water: wasn't that it?"

Yes, I had said something like that. I could not meet Greep's placid gaze. I studied his chest. Breitbart was right: his blouse was slovenly, his name illegible above the pocket. "You need a new blouse!" I yelled.

Duckworth stood to the side, his chin glistening, his blouse soaked and dark, his eyes morose. "What's wrong with you!" I yelled. I took an armful of pages and carried them out to the burn barrel. The group lingered and lagged. "Go!" I yelled, when I came back in. Only Duckworth and Kirk Frank helped carry pages out to be burned. Flames curled around pages of women and men and more women tangled ridiculously.

"What's the five day forecast for Baghdad," Kirk Frank said.

"Not now," I said.

"Two days," he said.

"That one's from the invasion," I said. "You need new jokes."

Ten minutes later I sat alone on my cot upstairs, studying my ugly knuckles. It had been a good day for a while. Remembering that was like looking back to the hours before a car crash. The video from Hillary had delighted me, and the news about Babylon had delighted me. I tried to recapture the happiness about the mission, but it was gone like water on the courtyard dust. I sat on the edge of my cot and tried. I got out paper and stared at it for a long time. I wanted to write a letter to Hillary that purged me of my anger and disgust. But my feelings were incommensurate with the act of writing. They were too much.

I could not bear to check the tape to see how much footage had been lost. I couldn't even think about it. All day I had been savoring the thought of seeing Hillary's face again.

"Sir?" The voice almost startled me off the cot. It was Eccles. "I'm sorry. I wanted to say I was sorry."

After a moment, I found the emotional stamina to play my role. "Why would you do that to him?"

"Schwartz said—"

"Is the transfer that much to get your head around?"

"The transfer?"

"This stuff dehumanizes you."

He blinked at me.

"It makes you an animal. Your job is not just to follow orders. It's to remain yourself."

Eccles stared at me in my weirdness. These were weird things for me to say. Or was he staring at something else? He was staring at the mailbag. He had not come to apologize, he had come for his mail. He longed for yet another letter from Pat Mapp in Fayetteville. Rage was a substance in me by no means gone. I despised him despite myself, despised him intimately. When I handed him his letters he opened one and stood there looking at it.

He was gangly and ill at ease with his gangliness. An unfaithful woman was breaking his heart every hour of the day. He looked like he was stooping under an attic roof. "She sent me pictures of a party." He held them out for me to look at.

"She's trying to keep her spirits up, and yours." I didn't believe my own words. "She misses you." It was impossible to stay angry.

"There's always that dude in the pictures she sends me."

I had seen other pictures of Pat Mapp. Preternaturally pretty eyes formed the sole locus of prettiness in a heavy face above a heavy body. Her cleavage was a heralded fact. In the pictures now she looked drunk and copious and indubitably well disposed to the dude standing next to her. Eccles was right, the dude was a dude, a real dude, a dude with a backwards baseball cap and heavy-lidded eyes and long tattooed arms you saw all of, because of the muscle shirt.

"You know this person?" I said.

"I kind of know him. Mike."

"Listen," I said. "Your imagination is running away with itself. She's just at a party having fun. She misses you and loves you." I studied the picture. It didn't look like that at all. I wanted the picture to vanish and Eccles to vanish. The blackest thoughts of Hillary overwhelmed me. "Don't psych yourself out. She loves you."

"I love her," Eccles said. Then he said, "You got a video camera?" His eyes had fallen on it on the cot.

"You can't borrow it," I said.

"Can I look at it?"

"You can't borrow it."

"What if I made a video telling her I loved her?"

"Write her a letter."

"I don't write good."

As I handed him the camera I wanted to hurl it at the wall. I should at least have swapped out the tape. Retrospect is astonishing.

In polite society people usually avoid getting specific about the hierarchies men form, but I can list the Babylon Seven, the men who would become the Babylon Seven, in order. Despite my rank, Greep ruled: Greep with his grin, Greep with his good looks, Greep with his sadistic sexcapades and his collegiate vocabulary and his major league father and his minor league past and his weird modulations from suburban argot to urban patois. You'll hear more about all these things. Below him, in love with him, at odds with him, in charge of him: me. Then J'Million, the heroic gunner—brave, toothy, weird in laughter, truly from the ghetto, truly black, whatever that means. Then Kirk Frank, with his full name and froggy eyes and seaweed hair and silent competence and fantastic skills at driving and his corny sociopathic jokes. Then Schwartz, the fat Brent, porcine, pushy, slack-jawed and awful, rotten-southern-sheriff-like, vying and gross. Then Eccles, the skinny Brent, Schwartz's punching bag, our Ichabod Crane, tawny with tan, craven, a lackey pining twenty-four hours a day for a woman busy partying with dudes named Mike. Then Duckworth, poor Duckworth, lachrymose Duckworth, poor him.

Looking back, I can say that Greep was guilty of crimes as far beyond the pale as the men who killed us. At the time, I forgave him the terroristic pranks that blazed the trail to our beheadings. I feel morally bound to remember this, that I allowed him to be him. It's so easy to will the memory from existence. We were often like friends, and often friends.

His place in my life in the army mirrored that of Hillary in my civilian life. The orderliness that I lived to crave and serve, he lived to blast through and upset. He antagonized the commanding officers that I could not antagonize. He infuriated Breitbart and hovered as a gadfly on Akana's far flank. Even the things he did that made me feel like punching a wall got metabolized in my moody brain like shots of firewater. The enzyme was his grin.

For Greep, the American operations were a dark circus, free from the rule of law. He mastered the art of taking advantage of the good-will of the Iraqis, an advantage more easily taken when there was still goodwill for the taking. But I barely actually *saw* him do any of what I suspected him of being responsible for. He was always the innocent face floating at the fringe with the camera.

Was it Greep who convinced Schwartz to run a tank over some bicycles, Malik to graze the corner of a house? Did Greep act without malice when he passed out the orange index cards the army issued to wronged parties in need of restitution? "The point of contact for this memorandum," he would write, "is the undersigned, available on hopset 452." Except there was no hopset 452. On the cards the signature would be one-quarter legible and four-quarters fictional. Later I would overhear him through tent walls laughing about the Iraqi men returning home with orange index cards, positively glowing. Iraqi men trusted paperwork as much as they didn't trust each other. They received the cards like purchase orders signed by President Bush. Under Saddam the faith of the average Iraqi in the sanctity of paperwork bordered on the metaphysical.

When I confronted Greep with a bogus card, he slapped his forehead and cursed his scattered mind. He sucked at remembering hopset numbers. He had always had bad handwriting. "Teachers hated me," he said, flashing that grin. I felt sick at this and drawn to it.

52

How did he convince Schwartz or Malik or Corez to commit small crimes? Eccles to torment Duckworth? Why did his own hands always remain so putatively clean? The men would shit in MRE bags and toss them to the kids who yelled for free stuff. At traffic stops they would smack off men's headscarves, claiming to be looking for bombs. They would distribute obscene magazines to little boys whose fathers and grandfathers later stormed up to me with faces so angry that the blood in their faces made it look like beaten flesh. Behind all of it I suspected Greep's will. I could prove nothing.

Many nights, as I struggled to sleep, his culpability hemorrhaged in my uneasy thoughts. In nightmares I lay the whole war itself at his feet. In the fitful darkness he roared as an evil motor at the heart of a perfidious machine. In the morning light, his grin absolved him. My forgiveness was not just weakness, although it was that too, it was also a distinct and ambivalent flavor of envy. He did not let the dangerous streets drive him deep within himself. He did not take the war too seriously. And he pulled pranks on Americans who deserved it as often as on Iraqis who didn't. On certain days, in certain situations, his subversions aligned with me, liberated me, cut like a righteous sword through the otherwise implacable ugliness of this entire misadventure.

For instance, this story: the time Greep accompanied me to a Fulbright meeting in the Green Zone. They actually held such things. "I'm game," he said. "What the hell is a Fulbright?"

"Money for nerds," I said.

"You'll do well," he said.

This was after the transfer had been announced but before it happened. With Babylon on the horizon, I was thinking that my background in classics plus my time at the ruins south of Baghdad might position me for a fellowship.

That morning Greep shook me awake. Greep was always awake, always wakeful, always watching everybody rise. Had I ever seen him sleep? He was also pathologically neat. His bunk was always the one in the shippest shape. Only his dress was slovenly, not even dirty, just torn.

In the darkness he grinned above my cot as I jolted from sleep. I emerged from a nightmare in which Hillary's vaginal secretions had the consistency of gravy and tasted like soy sauce. We were rising at 300 in order to latch onto a patrol to catch a ride to a meeting that

53

would not happen until six hours later. In Baghdad you didn't exactly go where you wanted when you wanted.

Ten minutes later we joined the patrol convoy in our Humvee. He drove. Baghdad in the darkness was a different city, empty and cool with stink instead of teeming and hot with stink. It was ancient and modern and dead. Dark palms stood motionless like crestfallen giants, rounds cracked in the distance, and I have to say that war is most frightening in stillness and darkness. I watched the shadows of alleys for portents of violent death. I had long ago resolved to take as few risks as possible, to do my job, skip the field trips, suppress the odds. These fantasies of Babylon got my guard down and gave the week a different feeling, an open one, at least until I found myself riding through Baghdad in the dark.

Sometimes when Greep was focused on a task and not looking at me I thought I saw a truer Greep in his eyes, a calculating, tragic person, unshielded by the priceless smile, anxiously laying the groundwork for the next charismatic blitz. In these moments I wanted to hear that person speak, the real Greep, to audit a serious voice that bore some intimate relation to the tense jaw and ambivalent eyes. But he could not speak without throwing the veil over that person, returning to himself. "I farted," he said.

"I don't smell it."

"Give it four seconds."

"Jesus Christ."

We reached the four-meter-high walls that divided chaos from order, poverty from wealth, heat from AC, anarchy from democracy, the dystopia of Iraq from the utopia of the States, the streets of Baghdad from the Green Zone. The convoy fed us into the chute of barricades, a maze that led us in. At the first guard post a U.S. soldier, drowsy and sunburned, dark and green-toned in the dimness, stood in a tower of sandbags next to an elaborate gate of more sandbags and Hesco bastions. Concertina wire covered everything, the ubiquitous shreds of plastic bags fluttering on the blades. A soldier from First CAV approached my window and asked for IDs. In a minute he was lifting a counterweighted guard arm striped like a candy cane while another soldier dragged clear the tire shredder then waved us on. Klieg lights rendered the shoot of concrete brighter than day, weird and penal. "I dreamed Hillary's secretions were like gravy and tasted like soy sauce," I said.

"Best of both worlds," Greep said.

54

"I also dreamed—not last night, but I wrote this one down—"

"Still savoring the first one."

"I was about to be beheaded. I had long hair. The rope was tied to my hair so that my head would swing free. I was standing on my toes and a hajji was readying his scimitar."

"The scimitar stereotype. You bigot."

"I was on this platform. Maybe there were cameras out in the darkness. Below the platform was a bed with white sheets. On the bed lay Hillary, naked, with a beauty-pageant-type ribbon around her chest."

"So you couldn't even see her tits."

"My fiancée's breasts."

"You're about to be beheaded, and you don't even get to see her tits."

"Her breasts were plenty visible."

"No tits. I hear you."

"I was on my toes, because of the noose. Then I had been beheaded. I was dead and knew I was beheaded, but also could see the blood spilling onto her, on the sheets, on the bed."

"Make sure to bring this up at the Fulbright meeting."

"I thought you didn't know what a Fulbright was."

"Because I'm black?"

That was another favorite Greepism.

An M1A2 tank with its main gun pointed at our windshield sat at the end of the tunnel of jersey barriers. The brilliance of the klieg lights differed from the sun we were used to, making the tank look harsher and taller. We got waved on by guards at a second and a third guard post. Then suddenly, for the first time in six months, since being on leave, we were clear of the threat of instant extermination. The villas were spaced comfortably and the stillness was not the stillness of imminent bloodbaths. Foliage grew twice as thick here as beyond the fortifications and smelled nice.

Greep steered the Humvee to a vast parking lot filled with Ford Expeditions, Chevy Suburbans, Range Rovers, and Yukons, vehicles used in the Green Zone like golf carts. The CPA could have used golf carts, why not, mortars would kill you regardless, but the technocrats were playing cowboy and loved chugging gasoline. It was dark as Greep pulled in and I was exhausted and he was cheerful because well aware that I was exhausted. I don't even remember climbing into the backseat and stretching out. Then there was an hour of the oblivion of exhaustion.

When I opened my eyes again it was not because the sun was up. Outside the window a skyline of palm trees and biblical-modernist architecture loomed in dark indigo against dark-blue sky. I saw pink stars and wondered what I had just heard. It had sounded like giggling. For a moment all my ears found was the drone, coming and going, of Apache helicopters. Then giggling again. "Live sex show," Greep whispered.

"Is the Hummer shaking?" I said.

He pointed with his toe.

The back of a man's head was pressed against the window.

"A weapon of mass destruction!" we could hear a girl saying. "A warhead!"

"Oh yeah," the man said.

"Such a large warhead. Let's hide it in the fertile crescent!"

"The Hummer is shaking," I said. "No doubt about it."

"Scud," the girl said, "or Tomahawk?"

Then a low moan.

But probably Greep didn't hear it in the shuffle. With blue ribbon timing he at once laid on the horn and started and gunned the engine. The sounds were explosive in the silent lot and his darkest laughter filled the Humvee. When the man and woman were scrambling away he hit the headlights. Two forms squinted and hunched for a minute in the sudden brightness. It would have made a great story even if it ended there. But Greep said, "That's Spencer Talent."

Only by studying his face could I place the name of the TEX News anchor. And sure enough it was him, that groomed, southern, black-haired tub-thumper who, in the mediated unreality of the soundstage, always came across as too young for his haircut and suit. He was one of the those who had spoken with gleeful rancor and sold the war nonstop. Now on cable each day he euphemized the war. "The increased violence proves the dead-enders are getting desperate"—that kind of thing. Before us in the headlights he was adjusting his fly and buckling up and already thinking better of standing blinded before unknown eyes. Next to him stood a woman with a gorgeous mane of red curls. She reminded me of Shamhat's Cabbage Patch Kid.

"Bitchery and abomination," Greep said.

Then they were gone.

Later when we awoke again the sun had transformed the Humvee to a hothouse. Clothes soaked, mouth dry, bladder full. "I have to piss like crazy," I said.

"Piss on the lot."

"We're in civilization."

"Quote unquote."

We drove down safe broad streets empty with dawn. We passed the Republican Palace, from each corner of whose magnificent edifice a head of Saddam surveyed his lost empire. "Saddam wrote novels," I said.

"In blood," Greep said. "It's the way to go."

"About reclaiming the glory of Babylon."

He pointed, and at first I thought he was illustrating the reclamation of that glory. Two great stone hands wielded two arced sabers that crossed high above our heads. Tied to the thumbs of the hands were wire mesh horns of plenty. Hundreds of helmets collected from dead Iranians (we later saw) spilled from them onto the dirt. But what Greep was pointing at was the line of green port-o-johns between the sabers.

"Praise Allah," I said.

"I'm starved," I said after I pissed.

"You're one bundle of needs," Greep said, but then added: "I could eat." For Greep to admit even this meant that he must be ravenous. I held out my palm with two dollars and fifty cents' worth of pogs from the PX. "I have this, and some sand," I said.

"You're supposed to buy your driver breakfast."

"Can you spot me?"

"Why would I have money?"

"They'll feed us at the meeting," I said. "A Fulbright meeting's the kind of thing they feed people at."

We drove back to the Republican Palace. At the entrance we declared our business to a white marine who bore a striking resemblance to O. J. Simpson. He barely looked at the IDs we flashed and asked: "CPA passes?"

"No," Greep said.

"We're here for the Fulbright meeting," I leaned over and said.

"Heard you the first time," the marine said. "CJTF-7 pass?"

"No CJTF-7 pass," I said. "We arranged it over e-mail. It's through the State Department."

"Gotta call Force Protection." We could hear him call from where we sat. "They say they got a meeting but they don't got badges." He looked up at us. "Point of contact?"

Two national guard privates first class pulled up behind us in an SUV. The marine set down the phone and waved them around us.

"I'm gonna cut his dick off with a donut," Greep said. We waited fifteen minutes for Force Protection to call back. If the meeting started on time, it had started already. Finally, the marine waved us in as if he had forgotten who we were.

Inside the palace a turquoise dome gave the rotunda an incongruous feeling of peace. Marble, sandstone, gilt, and ornament ascended, spanned, and spiraled around us. It was beautiful as long as you craned your neck. Even Greep might have gawked in this space that defied coolness, that forced a response, if he hadn't been busy surveying the floor. Cubicle dividers, power cords, office furniture, and spastic screensavers on new PCs congested things at eye level. Red marker on a whiteboard announced the day's business, including the meeting we were late to. "We've really improved the place," Greep said.

"He used to live here," I said.

"Writing novels in blood," Greep said.

The ample American checkpoints created the effect of standing in line six times to purchase a pack of gum. We passed a mural celebrating the Twin Towers, the four branches of the U.S. Military, and the fire and police departments of New York City. Then I was pushing open the doors to a conference room, Greep moving behind me like a gangsta at a quilting bee. He seldom moved like this. He knew how black he looked to white people. It was for the occasion.

Silence and cold air washed over us. A long conference table stretched toward a wall with two whiteboards on it. You could hear in the silence the fact that we had caused the silence. A score of fresh, clean faces peered at us with unapologetic and unselfconscious curiosity, alarm, and scorn. A middle-aged woman, silver-haired, dressed for success, stood between the boards holding a marker. The people around the table wore polo shirts and did not smile. The people were children. The Fulbright person smiled at us as if at hyenas free from zoo cages and redolent of carrion. It was hard not to catch sight of yourself, suddenly and awfully, in body armor, Kevlar helmet, and load-bearing vest. A year of sun had bleached our DCUs and turned our faces to masks. We were carrying M16s, five hundred rounds of 5.56 millimeter between us, and 9-millimeter Beretta sidearms.

"Counterterrorism Special Ops Top Secret Briefing?" Greep said.

"He's kidding," I said. "Fulbright?"

The woman told us to have a seat, and a man resumed speaking, except that he was a boy. Someday he would begin to shave, but for now he was running a foreign nation. "I'm writing new labor laws for Iraq," he said, "and I think it would be interesting to do a comparative study of various nations' labor laws." "I'm interested in urban planning and have been doing the traffic plan," a girl said. "I want to do something on the president's vision for a democratic Iraq," a boy said.

"Us too," Greep stage whispered. "Us too."

"Iraq will embellish any resume," the woman said.

"Iraq will embellish my resume," Greep said when we left. "Remind me to make a resume." As we drove out he gave the bird to the marine who had given us such trouble getting in. "And I quote, 'A Fulbright meeting's the kind of thing they feed people at.'"

"You don't feel like you were fed something?" I said. But my mind was racing with prospects. I had spoken with the silver-haired woman after the meeting, and she had brightened at the sound of my plan to study Babylonian history at a German university. "You're a born shoe-in!" she said.

"You really only have pogs?" Greep said.

"There's Chinese food." I pointed. "The Chinese should take pogs. I think China invented the pog."

We would have eaten parsnips, turf, anything. As we climbed down from the Humvee, men in dark suits with dark glasses emerged from the restaurant. "CIA?" Greep asked. They ignored him and climbed into an SUV.

"You're a moron," I said.

"Can't you feel that?"

"Feel what?"

"The absence of the unremitting threat of seeing your lower intestines?"

"Do you take pogs?" I asked the man behind the counter, who looked more Pakistani than Cantonese. The man declined the pogs. "Start a tab?" Greep looked ready to lunge across the counter at the food. Piles of chicken, fried and glazed red, steamed coquettishly. The man turned from us, shaking his head. Greep slammed his palm on the wall as we walked out.

"Listen, can I go in here?" I said. The sign next door read THOU-SAND AND ONE NIGHTS BOOKSHOP.

"No," Greep said.

"I have to go in here."

"Dude."

So I came clean: "Akana is sending us to Babylon to meet up with some Italians. I was going to tell you tomorrow. This is need-to-know for now. We're camera-fodder for a feel-good piece about protecting antiquities. Because I know some Latin."

This revelation sharpened Greep's attention to a point. For a moment I could all but hear the gears turning in his skull. His face showed nothing, but he studied me as he digested the news. I expected him to explode, be indignant, accuse me of cowardice, and curse the loss of a chance at combat. Or I expected a grin and for him to make fun of it. You could never tell with him. Now, as so many times before, he surprised me, saying, "That looting the museum stuff made me sick last year." So he gave his approval.

Inside the bookstore I found *The Complete Idiot's Guide to Understanding Iraq*. They had three hundred copies. In the back, under some dust, I found four volumes on Mesopotamian, British colonial, and Iraqi history. The storekeeper, Iraqi, eyed my excitement. I asked him if he took pogs. He didn't take pogs but told me I could pay him later. I walked out with a text presenting seven thousand years of history and a hundred and twenty-five years of historiography in one hundred and five pages. I also found a translation of *Gilgamesh*, with archeological annotations, from 1996.

"You know your men are just going to jack off all over that stuff," Greep said.

"If I don't eat, I'm going to lose my sense of humor," I said.

We drove around until we found the Al-Rashid Hotel. The Al-Rashid was the hotel of choice for people who needed to be in Baghdad but did not want to spend every hour shitting themselves in fear. The dark atrium of the convention center exuded 1970s affluence, but that was transformed by two decades of war and impoverishment. For a brief, happy time, the oil pumps had pumped and the peace with Iran held. In those years blunt facades, perpendicular lines, gold railings, square chandeliers, and sepia windows had struck Iraqis as the best possible instantiations of vast wealth.

"Did I mention my hunger?" Greep said.

The atrium looked like a student union at a declining state university in midsummer. Printed sheets of PowerPoint slides cluttered the square columns and directed visitors to various offices: "The Iraq Mine Action Center," "The Dutch Liaison Office to the CPA," "The Iraqi American Friendship Council," "Jumpstart.org," "The Royal Jordanian Airlines Ticket Office," "Office of Infrastructure," and so on. Everywhere was a sheet reading, "Due to Recent Convoy Cancellations Some Items are Not Available."

"By cancellations," Greep said, "they mean blown the fuck up."

"Let's try public affairs," I said.

At a table in the dirty light sat two officers, an E7 reservist old enough to have served in Vietnam, except female, and a much younger marine, also female. The marine had chocolate eyes, perfect skin, and a pug nose. She glanced at the names on our shirts and said to Greep with enthusiasm dazzling both of us, "Sergeant Green? I'm Sandra, we've been e-mailing! I'm so happy you agreed to work with us and TEX on this piece we're doing. May I call you Jackson? But who's this?"

It was the *P* on the patch on Greep's pocket that had been worn illegible. "We—" I started to say.

"Sandra," Greep said. "It's a pleasure finally to meet you."

The strangeness of the Green Zone and the Fulbright meeting, the radical difference between this particular day and all the other days, distracted me from the intuitions that generally distinguish me as a sensitive dude. I should have had an intuition thirty seconds ago. It was a no-brainer that Greep would take this mix-up and ride it all the way home.

"As I said in my e-mail, the idea is for you to mingle with people from all the offices of the CPA, sharing your important perspective on the war and on the president's vision for Iraqi democracy. After the interview there will be a brainstorming session on Peace and Prosperity Month." She paused, looked at me, and looked at the paperwork.

"I was riding shotgun," I said.

"He goes where I go," Greep said. "Else I get jumpy."

"He can come in, but we can't shoot him," Sandra said. "You were carefully selected by the people at TEX."

She led us downstairs.

In the conference room on the lower level celebrity disturbed the air. Elizabeth Slade was smiling and shaking our hands. In the flesh the woman appeared as a quotation of herself, a stunted simulation of her actual, vivid, televised eminence. She was a petite person with a small face and head, everything about her only two-thirds as large as you expected. Her hair was a blonde shell, her smile a red mechanism, her eyes more vacant without the blue glow of the teleprompter at their cores. Next to her stood a cameraman whose unshaven cheeks looked more cultivated than a clean shave would have. He was eating a donut. "Could we could get some donuts?" Greep said.

Sandra got us some donuts.

"I guess I should get them some more?" somebody said in a minute.

"Should we get started?" Elizabeth Slade said.

Wiping our mouths, we sat at the table, Greep having put on a face of radical disgruntlement. Sandra asked me to move out of the frame.

"I'd feel safer if he stayed," Greep said.

"Are you joking?" Sandra asked. He twitched in a way he didn't usually twitch in. "We e-mailed about this, Jackson. TEX is looking for a particular point of view. They decided you were perfect."

"Because I'm black?"

Uncomfortable pause.

"I get it," Greep said. "Straight from *Uncle Tom's Cabin*."

"We would like footage of you being honest about what being in Iraq means to you," Elizabeth Slade said.

The cameras rolled. "We're here to kill terrorists," Greep said. "After nine eleven I knew I had to go to Iraq to kill terrorists."

"So you enlisted after nine eleven?"

"America would not be safe until Saddam Hussein was killed. I was working at Taco Bell and would be proud to be killing the enemy."

"Stop the camera," Sandra said. "You told us you were getting a masters degree in communications."

"Taco Bell was to pay for the drugs," Greep said.

"Drugs?" Elizabeth Slade said.

"Talk about the masters degree," Sandra said.

"You look familiar to me," Elizabeth Slade said.

"It's because you vetted him," Sandra said.

"Are you an athlete?" Elizabeth Slade said.

He was a minor league veteran and the son of Bobby Greep!

"This war feels athletic," Greep said.

"Can we start over?" Sandra said.

The cameras rolled, and Slade asked Greep about his pride in enlisting.

"I was proud to be killing the enemy," Greep said. "I knew Saddam had weapons of mass destruction and that we could make a cradle of democracy in the Middle East that would smoke out Osama bin Laden and kill AIDS in Africa without condoms. I knew we could leave no child behind without killing stem cells."

Slade looked to me, perhaps for salvation. "Private—"

"Fleming," I said.

"He's a lieutenant," Sandra said, "but he's not vetted."

"No comment," I said.

Finally, Sandra said, "Elizabeth, did Spencer still want to do a conversation?"

"You're right. Sergeant Green might be more Spencer's speed," Elizabeth Slade said.

Sandra left the room and returned with Spencer Talent and the woman with the mane of gorgeous red curls. She followed Talent with a clipboard.

Talent shook our hands and said, "We couldn't do this without you."

"We certainly couldn't have done this without you," Greep said.

"Well," Talent beamed. He exuded buoyant anger, showed a kind of quick vigilance in his eyes. He set up next to Greep, the two of them in two chairs, like interviews you see on television. Talent crossed his legs. Greep planted his feet on the floor, spread his legs, and pressed his chin to his chest.

"Tell me about the good you do on a typical day," Talent said. "What kind of Iraqis you help, what kind of progress you see."

"I see democracy everywhere," Greep said. "The Iraqis are increasingly democratic each day. They do anything they fucking please."

"We'll have to edit that," Sandra said. "Jackson, you're clear on our policy about language?"

"Tell me what kind of things you see," Talent said.

"We painted a school. I think we painted a school in October. Flem? October?"

"With Iraqi schoolchildren?" Talent said.

"With democratic Iraqi schoolchildren. The children are growing up to love automobiles. We give them chocolate whenever we can. I hope that women stop wearing spooky outfits for democracy. Imagine Martha Jefferson in a spooky outfit for democracy."

Talent paused. "How is morale in the street?"

"Spectacular," Greep said. "As soon as we find hajjis who bleed white and hajjis who bleed blue, every intersection will put Betsy Ross to shame."

Somebody had appeared at the door. He was an African American sergeant who shared Greep's dark skin but had slender, regal features and narrow eyes. The vintage E7 from public affairs stood next to him looking anxious. "This man says he's Sergeant Jackson Green," she said.

"Two colors shy of ancient Athens," Greep was saying.

"Am I late?" Green said. "I thought I was on time."

"Who's that?" Slade and Talent said.

"Jackson Green?" the E7 said.

Everybody looked at Greep.

"Stop the camera," Sandra said.

"Who the fuck?" Talent said.

"You knew you were the wrong man." Sandra was furious.

"You racist motherfuckers," Greep said. He scanned the room with an expression of outrage. "We all look alike? That what you think?" He rose from his chair and strode over to Green. "Can't tell us apart?" He was standing square next to him. "Think we're twins?"

"I can't believe you're even thinking you can fuck with us," Talent said coolly.

"TEX News is for crackers, ain't it?" Greep said. He turned to Green: "You going to be part of this? First in News for Crackers? All us niggers look alike?"

"Get away from me," Green said.

"Get Bremer," Talent said coolly. The redhead had moved to his side. "Sandra, get Jerry on the horn."

"You're going to pay for those donuts," Sandra said.

"We have pogs," I said.

"Just find out what unit they're from," Talent said. "Whoever they are they're gone. This is over."

In my fear of authority and my aversion to conflict I was sweating it. I thought of Breitbart and of Akana, of the specter of a dishonorable discharge. Minutes ago, we had had before us an easy month of protecting splendors of antiquity followed by a plane ride home.

Greep was not the wimp I was. He was bearing down on Talent. "Listen," he said, "before this is over, can I ask you a question?" His grin arrested the room. "It's just that me and Flem heard about what a big Scud missile you've got. We've heard all about your weapon of mass destruction." He grinned at the redhead and said, "Scud or Tomahawk? I forget."

"Weapons of mass destruction?" Elizabeth Slade said.

"Scud or Tomahawk, Flem? You remember? I suppose we can just check the footage, since we got it on tape. Flem, where's that camera? Still in the Hummer?"

"Get them out of here," Talent said. "Sandra, don't bother Bremer. Get out of here, go on, go!" He was redder than red. The intern was blushing too, and her eyes were fixed on the clipboard.

"What is going on here?" Elizabeth Spade said.

"They owe us the donuts," Sandra said.

"Fuck the donuts," Talent said.

A half hour later we finally stopped laughing. We sat for a long time in the atrium, watching people come and go, at first happily but then slowly feeling haunted, me at least, I felt haunted by what we were laughing at. I couldn't help thinking about it too much. What is the morality or immorality of pretending to be something you're not around people pretending to be something they're not? What if they don't know that they're pretending? And you do? The war belonged to the media (thought the Henry Fleming who got shipped off to Iraq, having enlisted for Afghanistan); it was their war, not ours, not mine or Greep's, not anybody in Iraq's, but it was our bodies that cracked, crumpled, lost pieces, and bought the farm. It was better to laugh, I wanted to laugh, and Greep had no trouble laughing, but it was hard for me to, at least after a half hour it was, so I watched people and felt the laughter drain from me like the effects of a stiff drink on an empty stomach.

Twelve hours remained until the convoy would pass by again and pick us up. Late in the afternoon I found a friend from West Point who treated us to cheeseburgers, the best cheeseburgers in the history of America. He took us that night to three bars in the Green Zone. We could not drink but watched the pretty young Republican girls dance in hot pants and high heels. There was one pretty young girl for every ten ugly, lonely men.

At 2300 we drove back to the parking lot and bunked out until 300. I was exhausted and felt like crying. I experimented to see if I could make myself feel better by running my mind over the details of my conversations with Akana and the silver-haired woman. Tomorrow would be our last patrol of the Baghdad streets.

"Do you think we'll get to overhear any more GOP rutting?" Greep said.

"One can only hope," I said.

"It was almost as fun as being hungry for twelve hours."

Later I said, "Could you take it easy on Duckworth?"

"Dude, I was asleep. I was right there."

"Could you?"

"You're exhausted, Flem. You get sentimental when you're exhausted."

Later I awoke from a dream drenched in sweat and crying. The darkness of the Hummer contrasted with the yellow warmth of the dream. I had been in a restaurant with a picture of a sperm whale on the wall and distant accordion music, eating plates of pasta and mussels with Hillary and my long-deceased mother and a friendly man I didn't recognize. Everybody had been so happy. My mother had been smiling and shaking her head like she couldn't believe how good things could be. A dark feeling swept over me as I studied the faces of the people I loved. I loved them all. The words came into my mouth like spinal fluid. "Wait," I said. "Am I still in Iraq?" Everybody looked down at their plates in embarrassment. I moved to hug Hillary and grasped nothing and awoke crying. As I lay there in the darkness I listened to the Apache helicopters coming and going, that heavy machinery hovering in the sky as if weightless.

IV.

When John Townley was thirteen his uncle married an affluent northerner on a vast lawn filled with American dignitaries overlooking the
North Atlantic. Much later in life John would look back with an
awareness of the irony of the vehemence with which, at the age of
thirteen, he resisted going to the wedding. He could have met his
cousin Emily a year earlier, not to mention nibbled at the edge of
history, but all spring the talk among eighth graders at Apalachicola
Junior High had been of the adventure camp run by the Bible Church,
of rope bridges and zip lines spanning forest canopies in Georgia.
Stang told John how Rick Force said that his older brother said that
lots of girls from Apalachicola Bible Church gave their first blowjobs
there. "Plus the zip lines are totally mainy."

So when John's parents suggested he forgo adventure camp to attend a fancy wedding in Rhode Island, John rebelled to say the least.
He was not a mild person so much as a person whose intensity directed itself inward, so his outburst defied his basic psychology and
astonished Frank and Mary Townley. That it was the Bible Church
that ran the camp added insult to his father's injury. "Tambourines
instead of theology," said the look on Frank's face. Instead of meeting Emily, John spent the time living in tent cabins, memorizing dirty
jokes, being sweetly browbeaten to be born again, and bobbing from
zip lines. Each day for seven days with diminishing optimism he
watched and waited for any sign of blowjobs.

Sallie White, the name on the wedding invitation, was a famous
name in the Hamptons, Washington, DC, and on the Upper East Side,
but not to a thirteen-year-old who had never traveled further than
the Carolinas. She was the widowed third wife of Dickerson White,

an American statesman, a Kennedy crony, a third-tier Cold Warrior famous for a decade four decades ago, once a hero, now a footnote in scholarly articles. His successor in matrimony, Marion Townley, Uncle Marion, had escaped Florida by attending Princeton on a track scholarship, graduated from the medical school at Harvard, practiced family medicine in Santa Monica, and become an orthopedic surgeon in Vancouver. Marion's colleagues esteemed him highly, and his patients paid their bills with earnings from Super Bowls. In the eyes of Frank and Mary and John, Uncle Marion was himself a hero, subject to less gravity than normal men, somebody on whom Dickerson White, footnotes or no footnotes, arguably had nothing. Sallie White, dressed in black, selected Marion as the most unobtrusive replacement for her late great husband to be found among the alumni at a Princeton class reunion.

The year after the wedding, Marion, Sallie, and Emily traveled to Florida from Vancouver. John anticipated the visit from the confused vantage of intense changes and with no thought given to the cousin. Puberty was making a daily business of baffling him, his armpits freaking out, his skin staging insurrections, his affections and repulsions assuming proportions a hundred times what they used to be, and even in his boyhood they had never been small. He wondered in this case how to transform childish adoration into mature worship of the long-legged, slow-tongued, handsome, sardonic Uncle Marion. He did not wonder consciously but felt embarrassed at how easy it used to be to love him. It was hard to love anything simply anymore, including girls, which he loved incredibly. Marion shared Frank's features and color but made those things look distinctive and powerful instead of bland and mild. Growing up, John had seen Marion once a year at most, a rareness of exposure that gave the uncle an exotic air and nurtured in John the secret conviction that he himself would accomplish things far beyond the ambivalent pulpits of northern Florida.

When the rental car pulled into the driveway, John was standing by the garage and holding his BB gun and wearing old fatigues. Eighth grade had ended not two weeks earlier, and he was feeling pretty immortal with the freedom of early summer. He saw the three heads in the shadow of the no longer running BMW, then Uncle Marion hauling his aged track-star limbs from the cramp of the driver's seat, then a brittle, wincing, immaculate woman in powder blue emerging from the passenger side, then a girl. The girl wore a green sundress and made a conquest of his imagination in a clap. The blood rose from nowhere to John's face and he discovered the gun in his palm like a pair of dirty shorts. Marion was making introductions from behind the wall of wavy air and shame that stultified John's vision. "A soldier!" the girl said brightly. "You didn't say he was a soldier!"

"I barely recognize him," Marion said.

"Growing like kudzu," said John's father from the front walk.

"Not with that haircut," Marion said. "What ever happened to teen angst?"

"Don't ask Emily that," Sallie White said.

In a hilarious tone, Emily asked what kudzu was.

"You saw it from the car," Marion said, "you saw nothing but."

John's mother was there on the walk behind his father, they had a way of moving together, and he wanted to bolt for his room, vanish, dissolve, cease to be. The girl was objectively wonderful, smirking at him. "His voice changed this spring," his dad said. "As if a plank gave way."

"Multiple planks," his mother said laughing.

Aunt Sallie fanned herself and winced by way of smiling politely. Emily glowed, laying hold of and dismissing with pretty eyes this place and world, over and over, giving John knowing smiles. Marion and Frank hugged and smiled at each other at arm's length in the sun, sweating heavily. They looked like brothers, would burn easily and turn the same color red.

"Marion got lost," Aunt Sallie said. "We're so sorry we're late."

"Wrong turn at the Boredom Weekend Lodge," Emily said.

"The Borden place," Frank guessed.

"In the car it was the boredom place," Emily said. "Sallie said boredom by accident and Marion kept saying it." An awkward pause— awkward for everybody but Emily, who glowed. "Don't worry, Sallie, nobody believes in Freud anymore." She smiled at the Townleys as if to confirm their disbelief in Freud. These words about Freud in their sophistication, amazed John, who still wore the camouflage, who still held the gun. His childhood, which he had abided in until ten minutes ago, seemed a decade remote from him—or should have been. Freud? She was hardly a year older than he was but of another species, calling her mother like that by her first name. Emily had dark-brown hair, almost black, and pale skin that was blushing and fearless.

Aunt Sallie took in the Townleys and their property with the brittle cheer of a senator's wife surveying a constituent's yard sale. The

Townleys lived on a country road where palm and scrub pine mingled with the sundry junk and with the grass that grew up around the junk. Humidity ruined the eaves, and their two stinking sheepdogs lolled and trotted and nosed at phantoms in the backyard. Frank and Mary, cultured and proud of it, could blend in in a cultureless neighborhood. Frank was practically more religious about not putting on airs than he was about religion. "Let us help you with the bags," he said.

"We unloaded at the hotel," Marion said.

"You're not sleeping here?" Frank said.

"Please do sleep here," Mary said. "I made up beds."

"We wouldn't for the life of us let ourselves put you out," Aunt Sallie said.

"Emily already flopped on the beds," Marion said. "They'll charge us anyway."

"I flop on everything," Emily said. "I ruin everything."

"It wouldn't put us out," Mary said.

John could read his parents' hurt in the silence that followed, but Aunt Sallie couldn't read it, and Marion didn't try to. Soon everybody was being social on the porch, sitting on the cracked rattan furniture. Beyond the shade from the roof, the yard baked and stewed. Frank carried in the rotating fan from the living room and set it whirring. Uncle Marion's limbs dwarfed the furniture, his bent knees angled high from the low couch. He looked much like Frank but lanker and larger and better even, as if the womb tried twice and got it right the second time. Chittenango and Chattanooga, the dogs, circled and rootled the laps, dragging in their fur the affable stench of swamp as they searched for love. Emily petted Chittenango and smiled at John. "What are their names again?"

John looked at the floor and then back at her, but now she was smiling at her new Aunt Mary, who stood at the door, index finger ready to list and tally on her fingers the things she could offer them to drink.

"Chittenango and Chattanooga," Frank said.

Aunt Sallie crinkled her senator's wife's nose at Chattanooga, who plunged his nose at her senator's wife's crotch.

"This place has great words!" Emily said. "Kudzu, Chittenango, Apalachicola, what else?"

"Choctawhatchee," Marion offered.

"Choctawhatchee," Emily said.

"Chit and chat," Frank said.

"Water, milk, lemonade, and tea," Mary counted on her fingers.

"So how about it, Sallie," Marion said. "Vodka or gin?"

Mary disappeared to fetch lemonade all around. Marion asked about the church, and John's father went on about it. Frank Townley would never declare a literal belief in heaven or a literal fear of hell but spoke of the church with unwavering conviction, a certainty it mattered, that its existence was righteous and that the lives it shepherded held lessons for all. Each day at work he collected stories about parishioners and repeated them to others, transforming them through his tone of voice to parables, gossip delivered as parables over the telephone to other parishioners, or like this, now, to an outsider. Death accosted businessmen suddenly and left behind wives, young couples lost their jobs and had no health insurance, old people faced boils, tumors, and radical thyroids.

John did not often listen to his father with bitterness, but that afternoon he felt only bitterness at the droning chronicles, the pious details, the unwavering confidence and humility. He could not have felt more disagreeable nor less happy in feeling disagreeable nor less happy with himself. When, during the school year, his parents mortified him by appearing at school, he felt something similar. The sight of the idling station wagon at the curb (with all the other idling cars) touched him with panic; and relief inundated him when he slammed the door behind him and buckled the seatbelt. He loved them and felt guilty for allowing the sight of them to humiliate him. In the hot shade of the screen porch, in the thick familiar stench of the dogs, under the wincing smile of his new aunt, under the magnificent smile of his gorgeous new cousin, it was worse than having his mother call his name across the gymnasium floor during a snowball at a school dance.

"Here we are," Mary said, entering with the lemonade. Aunt Sallie received hers with a tense hand as she perched on the edge of the wicker loveseat, her back straight, her smile poised to shatter. "Why don't you give your cousin a tour of your kingdom," his mother said to John.

"Kingdom," Emily said, "or battlefield?"

Marion looked over his shoulder for the kingdom or battlefield.

The plastic soldiers on the back fence flashed in John's mind. He had been preparing to shoot down toys with a BB gun. Emily's smile settled on him again, and the adults had paused to see. She was free

71

from all heaviness. "I bet the kingdom lies just *beyond* the battlefield. That's how these things tend to go."

He shrugged and stood, too aware of his clothing, burning in it, wearing camouflage pants and an Optimus Prime T-shirt. Her skin against her sundress, her calves in the shade, her neck and arms, her breasts, her eyes, her smile—it astonished him she could even exist. In a moment the screen door had snapped behind them and the voices of the adults became a murmur. "Was that a machine gun you had?" Emily asked.

"BB gun."

"So, like a shotgun?"

He stopped walking. He scanned her face to verify the ridicule, but her face was blank with good nature. He couldn't tell. "Can we shoot it?" she said.

"Are you making fun of me?"

"You're making fun of me! I don't know the first thing about guns! But I've always wanted to shoot one! What's a baby gun?"

He did not answer, made for the house, entered through the back, retrieved the .22 from the closet, and returned. Then he was setting up targets in the range, tin cans, not plastic soldiers, with expertise that he longed to believe showed in the precision of his movements. She watched him, her prettiness blowing outward, radiant as if oblivious to itself, free from the flux of shame. He explained the gun to her, shot a few times himself, and sent the cans caroming over the fence. "John, are you firing the rifle?" his mother yelled from the porch, and he ignored her.

He handed the gun to Emily, corrected her grip, felt his blood double when his skin brushed her skin, and at last could study her instead of being studied. Her gaze, which until now had remained in precise but constant motion, seized on the target. He ceased to exist to her, having taught her something that engaged her. She shot well. After a few minutes she looked very happy. She was grinning between shots, whether she hit her target or not. She didn't hit anything for a dozen shots, then hit, then missed, then hit three in a row. He took the gun and shot well and gave it back to her. She laughed and smiled at John and was truly delighted and delightful. Then her face changed, and John heard the crunch of feet approaching. He somehow knew it was Stang before he heard Stang say: "Annie Oakley and Wild Bill Niggercock!"

"Who are you?" Emily said. "And why are you taking our picture?"

John had a sinking feeling that he would understand completely only ten years from now. Stang reached them in his jeans and bare feet and muscle shirt and stood next to John and looked Emily up and down. Emily glanced at John for an introduction as Stang whistled a catcall as if at some distance. "Excuse me?" Emily said, the gun in her hands suddenly like something caught from the air by accident.

"Marshall Franklin Stang. Oldest friend of Wild Bill Niggercock here."

"Why does he call you that?" Emily asked. "Why does he keep using that word?"

"Don't call me that, Stang," John said.

"Listen to the northerner," Stang said. "I can hear it. Even though John's from round here I always did think he had something of the Yankee in him, niggercock or no niggercock."

"Stop!" Emily said. "What are—?" She had lost the ground that had until now seemed unshakable beneath her.

"Innerductions," Stang said.

John felt frozen as in a nightmare.

"I'm Emily Elizabeth White, since we're being ridiculous."

"You sure didn't look ridiculous from back there," Stang said. "Still don't."

"What is wrong with you?" John said to Stang.

"I never quite believed people were still racist like this," Emily said. "I just couldn't picture racism like this."

The word hung between them for a moment. It was an abstract word, and the backyard and their faces were not abstract. "So it's not the cock part you have the problem with?" Stang said. There was a second awful pause. The color in Emily's cheeks was no longer that of effortlessness. John felt sick and was not acting with intelligent decision when he said, "This is my cousin."

"Kissin' cousins," Stang said.

"Cousin by marriage," Emily said.

John picked up the .22 and turned to the fence and started firing. Emily faced away from Stang and watched John shoot. John kept missing now. He could feel Stang taking pictures and between shots hear him talking. "I hook Johnny up with what he needs. He'd never've seen a pussy even today except for my baby stash of vintage porn. The Reverend Townley? Not so big on the *Hustlers* as far as we can figure out. But who knows? Every man has his vixens. I pretty much outgrown it, it's boys' stuff, T and A, a little wham-bang-thank-you-ma'am, but John loves it, loves them pictures of pussy, you get him in my closet where I keep the porn he's like a hobo in a vat of Nabisco."

John set down the gun and launched himself wildly. His swinging hand hit Stang's jaw like a bird against a window, wild and thumping and light, and Stang backed off laughing and holding the camera away from the blows. He was rubbing his face and laughing as if hit by a water balloon. Emily watched them with bright eyes and total amazement. "Nothing to be ashamed of, John," Stang said, "'tain't a man what don't love pussy."

"Go home," John said.

"Just wanted to extend some southern hospitality," Stang said, backing off. He turned and walked ten yards then turned back again and took a last picture.

They watched him vanish down the driveway to the road. He was practicing his catcall and didn't look back. Emily waited for John to say something, but he was wiping his eyes on his shirttail. "Let's get some lemonade," she said. He tried to breathe and only slowly did his breath come back to him as he watched her cross the yard back to the porch and their parents.

Marion complained about the hotel the next morning. For ten minutes in his laconic drawl he described the horrors of it. "I don't feel sorry for you," Frank said at last, not to his brother but to his new sister-in-law, as though she had been the one complaining. "I asked you to stay here."

There were other sticky points, especially regarding drinking. Marion and Aunt Sallie brought wine; Frank and Mary did not drink. Marion opened the bottle with a drill bit after a search for a corkscrew. "Emily will have a glass," Marion said. "Yes!" Emily said. Frank poured quarter glasses for himself and his wife and Emily and none for John. Marion gave Emily a full glass when he divvied up the remainder later on. So Marion, Aunt Sallie, and Emily drank the bottle and transformed from reserved and deferential guests to radiant ones, smiling with distraction and with fluid affection as Frank drew solemn conclusions from the non-Hodgkin's lymphoma of a local real estate agent who sang in the choir.

The next night Marion presented more wine to the Townleys and for a second time drank with his new wife and his step-daughter without reserve. Again, Marion and Aunt Sallie spoke freely and laughed in a spirit of sophisticated levity. They had done cocaine on their honeymoon and had a vital sex life even at their age. "No!" Emily protested cheerfully at the mention of it. Invoking sex in the Townley house was like crapping on the coffee table. Frank kept his eyes on his plate.

Later Aunt Sallie got it into her head to interrogate her awkward new nephew. "I'm surprised that you don't have to board. Is there a day school in Tallahassee?"

He looked at his mother. Board? he thought. Day school?

"He goes to the Apalachicola public schools," his mother said. "It did just fine for Marion and Frank."

"Democracy depends on public schools," Frank said.

"Good lord you sound like Emily's father!" Aunt Sallie said, meaning the late great Cold Warrior. "Dick graduated a high school of three hundred in a small town in Indiana during the Depression and to hear him talk about it it rivaled Exeter. He loved to recite the prologue to the *Canterbury Tales*, which he learned as a freshman. He went on and on about it. I couldn't stand the sound of it, all those drooly vowels."

John had never heard of Exeter. He asked Emily if she went there.

"This is the tackiest conversation ever," Emily said.

"Emily goes to Groton," Aunt Sallie said.

"Sigh," Emily said.

Color had risen in Aunt Sallie's cheeks, and she now looked sharp instead of brittle. Her questions paved the path to giving advice. "It's definitely worth checking what the school's placement rate is, how many of their students go on to good colleges. Clearly, John, you must be an excellent student."

"John's an excellent student," Frank said. "There are excellent colleges everywhere. Emory was excellent."

"Emory's terrific," Aunt Sallie said. "Put Emory on your list."

Emily finished her glass, and Marion poured her more wine.

On Sunday afternoon Emily and John walked up the road. Her eyes swept the woods and saw nothing but arbitrary emptiness while he saw textures, colors, shadows, and secrets indistinguishable from his personality. "I can see why you look at porn," she said. He was silent, and she watched his ears turn red and then laughed. "What do you *do* here is all I'm saying."

"I read a lot."

But he did not read a lot, not by any standard. He told her this only because she had admired his parents' books seven times this weekend. Books filled the house.

"What do you read?" Emily asked. He told her he had just finished *Catcher in the Rye*. He had finished it six months ago. "I am so sick of that book. I had to read it three times for school. I liked it until I was clobbered to death by it. It seems so fundamentally immature."

Immature?

"I just started reading Nietzsche," Emily went on. "Nietzsche is to *Catcher in the Rye* what *Hustler* is to *Playboy*." She laughed at this. John wanted her never again to say the words *Hustler* or *Playboy* and wanted Stang to be hit by a bus or a moon.

Even before Monday morning, when the BMW backed out of the driveway for the last time, he felt the shift. He had grown up telling himself the story of his life and saw he had gotten it wrong. Until that weekend his superiority, and the superiority of his parents, existed as one of the unquestionable and immutable facts. His fantasies of escape depended on his rejection of his parents but also and quite crucially on his difference, the family difference, from the men and women around them. His parents were solemn, modest, unassuming, unpretentious, earnest, quiet Christians who never would have advertised or even allowed themselves to describe to themselves their superiority. John shared the circumspection and the self-confidence. He had needed the self-confidence to fortify himself against other very different orders of insecurity that thrived in him in this particular local soil.

Since sixth grade and on an almost daily basis Stang had given John someone to compete with but also to define himself against. John envied the purely physical excellence, the unthinking and reflexive prowess, that Stang tackled life with. Without hesitation or misstep Stang performed stunts and feats and athletic miracles, he accepted dares, he ducked punishments, he got the other boys to fall in behind him. There radiated from him a kind of self-fulfilling certitude. Do whatever you want to do with sufficient boldness and whatever you want to do will be done. It was a lesson in audacity that John could observe and cling to and rehearse and enshrine and attempt but not come close to assimilating. His body, in junior high, was a hideous cage, a gorilla suit, a stifling contrivance, a blushing, sweating horror. Making matters worse, Stang mocked him for his occasional forays into boldness. "It's like you're such a *virgin*," Stang said long before either of them had had sex. The distance between theory and practice, between what John grasped mentally and failed to perform physically, between Stang's ease and his own awkwardness, formed the dark heart from which all his shame and sadness in those years flowed.

So John endured his schoolyard inferiority by nurturing a sense of superiority on other grounds. Precisely what he lacked he made a virtue of. At least he could *think*. But in a brief seventy-two hours, his uncle, new aunt, and new cousin had laid waste to this consolation. Being better than the county meant nothing more than being better than nothing. The rough punk from down the block showed him up from below, the wealthy northerners, from above. He had less force and less devilish intensity than Stang, less brilliance, grace, knowledge, and cleverness than Emily. He knew nothing and attended a school that would not change that. He was mediocre and stranded.

So from the moment she departed he resolved to hold onto her. He would look to her to drag him up and out. The idea had already crystallized when the house was still quiet with the sound of their departure. He would not let go. His parents were washing dishes and reflecting on the visit in silence. John was lying on his bed feeling desolated by having lost what seemed barely anything much to have while he still had it. He rose, took paper from the desk, returned to the bed, and lay down gently. He stared at the page and thought of Emily saying "I flop on everything, I ruin everything." He was too cowardly even to flop on his own bed. He wrote feverishly. Within two hours he dropped in the mailbox a letter meant to extend the liberation of knowing her.

Within a year he would understand the uneasiness that descended on him that day: in that first letter he revealed to Emily his failure to comprehend the necessary mutuality of love. He mistook the force of love for something original to him and also for something he was not beholden to control. It was adolescent. As soon as he mailed it he felt ill. The letter undermined the satisfaction he otherwise could have taken in the visit as it stood, breaking open the closed perfection of the three days. That perfection did not appear perfect until the mailbox flapped shut. It emerged as it vanished.

For a week, for ten days afterwards, the heat sat on the household, and John cried at night. He checked the mailbox morning and afternoon, certain it would contain nothing, pledging his soul to a devil he didn't believe in if an envelope would appear. An envelope appeared on the back of his eyes and vanished when he opened the mailbox. His imagination perpetrated this act of violence against his heart every hour on the hour. He barely had will enough to move through the day. His parents' eyes followed him and, despite their intended kindness, made him self-conscious and angry. It was the worst thing in the world to have others watch you want something.

Then after ten days his father brought in a stack of mail with her reply. Frank held out to John a small, blue envelope slightly dampened with sweat from his hands. The paper was lush to the touch, John could feel this as he hurried to his room, and ripping it open felt like plunging a finger in a living thing. Two pages dense with script repelled John's eyes. Reading the lines was like trying to run down a rugged hill without falling. He had to read the letter four times before he began to understand what it was about, and, as he did, a cruel coolness settled over him. She had written in jest, friendly jest, with humane, sophisticated levity. She had nothing to confess to him and knew already at fifteen not to write seriously. Her sentences erected winsome, facetious architecture. She attempted an effect and achieved one. She could do on paper what she could do in person while he had done on paper what he had done in person.

Stang had understood the need to make himself scarce after the moment in the yard. He knew he would be hated for a while, and kept away for two weeks. Then he came by the house in early July to show John fireworks from across the Georgia line, acting like nothing had happened. "You could blow up an alligator with this donkey dick." He held a Roman candle the size of a rolling pin like a boner from his crotch. "I looked for a black one for you." He studied John's face for a moment, saw the furious absence of forgiveness and said: "Stop storing that rat up your ass. She's in love with you. Head over heels. I couldn't have changed that."

"What are you talking about?" John said.

"She wants to mount you sideways."

They were out by the back fence, and Stang kicked stones with a weightless conscience. John braced his hands on the fence and just let his eyes rest on his friend. Stang's words—as close as he would come to offering an apology—stirred John's blood into awful hopeful confusion. "I did you a favor bringing up the pussy. Now she knows you're a man of passion. You should have seen how she was staring at you. She was drooling on the crabgrass."

John was so desperate to believe this he believed it.

"She wants to mount the niggercock."

"Could you really stop staying that?" But it was a protest weakened by the flattery, the enabling.

"I walk up to you guys and what am I supposed to do? Drown in the drool? It was disgusting and embarrassing standing there. Listen! I have the evidence!" He pulled from his pocket two pictures that melted John's heart: of Emily, and of himself and Emily, of their happiness firing the gun in the moment before Stang broke in on it. Stang gave him the pictures, and these, more than any words Stang could have spoken, cleared the air.

After that afternoon John allowed himself to float hopefully on the absence of total disbelief that Stang had planted in him. When he reread the letter from Emily for the twenty-seventh time, its words smirked gorgeously on the pages, not in jest but almost in flirtation. Starting with his second letter he tried to write as she wrote. His words should glance as effortlessly. He composed rough drafts in a notebook and revised each one twice before copying it out. It took him an afternoon to be at all satisfied with a letter. He pedaled the finished ones to the main road with triumph, the sunlight hammering the overgrowth, the roads empty, his blood possessing the universe. These bike trips to the mailbox were the desperate, ecstatic ritual that filled the rest of the summer.

Yet after even the best of his letters were posted, his insides turned sour. There was a perfection in each response he received from Emily that each subsequent letter of his destroyed. He reread the letter drafts in the notebook and perceived with perfect clarity their adolescent mediocrity. He had achieved a sneering, sniveling, florid, arrogant brightness of style. He was pompous and ponderous but also loose and obscure. He was slipshod and stiff. He had no better idea of how he sounded than of how he truly looked.

By the fall his memories of the visit had lost all texture, all reality, worn to smoothness and abstraction by the hungry touch of active recollection. It was a dirt path in the grass of his brain. Had he actually ever met her? The letters confused the situation instead of clarifying it. Who was Emily, and who was she to him? He lived for the brief seconds of hope that existed between his receiving a letter and his discovering the whole of its contents. Her letters burned out like falling stars.

That fall, she described a school and a town and a state and a region about which John could picture nothing. In the word "Massachusetts" he saw Pilgrims eating turkey and Indians planting corn with fish. The postmark from Groton dazzled him like the insignia of a king. Emily was a year ahead of him, beginning her sophomore year, and recounted reading philosophy in her room as her roommate withered from anorexia on the bed across from her. People shouted in the hall, smoked, drank, and channeled family wealth into cruel displays and bizarre transgressions. Jaguars got totaled and cocaine snorted, sex acts transpired with casualness simply insane. Plagiarism and cribbing sustained the atmosphere of excellence. John wanted to go to prep school.

More affecting even than the sordid gossip were Emily's treatises on literature and culture. She did not care about the Emerson and Thoreau he had to read but cared a great deal about Kundera and Bataille. In the library at the high school John could not find Kundera and Bataille. The librarian in Tallahassee could find Kundera but not Bataille. John opened Kundera and discovered incredible sex scenes and realized that Emily might soon have a sex life. He felt sick.

"I'm only getting around to Rilke now," she wrote. And: "You'll be horrified but I've never looked at a word of Hardy until today. You remind me already of poor Jude." He read *Jude the Obscure* and was not happy with what he found.

When she was a senior and he a junior she began to read and recommend novels without characters. There were proper nouns but no personalities to care about or follow from one place to another. Empty souls floated through abstract landscapes filled with improbable organizations and bright colors, all described in sentences too long to hold in mind at once. He read these books and others she mentioned, yet, even when he shared her admiration for a novel, she unwittingly said things that shamed him. *Lolita* he read in earnest, felt gravely moved by, and was dismayed to hear called a grand prank.

Throughout high school Emily took many trips and described them at length in letters and postcards to John. Twice a year she traveled with her mother and Marion to places too remote even to seem possible to be traveled to: Tahiti, Finland, Buenos Aires, Rome. One summer they went to India, and photographs followed: temples and elephants, Marion's triumphant height bent to fit a rickshaw, brown-skinned porters grinning beside beautiful Emily. John hung them above his desk and studied them in envy and disbelief and humiliation.

In his letters he attacked everything around him. Trapped by his upbringing, embarrassed by it, longing to be free of it, his language was scathing. He wanted her to know he perceived as keenly as anybody his parents' earnest goodness, their pious obliviousness, their sober morality, their dysfunctional temperance, their unshakable backwoods credulousness. How could his father preach the Christian Gospels? It was a world of chaos and capitalism, indecency, delight, randomness, cynical resolve, chemical emotions, and utter pain. John drafted and posted the letters as if he were a ten-year-old boy trying harder and harder to perform a stunt on a skateboard for a girl on the curb. Each time, Emily wrote back, "I love your mom and dad! They're so sweet!"

Between 1994 and 2003 John wrote a thousand letters to Emily. He spent the best energy of his adolescence crafting a second self in prose. He got nowhere in the schoolyard in his efforts to compete but held out hope that on the page he was growing less and less like his actual awkward self and more and more like the inhabitants of Emily's world. So that what might have been mere lovesickness after one strange June weekend grew to look to him in retrospect like an existential watershed. In equal parts he was in love with the person he was writing to and with the escape the writing provided. When, in 2003, after Stang's return, Emily asked to come visit, it blew his mind.

V.

Above the bunker wall the city was mauve and fuming. Dogs barked, cars honked, men yelled, children yipped, and bullets popped in the distance: another brief twilight. Shamhat, with her beautiful eyes and mannish nose and skimpy shorts and thirteen years, sat alone in front of the guardhouse looking long since bored with the day. Her thighs screamed at you: life was a flower. When she saw me she grinned as if we had just been making jokes. Ayad trotted into view from around the corner, holding a kitchen spoon like a gun. A generation ago in a distant prosperous nation at this time of evening children his age would already have been in bed. A spray of imaginary bullets riddled my chest.

Shamhat screamed. It pierced the dusk and sent chills across my skin. A spray of real bullets had riddled her chest. No. She had caught her finger in the rusty joint of something. No. Her new woman's body rose shrieking from the chair, and she closed the distance between her and us. Ayad turned and ran toward the far side of the bunker, away from his sister. Watching him I saw then that what I had taken in the dusk for a backpack, part of his imaginary soldiering, was Shamhat's Cabbage Patch Kid, strapped to his back like a papoose. Shamhat caught him at the edge of the bunker and threw him by the shoulders roughly to the ground.

"Any letters?"

I almost jumped at the voice. Eccles had come up to me.

Yesterday's mailbag, fetched today from Camp Triumph, contained mail for Eccles, J'Million, and Hornbuckle. Contact was crucial to morale, phone calls were, e-mail was, mail mail was. Half the men in the platoon had sons and daughters they focused on, usually wives or girlfriends, and the rest had siblings and nephews and nieces. Contact with the outside world helped them to picture summer BBQs, little bodies squealing in pools, trotting and dripping on decks, burning happily in the sun, eating hotdogs how kids eat hotdogs—intently, as cats clean paws. But most men did not have children yet, had girlfriends and siblings and nieces and nephews and parents. Eccles had Pat Mapp. J'Million loved his sister's son. Greep said almost nothing about his mother, the widow of the major league hero Bobby Greep, living in public housing in Chicago, but what he did say said a lot. Kirk Frank was married and his wife was expecting, and you always forgot it because he floated in silence like a monk.

Only Duckworth didn't have anybody. Yet often I felt as though I didn't have anybody. I had Hillary, but did I really have Hillary? Only in the first instants of opening the latest letter or hearing her strangely close voice on a satellite phone or watching her hold up a cat on a videotape did my dark fears ebb. Otherwise they flowed and flowed. Fears rushed in to obscure with sloshing blackness the warm blond ground of our love. Tonight, in this respect, was not a good night.

In the growing purple dimness, under Shamhat's gaze, I had been standing outside the bunker flipping through the stack of letters just to confirm what I already knew for sure. No mail from her. And the emptiness required no time at all to transform into a sign of the worst possible turn. A thing missing can carry the force of a thing hitting you in the gut. The absent letter made a shadow across the image of Hillary's face in my mind, and that shadow was the shadow of the body of a strange man. Her eyes flashed with lust for a mind different from mine. This man atop her lived to act instead of to think, had approached her in a glamorous locale with the dauntless libido of fantastic handsomeness and correlate cruelty. He was probably rich, too. It did not matter that she hated men like this. It did not matter that Hillary had just yesterday greeted me from a video screen holding up a member of a species she could not stand. The mailbag was empty.

Last night I had written Hillary a long letter about the tragicomic day in the Green Zone, the farce of it, treating it dramatically, making a scene of it, inventing some dialogue, capturing the minor players and Talent and Spencer and the red-headed intern and most of all Greep. "Look for us on TEX News no time soon," I wrote unprophetically. Three weeks ago she had asked in a letter: "Do you hate

83

Greep or love him?" My answer was yes. My Green Zone letter ran seven pages, and after the drafting of it I felt close to Hillary. Even though it would be ten days before she read it, I savored the feeling of closeness—until I opened the mailbag tonight.

Behind Eccles, the harsh light that we hung at the corner of the wall was glaring, now brighter than the dimming sky, and against it his form flattened. Even from the silhouette I could tell that a craven longing filled him. I should have been happy to have a letter to give him. "Did you film yourself yet?" I asked.

His features remained obscure. He did not answer.

"What's with you?" I said. "I thought you were going to make her a tape telling her you loved her."

"Oh yeah," he said. "No, not yet."

Ayad sprinted past us toward the guardhouse, Shamhat two strides behind him, screaming, holding her doll.

Eccles tore open the letter. He held it up to catch the light. After he read it I could tell that he wanted to show it to me. But then Greep's voice, coming from the bunker, distracted us both.

"That girl blew your mind 'cuz she seemed seven hundred percent normal. Seemed like a sweet girl, girl-next-door bullshit. Dressed normal, talked normal, I introduced her to my ma, I remember I introduced her, and my ma asked me where I found her, the country club?"

Greep was holding court. You could just tell. He had moved to within earshot.

"I hated that girl when she talked, you know how when they talk, but she had an ass, she was fine with her mouth closed, on all fours, an ass you would not believe."

"Damn," we heard Corez say.

"You make this shit up," we heard J'Million say.

"The only girl you ever got your dick beaters on?" Greep said.

"Your mom," J'Million said.

"Your sister," Greep said.

"When she and I fucked your mom," we heard Schwartz say.

"What the fuck you talking about Schwartz?" Greep said. "You make Duckworth look like Bobby Fisher."

Everybody laughed.

"Who the fuck's Bobby Fisher?" J'Million said.

"King of Prussia," Greep said.

"Why's Duckworth crying," Schwartz said.

"Ask him," Greep said.

"Why you crying, Duckwad?" Schwartz said. (Why was he crying? Months later I would finally know.)

It felt eerie standing in the dusk with Eccles, listening to the voices without seeing the faces. A shadowy body heaved atop Hillary. Eccles mourned a woman busy partying with dudes named Mike. I wanted the voices to stop.

"I hated this girl," Greep continued, "but that ass. That was the thing. Plus she loved it in the ass. She loved it. Might as well of found her at the country club because she was a lawyer's daughter, big shit lawyer from Ketchum, Idaho, used to take family vacations with Hank Sheffield, his family."

"Hank Sheffield as in—" Corez said.

"Hank Sheffield as in every movie you ever seen on Delta."

"You want us to believe that?" Schwartz said.

"Believe THIS." I could not see Greep's gesture. You can picture the gesture. "This girl hated her life. That's how rich people get. Trust me. I was one once."

"Your old man didn't hate his life," Corez said. "You saying Bobby Greep hate his life?"

"Sleeping with your mama?" J'Million said. "Everybody hate that."

"Everybody try it and everybody hate it," Malik said.

"I hate your life, right?" Greep said. "Give people enough money."

"Look at him," Schwartz said. "Blubbering."

"I thought Eccles's your girlfriend," Greep said to him. "Now you moved on to Duckworth?"

I studied Eccles's silhouette at the sound of his name. He stood there in the twilight that had almost sunken into full darkness, listening with a heavy raptness in the set of the head and a deadness in his eyes. My eyes had adjusted and our positions shifted so I could see his eyes now.

"She loved it up the ass," Greep said. "Rich people the most fucked up motherfuckers there are."

"Lookin' forward to it," J'Million said.

"How'd you get to be J'Million anyway?" Greep said. "And not "J'Ten or J'Hundred?"

Voilà, the birth of a Greepism.

"Shit," J'Ten said.

"Fucking her up the ass every afternoon," Greep said. "So then I figured sky's the limit. I pile-drove that shit three times a day. Her neck all scrunched, her face all red? Then I got bored with all that acrobatic monkey-bar bullshit. So you know what I did?"

"Proposed?" we could hear Kirk Frank say.

I loved Kirk Frank so much.

"I got her to shave her head."

"Shave her what?!" J'Million said.

"I said, honey, you really love me you shave your head. Turn me on. Then I said, honey, you really love me you shave your eyebrows."

"Sick," Corez said. "Just sick."

"You get a rich girl who vacations with Hank Sheffield who lets you fuck her up the ass," J'Million said, "and you want her to shave her eyebrows?"

"The fucked up thing," Greep said, "was she wasn't even my girl-friend. She was somebody else's girlfriend, you know what I'm say-ing? And what does that nimrod think, his girlfriend shows up with no eyebrows?"

Laughter and happy booing.

Eccles's watering eyes worked as a catalyst. My own emotions were not exactly weak. My voice ran ahead of me. I moved to the door, took in the circle of jocular faces, watched the smiles transform from unselfconscious to insubordinate, and heard the strange sound of my orders: "It's time for some PT."

"What's the prob, boss?" Greep grinned.

"You just doubled what I'm going to ask you to do."

"What the fuck?" J'Million said.

"Doubled again." I remained calm. They noticed the calmness. It scared the men more than shouting would have. "Up," I said.

In the courtyard, almost as if to humor me, shuffling and smirk-ing, they dropped and started doing push-ups at my command. I was sorry to watch Kirk Frank among them. "Why ain't Eccles doing 'em?" Schwartz said after two push-ups.

"Doubled again," I said.

Shamhat was sitting in front of the guardhouse again, stroking the head of the doll. Ayad scurried from man to man, watching. Eccles crept off, letter in hand. The scene only made me, too, feel worse. The sight of male bodies rising and falling in the darkness, mounting the prone ground, random and angry, pointless and angry, made me feel really just wretched. Even as he did the push-ups, Duckworth still was crying. Why was he crying?

VI.

Throughout high school John and Stang pulled countless minor pranks, although none as violent as the rock on the roof of Stang's dad's Town Car. They repainted PASS WITH CARE signs to say PASS WITH JOY; they made 35 MPH signs read 85 MPH; they substituted a blue bulb for the red bulb of Rudolf's red nose in the town Christmas display; they doctored the templates in crosswalk signs to read THINK and ACT. Junior year they tampered with the moveable letters on the sign outside the Camden funeral parlor, transforming

GEOFF BURR

DANIELLE SCHUTE

to

FRESH GROUND BEEF

Stang had waited for years for that one. He hung a remaining *U* above the front door of his mom's house like a horseshoe. Every last one of the pranks was captured by Stang on video, and John wondered at the time how these images would look to him in later years. "You should let me see my finger getting smashed," he said once.

"Wait until you're unrecognizable to yourself," Stang said.

"I'll always be recognizable to myself," John said.

"You think old people think they look like old people?"

Stang could be wise.

Since freshman year, Principal Wiffin had discovered a new product for his hair so that it no longer waved in exasperation to the side of his bald crown. Maybe Mrs. Wiffin had discovered the product. The hair now lay flat as if he had just emerged, drenched and sputtering, from a pool into which he'd been pushed by juvenile delinquents. Otherwise Wiffin was the same man with the same triple chin forming a cushion for the one true chin to rest on. John had never liked him because Wiffin had always been stingy where John longed for generosity: in estimating John's intellect. "You're not as smart as you think you are," was Wiffin's attitude toward John. "You're destined for the federal penitentiary," was his attitude toward Stang.

If Wiffin kept an eye on John he kept a rifle scope on Stang. They were opposite elements, sparks and gasoline. At various points Wiffin tried to numb Stang with legal drugs and test him for illegal ones. He harassed him with counselors, threw the book at him. Stang logged more hours in in-school suspension each week than John spent at the dinner table with Frank and Mary. Stang waged a war of charm on everybody surrounding Wiffin and accepted his punishments with sporting indifference. Nothing so much as martyrdom gave him the moral edge. Students loved him almost universally, as did the more subversive teachers. His ideal prank would best Wiffin in full view of everybody. The more punishment Stang suffered until then, the sweeter the revenge would be.

His ideal prank they pulled in their senior year. It was Stang's idea. "We need three hundred sheets of school letterhead," Stang said to John one day, "which Tom Monk can get since he works in the office, and three hundred biohazard bags, the little ones you put your cup of piss in, which Rick can get his mom to get, she's a nurse. But you have to write the letter, you're the letter writer."

"Tell me what you're even talking about," John said.

John perfected Stang's suggestion to read:

Dear Freshmen,

An outbreak of food poisoning among our student population has been traced by the Department of Health and Community Welfare to the cafeteria at Apalachicola High School. If you ate meals prepared by dining services during B Period on Friday, October 17, please use the enclosed bag to bring to school a sample of your stool for testing. Samples will be collected by a county employee in C214 (Principle Wiffin's office) between 7am and 8am on Wednesday, October 23. Your cooperation is appreciated.

Sincerely,
Harold Wiffin

Stang was dating Tina Linnabrink, who was aide to the secretary and culled the addresses for the families of the three hundred freshmen.

On Wednesday a hundred of them, the obedient ones, appeared at Wiffin's office carrying bags of their own shit. Stang and John shared a locker in C Hall and watched the crowd from twenty yards away. Meek girls with overbites, thin boys with acne, and deferential minorities formed a bottleneck at the office door. Ms. Blench, who joined the secretarial staff the year Stalin died, was trying with insufficient force of personality and dangerously low bone density to turn them away. Things got pretty heated for a crowd of meek girls, thin boys, and deferential minorities. From laughter Stang couldn't breathe.

Wiffin appeared in the throng shouting and waving his hands. "Dispense!" he shouted.

"Doesn't he mean 'disperse'?" John said.

During second period, Wiffin broke the classroom silence over the PA: "This morning some members of the student community have placed their peers at risk of serious illness. The school is in the process of identifying the involved individuals, who should know this matter is being taken with the utmost seriousness. Anybody with information regarding these events can speak directly to me. This is being taken extremely seriously." He paused. The school listened. The principal wheezed, and the microphone scraped. "With extreme seriousness," he said.

A week passed, nobody was caught, the prank entered the annals of legend, and Stang and John walked. The local newspaper ran a story about the prank and printed letters in response. John collected two sets of the clippings, one for his journal and one to send to Emily.

Stang in general made trouble in order to antagonize Wiffin and to define himself in the eyes of Apalachicola, but John did it to expand the version of himself he could describe to his cousin. She needed to understand that he humored the place he was from, that he toyed with it, defied and transcended it.

His heart was still glowing with this victory when his conspirators got busted. Not Stang, but everybody else. In his compulsion to capture on video every detail of every prank, Stang had shot the session when Tina, Rick, and Tom Monk printed and folded the letters and sealed them in envelopes. John had not been at the session or known about the tape. But when he came to school one morning the gossip was burning through the halls. Principal Wiffin had found the tape in the choir room. It had no audio, but the images incriminated the faces on it, Tina and Rick and Tom Monk. He called them in to his office and demanded that they tell him who was holding the camera. Of course they refused. Tina was dating Stang, Rick Force was a thug, and Tom Monk was almost as smitten with Stang as Tina was. Wiffin offered a plea bargain. They refused and were suspended.

"Why did you film it?" John asked Stang.

"How do you know I filmed it?"

"Come on. And how did the tape get in the choir room?"

Stang shrugged.

The next Saturday John found his father in the shade of the porch sipping water and staring at the yard. His father was a quiet man but also a constantly active one who rarely just sat. So something clearly was up. "Sit down," Frank said. "Look at them." He nodded at Chittenango and Chattanooga. In the distant shade they resembled corpses, slain havalinas. Both had lived too long and needed to die. Father and son gazed together at the lifeless scene. "I read in the paper about the prank," his father said. "A clever prank."

John's eyes lost sight of the yard that they remained on. He wanted to choose his words carefully. His father said, "The article said three students have been subjected to disciplinary action. That was the paper's phrase. Why don't they just say 'suspended'?"

"What do you always call this? An age of technobabble?"

"Torturous technoglossia. Do you know whose prank it was?"

"I think Rick Force got suspended."

His father ruminated or pretended to ruminate. "A clever prank for the likes of Rick Force. I know who he is because he's stupid. A town knows its stupid residents. I have no other reason to know him."

"You're a figure in the town."

"The clever ones stand out, and the stupid ones do. I'm amazed at Rick Force for coming up with such a clever prank. Do you think he came up with it?"

"Tom Monk also got suspended."

"The Monks are at our church."

"Dad, I know."

"Thomas shows just enough initiative to button his shirt. He couldn't get a bird to fly. That's just my impression. You might know a Thomas that I don't."

John was silent.

"I was just struck by the cleverness."

90

"I think Tina Linnabrink is the other one."

"Stang's girlfriend?"

"Not anymore."

"Oh? He disapproves of her character?" His father laughed. "I shouldn't say things like that. Is she the clever one?"

"She's nice."

"And clever?"

John could feel his ears burning as he stared at the yard.

After a long pause his father said, "I know your spirit is bigger than this place."

He did not want to look at his father. From the sound of his voice John suspected his father's eyes were watering. His father surprised him by rising from the loveseat and going into the house. From inside he called, "Wait there." John stared at the yard and tried to imagine how it looked to his father and wondered what punishment was coming. Could he be punished without evidence of guilt? Or was the evidence really that important? The pines and palms looked sodden in the sun. Long ago, Emily, Aunt Sallie, and Marion had been in this place. He still often flipped through the shots Stang snapped of him and Emily. Time did astonishing things. In short order it transformed Jesus from an anonymous homeless man to a God. You did not have to watch five years pass to see facts become something more than facts.

His father had a strange expression on his face when he returned, a look as though he had received but not absorbed some piece of news. He held in his hands, then handed to John, a leather-bound book that John did not recognize. Its pages released a handsome sour scent and creaked when John opened them. They were blank.

"Your great grandfather got that in Italy after the war ended." Frank meant World War One. The leather felt oiled, and the pages smooth. "He gave it to me when I was your age. He loved novels and thought his grandson should write. He loved Stephen Crane's *The Red Badge of Courage*. I wrote, but never novels, and never in this book. It seemed too nice. A novelist is an artist, and an artist is somebody with a certain relationship to the world, an imaginative one, a subversive one. A clever one. He plays hypothetical pranks and has all the freedom in the world to do so. Even when I was ten I knew I wasn't an artist. Wild imagination confused me. I liked pages that men better than I had filled with words. All my imagination, now like then, either flows toward God or to puns and jokes. The highest form of sense and the lowest. I don't live much in-between. You might have noticed." His father laughed at himself, set his chin on his chest. "The horizon doesn't interest me or entice me. What interests me is the heavens, and what pleases me is your mother and this house and the routines we have. But I know that these things don't capture your imagination. You're interested in the horizon, and some people are. Maybe everybody is now. I feel as old as those dogs. You're like Marion, and Marion was like our grandfather, so I thought you should have this book. Our grandfather tried to write a novel about the war, but even though he had the experiences he didn't have the patience or the gift with words."

John closed the book and held it on his lap. They sat for a while.

"Look at them out there," his dad said. "This is where I am. One morning my heart'll give out while I'm reading the paper."

"You're OK," John said.

"Your life will be different from mine. It's a blessing. You need to know how much I believe in you and love you."

"I'm seventeen."

"I know that better than you do. I remind myself not to be too proud or too worried."

"I just don't understand why you'd let them hang," John said to Stang a few days later.

"They get out of sixth periods for the next two months. They're lucky bastards."

"You don't feel bad about it?"

"I feel terrible. I'm going to throw myself on my sword."

"I'm not kidding. We should turn ourselves in. We could get them off in an instant. It wouldn't change anything about the prank."

"Feel free to say you were the one holding the camera."

"But it wasn't me," John said.

Stang smiled. "Who knows who it was? Except Wiffin does. That's the point."

"What's the point?"

"The point was getting Wiffin, and we got him. Every night he's going home and blowing fuses over his coleslaw. He knows it's me, but he's not able to prove it. It would make his friggin' year to hang this on me. It was the whole point from the start. I put him where I aimed to put him. A good rule of thumb is whoever's behind the camera is invisible. And whoever's invisible is innocent. Unless they open their mouths."

John's mind kept circling back to the moral line of thinking. "They're innocent, and they got suspended."

"Innocent?"

"You made them do it."

"Nobody makes anybody do anything. People do what they do."

VII.

Then an omen—a black day. The streets had changed a lot since a year ago. A year ago we did presence patrols, just driving to be seen, and at every corner Iraqis would mob us, shouting "Ali Baba!"—their way of crying thief—and looking generally glad to see us. Long ago I had felt magnanimous commanding my men to drive the streets looking for the thieves. It did not take long to discover we were wading into seas of implacable vendettas, that people were inventing stories about their neighbors and seeking revenge for tribal spats, religious differences, regime-era machinations and executions and atrocities. So we stopped helping, and they stopped yelling "Ali Baba!"

These days nobody wanted anything from us except for the kids, who wanted our chocolate, and the grown men, who wanted our extermination. As if to give visual form to the emotional change, the cars themselves had changed, it was a new world of traffic. During the invasion all you saw were orange-and-white taxis, red VW Passats, and white Toyota Coronas. But America, loving free markets, decreed free markets for all, and 2003 was a boom year for auto sales in Baghdad. It was also a boom year for our Korean allies, whose contribution to the coalition of the willing consisted mainly of unloading Hyundai Elantras at Umm Qasr. Never again would I feel at ease around Hyundai Elantras. I associated them with being profoundly hated. And the freedom of the market did not lead to the freedom of the roads. As a matter of simple math, the more traffic there was, the more dangerous doing checkpoints was—more cars that might explode, fewer alleys to drive down in order to escape death by ambush.

It was under such conditions that we ventured out to do our last traffic check.

Our unit covered two intersections. Kirk Frank and I walked down from our tank to Greep's and could tell something was up. On a hostile street Greep's squad was violating the rules of movement, posture, and position. They were standing around. They were distracted. Why were they staring at mud slung against a wall? I saw the words GO HOME spelled out in red paint. Then the mud was not mud, it was puppies. Duckworth's sobbing clarified it.

A day is a long time in the progress of a decaying corpse in a metropolitan area rife with flies and open sewers and evil. Somebody had driven spikes through the puppies into the wall above the box they lived in. From up close they didn't look like puppies or even mud but like rotten catchers mitts spewing black iridescence.

Duckworth's shoulders shook. His universe had collapsed to the space between his messy face and his giant hands, which covered it. The mother dog, I now saw, was lying in the trash by the wall, looking dead herself. I went over and prodded her with my foot, and she opened her eyes and gave me a glance of human desolation. She twitched an ear. It would have been a mercy to shoot her.

"Duckworth," Schwartz said. "Pull your nuts out."

"Leave him alone," I said.

"Tell you one thing for fucking sure," Schwartz said. "I'm glad we're getting out of here tomorrow."

"Deal with today," I said.

"Fucking did not sign up for slaughtered puppies and blubbering retards."

"Schwartz, I swear to God you don't shut your mouth you're going to regret it."

"What, more push-ups?"

Soldiers stood. Flies buzzed.

"He's right," I said to the others. "Duckworth, we need to get out of here." For four blocks in all directions crowds thronged, going about their business, streaming by to watch. We were exposed to getting our dicks shot off. Greep had his back to Duckworth and his face to the street and his M16 ready. Schwartz stood next to Duckworth, bullying and huffing and useless. Eccles and Hornbuckle were back at the other intersection. J'Million must have been in Greep's tank, manning the gun. With Kirk Frank and me we made five soldiers uncovered on a busy street distracted by carnage on a wall and a crying giant. "Duckworth, move it!" I said.

"Idiot," Schwartz said.

"Shut up," Greep said, turning.

Was Greep serious?

An old Iraqi man in man-dress and flip-flops crept toward us, staring and grinning and nodding at our crying man. Another man, younger and fatter, looked cheerful as anything. I gestured at them to get back. I gestured a second time. Anger inundated me, fear became anger on a dime. They shuffled their feet back perfunctorily—almost not at all—as children gathered around them, laughing and pointing. Greep ambled over and squared his chest against the laughing old man. At first I thought he did this in the same easy spirit he did everything. Then he was screaming. "Leave him alone you fucking fuck!"

"Greep," I yelled. "Back off."

"Wipe that fucking smile off your fucking sand nigger face!"

"Greep!" I yelled. Any moment we could be hit by insurgents. The laughter of passersby was nothing. Duckworth had sobered from his tears enough to watch. "Get in the tank," I said to him quietly, urgently. "Schwartz, pull Greep off."

"Fuck Greep," Schwartz said. "Fuck all of this."

Duckworth was twice the size of the Iraqis' largest relative. His sobbing hulking frame was a major entertainment. Dogs disgusted Iraqis, the idea of pets disgusted them. Interpreters were always asking us if we had dogs back home. "That you keep in house?" they would say. They knew the answer and were titillating themselves on the exotic and the perverse, as if we ate babies. Saddam used to pay a bounty on batches of dogs and cats brought dead to the palace. People believed he ate the animals. Greep was screaming, and the crowd was growing where the old man stood. I took Duckworth by the arm and started dragging him toward Greep's tank. "Cover us," I said.

"Got it," Kirk Frank said.

"This sucks," Schwartz said.

Greep whirled and shoved Schwartz, knocking Schwartz sprawling, driving him into an old Iraqi woman, who sprawled too. Stupid. I watched the faces of the gathered Iraqi men curdle. Schwartz stared up in astonishment at Greep, not brave enough for rage, oblivious to the riot waiting to happen. "Greep!" I shouted. "Everybody, move."

"He loved those dogs, you asshole," Greep was yelling at Schwartz.

Schwartz remained on his ass a second longer, then scrambled up and tried to shove Greep. Greep punched him. I forced my body between them. My eyes were blurring, going blind to the gathering crowed. Without a word and with great competence Kirk Frank helped me separate Greep and Schwartz. Blood was running steadily from Schwartz's nose. He let himself be separated.

I had wanted to take my platoon intact and happy to Babylon tomorrow, to see a safe end to this thirteen-month nightmare. "Take him," I said to Kirk Frank, meaning take Duckworth. Kirk guided him across the road to the tank. Then I glanced a last time at the black husks glittering like grackle wings, the words in red paint or dried blood: GO HOME.

VIII.

After graduation John did not leave Apalachicola to attend a university in the north as he had always claimed he wanted to. He stuck around as if bewildered. He let senior year pass without applying to college at all. When he thought of college he pictured an obstacle standing between him and New York City. Did he not realize there were colleges, too, in New York? His parents asked about his applications but did not push. Calvin's ideas about predestination confused their good instincts as parents sometimes. In the fall John started taking courses in English at the junior college and told Stang he was going to be a writer and move to New York soon. "Like in the olden days," Stang said. "Genius." In letters to Emily, John declined to announce these plans. He sensed their presumptuousness but also wanted the news to break with fantastic force when she discovered his first novel in a bookstore. Out of ignorance and delusion he believed this could happen within months or even at all.

Throughout the fall he referred to himself as a writer and thought often about writing but wrote little. In the spring he forced himself to write each night. Sweating over the keys, tuning his nerves to the brazen hum of the cicadas, sipping the beer he drank to taunt his parents, he wrote, and it felt like carving freedom from blankness. It was better even than writing to Emily. He began to tell the story of a southern boy whose influential northern cousin by marriage transforms his life. He wins her love through the brilliance of his pranks and the eventual genius of his manuscript.

Emily was beginning her second year at Columbia University. She wrote even better letters in college, and more of them, and recommended increasingly difficult and excellent books for John to read.

John relished the sight of the New York postmark and felt an immense proprietary feeling toward the city. When its skyline glimmered on the screen at the cineplex he regarded it as more his than anybody else's in the state of Florida. Crowds waving signs at cameras from the background on morning shows belonged to him. News footage about events there filled him with a conviction of special understanding. But the courage to uproot never dawned in him. As deluded as he was about publishing and love, he knew perfectly well that rent in New York was exorbitant.

It was understood that he had to get a job, and he finally got one canvassing for a city directory. Breitbart & Hornbuckle, Inc., compiled telephone numbers and counted heads, printed the information, and sold it to businesses while pretending to be a public service. Ten years later the Internet would annihilate such enterprises. The job made John familiar with expanses of backcountry that he had only ever driven past. Between classes at the junior college he canvassed suburbs and remote roads and discovered the deadest corners of Franklin County. Libertarians shook fists, dogs barked, snarled, and charged, and a handgun got waved in his face.

Emily began an internship at *Vogue*. Whenever John went to Tallahassee he would stop at the Barnes & Noble and flip in awe through the magazine. The lifeblood of the globe coursed through his cousin and did not run within five hundred miles of where he lived.

On his birthday in June the next summer, he burned the pages of the novel about the southern boy and the northern cousin. He began a new novel that dramatized the meaningless existence of a canvasser for a city directory. Snakes, shacks, junkyards, creeps, dogs, crappy bars, thick heat, and teenage girls with gaunt limbs and skin looking ready to bruise filled the pages of the manuscript. The pages came slowly and the days moved slowly and the weeks and months vanished in a blink. When he finished the manuscript he tried to figure out how to get it published. He sent query letters to scores of agents. One asked to see some pages. John mailed them in a manila envelope. Five months later the agent sent an e-mail underscoring the value of plot and the need for emotional urgency and the limits of the interest of descriptions of rural Florida.

Stang had moved to Quincy and drank a lot more than he ever had in high school. He worked at the kitty litter factory, holding a dusty, noisy, tedious job that he loved telling people about. "Cats shit and piss in style because I go to work each day." Mostly he told African

American people about it. He rented a one-bedroom apartment in a complex full of them. He played football in the courtyard with ten-year-old black kids and started dating a black girl still in high school. He got beaten up for this and refused to say anything about it. He kept the apartment and kept the girlfriend or found another one like her. Stang was racist how missionaries are missionaries, he moved among people different from him with the affable and unflinching condescension and confidence of a person with a faith. He had no faith. He listened to hip-hop and dressed like Eminem, who was just getting popular. Did Stang wish he himself were black? Although John drank with him, the fun had diminished since high school. Stang and John hunched their frames over bottles of beer or shot pool in a bar in Quincy called Lazy's, where everybody except Stang and John was black and John always felt nervous and sometimes scared. "John's a writer," Stang told everybody, "like in the olden days." The nodding heads ranged in mood from indifferent to hostile. "He'll be on the bus to New York City any year now."

John, who shared his parents' lofty and progressive view of race relations, and had never stopped cringing at Stang's free use of the n-word, was terrible at drinking at Lazy's. So there was theory, and then there was practice. It was a long drive for John to get from Apalachicola to Quincy, but Stang seldom came back to Apalachicola, and John liked getting out. Most weekends for a year and a half he got drunk at Lazy's on Saturday night and crashed on Stang's couch and drove back Sunday mornings feeling miserable. He tried to arrive at the house before his parents returned from church so he could crawl into bed and hide from them.

One day in August he looked up from his life and realized that two years had passed since high school. The impoverished span of those years struck him in an excruciating flash. As far as he could tell nothing had happened at all, no transformations, no revelations, no triumphs. A new president was in office but nothing had changed. It gave him his first taste of a full life passing with only the slow and terrible diminishment of any hope of doing anything that mattered to anybody.

That August, as every August, hurricanes congealed and threatened the Atlantic coast distantly. The sky took on moral force, minatory properties, weighing on the town like a verdict. Late in the month the nightmares began. It was as though he were suffering from

100

the symptoms of withdrawal, going cold turkey, kicking the intoxications of youth. Wasps the size of baked potatoes beset him in brightly lit rooms. He murdered somebody accidentally and tried to hide the finely ground body in the cardboard tubes from cheap clothes hangers. He fought alligators with a baseball bat in ankle-deep water filled with snakes. In early September the nightmares tortured all peace and rejuvenation from five nights of sleep. On the sixth night they stopped. He awoke that morning astonished by the pleasure of his sleep, amazed as if a fever had broken. He checked his brain as if patting his pockets to find a lost wallet and finding it. Standing on the porch, watching Chittenango and Chattanooga gregariously nose a Pepsi bottle across the dirt, he could feel the change in temperature, the sudden coolness of the air. The truth of his age and freedom dawned on him. He was young with a full life ahead. So when he turned on the television and heard the grave euphoria of the voices, voices euphoric with something really finally to talk about during all the hours of angry broadcasting, it was as though history had prepared his blood and bones for its unfolding. The smoke was pouring in its impersonal blackness from the towers in New York.

He found his mother in the sewing room. She glanced up at him and was cheerful with her good morning smile. He understood that she was glancing at him from another era, still innocent. "There have been attacks," he said, and she rose and followed him to the television. As he watched her watch he perceived for the first time how much she had aged since the last time he had thought about it. Later his father came home from the church shaking his head. He made a living metabolizing the raw nutrients of misfortune into the sustenance of wisdom and was at a loss. "With that bastard in office," his mother kept saying. It was thunderous language for her.

At noon John dialed a phone number he was almost ecstatic with being able to dial. How easy it was astonished him. He could have done it any time since 1993. Aunt Sallie answered. "This is John," he said.

"Oh God," she said.

"Is she all right?" John said.

"Emily?" Aunt Sallie almost shrieked. "Is it Emily?"

"I'm calling about Emily's—"

"Marion!" Sallie yelled.

"This is her cousin John."

"Cousin?" She seemed to be cupping the phone. "We need to keep this line free." She hung up.

Later Uncle Marion called and apologized and gave John the number in New York. "Let us know if you can reach her. We haven't gotten through yet. I'm not worried, but it's all busy signals."

Later still, Emily called. "I thought you were Uncle Frank!" she said when John answered.

"It's me."

"*It's me*," Emily said, like Cookie Monster. "I totally didn't think about your voice changing more!"

"I'm glad you're OK."

"The facts have gotten ahead of us. It's a nation of control freaks. So it's weirdly wonderful. Don't tell anyone I said that. Everything here smells like burnt foam. I'm heartbroken too."

After the phone call, in the wake of the attacks, Emily did not write to John again until February. This was the longest, by four months, that she had ever gone without sending a letter. He wrote twice in September, but as soon as he posted them, these letters, drafted furiously in response to great trauma, appeared tiny and tinny and pointless, vain and small. They returned him to the familiar shame of his adolescence, and he did not write a third. Emily's silence hurt his feelings but also amplified the already deafening roar of the great events, giving them even greater significance. Things had changed.

Each day from the day itself John felt pulsing in his chest the whisper of a conviction that there was more to come, more for him and for everybody. It was ominous and exhilarating, bracing and ultimately delusional, because nothing on the order of what he expected came: no mushroom clouds, no smallpox outbreaks, no suicide bombs in shopping malls. Anthrax letters came, and war in Afghanistan did, but these, unlike the attacks themselves, did not give you the feeling of having been swept personally onto the world stage. So that what, for a brief time, had felt like a fusion of John's private life and the epic drama of history, slowly revealed itself to have been a projection of preposterous self-importance.

In December John tried to return to the pages of the novel about the canvasser. He found paragraphs written in another age, empty, shallow, hollow, and glib. He reread the e-mail from the agent and agreed with it. He didn't know what to do. He floundered and paced. He let his course work slide. He changed what he read and tried more

Shakespeare. He marveled at plays in which hero and state fused bloodily and bodily in the lives and deaths of kings and princes. On television, newscasters, talking heads, businessmen and bureaucrats from the heights of ambition, were smaller than the terrorists they analyzed. That sheet of photos of strange dark faces showed men who had refused to acknowledge the impersonal scale of skyscrapers and jetliners and bureaucracies. Profit-mongers and psychiatrists were conducting a war against heroic scale.

The letter from Emily that arrived in February sickened John with an unprecedented kind of envy. He had been scooped. Or he had been trained so well by her that what he had taken to be his genuine intuitions and reflexes proved merely to be signs of her influence. His emotional response to the attacks followed hers, echoed it, anticipated it by her graces. What, exactly, did she feel? For months she had brimmed with restlessness, she claimed, feeling in the air an impending momentousness that she herself wished to possess and control. She used such phrases in her letter, putting with eloquence and precision what John had felt only with inarticulate vagueness. Worse—worse for his envy—she had resources, colleagues, and a plan.

She and her friends were founding a magazine to give voice to the opinions and ideas of young progressives in a nation whose air had been chilled by reactionary fervor. It would be called *Greater Than X* and it would bust the monopoly on moral seriousness that the political right was trying to hold and holding. With this letter John felt his recently expanded self contract. He had made no plans and founded no journals. He had not thought about events in partisan terms. He had merely cruised county roads with nerve endings tingling. He was a fool. More than ever before, he wanted to be in New York, inhaling the terror, witnessing history, breathing relevance in with toxic smoke.

What could he do but go see Stang?

But after driving an hour to the apartment complex full of African Americans he found Stang's unit vacated. The ten-year-old boys Stang used to play football with stared at John with naked curiosity. This was their turf. "He gone," said one with cornrows and a plastic Uzi. The superintendent came over. John asked the super. "He's gone," the super said.

"We told you he be gone," the boys said.

You could hear the roar of the kitty litter factory from the complex. John drove there. "Gone," said the foreman.

John drove back and visited Debbie Duncan, Stang's mom. "He said he said good-bye to you yesterday," she said.

"I just wasn't sure when he was leaving," John said, trying to cover his ignorance. "Where he'd go?"

She studied him as though he were crazy. "He joined the army."

IX.

Sleep. Then I could hear a huge change without understanding what it meant. The voices stopped and some yelling—a different voice—began. Night had fallen and I pulled myself up, readying myself to be ready, not having any idea for what. Then I could tell it was Breitbart yelling. Was this a late-night porn bust? I made out: "Intel on a building three klicks from here." He was using his war voice. "We're at the corner with Bravo Platoon ready to go. They got the Humvees, we got one tank and need two more."

"One and two are on," I was saying in an instant, descending without thought, "mine and Greep's," buckling up. In the chaos Breitbart squinted calculating eyes. His turkey waddle appeared to quiver in rage and anticipation. I hurried to stand between them, Breitbart and Greep. They were opposite elements, sparks and gasoline. Groggy bodies were rolling off thin cots, J'Million moaning, Duckworth plodding through motions with ponderous unflappability, Greep looking wide awake and fully prepared as if he had not been sleeping. "Sunnis or Shiites?" I asked.

"Militia laptop," Breitbart said. "Objective's the laptop."

"Sunni or Shiite?" I said.

"You following orders or asking questions?" Breitbart said.

"I thought that was Fifth Division's turf," Greep said.

"Greep," I said.

"Just asking," he said.

"Two tanks enough?" I said.

"Two," Breitbart said.

"You trying to kill us off?" Greep said.

"You want to see what being killed off looks like?" Breitbart said.

105

"Greep," I said.

We had seconds to mobilize. Breitbart was already out the door. In the scramble, an awareness of the futility of our training dogged me perversely. At Hohenfels and Grafenwoehr we spent days and days planning and rehearsing a single training exercise. Here in a combat zone with threats from all sides we had twenty seconds to prepare for a mission we never in our wildest dreams dreamed of. I tried to breathe deeply, to focus and operate, simply operate.

Amidst the fear and scramble Greep paused by Duckworth's cot and lay his black hand on the giant's broad back. It was a frank and fleeting gesture. It seemed to me to say, "The puppies are gone, but *we're* here." Perhaps I wanted too badly for it to say that.

But then, in a moment, to my total outrage, I caught sight of Duckworth handing Greep my goddamn video camera. We were out in the courtyard, but even from ten yards I knew it was mine. "Is that my camera?" I yelled.

"This?" Greep acted as if he had just discovered it in his hand.

"Where did you get that?" I said to Duckworth.

Dumbness. Fear skittered in his watery eyes.

The little box of plastic and silicon and copper and nickel and lithium had carried Hillary's face across the ocean. It was a cherished vessel violated by rude paws. I looked for Eccles and found him watching us. "You gave my camera to Greep?"

"What in bloody tarnation!" Breitbart yelled. "MOVE!"

"Greep! Duckworth! Get back here!" They were edging off. "Give me my camera!"

"MOVE!" Breitbart's face was a slapped ass. "MOVE!"

Eccles and I fell in line. There was no choice. I had to get ahold of myself.

Kirk Frank hit the start sequence for the turbine engine, engaging the AGB, which powered the fuel pump, hydraulics, compression fans, and oil pump, everything banging something awful. You could hear it turning the EMFS as the whine from the engine grew to a roar when the fireball caught. Then the engine was powering itself, the fuel pumps pumping and the air sucking in. Hornbuckle was already in the turret with his CVC on. "I guess they didn't think the rooty-poo berm guard patrol was up to this." He lugged a box of .50 cal ammunition to the machine gun, placed the box in its holder, and pulled out the linked strand. It clinked out like an anchor chain, each round the size of a carrot. He fed the first round in the feed

106

tray, snapped the extractor around its base, then slammed down the cover.

It takes four men to operate a tank, and in White One Hornbuckle was gunner, Kirk Frank driver, Eccles loader, and I the commander. In White Two, Schwartz drove, J'Million gunned, Duckworth loaded, and Greep was in command.

"Secure the building and fry the meddlers," were Breitbart's last face-to-face orders. "Let Bravo raid." Bravo was supposed to arrive a minute ahead of us to preserve the element of surprise.

"Command and signal," I said over the radio. "Three eight three. I got air-net five seven six. White Two, this is White One, prepare to copy, over."

"This is White Two," Greep said, "send it, over."

"White One, roger, let's roll."

The streets stretched before us in sick green. In a moment we joined Breitbart's tank as the Bravo guys rolled ahead. Like wind moving fog, fear finally swept my mind clear of noise. The hellishness of the city at night tyrannized your nerves. I never hated a place as I hated Baghdad. Sometimes I tried to imagine living here in a time of peace, to picture what kind of happiness you could hope for. The rank smells, the high heat, the oppressive architecture, the shabby beauty of even the prettiest Iraqi women, the men's grotesque mustaches and fulsome acne, their hand-holding, the crepitating fanaticism of the mosque calls, the sick spicy stink of burnt meat, the fashions culled from the remainders of trends in other nations years ago, the fading posters in CD stores of men in turbans and women in pop music videos, the beleaguered palms and rutted streets, the angular meretriciousness of 1970s architecture tarnished by twenty years of war—it was unbearable in every aspect. You could not think of a bed you wanted to sleep in, a table you wanted to sit at, a family you wanted to meet and dine with. Suddenly I saw in my mind my father at the kitchen table in the split-level in Waltham. Every day after work he drank a can of piss beer, pouring it daintily with dirty fingers into a juice glass, a third of the can at a time.

"Greep promised me he'd give it right back," Eccles said.

"Whatever you're talking about," Hornbuckle yelled, "shut up. No Mogadishus tonight please."

The men in Mogadishu had had their minds in the wrong places and had regarded as simple a raid that was anything but. Every time you had a sinking feeling, you thought of *Black Hawk Down*.

At the turn onto Route Wild we saw in the distance a blast of light lift from the roof a Bravo Humvee. The sound delay was perceptible. It blew loud. "We're hit," Cobra Six said over the radio.

"Shit," Kirk Frank said.

"Lock and load," Hornbuckle said. "They are messing with the wrong motherfuckers."

We could hear screaming on the headset. In the distance a second Humvee pulled up beside the first and put suppressive fire on an alley across the route. The popping sounded weirdly close, and then I knew we were getting hit too. Bullets pinged off us. They wouldn't do anything unless the shooters knew where to aim, which they did. RPGs could fuck up everything. Hornbuckle had good fire discipline and held tight because we couldn't even tell where the shots were coming from. Then they stopped. In the night vision scope the streets looked grainy and green like the bottom of a dirty pool at night. I wanted to see blanched Iraqi faces stumble in fear in front of us, but it was ghostly, deserted, unnerving. In the scope I could see the burning Humvee, white as phosphorous.

"Cobra Main, this is White One. Awaiting orders."

"WE'VE BEEN HIT," Cobra Six was saying.

"White One, this is Cobra Main, stand by," Breitbart said.

"Stand by?" Eccles said.

We sat there.

"Sitting ducks," Hornbuckle said.

The popping of rounds.

"White One, this Cobra Main. QRF's been called for Cobra Six. We got their backs. Bravo's got a fourth tank coming. Head to the site, lead the raid. Cobra Four'll be there. Grid is MB four three seven four eight eight."

So, suddenly, it was our show, whatever "it" was. I paused for a moment then told Breitbart I wasn't briefed for this.

"Third floor, on the left," he answered. "Search and detain. Get the laptop. TIME NOW. This is not an endless window. We've got Cobra Six. Take Florida to Copper and skirt the clusterfudge."

"'Clusterfudge?'" Greep said, "Really? Over."

"Florida to Copper," I told Kirk Frank.

Tanks stay safe by moving and firing—and by traveling with infantry to cover their blind spots. A single tank is a death trap. A pair of tanks is one tank away from a death trap. But our two tanks were heading solo toward a man we had never seen in an apartment we had never seen in a building we had never seen on a street we had never seen.

A huge department store, gutted and pathetic, loomed above a row of houses including the target house. We squared the tanks against the door. Hornbuckle manned the .50 cal, and against my better judgment I OK'd Eccles to use the free-floating junior, which could shoot anywhere, including at our own tank. In heated fighting, inexperienced gunners sometimes shot chunks from their own hulls. Eccles was inexperienced. But: "We don't have enough for rear security," I told him and Hornbuckle. "You *are* rear security. Don't count on backup. So listen hard. For now nobody's firing."

Kirk Frank and I hustled out. Greep left only J'Million in White Two and came with Duckworth and Schwartz. Five was half the minimum you wanted for a search team, rear security, pat down, and detainee control. Especially for a third-floor raid.

Blood on the wall: GO HOME.

"Do it now?" Schwartz said. "Or do you guys need a few more minutes to make out?" He was talking to Duckworth and Greep. I yelled Schwartz's name and told him he had our rear. It was the least desirable position of all the undesirable positions. I wanted to get Schwartz out of my face, punish him, abase him. "Stay at the first landing. Look both ways. Hear anything, discharge like hell."

"Great," Schwartz said.

I could have shot him in the head then and there.

"Greep, you and Frank do pat down," I said.

"Let's hope the wife is on the pill," Greep said.

"Duckworth will have my back," I said. "I'll search."

Then we had knocked in the door and were charging the three flights up. My mind saw grenades from nowhere, shadows of men with guns, ghosts in the blur. My heart thundered at the climb. The building was silent and empty. A frosted pane in a blue door shattered under the butt of my M16. A woman screamed on the far side, her babies screaming, everything screaming, all screams. Then the door was open, but for some reason Schwartz was stepping up with a laser pointer. He was supposed to be three flights down protecting us from attack from the rear.

"DOWNSTAIRS" I screamed. We were dead without cover. He hovered there, insubordinate, his mouth a hole, his eyes calculating, stupid, angry, vying, insane. "DOWNSTAIRS." Anger blurred my vision at the moment I needed it most.

109

"Downstairs, fatso," Greep said, and finally Schwartz went.

Duckworth spotlighted me from above, and I pushed into the apartment. Corners first—our eyes and sights swept the corners. Greep and Kirk Frank were crowding after me into a cramped living room. Kirk Frank's frog eyes and kelp hair looked even stranger in the shadows and jerky light. He held the door. Duckworth moved with the brute competence that stupidity actually can increase. He had reflexes and instincts. A wailing Iraqi woman gripped a howling infant. Twin girls, young toddlers, wading in squalor, stared with terror from the floor. The father simpered before me, late middle age, a heinous comb-over on a greasy scalp, a mint-green velour tracksuit showing his paunch, his breath crinkling with whiskey and rank lamb.

You don't humiliate fathers in front of wives and children. We learned this months ago and should have acted by it now. The man was terrified, ingratiating, abject. His children and grandchildren would recount this and seek revenge until the end of the twenty-third century. I would have no descendants to exact revenge from because I would have died in Iraq. A raid on Shiites might have made sense, but these were Sunnis, no doubt Sunnis, people who probably had lived in terrified fear of Saddam and simply went along—hopefully, fearfully, pathetically. The father was grinning with terror and ingratiation. Then he was holding out a packet of cigarettes. I raised my left hand from the stock of the gun to wave no thank you. Then time slowed with the shock of what happened next. He saw my hand. His face changed. Excitement filled it. He raised his own hand.

"Let's go," Greep said.

I could not go because there was a hand in my face, waving happily. The Iraqi man was missing the same finger I was missing. It excited him terrifically. We both were missing the pinkie on the left hand. I had lost mine in Germany doing tank maintenance. The man held up his hand and shook it like a revelation. He kept saying *eeRANtek, eeRANtek*, something sounding like that. It wasn't any Arabic phrase I knew, not that I knew more than four. Greep was patting him down, his black hands frisking the green velour. The man seemed not even to notice it, the groping, the touch, the violation, obsessed as he was with our identical hands. The baby was screaming, the twins stood on dirty laundry. Finally, I deciphered the sense of the sound. Iran had taken his finger, he'd lost the finger in the war.

"Let's go," Greep said.

I wanted to strike the father with my M16. It came over you. Your body had its own responses. Your body was the horrific majority of what you were, and it took a moment like this to grasp that. Your body was all of what you were. I cut from him rudely and searched. We were supposed to find a laptop, but these weren't Shiites, and they didn't even have a television. There was an empty stand for a television. Dirty clothes covered the floor of a back room that smelled like body. Flies rose and fell from the crusted dishes on the counter. A quarter inch of whiskey sat in the bottom of a bottle on the windowsill. In the closet of a bedroom I found the one weapon the family was allowed by law to keep for protection.

When Duckworth and I finished searching we returned to the living room. There Greep stood, filming the family with my camera. They were hysterical, and he was filming them. "Stop that!" He swept the camera across the faces of the screaming children and crying wife. "Stop!" I shouted. The wife was sitting now, and the baby had gone from crying to gagging and croaking. When the father saw me he shook his hand again at me. Greep captured that: the look on my face as I was claimed by a parallel soul not at all parallel.

X.

"Where's your pinkie?" a stranger in New York City asked.

He held his hand out and glanced at the missing finger. He was so used to his hand that he never thought of it anymore. He returned the three fingers and the thumb to the glass. He had lost his left pinkie on a table saw. He told her this. "For a year it felt like an adventure. We made a grave in the backyard. The dogs dug it up."

She laughed. She stopped laughing.

Why not mention the "meteorite"? Stang's dad's car roof? His thoughts couldn't go anywhere near it. New York City would belong to him alone.

"Chattanooga and Chittenango," he said.

"Those were the dogs?" She laughed some more. "You ordered what I ordered."

"I ordered what you ordered."

"It wasn't an accident."

"No."

"I'm calling the cops." She was a stranger being aggressive. She was three stools down but slid over one, then one more. It was vodka and cranberry. Her smile was flippant. "Can I crash the pity party?"

"There's no pity party."

"You look like a war's about to start."

The war had started last spring.

"I feel like a million dollars."

"There. You've got a great smile. I was betting, but who knows, right?"

"I feel like a million bucks."

"You're drinking alone." She looked at him to say it but returned her eyes to the mirror behind the bar to take a drag from her cigarette. She focused on inhaling as if patting the head of boredom. He drank from his glass. She exhaled. "The pinkie is attractive. The missing pinkie. The drink thing is just plain creepy."

He drank and she smoked. The bartender ignored them.

"Why did you order what I ordered?" she said.

"Do you want to go somewhere else?" he said.

"Somewhere public," she said.

On the street he made better sense of her. She had looked thirty in the darkness of the bar and closer to forty in the streetlight, he couldn't say for sure, he was young. She wore a billowy brown blouse and tight dark jeans. Her dark hair was up, but strands of it fell at her ears and neck. Fifteen years ago she must have been the most beautiful woman in whatever room she was in. She walked like she was out on business. They moved up the avenue as traffic streamed down it, crowds and cars. Anybody who looked at them would have seen two people together in the world, a couple, or a man and a woman on the brink of making a bond. Or would they see an aunt and her nephew? He had been taking imaginative possession of strangers for many nights, here in this city, his new home, which felt nothing like a home, but now a stranger had taken possession of him.

Then they were in a bar whose elegance clashed with the neighborhood. Dark domes and vague curves. Black leather furniture, modern and low. Light fixtures the size and shape of toilet paper tubes hanging at the end of long wires barely visible. Electronic music swelling and whipping goofily. She asked his name. "Marshall," he said, and frightened himself by saying that. She tried it out. "*Marshall.*" She kept her eyes on the bar, pulling smoke from the cigarette. "Well, *Marshall*, order a drink for yourself. Then I'll decide what I want." He asked her her name, and she said Nerissa. He ordered vodka and cranberry. "You're terrifying." She asked for a martini.

She rested the palms of her hands on the bar, spreading her fingers ceiling-ward, and the rings on her fingers called his attention to the aged skin, the wrinkles at the knuckles, the perseverance of bone. He counted her ten fingers. In the darkness, except for the fingers, she looked young again. Suddenly she was watching him look her over, her eyes vaguely hostile-seeming because unknown but also large and inviting. For a long time they sat in silence, drinking their drinks, watching the smoke gray the air between them. Finally, she said, "I'm going now."

"Don't."

"Then say something."

"So tell me about yourself."

"Wrong answer."

"Let me tell you about myself."

"Make it good."

What could he say? What did he want to say? There was only a past to forget entirely. No reason he couldn't talk about anything that had happened since the move, but nothing had happened. When he arrived a month ago to his basement apartment in a corner of Queens he picked up the key from Martin King, a blind black man who lived upstairs and wore always a beige cardigan crusted with beige clumps, and who showed no interest in talking. From the door King shuffled away and shuffled back with the keys. A television was turned up too loud, and from somewhere nearby a dog barked with profound alert futility. In the door to the basement apartment around back the key took jostling as the sky drizzled freezing drops. By the time John unloaded his belongings into the basement it had started to rain a cold, heavy freezing rain.

You entered and exited the basement apartment from the alley. The main room was immense, of the same square footage as the house upstairs, and unfurnished. A fuse box broke the drab uniformity of the far wall, and pipes braced the ceiling. Thin blue carpeting, smelling like wet couch, covered but did not soften the concrete floor. Swinging half-doors divided the tiny kitchen from the tiny bathroom, the kitchen and the bathroom having been built under the stairs that rose to a padlocked door and drew the eye from anywhere you might stand in the main room. From above came the sound of the barking dog and the whisk of its claws on the linoleum and the pregnant silence between barks. John placed his sleeping bag in the corner and left the rest of his few belongings to be unpacked later. He made a pile like a cairn in the center of the room.

For a few days after arriving he was at a loss. Everywhere he went he had the sense that a great bang or boom had sounded, a clap of destiny, a sound unheard by him at the time, and its aftershocks took the form of this city. Having heard nothing, having come into existence in the silence of the backwoods of Florida, he watched without full comprehension the people who, like planets and stars, streamed outward from this blast. The manhole covers steamed with the smoke of this explosion. The wintry city had a fiery core. Secret lives spiraled indoors and outdoors, on and off trains, everywhere. Everybody on the subway was returning from an assignation, drug deal, brawl, audition, robbery, party, trick, photo shoot, execution, poetry reading, funeral, wedding, or birth. It was all in plain view, and endless, and none of it his.

He had moved without job prospects with a box of saved cash. He would have come in October if he could, as soon as Emily left Apalachicola, but he had had to save. Now in December with his slim savings he realized just how stupidly he had assumed the city would assign to him a purpose upon his arrival. It didn't assign anything. After two days he was lonelier than he had been in his life, and he turned to bars. He found one near Washington Square that had no theme, only the dark basics, called Chewbacca.

"Live around here?" the bartender said.

"Down the block," John said. He was miles from Queens. He feared the bartender because he couldn't see him because John's lenses were fogging in the warm air.

"A new face. I never forget a face. Guy comes in to drink half a beer on Flag Day in 1987 I remember his face." The bartender sounded like he expected John to doubt him. He had dark hair cut short and brown skin and nothing distinct about him but both ears were pierced. He looked Italian or Spanish or Mexican and sounded like he was from New York.

"Names?" John said.

"Tell me a bazillion times I won't remember. No good with the names."

"I'm Patrick," John said. Patrick was his middle name.

"A wise guy. Nice to meet you, Peter, see? But your face I won't forget. A year from now I won't forget it. Five years. Ten."

"He'll never forget it," said a man down the bar. This second man had thin arms and long fingers and hunched his body around his beer. He looked like a gremlin guarding a pie. A cap brim almost hid his eyes.

John ordered a beer, and they left him alone as he drank it, letting him keep to himself in a way that made him feel OK. So he went back the next day.

"Here yesterday," the bartender said.

"He never forgets a face," the man down the bar said.

"I never forget a face," the bartender said.

The day after that John went to a different bar, and to a few more bars on the nights that followed. Things in New York tended to cost twelve dollars instead of three dollars or five dollars. After a week he counted his cash and a murmur of panic sounded in him. So he went out that afternoon to find a job. When he slinked into restaurants, nobody seemed to be able to understand the question, Are you hiring? That afternoon he collected newspapers. The next morning he made coffee and searched the listings, circling plausible openings in pen as he knew to do from TV. In the afternoon he called places. The donut delivery men laughed, the building managers cited the doormen's union, the taxi companies invoked the need for licenses and permits. These were short conversations. Then somebody helpfully said: "What are you, stooptarded? Them ads is so people don't get sued. Equal opportunity quote unquote. Crack whores. Nobody's going to hire you from the paper. Go to Marvel-Temp. My brother used to work at Marvel-Temp. You writing this down?" He gave John an address. "Marvel-Temp. Tell them Chip Douglas."

He told them Chip Douglas. The men at Marvel-Temp never heard of Chip Douglas. There were two men at Marvel-Temp, Chester and Todd, and they looked like each other, wearing thick moustaches and speaking with meaty vowels. They had meaty noses and heavy tan arms stretching the sleeves of defiantly pastel polo shirts. One of the men pushed John with sarcasm through tests and paperwork. The keyboards in the testing room were greasy, the light the color of a dirty fishbowl. John tried to fake knowing how to handle spreadsheets. He knew immediately that he was making a poor impression. "Kinda guy who wears shorts in February," Chester said of John in front of John.

"One of those guys, eh?" Todd said.

"Where's he from?" Chester said.

"From the Kingdom of no friggin' Spreadsheets," Todd said.

"A February shorts-wearer," Chester said.

"Shorts in February," Todd said.

But John aced the typing exam and was assigned to an insurance company starting the next morning. On the way out of Marvel-Temp he noticed everything he had failed to notice on the way in: the glowering black women dressed for success and treated by Chester and Todd with fantastic gallantry, an old man coughing and not getting called up, the greasy doorman at the battered station on the ground floor, the worn and dated mirrors and dusty plastic plants, the smell.

John went back to Chewbacca to celebrate the job assignment. He expected the place to be crowded but entered to darkness in which all of four bodies softened the sound of rock from the jukebox. At a table against the wall a couple appeared to be fighting in hushed tones. At the bar, the gremlin guarded his drink with skinny arms and long fingers. "Here on Wednesday," the bartender said. "Mr. Foggy Frames." John took off his glasses and wiped them on his shirt. Were all the men in New York assholes?

"Never forgets a face," the gremlin said.

"Wednesday and Tuesday too," the bartender said.

"You hear they bagged the son of a bitch?" the gremlin said.

"Saddam," the bartender said.

John had not heard this news. He focused now on the TV above the bar, which was showing it. Spencer Talent's closed-captioned words raced across the spangled screen.

"Miguel here has been protesting the war since it started," the gremlin said. So the bartender's name was Miguel. "How does he feel now that we bagged the son of a bitch."

"Screw you protesting the war," Miguel said.

"Putting flowers in his hair, singing what is it."

"Kum Bay Yah."

"Kum Bay Yah, singing Kum Bay Yah."

"Screw you singing Kum Bay Yah."

"We should've bagged him first time around," the gremlin said.

"It ain't him," Miguel said. "What do you mean him? Osama Saddam bin Hussein Laden?"

"All I know is what I saw one fateful day."

The bartender crossed himself. "You weren't alone what you saw one fateful day. I saw what you saw one fateful day. We all saw it."

"All I know is what I saw."

"What you saw was Israelis."

"Lee Harvey Oswald is responsible for 9/11 is what you're saying. Charlie Manson, Jim Jones."

"Jack Ruby is what I'm saying. The CIA."

"Deep Throat is what you're saying."

"You never know is what I'm saying."

"*They* know. That's for sure. *They* know."

"They don't know shit is what they know. What they know is oil."

"You want me to believe al-Qaeda attacked us over oil?"

"Al-Qaeda and Saddam they don't have a thing to do with each other."

"I've seen the pictures."

"You've seen what pictures?"

"Them pictures of them Arab dudes holding hands. They hold hands and walk around in dresses. The only question is who's on top? Saddam's the one with the moustache."

"Osama's got the beard. Cheney is making the whole thing up."

"Cheney's making up the crater down on Court Street, is that what you're telling me? That's pretty good."

"You gonna tell a lie? Then go big or go home. Joseph Goebbels said that. You even know who Goebbels is?"

"Wore a burka, walked around holding hands with Hitler."

"Go big or go home. Telling a lie? Tell a big enough lie." Miguel turned to John: "Another?"

"You guys here on 9/11?" John said.

"Where I'm standing," Miguel said. "Ka-bang. Sounded like a garbage truck dropped on a garbage truck."

"I was having my coffee," the gremlin said.

"Always has his coffee to get ready for his first beer," Miguel said.

"One then the other, he's right, and don't bitch, I keep you in business. Having my coffee and it sounded like a semi hitting a pothole and the trailer bounces and slams down. Like that in your car. How Miguel could of been in this city one fateful day and not want Saddam in the bag: beyond me. But hey, mi casa su casa."

"One of them hijackers used to drink here," Miguel said.

"He never forgets a face," the gremlin said.

"Drank here twice. I gave him ouzo. He wanted arrack. I told him arrack is a towelhead drink."

"Not in so many words."

"Frig yeah in so many."

"Where were you . . . Remind me your name?"

"John," John said. "I was in Florida."

"You said your name was Patrick," the gremlin said.

John felt something drop within him.

"Before you said your name was Patrick." The man, the virtual stranger, the gremlin, looked angry. Now both he and Miguel were studying him with hostility. "I never forget a name," the gremlin said.

"Never forgets a name," Miguel said.

John stared at his drink with burning ears. For the longest time he thought their eyes were on him. When finally he glanced to the side he saw he was dead to them, so that was that for Chewbacca.

When John reported to his job at the insurance company, the person from HR showed him to the door of an office whose window opened on the Chrysler Building. At the desk, turned away from the door and facing the window, sat a dark-haired, dark-skinned man whose voice John deduced was Indian from the words he was screaming into the telephone. The man mixed English and this other language and did not sound like he was selling insurance. John studied the office as the man yelled. Framed photographs filled the wall behind his desk, pictures of the man, it had to be him, beaming next to a beautiful girl John's age, it had to be his daughter, wearing saris in some pictures, dresses in others. The man wore an expression of triumph like that of a sultan. As John listened to the man yell, he decided he wanted to marry his daughter. Next to her in some photographs were a sad looking mother—this man's wife—and a lost looking son.

The Chrysler Building could have been a celestial embassy. The man slammed down the phone and gazed out for a few moments. John cleared his throat. The man turned and took him in. "The new one," he said. "Harsh," he said.

"Harsh?" John said.

The man said it again; it was his name. He was a brusque man from India, a brusque man named Harsh. John in response gave only his first name too.

"*The* John?" Harsh said. "The only living John in America?"

"Townley," John said.

"Details!" He did not rise from his desk. "Your name: that is a detail. That is success, details. Get details correct: get everything correct. Focus on the little picture. People say: big picture. I say: little picture. I say: not one big picture, a thousand little pictures. Only then, one big picture. Success is a thousand pictures, all very little. Tiny pictures."

The job was to distribute accounts payable forms to people in cubicles. It involved details indeed. The forms varied in color and text with endless and imperceptible variety, which made it easy to imagine how it would feel to have aphasia. After you discounted the details, there appeared to be nothing remaining. The people to whom John distributed the forms were easier to tell apart. Old black Maggie loved Senator Hillary Clinton as much as she loved her grandchildren and papered her cubicle walls with photographs of seven young African Americans and one old white woman. Wearing cologne that preceded him by fifteen yards, Roy, also black, processed the insurance forms with entrepreneurial gregarious as if auditioning for a job in sales. Preceded even farther by the smell of cigarettes, old white Alice flirted matter-of-factly with John. Her eyes with their mascara reminded John of exploded caps. She took six short smoke breaks each day instead of a lunch hour. "It adds up the same," she rationalized. Bob, old and white, liver-spotted, paunchy, gregarious and fragile, the office complainer-in-chief, questioned that math. He used a flaming stage whisper and flirted with John by attacking Alice and not only Alice but also everybody but John, except behind John's back, when he attacked John too, John had no doubt.

When John could not recognize a form he showed it to Harsh, who relished his right to be frustrated with John. It pleased Harsh to have grievances that threw his magnanimity into relief. He glanced over his bifocals, letting his mustache twitch. At the end of the first day John stood again at the door to the office and looked at the pictures of the daughter and said, "You have a beautiful family."

"I am a proud father," Harsh said.

"Do you still have a lot of family in India?" John said.

"I have six brothers," Harsh said.

"I'd like to travel in India," John said.

He was thinking of the pictures of Emily and Sallie and Marion. Emily and an elephant. Marion crammed in a rickshaw. Harsh was staring at him as if he had transmogrified into a hippopotamus. Then the phone rang, and in a moment Harsh was screaming in Hindi and English. "Details!"

Without Chewbacca to go to, John tried new bars and found himself one night up a flight of nineteenth-century stairs in a gutted tenement on the Lower East Side in a bar with a Russian theme. Tall, dark-red curtains hid the windows, and portraits of Lenin and Marx hung beside the bar. The warm, rancorous buzz of punk anthems dominated the almost empty space. It was seven on a Monday. The girl tending bar glared at John as he sat. He was an indictment of the punk girl's existence, was how her face looked, in his collared blue shirt and the bland trousers he had worn to his first day of work. She had spiked black hair and was very pretty. She moved up and down the bar wiping surfaces, shuffling glassware, filling the caddy with chopped lime. He waited for her to pause before him or make eye contact. Finally, he asked for a shot of whiskey.

"What kind?"

"What'll make my stomach hurt?" he said.

"You want that or you don't want that?"

120

"I want that."

She smiled but not at him. He downed the shot, and it warmed him and made his lungs feel temporarily powerless. The girl had ears with the compact puffiness of mushrooms and a stud centered beneath her full bottom lip. On one forearm was a tattoo of a fork stuck in the ground with its handle blossoming into a tree. On the other arm were the words LIVE FREE AND DIE. After another shot John was pretending in his mind that he was her. He as she had gone to NYU, studied classics, then kept books for her father's construction business until her father died of cardiac arrest at an ice cream stand.

"Your stomach hurt?" she asked.

"Not yet."

"Another shot?"

"A beer," John said. "I'll have a Budweiser."

"*That* would do it for *me*," she said.

He asked her where she was from.

"Jupiter," she said.

He drank the beer and critiqued his invention of her as until recently—but also so long ago now—he used to revise drafts of letters to Emily. He could do better.

After that night, when John drank, he went to new places and chose new people to base stories on. He went searching for stories and found them not by listening and talking but by imagining. He came from every part of the country and many parts of the globe and drank what his subjects drank. He was an editorial assistant enraged by a despotic editor who despised homosexuals. He was a cabby glimpsing hand jobs in a rearview mirror. He was a Polish engineer wearing an eye patch and a nicotine patch. He felt the violent oblivion of the glazed eyes of lupine lawyers insane with fantasy and bent on fucking him. He wondered about the word "lupine." He lamented the job he lost, the divorce he suffered, the cancer that progressed in his colon, the undeserved celebrity of his talentless friends, the infidelity of an ostensibly devoted spouse. Bartenders sensed he was strange. In his mind he became good at becoming the bartenders who sensed he was strange.

One night he saw a pretty older woman in a dark bar. She had grown up, he decided, in the Philadelphia suburbs with a father in insurance, never home, and a mother never not home. The mother charted her course through each day taking her bearings from the gin in the decanter on the bar in the family room. The mother pickled her aging beauty in gin while the father stewed in the old traumas of Vietnam. He worked fourteen hours a day or twelve hours a day and spent two secret hours a day screwing a mistress before coming home in a dour stupor. She, the daughter, this stranger, excelled at an affluent public high school, landing staring roles in plays, getting perfect grades, and distinguishing herself on the lacrosse team. But the excellence came so easily that it made her restless. In her sophomore year she discovered how much she enjoyed breaking rules, not for the sake of breaking them, but because her superiority grew by that means all the more apparent to her. She mastered at once a good world and a depraved one, and placed them in electric tension. She aced difficult tests and turned free tricks for lame jerks in the giant hollow metal mushroom in the city park. She did both things with her blood gauzy from hits from joints. In college—she went briefly to the University of Pennsylvania—everybody was smart and everybody transgressed. This robbed her of her strong sense of identity. It damaged her pride and killed her excitement.

The woman, in real life, interrupted: "Where's your pinkie?" And now, an hour later, she was waiting for him to talk about himself and he was failing to. She smirked at his silence and finally said, "Did I see you alone at Sebastian's? It's like you've been lurking at every bar I go to."

"I don't know the names."

"Do you live around here?"

"I just moved here."

"It shows."

She rummaged in a small purse and produced a glowing cell phone. The blue light of the screen illuminated her pretty nose. He asked how old she was. She came close to slapping him—faked a slap—and dropped the purse on the floor. She let it fall and slowed her hand and touched his face. "Sixty-five." In twenty years she might be sixty-five, John thought. She bent for the purse, and skin showed where the blouse raised. "Tell me where you're from," she said.

"Nowhere."

"Clearly." After a pause: "You know, nobody owns these bars but the owners. You're allowed to be in them."

"What's that supposed to mean?"

"I'm just saying you don't have to slink. Tell me where you're from." He told her. "You say Florida how most people say Chlamydia. You can't hate Florida. Nobody hates Florida. Florida is universally agreed upon."

122

"There's a huge exotic pet industry. Since Hurricane Andrew, Burmese pythons have been multiplying in the Everglades."

"Are you from the Everglades?"

"I'm from the panhandle."

She laughed. At that he understood that sex would happen later, if he wanted it. Arousal in John existed outside any notion of happiness. He understood what was happening and that such things happened. It differed so greatly from how he thought of himself that he did not feel culpable. It was like the current of a river. He told some stories about canvassing for Breitbart & Hornbuckle, Inc., that made her laugh.

After another drink they were standing on the street kissing. Later he was in her apartment, watching her peel her clothing from her body. Then she was letting him touch her as though nothing else could have been the case. Her black lace underwear looked indifferent to the flesh it covered. In the light she pulled off her underwear with flippancy that changed his breathing. She still wore the black bra. The small apartment was overheated and lighted only by a lamp in the corner. The elevator whined beyond the kitchen wall. The kitchen was all but part of the living room. The living room was also the dining room. All but undressed, Nerissa put on music and sat on the love seat and packed a pipe with marijuana as he sat next to her staring at her hands. In her fingers there was the perseverance of bone. She made him take the first hit and laughed out of sequence. They got high, and she laughed more until the music became fruitful and impacted. They kissed for a while, and as they did he couldn't remember who she was. He didn't know! She forced the progression of touches and did not wait for him. This and her strangeness filled him with fear and with a gasping joy that rode in on the prow of obscenity. He had believed that only boys ever felt so strongly as she appeared to feel. They moved to the bedroom whose darkness seemed an effect of the drug, which settled in in a sudden shift.

When the sex was over he felt annihilated. She had screamed the name "Marshall." He was foggy and spent and let himself slide away from himself. He woke a few times but only barely. Sleep kept him in place like some kind of device made of heavy cloth. Between moments of incomplete consciousness he nursed a dream in which Emily pushed her crotch against his leg. The crotch was shaven as Nerissa's was. She pushed it against him again and again without effect. Stubble and dread. Later he fell into a deeper sleep.

He tried to hear a pattern in the morning honking, opened his eyes, and saw that the light made the room simpler than it had been. The bed was empty, but then the stranger he had slept with appeared in the door to the room. He had to work to think of her name. "People don't do this here," she said. She was tying her robe and left again. She returned after a while.

"Don't have sex?" John said. Was he still high?

She held the end of the sash of her robe between her fingers and studied it as if for workmanship, then dropped it and looked at him and said, "Don't stay over."

He sat up into his hangover. He looked for his clothing.

"Don't bother running out now," she said. "It's amazing how you seem both creepy and harmless." She left the room as he pulled on his boxers, and he could hear her in the kitchen. "Stay for coffee," she called.

He looked young to himself in the bedroom mirror. He remembered how he had played Paul Bunyan in *Tall Tales and Heroes* in the fourth grade, and how Jimmy Kendrick, with his slow speech and lucky pencil, had played Johnny Appleseed. He remembered Jimmy grinning in a checkered flannel shirt wearing a saucepot on his head with the purple pencil even then sticking out from behind his ear. The thought of it slashed his sinuses with the impulse to burst into tears. After he gathered himself he went to look for her. There weren't many places to look, but before he got to the kitchen he peered in the room he hadn't seen, one painted pink. He pushed the door wide and saw a bed for a child covered with dolls.

"Flo's with Nasser learning about what a decadent Western slut her mother is." Nerissa had come to the hallway. "You can eat her cereal for breakfast. You seem like somebody who might get off on that. She's four." She smiled almost affectionately.

In the kitchen she had set a box of red, white, and blue puffs of corn on a miniscule table by the window. In a moment they were drinking coffee, and he was eating the puffs in milk turning purple. The woman across from him had been partying as a teenager when he was learning to crawl on the floor of the house on Hunt Road. She had wrinkles and a heaviness of spirit that old people have. She lit another cigarette. The smell of the smoke, the sweetness of the milk and cereal, the bitterness of the coffee, and the poison lingering in his blood came together, so he rose and found the bathroom, which he remembered only vaguely from last night. He kneeled above the bowl and watched the surface of the water. If you stared you could not tell where the waterline was because urine or minerals had yellowed the bowl. Soon the lavender vomit clouded the water. Sweat burst like relief from his temples as he rose and washed his hands and rinsed his mouth out, studying the Little Mermaid toothbrush on the basin rim. "That's why strangers don't stay over," Nerissa said when he returned.

"I'm sorry," he said.

"You're not sorry, you're embarrassed. But don't be. For some reason you chill me out. Maybe because you're so tense?"

"You're finally here," Harsh said. John wondered if he smelled or looked as bad as he felt. To his second day of work he had arrived an hour late in yesterday's clothes. He would not have showered at Nerissa's even if she'd offered, which she hadn't. He apologized as profusely as he could.

"Expected you at nine."

John kept apologizing.

"Waiting since nine."

John stopped apologizing.

"Come."

On the subway John had fixated on the idea he would lose his job. He had been replaying again and again the distorted memories of the drinking and smoking and sex. He never wanted to have to deal with Chester and Todd again. Shorts in February. In Harsh's office, beyond the windows, the Chrysler Building beckoned for the heavens to establish diplomatic relations with earth. The gorgeous daughter smiled from the photos on the wall. Everything was the same except John had squandered an opportunity. Harsh went to the window, preparing to fire John by gazing at the view.

But he returned with Tupperware and held it out to John with naked pride in his smile. "Gulab jamin. Go on. With your fingers."

John took what reminded him of bread cast into pond water for ducks. Harsh watched with supreme enigmatic pridefulness as John put the ball in his mouth. Harsh had been waiting since nine to feed him the gulab jamin. "Delicious," John said honestly. The fragrant tang had the right effect on his stomach.

"Not as good as you get in India," Harsh smiled.

"Your wife made th—"

"My wife!" A violent wave of the hand. "Yes, yes. I made them. But not good rose water anywhere. None in New York. I have my brother send me the rose water. Good rose water—all in the details." John took another. He understood he should not go to his cubicle until he took a third and a fourth. Harsh appeared to adore him.

He had planned on giving it a few days before calling Nerissa, but he didn't know anybody in New York and was lonely and under-slept and almost hysterical with uncertainty and confusion, so called Nerissa that afternoon after work. He called her from his cell phone from the bridge between Manhattan and Queens as he was walking home. He was walking to walk. His life was empty. "This is John," he said.

"Who?"

"John—we—" First the horror of Nerissa's failure to recognize him—then the horror of understanding his mistake. "John Marshall," he said. "Marshall." *Details!* She paused so long that he thought he lost the call. "I've got Flo tonight," she finally said. "We'll hang out tomorrow. I got more pot. Where *are* you?"

"At a bar with some friends."

"It sounds like a wind tunnel."

"It's crowded."

"I hear trucks."

"I stepped outside."

"I'll see you tomorrow."

When he arrived at her apartment again he had been thinking it over so incessantly for the last twenty-four hours that in his mind they had had a thousand conversations. He was ready to have a friend and to converse deeply and sweetly. The actual her surprised him. She answered the door in jeans and a green T-shirt and massive floppy slippers and said, "You're not supposed to call the next day. It seems eager and desperate." But he could tell that she liked that he had come. She was a mom and had been a mom all day today. He saw the lines under her eyes. She did not hug him or kiss him but pushed the door shut behind him as if he'd come to look at a freezer she was trying to sell.

"How tall are you?" she said.

"Five eleven."

"You seemed taller than that. Were you wearing platform shoes?"

"Platform shoes?"

"Of course not, I would have noticed it."

He went to the living room and sat on the sofa. The unfamiliarity of it was a gauge of how drunk and excited and eventually high he

126

had been two nights ago. There was a print of an elephant, graphic and vivid. There was a red chair next to the brown sofa. A different patterned throw covered each flat surface. The room attained a look by mixing looks.

"Drink?" she called from the kitchen.

"What is there?"

She entered with two bourbons and sat next to him on the sofa. He could not believe the fantasies he had had. He had imagined them melting into conversation as they had melted into sex. He had imagined them melting into sex as they had before. The television was on and muted. "I'm an *Omen* addict," she said. "It's a new one." She let the sound go, they watched *The Omen*, and at the half hour she rose and disappeared into the bedroom, returning with the pipe they had smoked with. She handed it and a lighter to him. As the show concluded he lost track of the plot and kept wanting to look at her face. He looked at it some. "You're looking at me," she said. The credits zipped up the screen. He was afraid of her, but he was here, so he leaned over and put his lips to her neck. She sat still for a moment and then leaned away but took his hand in her hands.

He thought she was going to tell him to go, but she leaned in and kissed him on the mouth as if doing something she had to do, resigned, unemotional. He studied her face when they separated. Her large eyes looked conspired against by her skin. They were looking out beautifully from it. He liked her dark hair, which was up, and the strands at the ears. He did not like her at all. It dawned on him suddenly. "Do you want to go to the museum some time?" he asked. She put the pipe to her mouth. At one and the same time she acted oblivious to the pipe and intent on it. She focused as the lighter flashed and the leaves glowed fleetingly. He was much more in command of his senses now than he had been last time. He was delighted and amazed and shy about everything that happened once it started happening. She peeled off her jeans and green shirt for him, but he felt like he should avert his eyes. He was allowed not to. Later it had all gone ahead. An hour had passed. They had said all of twenty words to each other. "I think I should go," he said.

"You think you should say you think you should go. That's what you think. Because of what I said before. Just chill out."

"What did you say before?"

"That people don't stay."

"I was just thinking I should go."

"To do what? Go home?" She was lying on her back and blowing cigarette smoke at the ceiling. She rolled her own cigarettes, making it seem of a piece with the marijuana. He had his hand on her belly, and her loins were right there. Then, like a day clearing up, she was in a good mood and wanted to talk. "Tell me your deepest darkest secret."

He took the command more seriously than another man might have. He could not begin with his deepest darkest secret because every single hour of his life since October he had moved through the world guarding it like the mark of a curse on his skin beneath his clothing. He wanted to reveal it to somebody who could see its horror and pity him. He wanted this badly. Nerissa could be that person, but he had to start small. He knew how to start small, saying, "Promise not to freak out?"

"You cut the women you sleep with into tiny pieces?"

"I'm telling you as a curious fact. Not to freak you out."

She frowned at his seriousness. "Don't tell me you're HIV-positive."

"I was a virgin the day before yesterday."

She rolled over and threw a hugging arm over his torso. She was shaking. Only after a minute did he realize she was laughing. A still burning cigarette still pointed ceilingward from the hugging hand and shook in the silence. When she eased she laughed audibly. When she caught her breath she said, "It's random crazy-ass stuff like this that makes this city bearable." After a moment: "Don't go getting all attached."

"I told you not to freak out."

Nerissa rolled back over and lit another cigarette. "Should I be flattered or insulted? Are you picky or even weirder than I think? Maybe I've lost my standards. What's wrong with you?" Between puffs she studied invisible hypotheses on the ceiling. He watched her profile and asked, "When did you . . . ?"

"Gawd," she drew out slowly. "About the time your mother was in the maternity ward." She thought about it. "I didn't have lots of boyfriends. But I felt like the sex belonged to me. I liked having it in my possession. I was fifteen?"

"That's so young," he said.

"It's not so young. It was so long ago it seems like another person. A cranky teenager in Saint Paul in 1976 had sex. What does that have to do with me? When were you born?"

"1980."

"Christ." It was the most peaceful, ruminative profanity.

"Who's your ex-husband?"

"You mean who's my husband? Do you want a cigarette?" When he took one she said: "I'm really doing a full job on you, aren't I?"

"I sometimes smoke." He followed this up with a fit of coughing.

"Hold it like this, or it looks like you're trying to get high."

She had lost her virginity when she was fifteen. This contaminated his secret, part of his dark secret, tainted it, and he regained a good mood only because he was in the arms of a lover, where he felt safe and free from the awful gravity of other people having sex, anybody having sex. Being in Nerissa's arms was like standing in the narrow circle of warmth and light around a campfire. He could see the darkness that would envelop him as soon as he rose from this bed and left this apartment. The warmth and light were the farthest thing from permanent.

He had run away from home to get away from what happened in October, to escape looking at it, to have it behind his back instead of before his eyes. The change of locale mattered not even so much as being in motion did, as placing himself amidst a parade of distractions. He needed to throb with the sensational novelty of wandering in new places in order to forget the captivating misery of what had happened.

"I never had sex because I was in love with somebody I wasn't near," John said.

"That's sweet and messed up and probably not true. Meaning, you're consistent."

"Can I tell you something?"

"So far your revelations have been more than entertaining."

So he talked.

He tried to make the scene as vivid in words as it was in his mind. He filled in the backstory about Stang and Emily. He sketched as quickly as possible his whole short adult life so that he could narrate the part that marked him as a curse. She needed the background, but he wanted to get to the central aspect.

Less than a month after he had picked up Stang from the airport, he picked up Emily. To the airport that day he drove the same roads through the same weather at the same time of day as he had driven to pick up Stang. He entered the terminal with not dissimilar feelings: uneasiness, excitement, envy, love. After ten minutes she rode the escalator down to the baggage claim area and like Stang astonished him in her new form.

She had become an adult, ten years older, the same self, a stranger, familiar and unrecognizable. The moment was a moment too anticipated, too severely mangled by a decade of having been imagined and longed for. It was underwhelming. Its actually happening, the fact of it, disoriented John in his ostensible happiness. Every fantasy he had about this moment had progressed instantaneously to lovemaking. (Nerissa laughed when he said this.) It was incredible that Emily had flesh, that it moved, that she moved and spoke and laughed and was capable of hugging you. She hugged him, he smelled her, he had never smelled her, she squeezed him and pushed him off and surveyed the space as if looking for something to mock, the provincial airport, the clothes people wore, but it was just like anywhere. Time had done nothing to her, had done great things, had hardened only infinitesimally the features of her face. She was an adult with the large-eyed, full-lipped, soft-nosed charms that only in really lucky and really rare people outlive adolescence.

"You're kind of judgmental," Nerissa said, "aren't you?"

Next to Emily's prettiness and confidence John felt shambling and smelly and heavy and awkward and zitty and shaggy.

"Yourself included, I guess," Nerissa said, laughing.

The man next to me on the plane, Emily said, *I think he thought I was with child, because of this dress. It makes me look pregnant. He raised his eyebrows when I ordered wine.* I took in her frock, John said.

"Nobody says frock," Nerissa said. "Nobody says with child. Are you just trying to use words?" He could not place this woman, next to him on a strange bed, in the same life that contained Stang and Emily. Through the window he suddenly focused on what he saw, a giant crazy clock with the numbers all wrong. Who was Nerissa? Who was he?

"I took in her dress," John said.

It was a loose sap-green dress without a constrictive waistline, but he could not see it, there were no signs of pregnancy. In a moment he had been detesting his own sweating body as he hauled her suitcase to the car. When they stopped at the car she started laughing and said, *I love it, it's tiny!* As they pulled onto the highway, she said, *You didn't tell Stang what I'm here for, did you?*

I didn't tell Stang anything, John said.

I need to make friends with him first, Emily said, *that's the only way this will work.*

He meets people on his own terms, John said.

I remember, Emily said.

In his fantasizing about the weekend, John told Nerissa, he had not pictured how it would go at home, had barely thought of his parents, had forgotten they would witness everything, but there Frank and Mary were, intrusive, hospitable, hovering, almost as interested in Emily as John was and too aware for comfort of his feelings for her. He was a transparent fool. It was embarrassing and difficult, and John was jealous of Emily's every movement, clung to her, not physically but in his brain as he accounted for her, following her through each room with his eyes, with his heart. She joked naturally and gorgeously with Frank Townley, who was not much of a joker but who discovered considerable reserves of charm around such a charming young woman.

"I see where this is going," Nerissa interrupted. He studied her profile. She was so weary and confident. She stared at the ceiling as if no ceiling could ever surprise her again. When John looked at the ceiling, it made the world seem vast and arbitrary. "Emily hooks up with Stang, right? Your cousin sounds massively stuck-up by the way."

John fell silent.

"Keep going," Nerissa said.

"You ruined it," John said. "You just ruined it."

Because yes. Of course. And of course, John saw now, anybody could have seen it coming. He was a fool to be telling it as a story with suspense. A perfect stranger could hear the slightest sketch of it and guess the ending. He alone had failed to anticipate the obvious, to see unwinding the most elementary plot in the universe of possible plots, with him at its center and blind to everything until everything reached its catastrophe. "The most painful part of it for me," John said, not ready to continue, "the most painful part of it for me is not even that they hooked up. That hurt, but I got over it. The most painful part for me is to remember myself that afternoon. To think about how I was with Emily in the house, to think about how it was looming over me, it was hanging over my head, it was inevitable, it was waiting to happen, but I was so happy Emily was there and in love with her and feeling important for what I could do for her and proud that Stang would see how profound my relationship with her truly was."

"Sorry," Nerissa said. "It sucks to be duped. You certainly surprised me with the virginity thing, if that makes you feel any better."

131

"It's not that you saw where this was going," John said. "It's that it was so easy to see." He wanted this depth of humiliation to belong to him alone. If the events had been uncommon and monstrous instead of banal and obvious, it would have hurt less. He breathed and focused.

"So what happened?" Nerissa lit another cigarette. It dawned on John that cigarettes in general were like little flags flagging the privacy of everybody's desires. Nerissa, like he, had a heart that wanted and wanted—blood that did. She was such a stranger to him, unknown to him the day before yesterday.

"There's more," John said, "You won't have guessed this part."

"Great," Nerissa said.

"But you could, actually," John said.

Emily and John had gone for drinks that night, not to Lazy's but to the fancy bar in the hotel on the waterfront in Apalachicola, and had watched the sunset and the surface of the bay break with birds and fish and sea mammals. The sun marked the time by nearing the water, measuring for John the fleetingness of the moment, a moment he had thought about for ten years and wanted to last forever. He had entered the hotel only once before, this fancy hotel on the water, once when he was eight, had never drunk at the bar, and since it was a familiar place from the outside, entering now and visiting with Emily felt like blowing a hole in the thick walls of provincial geography and pathetic cowardice and interminable stasis that confined him. There was a round, red-velvet Victorian sofa like a donut and a donut hole. Emily had so much to talk about. She told him about *Greater Than X*, their plans for a new liberal era, their belief in a literature of seriousness again, after all the years of froth, and the great excitement with which she anticipated the project with Stang.

What exactly is the project with Stang, John asked.

The war will speak for itself, Emily said, *Stang will speak for himself. I'm just giving him a little structure, a little grammar, a little polish. It will be his story, the story of his enlistment through his return home, written in his voice, with his flare and color, but on my laptop in my sentences. The war is an objective horror, so I want to write objectively. I want to commit Stang's heart to the written page.*

You're assuming he has one, John said.

"That's funny," Nerissa said.

I know from your letters he has one, Emily said.

The sun set, the night fell, the drinks flowed, and still they were at the bar. John could feel on him the eyes of a town that knew him, Frank Townley's boy, sitting in an unexpected place, drinking unexpectedly, talking intimately with a beautiful woman nobody had ever seen before. For, next to him, Emily was positively glowing, warm, fragrant, perfect. As the drinking progressed, things became less regimented, less polite, looser, happier, deeper. She put her mouth so close to his ear that his body brightened and tensed as though they were kissing. She began saying things he wanted badly for her to say. *All my life I've had such vivid memories of visiting you that time. It's bizarre to see you again.*

I've thought about this for a long time, John said.

I never thought about it, Emily said. *I mean, you became your words in your letters, that's what you were to me, a voice, not a person. Not even a spoken voice. It was bizarre when you called on September 11th. We had been so young the only weekend we ever saw each other.*

John could hear himself saying, through the haze of the drinks, *That weekend was the weekend I was born.* He could gauge his drunkenness by the stupidity of words like these. He had said too much already and tried to soften it. *It opened the world up. I saw there was something more than Apalachicola and Harold Wiffin and Presbyterianism and Transformers and Stang.* He heard himself saying, *It was the most vivid weekend of my life.*

It was in the running for me, she said. *And do you want to know why?*

Yes. John believed he wanted to know why. He had imagined something close to this conversation for nine years. But he had not imagined Emily saying anything like what she said. *I was devastated*, she said, *heartbroken, completely shattered, totally in trouble, totally in love. Do you have any idea?*

You were shattered by the weekend? he said.

Her tone and words—John realized he wanted her to stop.

I was shattered when you first laid eyes on me, Emily said. *I arrived that way. I was fourteen and no longer a virgin—*

Nerissa started laughing. It brought him back for a moment, but he pressed on, in Emily's voice.

—I had been sleeping with the English teacher at Groton since April, the school year had just ended, and he was getting dismissed, and I knew I would never see him again, and I thought—I was just a kid!—I thought I was in love with him—and Sallie was enraged,

133

and Marion couldn't do a thing, and the trip to your house had been planned, and it was the last thing I wanted to do. But as soon as we pulled into the driveway I felt positively restored. I felt rescued by you and rescued by your father. My uncle—your dad—is the sweetest man in the world. And so funny!

You had sex with your English teacher, John said.

We had had an affair all spring, Emily said. *He was twenty-two. It seemed ancient at the time. Now it's nothing. Can you believe it?*

Perhaps the darkness or perhaps the drinks in her blood had blinded Emily to John's expression. He stared at the slim slips of ice in the bottom of a glass of watery Scotch. He felt as though a blood-pressure cuff surrounded not his arm but his whole being and would forever.

"You sure don't shy away from the metaphors," Nerissa said.

For a week I had been fighting with Sallie nonstop, Emily said. *I had the perception that I was equal to her as a grown-up. I arrived at your house as a grown-up. But as soon as I arrived I felt welcome to a few more months of childhood. I think on some level I understood the shame of it. I was precocious in that way, at least. I knew that I was a child. But to argue against Sallie about Clarence—we didn't even argue directly about him—we didn't mention him—it was terrible and totally oblique—but to argue against her I had dug in as a grown-up. If I proved to myself I wasn't the child everybody thought I was, the situation wouldn't be the disgusting thing everybody thought it was. So much seemed to ride on my proving I was mature. But you—you were still a boy! And you gave me an alibi as a child on a weekend when only an alibi as a child could save me from going insane. Plus, your father seemed so measured and wise, compared to Sallie, who's been a teenage girl ever since she was one. When you're a teenage girl, and your mother is a teenage girl, you don't know how to act. Your father restored my faith in adulthood at a time when I didn't know what to think. Uncle Marion didn't harm things any. But he's a pushover compared to your dad. I'm glad your father exists, and I'm glad you exist. As soon as I saw you again today I had the weirdest flash of the same old feeling. You seem innocent to me, redemptive and pure.*

"All those things, plus creepy," Nerissa said.

I can tell from your face, Emily said, *you're not taking this as a compliment, but it's the biggest compliment I've ever given anybody. You remind me so much of your father. You're innocent, or you want the world to be innocent, but aren't naïve, exactly. You're free of the*

cynicism we all live in, you're not ironic, not in a superficial way—
I'm not saying you don't have a sense of humor—I just mean you
are what you are. I live among people who are jaded and cynical and
snarky and too afraid to make themselves vulnerable. They cover up
the most interesting part of themselves with glibness, with attempts
at cleverness that aren't even clever. You should try as hard as you can
to get yourself on paper, to be yourself on paper.

"I see why you fell for her," Nerissa said. "She's pretentious in addition to being stuck-up."

I've seen you do it in your letters to me. But I'm partial. But if
you could do for lots of readers what you have done for me in let-
ters, that would be amazing. Because when an innocent person writes
honestly, he can get away with saying things a cynical person never
could. Cynicism is a self-fulfilling prophecy. It makes impossible the
genuineness the cynical person decides is impossible. But all you have
to do is not be cynical. Which is like saying all you have to do to fall
asleep is to stop worrying about falling asleep.

La dee dah dah, Stang said, joining them at about that moment. He
might as well have said, *Wild Bill Niggercock.* John could hear, even
now, in bed with Nerissa, the sound of those syllables, *la dee dah dah.*

"I'm with him," Nerissa said, "But what kind of name is Stang?"

"His real name is—" John barely caught himself. "His full name
is John Stang."

"So John Marshall and John Stang," Nerissa said. "You guys sound
like gunslingers in a western written by third graders."

Stang had had to work that night and shower and drive down
from Quincy and do something for his mom before crashing in like
a warhead. *Johnny never takes Stang to the hotel bar,* Stang said, *I
see how it is, just out-of-town guests.* Stang ordered two shots of Jim
Beam. Drinking them fueled the bravado that he launched into for
Emily's sake. *I've seen some shit,* he said. *You want details on the shit
I've seen? You want pictures of the shit I've seen?*

You have pictures? Emily said.

Stang always has pictures, John said.

You will not believe the pictures, Stang said. *Fuck these crotchety
Vietnam dudes never saying what they seen in combat. I'll show you
what I saw. This shit belongs to America.*

Emily, who had just been loose and happy and intimate, became
different now—the first of the shocks. Long ago, her fourteen-year-
old self had recoiled in outrage at Stang's use of the n-word. A decade

135

later, John still expected her to feel that way. He assumed that, at least morally, his cousin by marriage here and now would be more or less exactly like his cousin by marriage back then. But prep school and college and the intellectual circles of Manhattan seemed to have destroyed the little earnestness she emerged from childhood with. Hardly did she balk at "nigger" anymore. The unacceptable thing, in her adult world, was to fail to avoid being too serious—was not to use scare quotes. You could tarnish your Williamsburg reputation faster than anything by meaning exactly what you said. But how on earth could John have anticipated this? He had been living a fallow life as a chronic teenager in a pious household. He was counting on Stang's offensiveness to be as repelling to Emily as it had been long ago. But now Emily treated Stang lightly, deferred to him, flirted with him, *worked* him, and Stang let it happen with total delight.

He presided over them as if he just got back from storming the beach at Normandy. He ordered two more shots and turned away from the bar and rested his back against it and his elbows on it and addressed the empty room and not just John and Emily. His eyes scanned the space as if searching for the audience he deserved. Until now he had told John very little about Iraq, and the details of the war emerged in blinding banality and grotesqueness: the cheerful abuse of helpless Iraqis, the shitting in the MRE bags, the American porn on the Muslim streets, the accidental deaths on both sides, the bikes crushed by tanks driven carelessly, the smells and the sights and the problems of skin—burning, chaffing, drying, molding, rotting, stinking. Stang showed no moral interest in the stories he was telling, did not pass judgment on himself or others. He just spun the tales. Later they talked about other things and got hilarious.

After they left the hotel Stang and Emily giggled in drunken conspiracy in the back of a cab as John attempted to appear sober and make small talk in the front seat with the driver, whom he vaguely knew as a face from town. Emily's giggles sounded false. The driver dropped Stang at his mother's house and drove four doors down to the Townley's. Emily paid the thirty-dollar fare. John was already dreading having to ask his father in the morning to drive him and Stang to pick up the cars at the lot at the hotel.

That night John did not sleep. He lay in his bed, his body divided by two thin walls from the sleeping body of his cousin two rooms away, his brain buzzing with a score of sentences from the evening, sentences he tried to herd without being fried by, as if standing in a vat of eels. He tried to piece together the whole of Emily's monologue, her version of the visit long ago. The main element gave him such a shock that he touched it again and again, marveling. He was a virgin a year older than the man who slept with Emily when she was fourteen. She had arrived in 1993 having slept with that man. That day, John had been wearing an Optimus Prime T-shirt and shooting toys from a fence with a BB gun. The adolescence that he had spent a decade escaping from returned from the dead to throttle him. Too much significance derived from the revelation of the sex for him to absorb it at once. It shifted the ground on which he had built elaborate structures of aspiration. Everything fell down.

"We're all whores," Nerissa said. "Either that, or we're no fun at all."

"I don't think anybody's a whore," John said.

"You wouldn't feel the need to say that if you weren't conflicted. You know I've done you a huge favor, right?"

"It would make it easier if I thought she was slutty, if I thought there was something cheap about it. It only makes you weak if you want it and aren't a part of it, it shrinks you to nothing, that's why I hate it, not because I think it's wrong, it's just horrible, it's not about you, meaning me, it makes me understand how much I overestimate the size of my will."

"It?"

"Sex. You're huge inside, but only inside. You're nothing but what you think of yourself."

"You're large enough on the outside." She was being flirtatious and kind.

"Everything, all of life, is only ever totally private. That's how it makes me feel: alone."

The catastrophic evening was itself banal. What could he remember about it? That night John was already trying to do the awful mental work of digestion. A body he had loved as inviolate, as parallel to his own, of its stage of life, had plumbed the mysteries without him, a decade before him, long ago, in childhood. It had—her body had—without his knowing it, been radically inhospitable to the fantasies he had projected on it. Were all bodies this way? It was not what he thought. It was not his, in any way. It did not wait for him or include him. So, the next night, the night with Stang, he was busy adjusting to this, was redefining Emily's body, not as a thing in the world but as a place his imagination had run to for all the years he had been writing letters to her. This labor, this adjustment, this recalibration, distracted him until the very moment when events had ceased any longer to allow him to be distracted. He was thinking of the English teacher, when what he should have been thinking of was Stang. Then Emily and Stang slipped off together. John had watched from the porch as she walked down the driveway to the road to meet him. Frank had come in and sat next to John. *I'm not quite sure I understand the nature of her project*, he said.

She's writing a book about veterans, John said.

That's imaginative, his father said.

GO AWAY, John had wanted to scream.

They sat there together for a while.

There are things we feel in this life, his father said, *more strongly than anything we ever feel again. They can be the most important things. But there are things that are brief and important and intense, and other things that are less brief and as important but less intense.*

Dad, will you leave me alone?

His father rose and went.

In the dusk Stang and Emily appeared on the driveway. John had been reading on the porch, or staring at a book, not reading. His cousin and his best friend laughed and talked. She was giving Stang everything he wanted, getting through to him, letting him be him. She was wearing a dress, and he was wearing a muscle shirt and jeans. "Even then I should have seen," John said. "But I was thinking about the English teacher from 1993. So even as I was thinking I had caught up to the horrific truth, more horrific truth was happening before my eyes."

"It sucks that she didn't like you back," Nerissa said, "But 'horrific'? Really?"

"I didn't see it coming. It wasn't one blow that week, it was two. You think you know who people are, you build visions of them, and you get it wrong, and the wrongness is your vanity, your own preoccupations. It's like you're trying to view the Grand Canyon through a peephole, and the rest of the door surrounding the peephole is your ego."

"Now you're being extreme for the sake of being extreme," Nerissa said.

"Nobody knows anybody," John said. "Jealousy is worse for me than love is good."

"You'll grow up."

The insurance company occupied two floors in a modest art-deco skyscraper across the street from Grand Central Station. Most days John ate lunch at a table in the basement of the concourse. He liked the low light and the relentless current of people. The archways to the subterranean platforms disgorged passengers like armies marching from the center of the earth. When he stood in the great hall he felt important and insignificant and lonely and hopeful. He always wanted to drink at the bar on the mezzanine, but never did. He wanted to be alive in 1945 and to be wearing a suit and to have a reason to drink there.

Each day he watched the headlines scroll across the digital board in the newsstand. He watched the closed captions stuttering beneath the newscasters on the televisions and browsed the front pages of newspapers. The war was losing interest as a story. It went on without meaning. What happened to the city of 9/11? John had missed it.

Some days at lunch Harsh fed John homemade dishes. John knew which days to stick around on because Harsh advertised well in advance. On Monday: "Wednesday I will bring a lamb curry. Very spicy. You cannot eat spice?"

"I can eat spice."

On Tuesday: "Tomorrow I will bring a lamb curry. You cannot eat spice?"

"I can eat spice."

On Wednesday: "Today I have brought a lamb curry. You will like."

Alice, the flirtatious smoker, once appeared at the office door when Harsh was feeding John. She looked startled and apologetic, as though she had found them kissing. "Harsh *loves* you," she said later.

By now John had fallen completely in love with the girl in the pictures on the wall. Was she fifteen? One day Harsh seemed to read his mind by asking him if he wanted to marry soon. "I'm still young," John said.

"Twenty-one? Twenty-two?"

"Twenty-three."

"I was married when twenty. In India marriage is the first thing. Everything follows. In America it is the last thing. I think it is better the first thing."

John studied the sullen face of the wife in the photographs.

He never saw Nerissa again. He remained in New York for two years, and in his moments of greatest loneliness he never considered calling her. As soon as he left her apartment that second morning, he felt exposed and ashamed. He had revealed to her the rawest, most searing, aching thing in his heart, his deepest darkest secret, had held it up for their joint inspection, and had diminished it; he could have told her anything else instead. He could have told her, when they first met, that he had lost his finger in the gears of a tank.

That second night marked not only the end of his relationship with Nerissa. It marked the end of a phase of pain. John had moved to New York to lick his wounds but had expected also that something magnificent, something tragic and grand, would come of their healing. He had brought with him the most powerful story he would ever play a role in, had had his heart broken with such force, had been humiliated with such egregiousness, that the future appeared without prospects for happiness or even tolerability. But confessing the story to Nerissa, seeing how readily she anticipated its logic and guessed its ending, feeling how oppressed she was, even in a brief hour on a bed, by the intensity with which he wished to endow such banal stuff, by the articulation he wished to give it, John grasped, with despair, that nothing tragic and grand, possibly nothing at all, would come of the healing. He had not been initiated into a wider significance; he had not discovered a plot for the ages; he simply had been asked by circumstances to stop being an adolescent. In exchange for an almost fatal blow to the heart, he once believed, he had received a story worth writing down, the novel he was searching for. Now, gradually but fairly quickly, he stopped thinking so. In the weeks and months that followed his arrival, as he changed from a temporary to a permanent employee of the insurance company, as he told to strangers at bars bigger and bigger lies of less and less importance, as he moved like a ghost through the side streets of the greening metropolis, the rich, thick, heavy, awful sorrow he arrived with became a poor, thin, weightless, windy trace of itself. It appeared destined to whistle through his chest for the rest of his life and do nothing more than that.

XI.

From behind his large desk Akana looked up at me from his sedulous little body and asked, "What have you learned?" A grimace was the best he could do for a smile. In the army you often feel like a phony as you deliver your half-assed reports with great confidence, and that was how I felt as I said, "Basically we're dealing with young artifacts—Neo-Babylonian, seventh century BCE, not much older than the classical record in the West."

"You can say BC, for Christ's sake."

"Collection, collation, nostalgia, an attempt to preserve the Sumerian legacy—basically, Nebuchadnezzar's latter-day ego trips."

"Sounds familiar."

"You mean Saddam. Everybody's always looking back. I have to admit I barely know anything. I read everything I could find. I found four books. The Barnes & Noble in the Green Zone has been closed for expansion."

"There's this thing called the Internet?"

"I did all I could with this thing called the Internet."

"I expected nothing less. Do you want to talk details, then?"

"I've been meaning to ask: You think we need tanks? Against looters and smugglers?"

"The journalists love tanks. Elizabeth Slade loves them."

He was sharp enough to see my expression change. He thought I had a bone to pick with TEX News. I did have one, but I don't have to tell you that that wasn't why my expression changed. Working with Elizabeth Slade at this point might pose some first-class challenges. Greep and I had not made a favorable impression I was betting. Akana interrupted himself and waited. I said, "It's Slade's crew we'll be working with?"

"She's excited about it. Not a fan?"

I decided on, "I had no idea it was such a high-profile story."

"She wouldn't be going if we thought the danger from smugglers was high. But yes, if you see the smugglers, please scare the shit out of them. TEX News is putting half their bureau on this, which is huge. The other networks are reporting on Karbala and Fallujah. Everybody thinks it's high time for archaeology and smiles. I don't have to tell you this is unconventional. There's the good of saving the antiquities, and there's the good back home. You agree?"

I said I agreed.

He was silent a moment. "I'm trusting you to cooperate. If they have ideas—"

"They, meaning TEX?"

"If they have ideas, I'm trusting you to cooperate. We all want the same thing."

Then he leaned forward and paged his assistant. "Send in Ms. Slade."

We left the next afternoon. We drove our tanks from the bunker to the pre-staging area at the FOB on the island, and for the last time I took in the sacrificed, scarified avenues, their litter, carnage, garbage, misery, heat, dust, cacophony, and slop. Iraqi men, drunk on Turkish whiskey, shook fists and yelled, "Fuck you, America!" Boys chucked rocks, old women stared daggers, drivers drove cars in lazy or speedy defiance of the heft and girth and firepower of our useless tanks. I could tell from how he did his duty and set his jaw that Eccles— afraid that Pat Mapp was screwing around on him, afraid of death— had succumbed to a deep stultification. On days like this, superstition consumed you. You were haunted by stories of soldiers who died on the helicopter delivering them to the airplane home. Deliverance from the horror seemed at every moment equally distant, which means that as it approached in time it receded behind the clouds of invented, imagined disasters. You would finally experience the fatal ambush that had filled your nightmares since June. But now, to us, nothing happened.

To get a unit of tanks from Baghdad to Babylon you don't drive them there. Nearly a hundred kilometers divide the cities. You load the tanks onto a tractor-trailer that makes a car-carrier look like a

142

Tinkertoy. On the Ba'ath Party amusement park island, in the bizarre shadows of roller coasters, under the weird gaze of cartoon mice, our 1070 HETs sat rumbling in the mid-morning blaze, throwing from their hoods clouds of heat that crinkled enough air to fill a ballpark.

My platoon was gathered in the shade and a half-dozen men sat near me, fishing for news. They knew the broad strokes—that we had been tapped to become television celebrities—but I had been tight-lipped about the details. As far as they were concerned I was being an asshole, a hog, a dog in the manger. It seemed like pure selfishness and poor form. I was supposed to share the wealth, facilitate rather than take strict control of their impending fame.

At the beginning of the war the press was all over the place. A surprising number of tubby dudes nearing middle age believed that visiting a war zone in an impoverished nation was the best way to get laid in Manhattan. A less surprising number of mannish women believed it was the best way to buck norms, which it was. The tubby dudes passed out cigarettes, condescended to talk on your level, botched slang, fumbled with their MOPP suits, wheezed, sweated, pissed from fear, and got in the way. The mannish women possessed superhuman endurance and tremendous competence and no sense of humor. Both the tubby dudes and the mannish women held the power by which our squalid, often deadly struggles might become quadraphonic, digital, glossy, orchestrally scored, glamorously peopled, wittily scripted movies. The mythology of such movies had landed three-quarters of us here. Being excited by the press showed everybody that you were vain and pathetic and desperate, so you couldn't look excited, except you were excited and looked it despite yourself.

Of all the men gathered around me now, in the shade of the HET, on the sweltering staging ground, it was Schwartz on whom the prospect of celebrity appeared to have wreaked the profoundest changes. I had known him for a year, and in that year I had never seen him reveal a glimmer of generosity, earnest interest, vulnerability or happiness. With his blistering red face, his porcine features, his slack-jawed outrage, his unremitting hatred of women, his heft and his hideousness, he repudiated his own needs by deriding the needs of others. Mostly, as you've seen, he picked on Eccles, bullying him about Pat Mapp, fostering the self-doubt that needed no fostering, urging Eccles to hate her as Schwartz hated all women. Any soldier, not just Eccles, who showed the slightest longing or weakness opened himself up to a snide swipe from Schwartz. I had made a point never to mention

my jealousy for Hillary to him or for that matter to anybody, in case
Schwartz caught wind of it. It was as though the war had compressed
Schwartz to the densest form of his own worst self. Which was what
made his new abjectness, his transparent desire, his sudden vulnerability, so fascinating. He badly wanted to be on the news, and it
almost sweetened him.

"What network is it?"

"That's need-to-know," I said.

"How's that need-to-know?"

"Don't be insubordinate."

"Who's riding with the reporter?"

"I'm still deciding."

"I volunteer."

"I'll consider it."

"When will you decide?"

"I'm working things out."

Elizabeth Slade was neither tubby and male nor mannish and was
the secret I was keeping. The day before, when she entered Akana's
office and shook my hand, her gaze lingered only briefly on my features. I made a concerted effort to smile and be talkative and dispel
any resemblance I might have borne to the quiet nervous person I
was in the Green Zone. It was remarkably easy, I found, to become
somebody else, at least from the starting point of obscurity. It probably helped that I looked like every other skinny white guy in the war:
average height, average build, neither ugly nor handsome, sunburned,
rangy, plain. If Slade remembered anything, it would be Greep.

So when Schwartz begged to ride with her I was, despite my
contempt for him, glad. I had four seats to fill on the HET carrying
my tank. I could take Schwartz and Duckworth along with Slade
and me, tucking Greep further back in the convoy. If we could get
to Babylon, or even just clear of Baghdad, the news story would be
un-call-off-able.

Of course it was probably the case that I was being paranoid and
that nothing was in danger. Probably Slade and Greep could have
reunited in Akana's office and the mission would have gone ahead.
But superstition consumed you. The Babylon assignment obsessed me
as a kind of premature deliverance from fear. The greatest dream no
doubt was to set safe feet on the tarmac in Germany. Until that happened, I could think of nothing better than puttering in ancient ruins
far from the fatal claustrophobia of Fallujah and Karbala. In this

state, I fixated on even small contingencies, and Greep was forever a large one.

"Why don't you ride with me and the reporter in the lead HET?" I finally asked Schwartz and never saw him look so happy. He looked impossibly happy, his face glowing and relaxed. All at once I could imagine him as a child and sickened at my hatred for him.

Moving lots of troops (somebody in the army believes) requires the pre-staging area, the post-pre-staging area, the staging area, the post-staging area, and the post-post-staging area. Imagine sitting on a scorching interstate as the wreckers clear a fatal pileup. Imagine that for an hour. Imagine that feeling: the heat, the impatience, the ignorance, the total absence of motion, the underlying premise of motion. Then imagine driving a hundred yards and doing it again for an hour. And again. And again. And one last time.

So six hours later, we hit the road. There were four HETs for our platoon, and, like me, the three other tank commanders—Greep, Tuttle, and Corez—rode shotgun in the massive trucks with a few of our men. The remaining soldiers pulled security from half a dozen Humvees. The archeological crew, just us, would split from the main convoy at Musayyib, drive to Hilla alone, then meet up with the Italians and head to Babylon. The rest of the battalion would drive on toward Karbala, where they would face harrowing urban warfare.

The last thing we did before pulling out of the post-post-staging area was to pick up Slade, who had chosen to keep herself cool in the air-conditioned FOB. Relief washed over me when this moment arrived, when she slammed the door and buckled in, not having seen Greep among our number.

In the Green Zone she had looked tiny to me, smaller than her televised self, and the impression remained in the cab. Her body looked slight in the seat, her blonde head tiny in the helmet, her chin too dainty for the strap beneath it. I wondered how she kept herself so clean and groomed. It was honestly like watching an angel float into a stockyard. I rode shotgun, a sullen sergeant named Blunt drove, and Slade sat between Schwartz and Duckworth in the back. When we spoke we had to shout over the seven-hundred horsepower Cat C18 diesel engine. The trip involved twelve hours of shouting and silence and shouting and silence and watching the often immobile rear end of the Humvee in front of us.

In the backseat Duckworth and Schwartz stared at Slade from either side. They barely noticed each other, they stared at her so intensely. Maybe I stared in the mirror in the same way. Schwartz rubbed his ruddy hands together nervously, as if preparing to show off his reflexes in a game of chance. Duckworth chewed his bottom lip between instances of gaping. He might have been realizing for the first time that the people on television were also people in the world.

Around us was nothing, miles of nothing, the strewn and tattered distant outskirts of a major city fallen in war. Downed power lines empty of juice wound around tire shards and car doors and rusted drums and broken hulks. Iraqi officials under Saddam had driven four-wheel-drive Nissan Pathfinders whose bent black frames still lined the highway a year after their drivers expired in flames. The vegetation looked slummy and incidental, the sand more like dust from a concrete wall than alluvium from the ancient mountains of Turkey.

"Look," Blunt said soon after we cleared the city. At first I thought he was pointing simply at this, at the diffuse and minor wreckage and ancient desolation. But then I saw the moving things, the sentient things, a goat and its offspring, or two goats, or a goat and some weird puppet-like trash swaying in a breeze not blowing. Then I saw that it was a single goat with a toddler. A delirious boy wearing no clothing tottered after the goat as the goat moved. The boy looked smaller than a real human being. He trailed the goat and did not look at us or appear to hear the thunder of the convoy. The goat was chewing on the hair of a body lying prone.

Long ago we had received orders never to slow or stop—even when civilians leapt on our vehicles or jumped in front of them. The Iraqis did this, the women and little boys and girls. Sometimes they were forced to by men preparing to ambush us who bet that American sentimentality would compromise us. Other times, the worst times, it reflected the desperation of people willing to risk their lives to beg for candy bars. Even American soldiers who did not hesitate to lay suppressive fire on rows of houses or unload weapons into the bodies of men and women whose eyes their eyes were locked with, even such soldiers could not tolerate the hit-and-runs. We hit people and ran. We ignored those in many kinds of need. So when Elizabeth Slade craned her neck to watch the child in the road vanish behind us, I was overwhelmed by the desire to underscore it, point at it, push her face toward the window for a clearer view. Here were the consequences. "Look what you get for what you wanted," I wanted

146

to say. "That's what you've done." Except that, at that very moment, she turned to Duckworth and said kindly, "So, you must be ready for a change."

Never had a man needed so little prompting. Within thirty seconds Slade knew all about the slaughter of the puppies. I craned my neck to watch and listen. She focused her energy, her very soul, on Duckworth's soul. She drew him out simply by yelling over the engine softly and kindly and by studying him with compassion in her eyes.

Schwartz shifted in his seat. He surveyed the landscape and rubbed his hands together. Finally, he looked at me and blurted, "Can't believe you friggin' learned Latin. Like, *opted* to. I guess that's why they call you Dr. Jones."

"Who calls him Dr. Jones?" Slade said.

Kirk Frank had made a *Raiders of the Lost Ark* joke. I explained this to her.

"I enlisted to get *away* from school," said Schwartz. "The army sucks, but school? Friggin' A. Lesser of two evils. Et CET tra, et CET tra." He spoke with indifferent bravado, unconvincing confidence, a stilted intensity. He was riffing, starved to be heard, saying nothing substantive.

"So you weren't big on school," Slade said.

"I wanted to go to school," Duckworth said, not willing to lose her attention. It was a remarkable show of backbone for him.

"Gluttons for it," Schwartz said, looking from me to Duckworth and back again. "Weird bastards."

"My dad said school," Duckworth said.

"Worst of both worlds," Schwartz said.

"I wanted to," Duckworth said.

"Too much sugar for a dime," Schwartz said.

Slade attended to both men, did her best to be kind and neutral.

"Dad never did school," Duckworth said, "and so for me he always said school. I wanted to do it. But it was always like dizzy what I was looking at. I mean, reading."

"Wanted to kill my old man," Schwartz said. "Used to dream of rigging a gun to go off in his face."

"Like the words or the numbers was in my stomach," Duckworth said. "Like in my stomach how when we're heading out to do a TCP. Like, being scared. But it was more different than being scared."

Slade had inspired a monologue twice as long as anything I'd gotten from Duckworth in a year.

"Do you understand what the fuck he's talking about?" Schwartz said.

"Let's watch the language," I said.

"Just hard to see." Duckworth pushed ahead. He was trying to get it across. His eyes watered with the effort. "I looked at the words or the numbers and my head, it hurt. Teachers, I give them paws. They said that, I give them paws. They give the test for . . ."

"Yes, for?" Slade said.

"Dyslexia," I said.

"Oh, cry me a river," Schwartz shouted. "Don't even believe that bullshit! That's welfare mama bullshit! Post-traumatic stress disorder bullshit! Rub some dirt on it, you know? *Dyslexia?*" He paused and studied Slade as if with a revelation in mind. "Can I say bullshit?"

"We'll consider this conversation background," Slade said. "How's that?"

"When I swear you can consider it off the record," Schwartz says. "I can't help swearing. I'm a man who swears."

"They was starting to test for this lexia," Duckworth said.

"You're fine," Schwartz shouted like a coach. "OK? It's in your head, OK?"

"In high school they was testing for it," Duckworth said. "But they said I ain't got it." His voice was low and his hands large, his nose large, his eyes watery, his hair like a kid's hair, blond and buzzed. "What I got was something else. It wasn't just words. Timmy Kendrick had a birthday. It was skating. Everybody on roller skates, and I put them on but I couldn't do it."

"Roller skating is for faggots anyway," Schwartz said.

"Let's watch the language," I said.

"She said I can say what I want," Schwartz said. "What's wrong with faggots?"

"I fell down," Duckworth said.

"I remember there was a kid on the base once who got new roller skates," Schwartz said. "He was a total dweeb."

"How old were you?" Slade asked.

"Eight. I can't remember a goddamn thing about it. Sorry, Lieutenant. But we stole them things from him and put wood blocks in the boots, scraps of two-by-four. The skates had them toes with the stoppers, them brakes like red noses. Before we crammed the wood in we bore a hole in the wood and in the heel of the boots and stuck rocket engines in them fuckers. You remember Estes?"

"I remember Estes," I said.

Schwartz, too, before Slade, had never said a word about his child-hood. Until earlier today he had struck me as an eternally shitty grown man. Apparently he had also been a shitty child.

"Dad was there, at the roller skating, with Timmy Kendrick," Duckworth said. "I fell and he hit me. Like I meant to do it. But I couldn't do it. Everybody could but me. I just fell."

"What we were thinking," Schwartz said, "was that them fuckers, sorry, them sons of bitches, sorry, Lieutenant, SOBs, would cruise down our street like tiny racecars, like the Batmobile in them movies? You get it?"

"I'm not sure I follow," Slade said. "What's estes?"

"I took the skates off," Duckworth said. "There was Miss Pac-Man, but dad said no way. I was crying. So I sat on one of them things with the carpet."

"It's an engine," I said.

"You listening?" Schwartz said to Duckworth.

Duckworth fell silent and looked at me as if a major decision had to be made.

"So first," Schwartz said, "we make sure that little faggot, sorry, Lieutenant, was outside to see what we'd done."

"Can you give him a name?" Slade asked.

"I sure can," Schwartz shouted. "That little faggot was Kent Clark."

"You mean Clark Kent?" I said.

"I say Clark Kent?"

"His parents named him Kent Clark?" I said.

"Told you he was a faggot!" To Slade: "Off the record."

"There was hot dogs," Duckworth said. "It smelled like them. Everybody skating. They could just do it. School was like that. I wanted to."

"Can I finish my friggin' story here?" Schwartz said.

Duckworth stared at his hands.

"So word to the wise," Schwartz said. "A roller skate with a rocket engine in it ain't gonna go in a straight line."

"Duly noted," I said.

"I'm still trying to picture an estes," Slade said.

"An *Estes*," Schwartz clarified. "Them fuckers spun like a moth-erfucker. Off the record. They *moved*, too. They was all over the place. They was hopping like a man a'mowin', lifting three feet off the ground."

Duckworth watched Schwartz talk.

"We was laughing our *asses* off, sorry. It's because we put a D engine in. So that faggot—"

"Kent Clark," I said.

"So he's watching with them faggoty little eyes wide, his roller skates, bouncing and skimming and hopping all over the neighborhood. And after a minute one of them gets stuck in a hedge. The other one bounces up his driveway. And then what?"

"And then what?" Slade says.

"That fucker, sorry, Lieutenant, SOB, hops up and cracks through the picture window. Of his house? SMASH. No shit. So his mom comes running out. She sees what happened. Sees that it was that little faggot's roller skate what smashed it. And she whips him up, drags him in, beats his pussy till it's pink."

"Watch the language," Blunt, the driver, said.

"Me and Duffy Dempsey was already laughing our asses off. Now we *really* was."

"So you didn't like school," I said to Duckworth.

"I couldn't get it. All the way through. Then Bobby got me a job. So no more school."

"You dropped out?" Slade said.

"Friggin' right," Schwartz said.

"What job?" I said.

"Ventures," Duckworth said. "I worked at Ventures. I had that job for until before the army."

"But?"

"Dr. Bonneville. His son was below me in school. His dad made him—Bruce—work at Ventures. He was smart and rich but he was in trouble. We had teams. We had machines what did gaskets in boxes in three steps and it took three on a team. My job was closing the top. How fast it went was how fast everybody could go. Before that I worked with Chuck and Hey Zeus. But I worked too slow so they changed it and put me with Bruce."

"Who was smart and rich," I said.

"My fingers," Duckworth said. He had held up his hands. "They put us in groups for how fast we are. So then I worked with Dale and Bruce."

"Tell us about Dale," Slade said.

"He was a black person, from prison. I'm not prejudice."

"Everybody's prejudice," Schwartz said. "Greep's prejudice. J'Million's prejudice."

150

I winced at the sound of Greep's name. Slade's eyes were on Duckworth. "His arms had marks," Duckworth said. "He always talked about giving you the cock."

"Just say it," Schwartz said. "He was a faggot and a nigger."

"Hey," Blunt, the driver, said. "Not in my cab."

"What?" Schwartz said. "They can say nigger, and we can't say nigger? Greep says nigger all the time. Plus there ain't even nobody black in this cab."

"Schwartz, you know I won't stand for it," I said.

"Do I know that?" Schwartz said.

"You want to get out and walk?" Blunt said.

"He talked about the ladies there," Duckworth said. "Giving them the cock." He turned to Slade looking afraid to go on.

"It's fine," Slade said. "Go on."

"So I was with Dale and Bruce. Mr. Krieger thought Bruce—that he'd be good. He put him with us for that. But Bruce never did nothing."

"Them rich fuckers don't never do nothing," Schwartz said. For some reason, to me: "No offense."

"My dad works construction," I wanted to say.

"Bruce never did nothing. He went to college later. He also crashed his car. Dale said he'd give him the cock. I tried to do all right. Sometimes Dale was on Mars. That's what Mr. Krieger said. Dale said he'd give Mr. Krieger the cock."

"You didn't like the job after that?" I said.

"I liked it with Chuck and Hey Zeus. But the new group, I didn't like that. It was me, Dale and Bruce. Stupid, jail, and rich."

"People have trouble with people who are different," I said.

"Because usually they're queers," Schwartz said.

Duckworth was finished. To reclaim the floor Schwartz said, "Give us your expert opinion, Ms. Slade. You think he had them?"

"Who had what?" Slade said.

"I don't think he had them," I said.

"Didn't ask you," Schwartz said. "I know what you think." To Slade: "WMDs."

"I don't have an expert opinion on that," Slade said.

"I don't think he had them," Schwartz said. "So the question is: oil, or the vendetta for pops?"

"Oil or vendetta?" I passed the question on to Slade.

"No opinion," she said.

"Son of a bitch!" Schwartz's laughter widened his mouth. "Fair and balanced! Fair and balanced my granny's last rimjob! What *I* think," Schwartz shouted confidentially, "is that they smuggled them motherfuckers, sorry, SOBs, into Syria. Buried every last canister just across the border. It'd take all of three E1s, two garden shovels, and a wheelbarrow to do what half the CIA is trying to do right now. *CIA.*" He positively heaved the name. "Don't doubt the bastards planned 9/11. Split the proceeds? With the Russians? Get it? You know what they are? A bunch of spooks. Plus Warren Buffet and the laser cones on them airplanes. Riddle me this: was there any wreckage in Pennsylvania? Never saw it. Plus I had a friend on that flight, and you know damn well she's at an army base in Canada and not dead or nothing. Five to seven of them hijackers, the ones they showed on TV, were still alive two weeks after. Cheney and them. There's fair and balanced for you. Why don't you do a little reporting on Buffet and them laser cones?"

"If it's news, somebody at TEX is on it," said Slade.

Slade did not embody my understanding of journalistic excellence or even basic objectivity. She gave hyperbolic voice to reactionary anger. I had watched her spout vitriolic hype on unreal soundstages against truculent graphics and martial drums. She had helped inestimably with the pounding of the drumbeat that led to this war. If she had only chosen to do so she would have found ample employment checking the hysteria of candidates for office, offering nuanced perspectives on complicated issues, corroborating facts, calling bluffs, and correcting mistruths. But what had emerged, in the America that launched this campaign, was a media committed to protracting the lives of falsehoods by repeating them in screeds.

There are people in the world whose opinions differ from yours so much that the difference implies violence, urges it, supplies a will for it. And if you stand on the side of moderation, this implication, this will to violence, upsets you even more than the mere difference of opinion itself. Because you are complicit in it—you become complicit in extremism by loathing extremism. You are reduced by your enemy to what you despise in your enemy. The world excuses only saints and lunatics from its economy of hatred, is what you realize. Pick a side.

In the weeks to come, Slade's network would contribute to the transformation of Antoine Greep from an obscure sergeant to a national hero. TEX News and the Department of Defense would produce from a public relations nightmare the harrowing and heartening story of the year. Insurgents, the story would go, captured and killed half a dozen Americans—but not with impunity. The forces of evil suffered four times our losses and displayed half our decency, bravery, and grace. Of course Slade herself, as you know, would not live to contribute to the mythmaking, which only now, months later, I am revealing for what it was.

I just want to make clear that at this moment in the HET my hatred for her vanished. For despite everything she stood for, her compassionate treatment of Duckworth and even of Schwartz made me wonder whether I actually might like her. I'll say again that I had never seen Duckworth—or even Schwartz—speak with such free and happy spirits. I felt in the cab of the HET, as I had never quite felt before, the confusion of the disparate scales of modern experience. I could almost put out of mind everything I hated Slade for because of how she treated my men. It was this confusion, on my part, that lent an increased feeling of unreality to her violent death, which happened not an hour later.

Watching the town of Musayyib materialize from the intermittent farmland I saw nothing more or less dangerous, more or less squalid, more or less dusty and ugly, than you saw anywhere else in central Iraq. Intel showed a hospital, a chemical plant, a power plant, and the crucial bridge connecting Baghdad to Karbala. Something shy of three hundred thousand souls called the city home. Stone and mud structures lined the bleached and charred streets above which power lines hung like grim rigging. What from a distance I had mistaken for a smokestack revealed itself to be a small, green minaret wrapped in a beaded stripe like an oriental barber pole. It was the shape of an Apollo rocket. Beside it was a billboard showing the faces of imams or ayatollahs, their white-bearded faces and black turbans rendered in airbrush in a garish modern style. Iraqis took seriously graphic techniques from the early 1980s that American advertising companies now used only in ironic reference to the early 1980s.

Our four HETs and half-dozen Humvees pulled aside as the rest of the convoy slowly rumbled toward the bridge to Karbala. We were doing a marvelous job jamming up the traffic for the locals. The locals watched us with the pious, self-sufficient, dignified hatred that I associated with Shiites. Or maybe I just knew this was a Shiite town.

When we got the sense that we would be here a while, I climbed down from the HET and assembled some men for a defensive circle in the shade. It looked like a safe enough spot to stretch our legs. Slade climbed down and reunited with her news crew, which was setting up next to a two-story windowless wall. Two specialists pulled security and in a moment the camera men were filming and Slade was interviewing a specialist from another platoon. I was watching them when J'Million came over to me.

"I'm not ridin' wit' them! After what they done?"

"Riding with who?"

Greep and Malik and Corez sauntered up behind him. They stood back, and my inclination was to stand back, as anger distorted J'Million's face. At a distance, Iraqis had already begun to gather and watch this mass of men and vehicles messing up their afternoon.

"Never again!"

"J'Million," Corez said.

"I fuckin' *saw* that shit." J'Million eyed me. "They be dead to me. *Dead* to me. Can't even say their names."

"Not the time for this," I said.

"Fuck you," J'Million said. "Now or never is the time for this."

"I really don't care what this is about."

"Oh, but you do," J'Million said.

"Nobody's dead to anybody," I said. "Greep?"

Greep, standing behind J'Million, shrugged and grinned.

J'Million stared through me. His eyes always looked spaced too widely, but especially as he was staring through you. This was the moment I should have listened to him. Things would have turned out differently if I'd listened to him. You've watched the consequences of my failure if you've watched any news at all.

Blunt blasted the HET horn. It looked like we could get going again.

"You guys are man enough to ride in the same HET," I said. "Who are you riding with?"

"No fuckin' way." J'Million shook his head and stared past me. Greep just shrugged and grinned. Blunt laid on the horn. "Listen, we don't have time for this," I said. "J'Million, you ride with me. I'll send Duckworth down," I said to Greep.

"Ain't ridin' wit' Duckworth," J'Million said. "I ain't going near Duckworth. All them be fuckin' dead to me."

Duckworth? Dead to anybody?

"I just told you. You can ride with me and Schwartz. I'll send Duckworth down to Greep."

"Who's the reporter?" Greep asked.

At that moment I noticed that across the intersection Schwartz had turned even redder than usual. He was screaming at a HET sergeant across the way. He and the news crew and I formed a triangle, three points on a four-cornered intersection. Sometimes when you hear rounds being let off, a sixth sense tells you that they found their mark even before you turn and look. I was watching Schwartz screaming and heard rounds and turned and understood even before I saw that Elizabeth Slade had been shot. I understood from Schwartz's face.

It speaks to the inescapable narcissism of even a sane mind that I considered myself responsible for the death. I mean responsible in a frankly occult way. My unconscious had willed her death. I had wanted for months to blame this war on her and her colleagues and make her answer for it. The media should face the consequences of its criminal amplifications of bald mistruths. The bullet that killed her issued not from a darkened window across the alley but from the recesses of my own thoughts. This was not true. The sight itself was terribly small; a petite woman taking a bullet to the brain is unspectacular. My pelvis bristled with electricity. I realized only as the sound of the shots and the collective whoosh and gasp of the crowd receded that I was standing next to Duckworth. His eyes followed the action with ghostly blankness.

Schwartz and I sprinted toward each other to the spot. Two soldiers had dragged Slade to cover behind the Hummers. But it was one of those things. No other shots were fired. A medic knelt by her side and made a demonstration of tending to her. But her brains were on her shirt. Her eyes played over us even as the exposed matter glistened in the flat sun. She was what they call expectant. Somebody else was radioing Akana.

The most gruesome part of war was the simultaneity of events of radically different importance. Two dudes bickering over who stole whose Pringles and fifteen minutes later one of them missing a leg. When, in a moment, I heard J'Million still fuming, I lost it in the sense of the Pringles. It didn't matter. "It doesn't matter!" I yelled. "Screw all this fifth-grade seat changing," I said. "You're riding with Eccles and Duckworth."

"You gonna regret this," he said.

"Don't make me give you something really to regret," I said. I heard how stupid I sounded—at the time I did, and now, much later, I especially hear it.

Part Two

XII.

Heather Kloppenberg went to the foyer, undid the chain, opened the door and looked out at the carnage of the student ghetto. It appeared endless and made you want beer and cigarettes eternally. She would have another cigarette and another beer. The evening heat pressed on her face, which was freshly washed, and the skin felt dry. Later she was supposed to meet the other poets for dinner at Captain Weatherbee's. She washed her face three times a day because of a force in her that if left unchecked made her feel like tearing the skin off. Across the street, in humid twilight, two sophomores were crouching at a hibachi grill, but she was only guessing they were sophomores. It took skill not to break out across the chin or on the other hand to flake around the lips. It took products and skill, and she employed the products and possessed the skill, and on one level she knew she was very pretty if not beautiful. On another level she was a thing never to be seen. Rain had bloated the sofa on the lawn behind the sophomores, and sun had dried it into something rank and faded. They were undergraduates, and she was a graduate student, but she had to remind herself. It was a new fact, being a graduate student, like becoming an amputee. The fat, dark undergraduate rose from crouching at the grill and sat on the sofa, sipping his beer, knees wide, feet bare. Then he stared across at her.

She shut the door wanting to be loved. She was supposed to go out but did not want to and wanted to be loved through the mysterious miracle of the universe moving toward her and through her, with no effort from her, which it never did. Plus tonight TEX News was showing newly discovered footage of Antoine Greep from right after his escape. The Antoine Greep story meant more to her than anything that could possibly happen at Captain Weatherbee's with graduate students in poetry. She would have to TiVo it, and then it wouldn't be new. The whole town of Shakopee, Illinois, would be glued to their sets while she was watching writers eat with ironic gusto and false amazement the grilled cheese cheeseburger at Captain Weatherbee's. Antoine Greep, son of Bobby Greep, had gone to her high school in Shakopee five years before she did. Her mom had had him in math class. He was the most famous person to come from Shakopee since the nineteenth century, and the famous people from the nineteenth century were pioneers known only to fifth graders. She wanted to watch on television tonight his pained eyes and gorgeous smile as he reviewed with Spencer Talent the newly discovered footage. Antoine Greep was the rare guest Spencer Talent was nice to. Heather missed Elizabeth Slade almost as much as she missed Neil Dubuque.

She could not believe that the Midland Program in Writing had admitted her, that her aspirations as a poet had received such sanction, but most of all that she was in graduate school at all. Every time she tried to explain it to somebody who had never heard of the program, which was most people in Shakopee, its strangeness dawned on the part of her from Shakopee. So most of her. It was not anything like college. She was seventy-two hours into it and could say so with confidence. College had ended in a haze of pointless hope and massive disappointment. Graduating was supposed to be a beginning, but it had reminded her of last call. She had felt bad since graduation. She had more or less been feeling bad since her thirteenth year of life, but feeling bad in college felt good compared to feeling bad in graduate school. She knew this already. She had just turned twenty-three, which put her half a decade past the age all men loved best whether they knew it or not. The skinny sophomore at the grill had paid attention to the grill. The fat one had stared. She was not an undergraduate. Her skin was dry. She returned to the bathroom to deal with herself in the mirror.

Five years ago she had been valedictorian at Shakopee High School. She could go anywhere, the career counselor told her, meaning Urbana-Champaign or Northwestern or maybe even Chicago, yet her parents sent her to Shakopee Junior College. Nobody understood how it was to have the parents she had. She was nervous like her mother and literate like no Kloppenberg in Kloppenberg history. She knew this and carried it around like a gorgeous dress you never found the occasion for. At Shakopee Junior College she could not have belonged less utterly or fit in more brilliantly. She devastated the place. She dominated the sociology seminars, irradiated with intellect and energy the Department of Women's Studies, drank, smoked, and had sex with boys. From the first day of high school to the last, she had vigilantly captained the skiff of chastity, but at SJC no longer. When she graduated from junior college she transferred to the university at South Coke, where there was more devastating, dominating, drinking, smoking, and sex-having.

In the mirror: her skin a nightmare. Her hair: ranking only behind her parents as a curse on her existence. She took that back; she loved her parents. After her shower, feeling lazy, she had let the hair dry and curl. To this day, a box of school pictures under her childhood bed revealed the stages of her mutation from a frizzy child to a frizzy teen to her current state of tenuous subterfuge. In the phase of greatest horror at age twelve she stared at the world through gargantuan eyeglasses whose frames appeared furrily capped by the monstrosities that were her adolescent eyebrows. For years she had been reducing her eyebrows to chic arcs and wearing contact lenses. But in her brain the past lived like a monster on the far side of a thin wall, always on the brink of bursting out. She had to summon all her will not to see in the mirror the frizzy, goggly, horrid self. It took a heroic act of will not to pluck the eyebrows bare. When you thought about eyebrows—but you couldn't think about them. Sometimes she dreamed her tongue grew hair. Almost always she straightened her hair, flattened her unruly curls. It was always fatal when she gave the curls another go.

Her new friend Marie Shea had invited her to the dinner. Marie had perfect hair, straight perfect raven hair, cut in devilish, ravishing, glamorous layers. Instead of going to Captain Weatherbee's to watch people from far away dine ironically Heather wanted to sit on couches with sophomores in college. She wanted to mesmerize unshaven boys dumber than her and desperate for her yet also wanted such boys to cease to exist.

In the bedroom she pulled off her skirt and studied her thighs in the full-length mirror. It was impossible to make sense of your own body, but she squinted at thighs resembling liquid. She turned and studied her ass. The thong reminded her of what a nurse wraps around your forearm to get a vein. She could not believe she was not fat. She could not believe it. She was happy she had small breasts. There was no way to have big boobs that weren't fat unless they were big fake tits. She hated the word "boobs" because it sounded fatter than the word "tits." She hated the word "tits" because she had irradiated the Departments of Women's Studies at two colleges. Her grandmother had once said, "Where're yer boobies? Y'look like a boy!" Her grandmother grew up in the hills, literally grew up in the hills. She had married at fourteen a boy of sixteen who had seen her in blackface at a Halloween party in the hills in 1930 and said, "I'll take that sweet li'l nigger in the corner." She had killed backyard chickens with dirty axes for seventy years and worked in a chicken plant, and now had a tube in her nose at a home in Joliet. She looked like a withered potato with bright blue eyes and had developed a crush on Corez, the huge black male nurse, whom she called in her fading state of mind "a right good-lookin' feller." Heather visited her grandmother every other week and despite the frequency with which the old woman used the n-word Heather liked her more than her mother or father or either sister, although she loved them all equally. "Them men all they wants is boobies," her grandmother argued. Corez, despite the n-word, liked her grandmother.

Heather got jeans from the closet and held them up in front of herself in the mirror. She thought about the fat, dark sophomore staring from the couch like a goat from a pen. Boys were animals. Under their gaze girls became animals. Heather wanted to be an animal and forget about being a girl. She hated animals. She had a rodent phobia. She held the jeans aside, looked at her legs in the mirror, and considered changing the thong for boy shorts. She kept the thong. Nobody would see the thong. She pulled the jeans on and then a red polo shirt. This would have to be it.

She exited by the side door to where her daddy's truck was parked on the driveway. Cicadas roared. She wanted the sophomore boys to see her leaving. She wanted them to imagine she was going somewhere they could never go. In fact she was driving to Captain Weatherbee's to eat dinner with graduate students in poetry. She climbed into the high cab, slammed the door, and tried as she always tried to smell the smell of smoke in the cab. Even in her daddy's truck she smoked when she drove. She aimed the exhalations out the window and held the cigarette at the window and officially her daddy did not know she smoked. Unofficially you could not miss the odor. Her daddy was a quiet and loving man. He mumbled and demurred. When he wasn't working at the plant he was watching the game and lubricating his happiness with RC Cola or Miller High Life or Crown Royal Whisky. She had seen him cry exactly once in her life. When she was still at the Junior College and living at home she had failed to come home one night because she was having sex with Brian Poore-McCallahan. When she came home in the morning her daddy had kneeled sobbing on the living room floor. Her smoke filled the cab of his truck now despite the window and the vents. Even if her daddy knew she smoked he would never tell her mother. Her mother was heavy, nervous, fidgety, prone to cooing, and had not smoked a cigarette in her life. Even if her mother knew she smoked her mother would repress the fact and never mention it, like everything else unpleasant in the universe.

Four days ago her daddy had loaded this truck with her belongings, and they had driven the hundred miles from Shakopee, Illinois, to Arden, Indiana. It seemed like a month ago. She had driven the truck, and her daddy and mother followed in her mother's sedan. Then they unloaded. "You should put the CD rack over here," her mother said. "The toilet paper's backwards," her mother said. "You hung the hangers the wrong way," her mother said. "You'll probably want green curtains," her mother said. "You need Triumph Max to get off the mildew," her mother said. "You'll need food," her mother said.

She did not need food. She needed beer and cigarettes. This phase of her life would be a betrayal of her parents. Every phase of her life had been one. Her parents and her sisters did not understand about poetry. They and all the good people of Shakopee loved baseball and NASCAR and TEX News and Antoine Greep, even if he was black, and grilled cheese cheeseburgers at Captain Weatherbee's. She loved baseball and Antoine Greep and poetry. In the spring when she had received the acceptance letter from Neil Dubuque, she had had nobody to show it to. An acceptance letter from Neil Dubuque was to the good people of Shakopee like a Platinum Visa to hunter-gatherers.

Last winter her parents had moved from the decaying ranch house on Watercrest Drive where she had grown up to a neighborhood too new for neighbors. They had moved to an empty new subdivision because black people were moving onto Watercrest Drive. It did not matter that the black people could have been Antoine Greep's family. The letter from Neil Dubuque arrived at the new house, a house Neil Dubuque would have loathed even more than the old one. Heather had graduated from South Coke the year before and was living at home as she got her teaching certification. She was temping as a receptionist at her dentist's office and on a lark and out of deep love for Neil Dubuque had applied to the Midland Program in Writing.

She read the acceptance letter standing on the unfinished mud porch of the horraculous new house and then went outside to listen to the Tyvek ripple and snap in the wind. The spring earth cast up the smell of bulldozed mud. Trucks made lonesome music on the distant interstate. Two days later she learned on the Internet that Neil Dubuque had died. She reread the acceptance letter in disbelief. She cried for a week. She received a second letter from the Midland program, which mourned the death, reaffirmed the admission, and announced the acting director, Karla Worth. Heather drove to Barnes & Noble and read some poems by Karla Worth and cried for another week.

To get to Captain Weatherbee's she'd take the freeway. College students had destroyed the residential streets she was driving down to get to the freeway. They had done it without knowing it over the course of sixty years. The destruction gave her a luscious sadness the way the best songs by Roger Ranger did. Then the gardens thickened and the trash thinned and she reached the houses where real families lived and she no longer felt the luscious sadness.

She had met Marie Shea two days ago at the orientation potluck, which was unlike anything she had ever experienced. Throughout her childhood, every third week or so, her parents invited the Wilkinses and the Henningfelds over for Miller High Life, Diet Pepsi, RC Cola, pretzels, cheese logs, wine coolers, chips, more chips, and the TV on. There would be kids screaming in and out of the TV room, making the circuit from kitchen to bedroom to TV room and round again. John Jones would tell dirty jokes, and her daddy would laugh bashfully, and Julie Jones would roll her eyes. Beverly Henningfeld would cackle like she was going to shit. Everybody hated Beverly Henningfeld except Heather's daddy, who didn't hate anybody. Later the kids would melt down totally and the grown-ups would bask in the buzz of five beers.

The orientation potluck had not been not like this.

The day before yesterday she approached the Victorian house that housed the Program in Writing carrying Jell-O salad from her grandmother's recipe. "Nobody don't love it," her grandmother traditionally argued. From the front sidewalk with a premonition of terror Heather saw through the lavish windows the darkly dressed grown-ups clasping wineglasses and standing in small groups. She had spent the afternoon drinking beer and keeping an eye on *Animal House* and making the Jell-O salad. Her daddy always kept an eye on *Animal House* if it was on. He would sip Miller High Life and chuckle almost inaudibly. Adults in black or olive or taupe or rust clothing crowded the room that she pushed her way into. Nobody looked at her. The Jell-O salad in her hands was like a clown wig on her head.

"The idea behind the magazine was to get away from irony without losing its seductive magnetism and inarguably illuminating consciousness," a man said.

"Did it work?" a woman said.

The parlor extended to the left, a crowded box, fronted by a bay window molded in oak, furnished with tufted horsehair Victorian sofas and potted palms and creaking and echoing with all the feet and voices. She could tell that the food and drinks were against the far wall. She had to squeeze past bodies to get to the table to set down the Jell-O salad. She wanted it out of her hands. Grainy, leafy, crusty, delicate, delicately arranged platters filled the potluck table. She considered dumping the Jell-O in the trash. An emaciated middle-aged woman in black standing nearby was saying, "The connections with that movement have been done to death." Heather set down the bowl and pushed back through the crowd to the hallway to find a restroom. She found a single one under the stairs and exhaled tearfully as she locked the door behind her.

First Neil Dubuque had broken her heart by dying, now he was ruining the potluck by being dead. His poems rocked with unhinged, poignant, lucid, endless, meaty, salty drive. They embodied the breathlessness of fashion, the shape and color of bottles of beer, the warlike blare of marching bands, the tragedy of power lines, the dead eroticism of the blue glow of TV sets in shaded windows. They deserved to be wailing from loudspeakers above suburbs from coast to coast. Plus, Neil Dubuque had written the best Charles Manson poem ever written. Heather lived in mortal terror of serial killers and basked in that terror as if it were lust. She read Dubuque's Manson poem like scripture. She trawled the Internet for psychopaths to rival Charles Manson. She would die a happy poet if she wrote one good serial killer poem. What the potluck needed was serial killer poets. What it needed was Neil Dubuque. Just standing in the same room as him would have been like taking hits from a joint. She would have glanced across the crowd at him knowing that he had read her poems. Neil Dubuque had! He had read them and liked them and drafted and signed the letter of admission, and then died.

The stairs above her creaked and drummed with feet descending. She closed her eyes. She opened them and studied her eyebrows in the mirror. She got it together and went back out. "His father had known him at Merton," a man said. "I write short fiction but I only read novels," a woman said. "His Catholicism? Totally irrelevant," a man said.

The variety amazed her: in age, in dress, in race. Everybody looked something: Californian, WASP, Jewish, international. She could see differences but had no names for them. It was the elegant women in sandals and dresses and bracelets who made her feel most stupid. That was, until a man said to her, "Not only am I in Indiana. I'm eating Jell-O salad. At a potluck." He had approached her and was being friendly. At the center of his plate jiggled a giant scoop of her salad. It must have been a third of the bowl. He was holding it out to show her. He wore cargo shorts and an orange T-shirt and sandals. His skin was tan and his arms hairy like those of men over forty and rich. He must have been going on thirty. His grin was pure teenager. Heather introduced herself.

"Marco Spakovsky," he said. "We're in a three-way tie with Frannie Kingdinger-Dollenmaier for best last name. Have you looked in the bookstore who your books will go next to? I'm right before Muriel Spark."

"I don't know who I'd be between."

"*Whom* you'd be between? Or are you speaking the vernacular in an avant-garde slash casual kind of way?" Then: "Who's *that*?" Marco said this loud enough for the woman in question to look. The woman in question came over when she saw this man grinning at her. Marco clearly liked how the woman looked. Heather did too. She looked beautiful and stoned. She was wearing jeans and a western shirt and had raven hair that fell in elegant layers that a girl with curls couldn't dream of. It was Marie Shea.

"You lose," Marco said when she introduced herself, "Kloppenberg and I are in a three-way tie with Frannie Kingdinger-Dollenmaier for the best last name."

"You lose too," Marie said. Her pretty smile pushed her eyes mischievously into a squint. Whatever she was smiling at, she looked like she was smiling at scandal. She was not too warm with Marco. "Do you have a cigarette?" she asked Heather.

On the porch smoking cigarettes with this potential friend, Heather felt like everything could turn around. She inhaled happily and studied the fraternity houses across the street. Except for the Midland Program in Writing, the University of Indiana at Arden resembled every other state university in the Midwest. The bars downtown belonged here, the farm kids belonged here, the practical majors belonged here. This pack of American foreigners devoted to fiction and poetry was an aberration. But she was part of it, and it suddenly excited her now that she had a potential friend.

"It's such a relief to meet somebody I don't already know," Marie said. "I'm exaggerating but just barely. I had this fantasy of getting away from it all for a couple of years and meeting new people and writing without distraction. It's like one big college reunion in there."

"I don't know anybody in there," Heather said.

Marie exhaled and smiled and squinted. "Practically the only one I don't know is the soldier."

"There's a soldier?"

"There's a creepy looking guy in a wheelchair."

Marie's effortless ultimate dismissiveness terrified Heather. Marie's hair fell perfectly and filled Heather with sorrow. Marie had full breasts and long slender legs cresting in real hips—had everything! She wore a faded, slightly fraying green cowboy shirt with pearl snaps, and sandals that could not have been simpler. She finished her cigarette and held out her hand for another before saying, "I slept with Eric Sprow. Did you meet him? No? You'll see him, he looks like a malnourished Rodney Dangerfield. We were both at the Bramble Mountain School last month and were both coming here and I was bored and drunk and I was so excited about coming here, and he was part of it, coming here. He was *not* a good fuck. I have long fingers, which means I need a guy with large hands. His hands were identical to my hands." Heather studied Marie's pretty fingers. "Big hands like Alaskan king crab, it grossed me out. I didn't want to see him again. But there we were. Bramble Mountain is in the middle of nowhere and Eric Sprow is ubiquitous like a dog." She exhaled emphatically. Heather was pretty much mesmerized. Marie seemed to assume that she'd pretty much be mesmerized. "At the Berlin Zoo one summer I remember watching a boy elephant chase a girl elephant. They went in circles. He was a teen, and she was a woman. By chase I mean walk after her. The thing had the biggest cock I'd ever seen. It was the size of a scuba tank. But the girl was twice his size and walked faster, so they went in circles, he couldn't catch her. I also remember the lions fucking." She gestured for another cigarette. "The happiest thing ever. The boy lion stood there bored and massive and preoccupied. The female crawled under him, like, offered it up. She was a slut! He settled onto her. When he came, he *roared*. Have you seen lions fuck? These were German lions, I mean raised in Germany. After he came, she flopped over. She was out, just out. He stood there staring at her. Then he started licking her head. She just slept. Later he flopped over and slept. They slept head to head with their bodies in opposite directions and their bellies showing. I'm writing poems about animals fucking. I'm going to have to sleep with somebody else just to get Eric to leave me alone."

"Not only am I in Indiana," Marco Spakovsky said, emerging from the front door, holding out the plate. "I'm eating Jell-O salad. At a potluck."

"Except you're not eating it," Marie said. "You're walking around with it, saying that over and over."

They stood in tableau: Heather and Marie glamorous with cigarettes, the guy not glamorous with Heather's Jell-O. "The worst part isn't even Eric Sprow," Marie said. "The worst part are the *Greater Than X* boys. They ruined the literary scene in New York, which I was fleeing, and now they're here to rain on this parade."

"Rain on the parade is a cliché," Marco said. "I eschew clichés."

"Eschew," Marie said. "That's great." She turned back to Heather. "The whole thing of treating literature as a platform for big ideas makes me want to puke."

"I'm working on a novel about the faking of the moon landings," Marco said.

"Tell us about it," Marie said, meaning, "Don't tell us about it."

"Oh! I saw that documentary!" Heather said. It was her kind of thing. There wasn't a high-profile or even medium-profile conspiracy theory that she hadn't spent hours on. The ambiguities of Antoine Greep and the Babylon Seven would have attracted her almost as much even if Greep hadn't been from Shakopee. "Do you believe they were really faked?"

"Of course not," Marco said. "It's symbolic."

"Of what?" Marie said.

"Just itself," Marco said.

A guy who looked like a malnourished Rodney Dangerfield emerged from the house. He wore baggy khakis and an untucked blue dress shirt. In Birkenstocks he rocked slightly from ball to heel while gripping a bottle of beer. "You won't believe what I just heard," he said to Marie.

"Probably not," Marie said. "I want some wine," and she pushed into the house without looking back. Eric Sprow followed her back

168

in. Heather ground out her last butt with the sole of her sandal and gazed once more at the row of fraternity houses across the street.

"Can you believe this?" For a third time Marco presented her with the Jell-O salad.

"I can honestly say I can't," Heather said.

So that was pretty much the potluck. Now she was entering the city bypass, picking up speed, feeling the wind from the window and the air from the vents blow her curls. She could not stop smoking. She never quite ceased believing that the person smoking wasn't her. There was the Heather who smoked and the real Heather who existed nowhere, lived outside of time, and would always be beautiful. Cigarettes were what she needed in this life because of how life was. You smoked cigarettes against fatness how people used to wear garlic against the plague. Heather could not see a fat person without thinking of her mother. Her mother had always been fat with the exception of three months ten years ago during the liquid diet. Heather had been thirteen. Ever since then she had despised the word "liquid" and vowed never to be fat. The liquid diet coincided with the one time in life when her daddy attempted to assert his independence. It had been a memorable three months.

John Jones was going hunting up in Michigan, and her daddy had wanted to go too. John Jones went to Michigan every October and came back a new man. Her daddy said so each November, "John Jones is back. He came back a new man." John Jones never looked any different to Heather, and she would never think to describe him as looking new. Her daddy was the one who looked new whenever he talked about John Jones going to Michigan.

Illinois to Michigan, for her daddy, would have been not too different from Topeka to Siberia for a resident of Topeka. He usually did not ask for anything for himself. The only thing he ever asked of anybody, he asked of Heather: "Baby, could you get daddy an RC?" He asked it when he watched the game. He asked with no presumption she'd say yes, but she always said yes. Her father had always asked her and never asked her mother or sisters, who called him hopeless, because Pepsi was clearly way way better than RC.

Heather brought her daddy RC obediently and happily until the era of the liquid diet. That year she put it together that his other drink was Crown Royal. So he drank two things: Royal Crown Cola and Crown Royal Whisky. That would have been fine, except she knew he didn't put it together, did not perceive the pattern. The revelation ushered in a feeling of tragedy, as if her daddy lived dwarfed by cruel forces he could not even catch sight of let alone comprehend. Everything seemed to happen that year when she was thirteen, the year of the liquid diet.

John Jones had asked her daddy to go to Michigan.

"I'd kinda like to do that," he said. "I'd kinda like to."

He said it one day, and he said it the next. Coming from her daddy, the words were a nuclear warhead of self-assertion. Her mother, who never stopped talking, stopped talking. "I'd kinda like to," her daddy said.

The time approached. Her daddy packed a duffle bag and set it in the front hall. It sat there for two days. Heather felt joy. She pictured him in Michigan with John Jones drinking RC in the afternoon and CR at night. But on Friday she came home from school and found him on the couch watching the game. The duffle bag was gone from the hall. He asked her to get him an RC. "Daddy," Heather said, "what happened to your bag?"

He didn't answer. Then she noticed a strange sound. It sounded like a washing machine trying to shout down an air conditioner. "Daddy, what's that noise?"

"Could be your mother," he said.

Heather followed the sound down the hallway toward the back of the house. The sound was coming from the sewing room, where nobody sewed. There Heather found her mother striding precariously and statically. She was on a treadmill. The treadmill was roaring and shuddering and whirring. Sweat was running down her mother's face, and blood was flushing her cheeks. She looked at Heather with a raised chin, like she was trying to glimpse land over the waves of the ocean. "Liquid diet," she gasped.

Heather went back to the living room. "Daddy!"

He could hear it in her voice. "Maybe next year," he said.

Her mom walked on the new treadmill each day for three months and consumed liquids. She transformed from a heavy person to a normal person, which, in Shakopee, meant still heavy. Then she started eating again and stopped walking on the treadmill. Then nobody ever got on the treadmill ever again. Ten years later it was still in the sewing room with the dog carrier on it and boxes of Christmas decorations. So Heather smoked.

The interstate was the fastest way to get from the student ghetto in Arden to the Captain Weatherbee's in Hopkins. Heather learned things like this quickly. She had a mind for the logistics of the suburbs. Malls factored into her existence considerably. She had worked at four malls since high school, engraving clocks and goblets at four different Silver Moments. Driving to the mall you saw how Arden had merged with Hopkins to make a single sprawling noncity. Each town had its exit on the interstate. Cornfields flooded the shoulder of the freeway from the north. Storage units, dwindling suburbs, fast food restaurants, and billboards filled the land to the south. There were oak trees and maple trees thick in the late summer air.

The sight of the Captain Weatherbee's sign warmed her heart despite herself. Her sister Kendra had worked at the Captain Weatherbee's in Central Center for three years. Heather and her parents used to eat there during Kendra's shift. Her daddy got the ribs basket and her mom got the salad with chicken fingers. At every restaurant they went to her parents had the things that they got. Heather always got the club sandwich, ate half, and gave the fries to her daddy. She drank Diet Pepsi and when she got older Miller Lite. Her daddy drank Crown Royal until the food came and then drank RC or Miller High Life. Her mom batted at the smoke that hung in the air and frowned. Like all the waitresses, Kendra wore for a uniform black clothes smeared with food. She never smiled and was heavy like their mother. Katie, the third sister, anorexic, never wanted to come. When she did come she ordered the steak platter, the most expensive item on the menu, and didn't touch it. "Dad, no gross!" she said if he tried to take it home. "I'm never going to come here again."

Her daddy's truck fit right in in the lot. From the outside she could tell that this was an old Captain Weatherbee's and not a new one like the one Kendra worked at. Seeing the inside made her nostalgic for the old kind, which she remembered from junior high. Tiers of booths radiated from the bar in the middle. Worn carpet covered the floor but was rubbed to nothing at the busy spots. Brass railings lined the walls and booths. Crap hung everywhere: trombones, Norman Rockwell prints, rocking horses, sports jerseys, stop signs. A Goth girl in a dirty black apron asked Heather how many. It felt strange to hear herself say, "I'm looking for friends."

It was the same here as everywhere. Sitting at the bar were taciturn men with eyes debauched on porn and guts grown fat from long shifts at doomed plants. They had buzz cuts and baseball caps. They gripped glasses of domestic beer in cracked freckled hands. They squeezed weightless cigarettes in heavy fingers and smoked and flicked ash automatically. Their unused hands rested on cigarette packs that rested on the bar. Their fat blonde wives sat next to them with bangs like malnourished pineapples. You studied the wives' bloated faces and tried to see the hot waitress or aspiring dental hygienist that had given those introductory and fateful blowjobs fifteen years ago. You tried to picture blowjobs and '80s rock. Aging was the pits, pretty much worse than death. Her daddy ate all day and drank beer at night and never got fat. Her mother and Kendra alternated rice cakes and Diet Pepsis with french fries and chicken fingers. The men and their wives wore mutually indistinguishable sweatshirts. They kept an eye on screens above the bar. The husbands watched the bartender, a plump brunette, young and still pretty, focusing on her lower back where the enigma of a tattoo, jagged like a sprocket, came into view when she bent for a glass. Heather had a tattoo of Shmoo from *Space Ghost* on her ankle that she would loathe until she died.

She made her way to the back of the restaurant. As a native she could feel the alien energy radiating from the back booths. You could hear the strangeness.

". . . or the co-op and even there it's expensive and you can't count on the fennel."

". . . like the bizarre spawn of Jacques Derrida and Barry Manilow."

". . . like Wallace Stevens skinny-dipping on Quaaludes was her phrase."

Marco Spakovsky caught sight of her, puffed his cheeks randomly, and waved a tan, hairy, handsome arm. The writers filled a rounded booth in the back corner. She arrived and hated the feeling of standing there being looked at with her curly hair by strangers. She could feel the irritated gaze of the normal patrons on her back. Marie's smile pressed her eyes to a scandalous squint. My hair, Heather thought: a ghastly mess. Then she realized the writers were high. Marie looked high. It was a table full of high people. It made her feel both better and worse.

Around the booth sat a black-haired boy with glasses with wire frames, a blond-haired boy with glasses with wire frames, Marie, Marco, and a guy in a wheelchair. The guy in the wheelchair was the solider. The soldier looked like Henry Fleming. This was Heather's first wild thought. The soldier was Henry Fleming. The soldier could not possibly be Henry Fleming, dead Henry Fleming, the lost lieutenant, Antoine Greep's vanquished buddy in heroism, whose face from three old photographs she'd seen countless times on TEX News. Disbelief chased astonishment.

She loved books about modern warfare and read *Black Hawk Down* every summer. The guy had the glasses and the wheelchair and the biceps and the T-shirt and the crew cut of a soldier. He rolled back and over to make room for her chair. He craned his neck to take her in as she took him in. A blanket covered his legs. She decided that he was not high, the only one not high. He offered her his hand to shake. It was the wrong gesture for the moment and felt uncomfortable for this reason and uncomfortable and thrilling also because he so closely resembled a dead celebrity, and also because he was missing a pinkie. She knew already she liked him quite a bit. "Patrick," he said.

"Heather," she said.

Marie introduced the boys in the wire frames. Even though Heather was bashful to gaze any longer at Patrick the Soldier she had a hard time taking in anybody else. Seth Rosenberg and Caleb Beck were twin intellectuals, black-haired and blond, curly and straight, Jewish and Aryan, brown-eyed and blue, but both pale, both slender, both keeping emotions like an asset not to be spent. Sitting across from them Heather felt scrutinized by a single intelligence. But they were eager to resume a conversation.

"I'm being consistent and thoughtful in response to a population that's forced to be Manichean," Caleb said. The sentence rose in pitch from beginning to end. It was the oratorical equivalent of turning a screwdriver.

"The idea isn't to do away with irony," Seth said.

"Why not do away with it?" Caleb said.

"The idea is to turn irony on the deeper complacencies," Seth said. "One of the deepest is death, how we think about death." He talked with unhesitant mastery, with confidence in the self-evidence of his assertions and the rightness of the order he presented them in. He was like a detective at the end of a crime drama drawing back a curtain of misunderstanding.

"The idea is to make it possible to speak seriously again," Caleb said. "The sanctimoniousness is based on nothing. This war wouldn't have started if people could speak intelligently. But they can only joke profanely or scream in demented zeal."

"You agree with that?" Marco asked Patrick.

"People don't take death seriously," Seth said.

"People don't take death seriously," Caleb said. "For tens of thousands of years life was built around it. It was the center of culture. It was always in mind."

"Every other baby died. Every fourth mother."

"Now life is built around psychiatric norms."

"Which presume life."

"Which presume life. The whole metaphysics, if you can call it that, presumes life. Nobody's supposed to die. If somebody dies, it's a lawsuit, because they weren't supposed to. Think of funeral homes. Once upon a time the bodies of loved ones were viewed in the living room. The daughter washed the mother's corpse a final time."

"Addie Bundren, et cetera."

"Now death is kept out of sight until the last minute. It never enters the home. Instead we eat popcorn and watch simulated carnage."

"*Texas Chainsaw Massacre*," Seth said.

"War on television," Caleb said.

"The zealotry of megachurches," Seth said.

"If you want to be polemical," Caleb said.

"Heather and I are bored," Marie said. She nudged Marco so she could scoot out. "Maybe you'll decide to entertain us when we come back."

Heather followed her obediently to the restroom, her mind spinning with what she had just heard. People simply did not talk like that in Shakopee. Then she was standing with Marie at the mirrors, envying the effortless straightness of Marie's raven hair. "Marco's a douche bag," Marie was saying. "He thought it would be fun to stage a battle royal between the *Greater Than X* boys and the Iraq War vet."

"I like Marco," Heather said.

"I fucked the shit out of him last night. I started making out with him in front of Eric Sprow just to get the point across. Then before I knew it I was in his apartment with his dick in my mouth. Which I wouldn't bring up except his dick is miniscule." Heather glanced to see if there were any feet in the stalls. "Can you believe it? It's amazing, it's tiny, and it totally turns me on. It's not like medical-condition tiny. I couldn't deal with that. It's small small small, and I'm used to COCK. My fiancé is hung."

"Your fiancé?"

"Marco drove me nuts with that dick, he's great with it, that miniscule little dick. It's not just mechanical. He doesn't shut off."

"I've noticed."

"It's how fat comedians work. He's got a small penis how Chris Farley was fat. His penis is, like, this hilarity at the center of the fucking. It's better than a big one. Think of laughing as hard as you're fucking at the same time that you're fucking. I want to marry him. I want to be his unfaithful wife." She added, "I love your curls."

"Patrick looks like Henry Fleming," Heather said.

"I'd kill for curls. Let's have small-cocked boyfriends together."

Back at the table they found something was going on. A stranger was standing before the booth. You could tell from a distance that he did not belong. His face looked like hell. He had a graying, drooping moustache and the mutton chops of a hippie. He was holding a burning cigarette he wasn't smoking. He was standing at the edge of the booth looking everybody over. It was the no-smoking section, and a mother and father in a booth of kids were glaring at him in murderous unanimity. Heather and Marie stopped and watched from a few yards away.

"Only reason I got through was the grass I smoked," the man was saying. "So I know about the grass." Patrick seemed to be nodding. "So to be fair I can't say nothin'. I smoked the grass when I was over there. I smoked it when I got back." Marie whispered something in sheer delight, but Heather couldn't hear her and wanted just to listen.

". . . what you've been through over there," the man was saying to Patrick.

"Yeah," Patrick said.

"Baghdad? You was lucky to come back in one piece."

"I've been lucky," Patrick said.

"You had buddies."

"I had buddies."

"My buddies, your buddies," the man said. "God bless 'em all. They're the ones who should be here." He looked at the table again. He was swaying. "To be fair I can't say nothin'. I smoked the grass way through the '80s."

"They're stoned," Patrick said. "I'm not stoned."

"To be fair I can't say nothin'."

"I'm not stoned."

"I can't say nothin'. I just came over to give you my thanks."

"I give you my thanks."

"Just think about who your friends are. That's all I'm saying. Think about your buddies. Nothin' about the grass. But these kids. I listened. I watched them come in. Then I watched you."

175

"I give you my thanks."

"Hippies threw bottles when I came back. They spit on me."

"I give you my thanks."

"Broken bottles. That was my summer of love quote unquote."

A waitress appeared at the man's side. "Beer's getting warm, Jerry."

"I give you my thanks," Patrick said.

"People like you don't deserve America." Jerry said generally. "People like you aren't worth the spit you spit." There was a silence. Then he let the waitress lead him back to the bar.

"We're ready to be entertained," Marie said as they sat.

"You missed the entertainment," Marco said.

"No we didn't," Marie said.

"So what are you going to write about the war?" Caleb, the blond intellectual, asked Patrick.

"Ernest Hemingway stuff?" Seth said.

"Write what you know?" Caleb said.

"I'll write what I write," Patrick said.

The food had arrived, and Patrick ate his without looking at them.

"You know what you should read," Caleb said.

Patrick barely looked up.

"He probably read it," Seth said.

"*The Marshall Stang Story*," Caleb said.

"By Emily White!" Heather practically yelled before she caught herself. "I love that book!" Everybody shamed her for her outburst with a brief blank pause.

"She's obsessed," Marie said.

"I *am* obsessed with Marshall Stang. But I'm *really* obsessed with Antoine Greep."

"Pawn of the media," Caleb said. "An African American patsy."

"He is not!" Caleb stared at her blankly. She changed the subject back to the thing they agreed on. "It's a great book," she said to Patrick, "I loved *The Marshall Stang Story*. The photographs are unreal."

"Emily sweated blood over that book," Seth said. "The photographs are obscene."

"She obviously cared a lot about it," Caleb said.

"Marshall Stang took the pictures," Heather said.

"But I'm not sure you can really do anything true with the war," Seth said.

Heather was reeling with amazement and envy. "You know Emily

176

White?" Caleb and Seth blinked and nodded and made her feel stupid. "It's an amazing book," she said to Patrick.

"I'll check it out," he said.

But he looked pained and disgusted by the whole drift. When she drove home that night she fretted about this. Did he think she was one of the *Greater Than X* people? She looked up *Greater Than X* on the Internet and couldn't figure it out what it was all about and totally hated it.

On Monday Heather stopped by the Program in Writing to meet for the first time with the world famous Karla Worth, a kind of entrance interview. Standing in the hall she could hear the droning voices of praise and criticism coming from classrooms upstairs and in the back of the house. A woman laughed again and again, a high squeaky laugh. "Oh!" she said as if at a marvel. Through the open office door Heather glimpsed jade plants before a grand fireplace and could hear the administrator arguing softly and confidentially with somebody on the phone. There was a great air of importance. There was the oaken, prosperous scent of the century of the life of the house. It creaked with handsome familiarity. Rural light glittered in the small beveled panes of glass on the landing. Potted palms drooped over the horsehair sofas in the parlor. Heather almost cried to think that Neil Dubuque had been here, and how recently. The woman in the office said, "we had better luck the second time around."

Above the photocopier on wooden shelves lay the worksheets. The poems for tomorrow were there. She was expected like all her classmates to get them and read them and write comments on them. She would find her own poem stapled between other poems, and her face burned with the realization of what she had shared. She found the worksheet labeled KARLA WORTH—2 PM TUESDAY and turned the pages. She had submitted "Blowjobs in the Interregnum." The title made her queasy with embarrassment.

She glanced over the other packets and worksheets. Her eyes did not stop on any in particular until they fell on his name. "Circle Jerk" by John Patrick Crane. Somebody else had a dirty and embarrassing title—him of all people! It was a relief and a joy. She picked it up and wanted to read it at once but also to save it for later. She had the strongest sensation that it would tell her something. She saved it because it was time for her meeting.

Inside the office, the world famous Karla Worth was pacing. She saw Heather at the door and ignored her. Heather sat on a bench outside and listened. Karla could not have weighed more than a hundred and ten pounds but the anger in her frame reached her feet as her feet punished the venerable floorboards. It was an old house. Heather thought about the world getting electricity and about Mark Twain still being alive. Her parents remembered the fifties and had grown up without TV. Her mother grew up in the hills where Ohio became Kentucky. Her grandmother from the hills, born long before the Depression, wanted her granddaughter to have boobies.

Karla Worth came to the office door holding a phone to her face. She stared at Heather with rage. "This is fucking unbelievable." She was verbally excoriating somebody a thousand miles away and waved Heather in irrelevantly. Heather followed and sat in a chair before a massive oak desk. Karla slumped her frail slender body into the chair behind it, still excoriating. "Tell him it matters. That's all I'm asking you to tell him." She hung up and said, "No more Blowjobs in the Interregnum. This isn't MTV. You're here, so you're here, so you're here. Do you want me to recommend some books? Oh god. Please do *not* cry. Stop! I assumed from how you wrote you had spine. There's an obvious facility with language. I don't doubt that you feel things. But no more blowjobs, and no more cigarettes. No more four-letter words. Your teenage rebellion should have ended with your teenage years. What we're doing here is bigger than that. I've smoked, we've all smoked, the reader doesn't care. Take Kleenex if you need Kleenex. Do you see the Kleenex?"

Heather knew her face was a mess.

"Heather," Karla said. "It's Heather, right? *Read*. What are you reading now?"

She took in the woman's face. The long hair framed it. The woman's eyes were savage and her voice precise, like civilization honed to a scalpel. She was the most powerful poet in America; she hated America. Heather loved America and hated America. Karla had studied in Italy and France. She had lived in Italy and France. She had been raised in Europe. She didn't know *Soul Train* and Doritos and Seymour Butts. "I can't tell what's going on. It's all surface. You're not talking to anybody. It has no roots. What do you read? Stop crying!" Karla sighed and seemed to be searching the cobwebbed corners of her soul for a remnant of sympathy. "Poetry isn't only about how you're feeling. It's about how what you're feeling fits in with how everybody else has felt and how everybody else has described how he's felt. Or she, if you're a feminist. Are you a feminist? I can't even tell. Anyway, poetry's about a legacy of language. It's about ideas and traditions. You're making clever but meaningless splices of true crime novels, bad rock lyrics, and fashion magazines. You can have a great eye for good trash, but it's still trash."

Heather had to collect herself before she could say, "Neil Dubuque didn't write about ideas and traditions."

"Neil Dubuque died, Heather," Karla said. "He died last spring, but he'd been dead since 1971."

She was still crying when she descended the stairs. Then she was crying harder. She thought about how her parents had not wanted her to come to the Program in Writing. She thought about how much effort they had put into driving her here from Shakopee and how lovingly they had unloaded her things and meddled. She wanted to call them and have them pick her up and take her home. It was impossible. Half-blinded by tears, she went into the bathroom under the stairs, ran cold water, and splashed her face. Somebody knocked, and the sound of it made her cry. The person knocked again, harder now. She opened the door and found Patrick Crane. He looked up at her from his wheelchair. "You've been sobbing." He spoke honestly before he caught himself, then caught himself, which showed on his face apologetically. "Sorry, I really have to go." Meaning, pee. It came across as a tender thing to say.

"I'm fine," Heather said.

He was slender and powerless and interested in being friendly. The wheelchair had strengthened his arms. His eyes were green and his skin was pale and freckled and his hair sandy. "Did you like that?" he asked.

"Sobbing?" she said. "Karla—"

He pointed to the paper in her hand. "My story."

She blushed. She blushed harder when he said, "'Blowjobs' is the best poem in that packet. I couldn't get a thing out of the other ones."

"I guess that means I'm too easy." She didn't mean for this to be an innuendo and blushed as soon as she heard herself. "Thanks." Her voice was lame. "We both had dirty titles." She couldn't think of anything else to say. She asked him if he was going to the party on Friday.

"You know me and Marco." He raised the hand missing the pinkie and twined two fingers. It was an ambiguous answer. In a moment she was standing on the porch, smoking a cigarette. She wanted to know where he lived and how he took care of himself and whether he hated her or liked her a little.

The boys across the street could see Heather on her porch smoking cigarettes, drinking beer, and browsing the pages of the worksheet. She wanted to build a buzz. The sophomores were throwing a football back and forth and had their shirts off, and the fat dark one wore a carpet of hair up and down his chest and back. It gave shape to the fat that quivered as he moved. There was an ecstasy in male fatness since it didn't matter. She tried to imagine Marco Spakovsky's small dick. The skinny sophomore looked concave and tan. Both sophomores moved their bodies with the happiness of showing off, of being naked and feeling the air. Everybody is a hero to himself. She wanted to own her body as those boys owned their bodies. She looked down at her thighs.

When she looked up again there were girls approaching. One wore short shorts and flip-flops and a tight T-shirt that showed belly at the hem. One wore a miniskirt and sandals with cork heels that lengthened her legs and shortened her steps. The boys didn't stop. The girls moved to the bloated couch and sat. They were four years younger than she was and a hundred years younger than she was. She could imagine how it would feel for it all to be over, to be thirty. A third boy came along, caught a pass, and disappeared into the house. When he came back out he joined the girls on the couch, handing them beers.

She went inside. Her apartment was nothing special but because it was hers she loved it. She had never lived alone until now, and shutting and locking and bolting the door felt wonderful. She turned on the television and turned down the sound. She loved cooking shows. A woman was making carbonara sauce, which nauseated her except for on TV, since she hated creamy things and hated cheese. She could fuck whoever she wanted in her apartment. Distantly she could hear the shout of the boys playing football. She finished her beer and got another beer, and the refrigerator light made her slender arms look pretty and actual, and her soul was pretty and actual with a fresh beer. She curled up on the love seat and began to read Patrick's story. There is a Methodist minister from the Florida panhandle, his wife, and their grown son living at home. The son feels stifled by his relationship to his parents. He tries to write fiction, he masturbates, he walks in the woods, and he bickers with his parents. The story grew interesting only in the last third, when early one late summer morning the young man masturbates to images in magazines and feels disgusted by himself after he comes and so bags up the magazines and disappears into the woods to get rid of them. Urged on by an ineffable force (Patrick's phrase) he pushes deeper into the woods, then even deeper until he discovers a tiny *cenote* (Heather had to look it up and wished he had just said it in English). He tears the pages one by one from the magazines and casts them onto the surface of the luminous pool. The abstraction of human depravity, the arm's length view, arouses him powerfully. He masturbates again, now onto the pages floating on the surface of the *cenote* deep in the forest. Despondent with another spent load, dreading his parents, and sad at the light in the woods, the young man returns home. He expects his parents to scrutinize him as he enters the house. He prepares himself to be annoyed. But he finds their gaze riveted beyond distraction by the TV set. On the screen are skyscrapers billowing smoke. Then the story got theoretical. Patrick tried to equate the images on the screen to the porn on the *cenote*. For the young man, no experience is primary: there is no actual flesh and no actual violence. There is only a wasteland of mediated lust and objectless fear, fed and bounded by images from thousands of miles away. The story ends with the young man deciding to enlist in the army. Heather could relate to the part about the parents, anyway, and she got herself another beer.

XIII.

If a tree falls in the forest and nobody's around to hear it—you know the trope. If a platoon receives orders to protect antiquities and the anchorwoman gets killed, do the orders stand? Does anybody care if nobody's watching? If it's not mediated, does it even exist?

Without God, only TV cameras.

The same irrational obsessiveness that urged me to keep Greep and Slade apart, that inclined me to fret about the mission, now filled me with gloomy certainty: it was over. Akana would call off the Babylon jaunt and order us to get to Karbala ASAP. It was the fitting ending. The more badly you want something, the easier it is for you to imagine its not coming to pass.

Yet as it turned out, the orders stood because the army never turns on a dime, it turns on ten thousand bars of gold worth forty billion dimes. It was as though our tiny group were cut free from the master plan, forgotten about, allowed to wander into antiquity with all the momentum of a CENTCOM brainstorm defeated and forgotten. "Proceed as planned," they told us over the radio, "and stay ready for new orders," whatever that meant. It turned out to mean nothing, the new orders never came, the old orders saw five men through to their deaths. I get it, it's hard to look up from large-scale urban warfare on two fronts to worry about four tanks and twenty men and the cultural legacy of three millennia.

TEX News, I'm sure I don't have to tell you, lost itself to its own story that week, covering with great fanfare the details of Elizabeth Slade's death. To judge from the hours and days devoted to it, it was a major turning point of the war. It was news far meatier than whatever minor ersatz piece Slade might have done on the archeologists.

It served its purpose. Ratings had to have soared. A viewing public turned its eyes from the bloodshed and bomb clouds in Karbala and Fallujah to something they could get their heads around. Elizabeth Slade, shot in the head! Our platoon appeared in that coverage as a footnote, as extras, as dolorous background. Schwartz got his moment of fame, his first and only living moment—posthumous fame came soon enough—saying briefly on camera with tears in his eyes, "She was friggin' great. She was stand up. She was the best. She was good people. I can't believe she's gone." The crew shot Duckworth sobbing, his dumb mass heaving with sobs. This clip got major play after his death, suddenly doubly poignant. As for Henry Fleming, he declined an interview.

It is hard to write about war without using the language of dreams and nightmares. I have used that language already and can't promise not to use it again. But it was only at that moment, when Slade's body crumpled on a nothing corner of a nothing street in a nothing town, that reality seemed to slip fully out from under me. Which might only be my way of saying that I finally awoke. These are clichéd philosophies, but it's hard not to conclude that life is the dream. You get through it by rounding up and rounding down, treating minor badness as major badness and major badness as total evil, treating goodness as greatness and greatness as divinity. You perceive in an ambiguous muddle a world of stark antagonisms that really only live in your mind. Coworkers are absolute antagonists, other motorists are, other nations. You rattle your sabers at axes of evil. You invent heroes and villains when all there really are are variations on mediocrity, greed and good intentions. Being at war strains beyond all plausibility the instinct to perceive moral poles. You stare at your hands and wonder whom they belong to. Dreaming provides the metaphor for this because (whatever else Freud may have gotten wrong) it unearths the buried psyche.

What are the standards? Against what unmovable thing does moral experience come to rest? Was Elizabeth Slade the wicked voice that cheered from the soundstage the movement of two hundred thousand American bodies to Iraqi soil? Or was she the compassionate woman who drew Duckworth out? Was Greep a bully adding a fine glaze of terroristic cleverness to the dull injustices from which Iraqis suffered? Or was he a righteous joker? Was Henry Fleming a sensitive humanist trying to keep the liberal spirit from dying under despotic conditions of great duress? Or was he a dithering wimp?

In the moment you simply pick up and move on. Greep joined us in the HET and razzed Duckworth in condolence. Duckworth was inconsolable and, as the day advanced, increasingly withdrawn. Schwartz was worse: the euphoria of performing grief before the camera had drained from him, his moment with Elizabeth Slade was over, and now he had to share a small space with men he hated and a commanding officer he hated more.

Greep had jacked him in the jaw four days ago. It had not blown over. Schwartz simply refused to speak. He was enough of a talker that I felt this as the hysterical gesture that it was. It was all too distracting. The thought of J'Million also distracted me. What was his beef with Duckworth and Eccles? There was no reasonable beef to be had. They were too sweet and too pathetic. I truly believed that. My platoon, in short, was a mess.

So my attention clung to the landscape and its immediate dangers. When you're on the road between Musayyib and Hilla, the Euphrates flows a few miles to the west, the Tigris an hour to the east. Between them lies this patchwork of fields and palm groves watered by irrigation canals. In many places the road divides waste land from farmland, brown from green. Palm groves shade long stretches, and the sunlight on the green lulls the mind, which is the heart of the danger, as the ditches along the fields provide premium cover for ambushes. But no ambushes that day, just dysfunction: Greep joshing, Duckworth morose, Schwartz far past morose—angry and silent. Fleming paralyzed.

We reached Hilla at 1900. Moving in a convoy too small for comfort, with HETs as targetable as pachyderms, we scanned the streets and clenched our teeth. Twilight stained the concrete blocks of squalid homes an ominous violet. Older Iraqis gathered and stared as Hornbuckle and Corez pulled security and I met and shook hands with Captain Scibona of the Carabinieri. He broke easily into a wide smile. "The American expert! Like Indiana Jones!"

"How was the drive up?" I said. They had come from Nasiriyah.

"Beautiful, beautiful. We have with us Adnan Antoon of the museum there. A great man. You will meet." Scibona glanced around. "He was just here." He ducked his head into his vehicle and radioed.

Adnan Antoon appeared on his own. He strode up to us from the mouth of a shop. I could tell it was the archaeologist. It was perhaps the only time in my thirteen months in Iraq that I wasn't unnerved by an Iraqi man striding up briskly. His clothing and comportment belonged to the faculty club, to Europe, to Eton or PBS, to the international intelligentsia: a dusty tweed jacket, a bow tie, a sense of impatience you recognized from train stations in Bonn or London. He was short with a huge nose and you saw why he might retreat with such a mug to the sedulous life of the mind. A mustache twitched with persnickety sensitivity. He gave Schwartz a withering look, then me one. He kept his hand in his pockets defiantly, as if we had not yet, and might not ever, earn the right to see them.

"A great pleasure," Scibona said, "to introduce Professor Adnan Antoon, deputy inspector general of antiquities."

Antoon addressed me in Arabic. I had to apologize. He spoke to Scibona in Italian. I could make out the language but not the words. He looked angry, but Scibona laughed. Antoon addressed me again, again in a language I didn't know. Was it Arabic? The third time the language had changed once more. When he finally used English he was livid. "An Assyriologist who knows no Arabic, no Hebrew, and no Aramaic." His accent was pristine Oxbridge, far better English than my own.

Assyriologist?

"Perhaps you have spent your time on Hittite? Greek? Latin?"

I did not want him to try it. I had never spoken Greek or Latin. People didn't speak Greek or Latin like that—or Aramaic, for that matter. "I'm not an Assyriologist," I said. "I was what they had."

"As we've been getting." Antoon turned and walked off again. His hands remained in his pockets.

"You really have a way with people," Greep said.

To get to Babylon you head east down a nonevent of a road on the Hilla outskirts. We could have been looking for a place to crap on the side of the highway in the Missouri Breaks. The HETs roared over scrub and past berms until the road split to two lanes divided not by a median but by a ditch. Water from who knows where lay stagnating in it. Epochal time had nudged the Euphrates miles to the west of us. I scanned the roadsides looking for bad guys. It was like looking for white collar criminals in Death Valley. Yet then a figure appeared, standing on a rock in the distance, facing us in arrogant stillness, not scared, not moving at all, ambiguous in size and girth in the crepuscular dust, but enormous, bigger than Duckworth.

"What the—?" Schwartz said. His first words all afternoon.

The figure was too large to be real. We slowed. It didn't move. It was a statue of Hammurabi. "Civilization's first lawgiver," I said.

"Didn't really pull it off, did he?" Greep said.

Babylon smelled like a gravel quarry when it didn't stink like a beer hall and a high school gymnasium. The deadest and the most living odors mingled. We had arrived at Camp Alpha after the last rays of twilight vanished from the desert and before the moon threw the sky into blue relief against the dark, high walls. Blinding floodlights created arenas where foreign soldiers lazed and wound down and kicked soccer balls and sometimes hooted. Poles and Germans fried meat that stank differently from the native lamb and goat. Their sadistic, chauvinistic, easy, oversimple laughter differed from American guffaws. "See you tomorrow, Indiana Jones," Scibona bid me good night.

The Carabinieri had gotten us tent space. People crawled onto cots without saying much. Kirk Frank and Eccles snored almost before they were down, but Duckworth, crammed on a cot, lay on his side gazing at nothing. Schwartz still was fuming. J'Million still was glancing at me every other minute and seething. I should have called him out of the tent then, gotten the facts of what I assumed was only a squabble, so much puppies and porn and crotch water, but I failed. I failed, I failed, I failed.

George Lucas got a lot of mileage out of setting futuristic armies against ancient backdrops. The base at Babylon, I decided the next morning, called that to mind: European soldiers moving in high-tech gear through styles of architecture defunct since clay tablets were the scribal medium of choice. Having witnessed once the elegance of the Ishtar Gate in the museum in Berlin I expected Babylon to be a heap of royal-blue shards. I was surprised to find that it was brown upon brown and evoked the worst of the new—the flat sides of a cineplex or a casino in Las Vegas or a castle made of Lego or video game graphics from 1983. It was a maze of beige rectangles topped by blocky crenellations. Saddam had undertaken a massive restoration project, not in the painstaking, authentic, deferential way of Western academics, but how you'd restore a shed in the backyard. He rebuilt it with new bricks stamped: "This was built by Saddam Hussein, son of Nebuchadnezzar, to glorify Iraq."

After getting coffee, I went looking for Adnan Antoon. You can guess how excited I was about another conversation. But you go to war not with the archaeologist you want but the archaeologist you have. A Carabinieri pointed out his tent, which, from the outside, looked like the rest. I stuck my head into the darkness, could see nothing, and thought nobody was there. Then a low voice asked me in.

Antoon had space enough for eight soldiers, and he filled it with the accoutrements of a career—a vocation—an aesthetic. Books bound in leather, pens cast in tortoiseshell, a typewriter, an elegant globe, a bust of a face, maps upon maps. Queen Victoria would have marveled at the futurity of almost none of it. Only the AC introduced anachronism—or chronism. Among the unlikely objects in the space, one above all caught my attention. On a small table by the door stood a framed picture of Antoon and what could only have been his family: a sullen-looking wife, weary and grim; a lost-looking son, skinny and sad; and a radiant daughter, gorgeous and smiling, wrapped in the arms of a father clearly loving and proud. I saw her and wanted to marry her.

Antoon waved me in. His brusqueness verged on anger. Tea was ready, English tea, and it almost could have been the case that he had been waiting to give me this brusque but flawless reception. I felt tall and foolish. His tie and shirt looked sharp and fresh against the dusty tweed. He said something I could not make out. He breathed out the universal halitosis of his profession. He huffed and then translated. "That means please do have a seat."

"In Aramaic?"

He did not answer. I asked nothing more. Tea first. It was English tea, but an Iraqi ritual. Silence filled the tent, and disdain filled the silence. When he offered me another cup, I accepted. "You are not an idiot. You know a little something."

"It is a great pleasure to visit you here."

"Your army seems not even to know the simplest thing. Taking tea well can change the course of a war. Victory is in details. You think in terms of grand visions, but where are the details? You are not winners because you botch the details."

"Because of the army I belong to," I said, "because of its civilian leadership, and because of my own demonstrated ignorance, I am in no position to convey to you—" I dropped it. I wanted to apologize but had not planned an apology. And apologize for what? He stared at me in bemusement. I tried again. I wanted to show him I was thinking. "So Gilgamesh existed historically," I tried, "but the myth of his—"

"No!" he said. "Not myth." His fingers he knitted reproachfully on his paunch. "You want to tell me about Gilgamesh?"

I was a college freshman daring to engage the professor emeritus.

"A myth is Genesis," Antoon went on. "A myth is Prometheus. Even your Big Bang, that is like myth. When you speak of myth you speak of mankind trying to make a supernatural approach to its origins. *Gilgamesh*, it is fantastic, it is a fantastic epic, but it addresses the conditions of life as we know them. It portrays a king afraid of death. It is a poem of this world. It concerns wisdom and tragedy, not magic, not myth."

I made to speak. I had nothing to say.

"Gilgamesh crosses the waters and reaches Uta-napishti," Antoon said, "and what does Uta-napishti do?"

"He gives him advice," I said.

"He gives him advice. Like Solomon in his Proverbs, you might know. Like your Benjamin Franklin. You know Franklin? And Solomon? But not Uta-napishti?" He was scolding me. "In the ancient Near East, this was a genre, the wise man passing his wisdom to his successor. The kings of France did such a thing. Even your Benjamin Franklin addresses his autobiography to his son. You have read *The Autobiography*?"

Shame consumed me. I shrugged.

"The only myth in *Gilgamesh* is the myth of the flood. Man dreams of his fellows destroyed and wiped out, of life purged, of a new, immaculate era. You have Noah in your Bible. Your Noah descends from Uta-napishti. Before Uta-napishti, the Sumerians had Ziusudra. Your George W. Bush bases himself on his Noah. He believes his Bible and forgets that before Noah were two others. Your government bases itself on your Noah. Each season a new, proud, arrogant, foolish Noah appears. Your allies have Tony Blair. This war is nothing but a dream of a flood. It is a dream of a world without details. Bush and Blair say democracy in the Middle East. By democracy they mean war as a deluge to be survived by a single virtuous tribe. But there is no single virtuous tribe. There is tribe upon tribe and clan upon clan, all vicious, all selfish, all wicked. This is not even to mention Sunni and Shiite and Kurd." He spoke with urgency but without any change in pace or volume. Then he changed. He said slowly and quietly, "What do you read?"

"I have been reading Russian novels here."

"Do you not read poets?"

"I discovered Ezra Pound in—"

"You in the West are proud of your poetry." His anger flared and revealed how little my words had to do with his ideas. "Your Odysseus descends into the underworld and converses with the shades. Virgil sends Aeneas, Dante sends himself, Milton sends Satan. James

Joyce sends Stephen Dedalus and Leopold Bloom. But long before any of these descends, the Akkadian Enkidu descends in a dream. Before him, the Sumerian Enkidu descended. Your country, you Americans, you have whom? You have Rip Van Winkle. Even your fantastic moments, your visions of transport, reach toward the future, always toward the future. You mistake our past for your own. You are proud of your lions guarding the entrance to your libraries? Those are our lions. Our lions were guarding palaces for three thousand years before your Christ was born. The terra-cotta lion of Shaduppum had endured the tribulations of history since the early second millennium. It was smashed last year. You failed to protect our museum. This invasion of my home, it shows you have no past. You don't know your own brief past. You have Rip Van Winkle, and we have our treasures smashed."

The atmosphere in the tent and the intensity and headiness of his words broke violently with all that had led me here. It followed strangely from the death of Elizabeth Slade. His body did not belong here, the suit, the pride. Other Iraqis I had met—men twice my age and twice as educated—never were able to ignore my power. Again and again it had filled me with embarrassment to see in mature eyes the knowledge that engineering degrees and tribal connections and trilingualism meant nothing in the face of tanks under the command of monolingual twenty-three-year-olds who might never finish community college. Antoon maintained a ferocious dignity as forceful as invisible machinations in dreams.

"You understand death as poorly. You turn away from it as you turn away from history. You fear death so much that you have ceased to acknowledge its reality. You hide living bodies in sterile institutions until they become corpses. You never have to watch. You pay the poor to watch as you coerce the poor to fight. You buy insurance policies promising each man the right to live forever. Who owes him this right? Your God? Gilgamesh fears death and envies Uta-napishti his immortality. That is the theme of the poem. Do you remember what Uta-napishti tells Gilgamesh when Gilgamesh asks about immortality?"

I did remember. Uta-napishti tells Gilgamesh to stay awake for seven nights and six days. Gilgamesh tries and fails. He cannot last a week without succumbing to oblivion. How, therefore, could he last eternally? I remembered all about it. But under the pressure of Antoon's gaze I could not find my tongue. His expression suggested that I, in my silence, had redoubled the shame of this war.

"Our soldiers," he said, "they fight with their chests and faces toward death. Your soldiers fight with their backs to it. You use robots and chemicals and magical plastics. But these only increase your fear and make valor impossible. Death is what we owe Allah. We owe Allah our deaths, whether we believe in him or not. I am not a fervent believer, but I know what I owe. For you, death is not what you owe. It is the opposite of what you think is owed to you. Your country is godless. I do not say that as a man of faith. I observe what is so. Affluence and piety mix poorly. Scarcity reminds man of his smallness. In the face of his diminution he has tremendous powers to imagine that which is larger than he. Your country lives far from the brink of scarcity and far from these basic human powers. The muscles of your souls are as slack as those of your bodies. Do you believe in God?"

I stammered. What did I believe?

"If you know anything—" He caught himself, or thought of something else. The elegant accent conveyed sanity. Against a backdrop of insanity the balance and clarity of his voice took on fantastic properties. To my ears they became a kind of madness.

"In the netherworld, the Sumerian Enkidu meets those who have suffered many kinds of death and died in many different states. The comfort or discomfort of these dead depends on their final condition on earth. Those without children suffer, those with children suffer less, those with many children suffer least of all. Do you have any children?"

I did not.

"The children slake the thirst of the dead with fresh offerings of water made from above. The childless endure great thirst. Also miserable are those who died in pieces—the leper, the man torn asunder by a lion, the man cut up by his enemy. In this war there have been beheadings, and there will be more. In this land people believe you should leave this world in one piece. They have believed this for five thousand years."

"I think I believe that too."

"You joke." He shook his head as though I had failed. "For them, this is a serious belief. It is an ancient belief. It is far older than Islam. Tell me, what ancient beliefs do you hold?"

Outside, the desert made noises I could not understand. Was it wind? Or my ears? The dimness and cold air in the tent became a property of my eyes. Had Antoon fed me drugs? Now I felt as though I had been here for much longer than I probably had been. Was it night? But no, harsh ribbons of sun glowed where the tent met the dust. Perhaps I needed water. For certain I needed sleep. The other-worldly elegance and anger of his voice functioned as a contagion. I had forgotten the question.

"I want to help," I said. "I am here to help."

"This the Americans always say. You sever a man's limb and offer him gauze and a handshake."

"If you want me to apologize for my ignorance, I'll apologize." My words sounded distant from me. "My army could be wiser."

"Armies are never wise."

"I am here as I am. I believe in what you're doing. I want to help, so tell me how we can help."

Antoon had maintained his brusque manner unflinchingly, so it surprised me to see his face relax. "Before the war I was very close to a great discovery. I remind you that *Gilgamesh*, the poem as we know it, has eleven parts. Some parts are more complete than others."

I nodded.

"The standard version establishes the eleven parts by collating seventy-three manuscripts. Almost half are from the library of Ashur-banipal at Nineveh, tablets from Nineveh. It is an epic like a patch-work quilt. *There* is an American metaphor."

He poured more tea. The dimness and coolness of the tent played on eyes and skin accustomed to heat and light. The air threw me off, the mood, the windy flapping silence. Was the tea doing something to my soul? Did I have a soul?

"Do you know where Nineveh is?"

"To the north," I said.

"Eight of the seventy-three manuscripts come from three other an-cient Assyrian cities: Ashur, Huzirina, and Kalah. Do you know these cities?"

I shook my head.

"Thirty come from Babylonia, most from Babylon itself, but some from Uruk. These tablets are much younger than those from Ashur-banipal's library. They would be like European editions of Virgil from the seventeenth century. By the second century before your Christ, the Akkadian language had ceased to be spoken. Men spoke Greek and Aramaic. But Babylon still remained a stronghold of the ancient culture. In the temple there was an astrologer-in-training named Bel-ahhe-usur. He was not a poet, he spoke another language, he lived in a modern age. But he wrote out the lines of the ancient epic, and he saved them. His transcriptions contribute essential portions to the poem as we know it."

He paused so that I could feel this.

"Your country could learn from Bel-ahhe-usur. Your country has never heard of Bel-ahhe-usur. It has not even heard of itself anymore. I spent two years at the University of Pennsylvania. I paid attention while I was there. I watched what there was to watch and read what there was to read. Everybody in America believes he is sacred and that his sacred self deserves celebration and celebrity and immortality. Every voice has to be a new voice. But this means that nothing is conserved and even less is transmitted. Your lawyers argue about intellectual property, but your intellectual property is worth nothing but dollars. That which matters belongs to nobody, meaning to all. *Gilgamesh* belongs to all. The *Aeneid* belongs to all. *King Lear* belongs to all. These creations have lasted because they have been conserved. To conserve the past is to renounce the self in the present. It is to accept history as a resource powering all feelings and all meaningful ideas. It is to escape the miniscule and negligible confines of the self. Who is Bel-ahhe-usur? I do not know. We will never know. He did not describe how his preferences, tastes, and perversions differed from the preferences, tastes, and perversions of all the other astrologers in training. He did not base his art on tantrums of lust and will. We know more in a day about your bloggers and your American Idols than we know about all of Babylon during the years of his life. But what we have received from Bel-ahhe-usur matters more than any blog post or television episode. He preserved and transmitted a poem two millennia in the making. You would say he plagiarized. Your Winnie Wilson and your *New York Times* would have chastised him. But you Americans value things which matter least, things which last the briefest interval, things which mark your banal and prurient differences. Truth begins with the universal. It does not begin with the personal. You might learn something if only you would try to escape yourself. You might feel freer than you do in your narrow freedom. You might be less arrogant exporting this narrow freedom."

He paused and watched my face. He seemed to be surveying the insides of his skull at the same time. Then he was talking business. "Yes, let's discuss the matter at hand. It is my suspicion that more of his tablets exist. My crew has been trying to dig for them in a tell four kilometers to the northeast of the city. New tablets could reveal what has not been known for two thousand years."

"Which is?"

"In the great poem, Enkidu is a wild man, crafty and strong, but uncultured. A harlot seduces him, feeds him bread made of flour, which he has never eaten, and draws him from the wilds. He hears tell of Gilgamesh, the king of Uruk, who rapes each bride in Uruk before her wedding day. Such behavior appalls Enkidu, who goes to Uruk, confronts Gilgamesh, and engages him in combat. There the text vanishes." He paused. He did not expect me to speak. He was letting the silence signify. He was mourning the vanished text. "When the text resumes, Gilgamesh and Enkidu are friends."

Another pause, to let this sink in.

"Think of that! They have just fought, but now they are friends. How mysterious! Yet how true to the nature of man! Your America befriends the Germany and the Japan it vanquished. Your America befriends Vietnam. Germany, France, England, and Italy join a single union. Sunnis and Shiites find common cause against the invader. Today your America destroys my country, tomorrow you will embrace it. Today my clan is at war with another clan. Tomorrow they are allies and brethren. Nobody knows how this happens. You must pardon me, I am superstitious about this. In our oldest epic, in the first literature mankind produced, what is missing? The lines describing the mystery. It is a recipe for peace, and it has never been seen, and it lies in the ground mere meters from where we sit. Bel-ahhe-usur left tablets we have not yet seen. Last year I had almost unearthed them, I believe this, but then the war came. Tablets safe in the ground for twenty-one hundred years could be destroyed yesterday, today, tomorrow."

"Who would destroy them?"

"Islam is very young, and those who dream of a new caliphate have no need for old artifacts. It differs little from the destruction by the Taliban of the Buddhas of Bamyan. Do you remember this? It is no different here, except more profitable. Muqtada al-Sadr and his followers take umbrage at nude Sumerian forms. It is a radical campaign. What could better serve the jihad than the exchange of obscene statuary and profane texts for money for guns and bombs? The wealthy collectors in the West in the end are paying for the weapons that kill the poor from the West. You destroy us, we destroy you, we destroy us, you destroy you, the museums vanish, and the fragments are dispersed."

"We want to help," I said.

"They send twenty men to do the work of two hundred."

Emerging from the tent felt like emerging from a fever, except the temperatures were reversed. The sun shocked me from the dizziness of the tea and his voice and the light. I headed toward a minor gate of the reconstructed city simply to get my blood to do something new. An Iraqi boy ran up to me and sold me a bottle of water. I drank it at once and gazed around. Babylon looked rendered from sand, designed by a Bronze Age bureaucrat instead of any kind of artist. It was heavy and ugly and endless and blocky. I followed the shade through it, hugging the walls, overhearing the medley of languages. The soldiers of each nationality lazed in their own proud way.

I found Scibona in the shade of the amphitheater. The amphitheater dated from the time of Alexander the Great, who had died here. Kellogg, Brown, and Root, the American contractors, had put heavy equipment in it. The army built a helipad nearby, and the wind and vibration from the rotors were shaking the walls. Two of Scibona's men dozed near their captain.

Scibona gave an impression familiar to me from other foreign officers in the coalition of the willing. My country had bitten off more than it could chew; it pleased him to belong to an army that would never display such hubris; he was glad to be on hand in order to be superior. But Antoon had mesmerized me, had played on something deep in me, and I need Scibona's help to do what I believed needed to be done. "We have to guard the tells around the clock," I said.

"Looters, they loot at night." He addressed me without getting up. "We guard at night. Very simple. You help by napping now."

Yes, it was a hundred and twenty degrees. But he exasperated me. "You're promising me there are no looters out there now?"

"Promise you?" He laughed and laughed. "This is a bad time and place for promises. But you, you like this weather for digging?"

"I'm not an Iraqi."

"I can see. You stand in the sun."

I stepped into the shade. He said, "The tanks are important. We take them tonight. The looters flee, it's good, this plan."

"I would love to see where we're going by daylight. It's safe to drive out there now?"

He laughed with gusto. "Nothing is safe. Your enemy now is the sun." He closed his eyes rhetorically.

It took some persistence to get him to rise and look at the maps with me. But we went into his tent and spread out maps and he showed me the site that Antoon most wanted to protect. "My unit is still on our battalion net," I told him, "but the battalion is fighting in Karbala."

"I'm sure you remain very important to them."

"If we need a QRF, is there somebody on the Carabinieri net we can call? We'd have to borrow a radio. Or some of your men could come with us to show us the way."

"The way, it is very easy," Scibona said. "You borrow my radio. It is perfect, this plan."

Back at our tents men were napping or resting their eyes. I stepped into the dimness prepared to rouse them, readying a speech in my head. Then, next to Greep's cot, on the floor, beneath his dangling, sleeping, ebony hand, I saw it: the camera from Hillary, my camera, still circulating, still lost.

I wanted to strike Greep in his sleep. But already he had opened his eyes. He reached for the camera as I lunged for it. I beat him to it. I backed away and held the camera, watching to see what he would do. He shed all urgency and sat up on the edge of the cot. He got convivial. "You don't mind if I keep the thing for one more day, do you?"

"Of course I do!"

"That's fine," he ho-hummed. "We just wanted to surprise you with something. No biggie."

"We?"

"Making a little something special for Breitbart to watch."

It was exactly his brand of cunning and bullshit. "Who is?"

"Me and the boys."

"There's no way I'm ever letting go of this thing again."

"You need it for something now?"

In fact I did. I wanted to film Babylon. I wanted to document antiquities. For once there was something worth filming. But my anger cut me off from saying this. It was my camera! Greep could see on my face that I wanted to scream something like this. *It's my camera!*

"We're heading out to the ruins." My blood pounded. "I need you to get everybody together."

"You think Schwartz is going to do anything I say? You think J'Hundred is going to do anything you say? You think Duckworth has an inch of morale left in him?"

"What are you saying?"

"I'm saying good luck mobilizing this crew on your own at this particular moment in time."

"You're bribing me."

"We're a team." That grin. "They'll listen to Greep and Flem together. But just Flem? You haven't exactly greased the wheels of discipline."

I almost threw the camera at his head. In terrible retrospect I wish I had—wish I'd smashed it right then. It might have saved five lives.

"I can finish our little video project by tomorrow," Greep said.

"Is the tape in here?" I made as if to preview it.

With a hint of resistance from him, I could have looked. But he just shrugged. It put me in the weak position. I tossed the camera back. "Tomorrow," I said. "I need it back tomorrow. Let's head out. You're with me?"

He was with me. We got the men to move. J'Million glared like a caged lion but could not resist Greep. Schwartz glowered too, but didn't refuse. Duckworth dragged himself from the cot. Eccles looked uneasy, but Eccles always looked uneasy. As for Kirk Frank and Hornbuckle, they specialized in reliability.

Fifteen minutes later we were rolling out of Camp Alpha plugged into the Carabinieri net. The map showed a distance no greater than eighteen klicks, half of them along the well-traveled route we had come by. These details may be familiar to you from whatever television specials you've watched. Kirk Frank drove first Humvee, I rode shotgun, and Hornbuckle and Eccles sat in the back. Schwartz, J'Million, Duckworth, and Greep rode behind us, Schwartz driving and J'Million manning the .50 cal on the roof. I would have felt better with a second .50 cal on our Humvee, but we had what we had. I also would have felt better with better squad morale. I had maintained a farcical semblance of discipline not through the power granted to my rank but through weakness and barter. I had traded my camera for it.

I tried to feel again the pleasure of anticipating a transcendent glimpse of ancient civilization.

"What do you get when you stick a knife in a baby?" Kirk Frank said.

"You tell this once a month," I said.

"An erection," Eccles said. "I hate that joke."

"What's the hardest part about eating an Iraq War vet?" Kirk Frank said.

"The prosthetic legs," Eccles said.

Scibona and I had reviewed the coordinates three times. I had committed to memory the lines and shapes on the maps. I prided myself on my sense of direction, and with reason. But still I counted on the approach to the tell to be a squinting, groping, uncertain affair. There were natural hillocks and little ridges everywhere. What, from a distance, would distinguish one pile of dirt from another?

I shouldn't have worried. Looking for a tell in Babylon in May of 2004 was like looking for Woodstock the day after it ended. The land was ravaged all around and drew your intuition toward the center of the destruction.

"Them mortar hits?" Hornbuckle said.

We gazed at the field of endless holes.

"Our dog did that," Eccles said. "To the yard. When I was a kid."

"That ain't mortars," Hornbuckle said.

"It sure ain't dogs," Kirk Frank said.

Acres and acres of earth bore the crude divots of lone teams of looters with shovels. It looked like a pirate with dementia and eternity to kill had been searching for buried treasure. Hole after hole after hole. At the center lay the tell itself, much less striking than the craters surrounding it.

"So we're supposed to park our tanks out here and wait for seven hundred midgets with lanterns and pick axes?" Hornbuckle said.

"Dwarfs," Kirk Frank said. "I'm pretty sure you mean dwarfs."

As for the transcendent awe? I had been dreaming of something spectacular and happy. This was not what I had in mind. I felt sick to my stomach. The Humvee hit a rut and jostled us. "INCOMING," Kirk Frank screamed. It had not been a rut. It had been a mad swerve. Then the whoosh of the RPG came, the cone scraping across the hood of the Humvee.

When I rose deafened and addled I was outside the Humvee. How had I gotten there? Was I standing? Time froze for a while and all sound was gone. Both Humvees were smoking, we all cowered behind them. I could not remember. J'Million was manning the .50 cal still and unloading soundlessly into the berms across the way. Ten yards down, Schwartz and Eccles, fat and thin, knelt at the side of burnt tires. It was not burnt tires, it was Hornbuckle. It had been Hornbuckle. Greep and Duckworth were firing across the hood of our Humvee when they could. I remember thinking, "All this for a poem?"

XIV.

The fiction workshops were in session, and Heather Kloppenberg drifted down the hall listening to voices echo in the old house. The hardwood floors tracked her movement and broadcast her infatuation. The sound of echoing voices blended to a single sound, but as she neared the door of the room she knew him to be in, she heard a woman saying, "I don't know, maybe it's just me, but I didn't get it. What does masturbation have to do with terrorism?"

So much silence followed the question that Heather doubted the acoustics. She leaned forward to peek through the half-open door and saw in fact a table of people being silent. "There were some great sentences," a man finally said. *Mere images of sex*, he read, *had become images of images of sex, twice again as far from sex, spread in the wild sun as abstract evidence of the secret and the human.*

"What do you like about that sentence?" somebody asked.

"Personally that's about where I zoned out," the first woman said.

"I have no idea what 'the secret and the human' are," another woman said.

"Let's you and I have a drink after class," Marco Spakovsky said. "I'll demonstrate."

Laughter.

"What this is," another man said, "is a valiant if failed attempt to fuse the autobiographical and the universal." Heather knew the voice. She leaned further and caught sight of the blond-haired wearer of wire frames, Caleb Beck. Sitting next to him was the black-haired wearer of wire frames, Seth Rosenberg. "It shows more boldness and creativity than anything else we've seen."

198

"Let's try not to be comparative," the teacher said. He was a Chinese American man with golden skin and goading eyes, the kind of man who winked at you without knowing you as if you and he were together in a room of fools. He had winked at Heather in the hall one day. Winkers skeeved her out.

"This is after all twenty-first century America," Seth said.

Heather didn't follow.

"Joyce seems no less autobiographical than Richard Ford," Caleb said. "But Ford mopes around like a neoconservative asshole. Joyce attaches the sense data of the material world to the firings of a soul to the fragments of a culture's vast mythologies and discoveries."

"Which is why I like plot and character," the first woman said. "We don't need another *Ulysses*. One is more than enough."

"Joyce does what he does throughout the whole career," Caleb said. "Even in the books you could understand or half-understand if you read them."

"Why should I read them?"

A long pause. A cleared throat.

"You're really asking why you should read James Joyce?"

"I'm really asking why I should read James Joyce."

"Without a tradition, what does any of this mean?"

"You think tradition is the source of meaning? For me? For any of the half of us? Maybe the *Updike* tradition? Or the *Mailer* or *Roth* tradition? In which women are cartoons to be fucked into silence?"

"Might we do best to talk about *traditions*?" the teacher said. "Plural?"

"For them," the woman said, "plurality is exactly the problem. Vibrators are a problem. Semicolons are a problem."

"We're discussing Patrick Crane," somebody said.

"I was just thinking?" another woman said, "what if, like, he wrote about, you know, the war? I love the language and the power and the images and would love to see this power tied to his experiences? As a soldier?"

A crash and a clatter from the classroom. Heather almost gasped and skittered two steps back in embarrassment. Then Patrick's form rocketed from the classroom on its wheels, the door banging wide against the wall. Silence redounded in the room he left. Heather had stepped back but still appeared in view of the class through the now wide open door. It was obvious she had been eavesdropping, it had to be obvious, and blood rushed to her face. People were staring, and she was blushing and backing up further. Patrick hooked the door with his footrest and slammed it shut, and she and he were alone.

"Shouldn't I be the one blushing?" he said. He waited a beat, then asked if she wanted to get a drink. It was the last thing she expected. It was not quite noon. He gestured toward the front door with his hand, as if shoeing her along. In a moment, after holding the door for him, she was on the front walk walking to keep up with him. She thought she needed to talk him down from great agitation and improvised. "I dreamed of coming here since high school. I worshipped Neil Dubuque. I had this picture in my head of how it would be. It's nothing like that."

He asked where she was from.

"Shakopee," she said. "Hometown of Antoine Greep, actually?"

"Antoine Greep." He didn't seem to recognize the name.

"One of the soldiers captured near Babylon? The ones who got killed in a totally unspeakable and public way? How can you not know about it? You even look like one of them."

"I look like one of them?"

"Henry Fleming?"

"Henry Fleming?"

The line of conversation was going nowhere fast. So she asked him where he was from.

"Florida."

"I'd love to be from Florida."

"It's all Burmese pythons down there."

"You must have missed it during your tour. Or tours?"

He shrugged.

She sensed he wanted to talk about Burmese pythons, and asked.

He explained about hurricanes and the exotic pet industry and filled her brain with images she loved. The only thing that could have made her happier would have been not to be sweating so much, which she was. "Hogs don't sweat," her grandmother always argued, "but I'm sweatin' like a hog." Heather harbored the suspicion that she sweated four times as much as the average woman but maybe it was really only twice as much or maybe it was the same amount and she minded it more. September was warm in Arden. It baked the cruddy yards of the gloriously ramshackle houses they passed on the way to the bar. It made the bugs happy and fat and fierce. Patrick was wheeling toward the Krieger, explaining the exotic pet industry. He was sweating like the most handsome thing she'd ever walked next to. She loved the dampness at his temples and his erratic awkward irritability. The emotion that drove him from the classroom did not appear to hold.

At the Krieger she carried Patrick's chair up the steps as he dragged his body along the railing, heaving with strong arms. His legs seemed not entirely useless after all. He had knees of some kind. She helped him back into the chair and walked behind him as he rolled into the darkness of the bar. She did not quite know what to do with herself and got out a cigarette and pretended to focus on it as she took in the space. The Krieger was the legendary bar where legendary writers had exacerbated legendary alcoholism. Neil Dubuque wrote two great poems about it. It could have been any bar in any town in the Midwest. Smoke and darkness softened two rows of booths, one down each long wall. There was room between for a pool table, and two bathroom doors and a jukebox at the far end. The bar itself lined a wall covered with random pieces of dark junk—clocks, busts, amber bottles, a medieval shield, and one of those weapons with a spiked ball on a chain. In rangy shirts one fat and two skinny lifers leaned elbows on the bar, their backs hunched against outsiders.

She wondered if there would be issues of pride and self-sufficiency, did not want to be presumptuously helpful, but Patrick handed her a ten dollar bill and told her to get the drinks. She asked him what he wanted. "What you're having," he said.

"That was more than ten dollars," he said when she came to the table with two shots and two beers. "It's Crown Royal and Miller High Life," she said.

"You've got your combination," he said.

"I have lots of combinations."

"Maybe you'll let me get to know your combinations."

It thrilled her, and the shot thrilled her esophagus, and she wanted to say so, but didn't want to spook him with the word "esophagus." She would be a girl for him, a total girl, until he showed he could deal with words like "esophagus." "My daddy drinks these things," she said. "But I'm not a daddy's girl. Or I am a daddy's girl, but my daddy's not a daddy's girl's daddy."

"My father drinks seltzer," Patrick said.

"My daddy never scared my boyfriends away," she said.

"My father's a preacher," Patrick said.

"Are you a Christian?" she said.

"I should be, shouldn't I?" he said.

"Are you a momma's boy?"

"My momma might be a momma's boy's momma. But I don't think I am a momma's boy. I'm an only child, which confuses things."

"My favorite part about your story was the parents."

"Ah, my story."

"Not that it was autobiographical."

"Not that it was," he said. "What about your mom?"

She thought about it, looking at his hands on the table, his nine fingers, feeling magnificent as he sipped his beer across from her and gazed at her patiently. They were talking first thing about parents? "You make people nervous," she decided on, "but you don't make me too nervous."

"It's the wheelchair," he said.

"It might be how you look at us?"

"Right. It's probably the wheelchair, but I think it's also social class. Do you know what I mean? What kind of high school did you go to?"

"What do you mean, what kind? A high school!"

He liked that. "So you know what I mean."

"In Shakopee, 'What high school'd you go to?' means 'Who do you root for?'"

"Do you make people nervous?" he asked.

"People make *me* nervous," she said. "I make people sexist. Without trying." She liked that she could feel him trying to figure out how to respond. "Would you have minded if I'd have said 'esophagus' a minute ago?"

"Do you want another shot? To wash down these beers?"

"Are you asking me to wait on you?"

When she set down the second round on the table she said, "My mother, since you asked, is an international champion of denial and repression."

"No kidding, mine too."

"For example?"

"You first," he said.

"I'm recovering from my trip to the bar."

"Fine. So growing up I had a close friend who my parents hated. He was more extroverted than me, charming, charismatic, and always getting in trouble."

"What was his name?"

He hesitated. "Rick Force."

"Are you making this up? That's too perfect."

"Rick was rough, and he was smart. I was smart but maybe more withdrawn and, like, contemplative. I took everything that happened to me personally and seriously."

"So you've changed a lot since then," Heather said.

He smiled at the razzing only as if he knew he was supposed to. "Rick took nothing seriously except the shit people talked about him. He got in fights, he stole things, he laughed and laughed, and he played pranks."

"And your daddy drinks seltzer."

"You got it. So one day early in our friendship, I was probably in sixth grade, and I was naïve even for a sixth grader, one day St—" He paused. "One day Rick says to me, Patrick, you're, like, such a *virgin*."

"You actually were one at this point I hope?"

"In sixth grade even Rick was still a virgin. So, of course. But what amazes me, looking back, was how apt it was. He couldn't have known how well he nailed it. Or maybe he did. I was such a virgin, anyway, that I went home and asked my mom what a virgin was."

"So what did she say?"

"She was horrified."

"What did she say?"

"She said, 'A young woman wearing a white dress in a king's court.'"

She could imagine her own mother saying it, which she told him, but only after she finished laughing.

"I was like, what the hell?" Patrick said. "Is Rick nuts? I felt superior for months until I saw how astute he had been."

"You learned firsthand? What it meant to be a virgin by stopping being a virgin?"

"No, that took years."

They drank happily.

"Your turn," he said. "Maternal denial and repression."

"We got a VCR early," Heather said, "like, early '80s, before I can remember. Back then the only place you could rent tapes was at a video store called Alfredo's, run by a man named Omar. It was in an empty strip mall halfway between nowhere and nowhere. A few years later, Shakopee got a Blockbuster and a Cinetime. But my mom got in the habit of renting from Omar at Alfredo's. All their boxes were faded from age, basically blue and white, and Blockbuster and Cinetime were in the same place she bought groceries at, in Central

Center, but she still went there, to Alfredo's. By the time I was in middle school, Omar had pretty much given up on renting videotapes to families and had started selling hardcore DVDs, gay and straight, to gay men and teenage boys and fat dads and all of mankind. By the time I was in high school, Kathy Kloppenberg was the only non-down-and-out woman in Shakopee who still went into Alfredo's. The family rentals had shrunk to a little island of boxes near the front between the fourteen-inch black plastic penises and the twenty-dollar nurse costumes. Kathy Kloppenberg's brain didn't see such things. It just saw the boxes for *Ordinary People* and *Terms of Endearment*. She wasn't going to live in a world of four-hour *Anal Schoolgirl* compilation discs."

"You win," Patrick said.

It was too good, being here with him, and she didn't want it to end. She didn't want other writers to arrive. She wanted this to last and last. "Should we go?" she said.

"Let's go," he said.

Outside, day blasted their buzz, heat and light did, muddying it, shaking it up. The dimness of the Krieger had created a false sense of nighttime. They were moving down the sidewalk past the quiet hospital by the Krieger. He did not look at her but at the sidewalk ahead of him. Had they been feeling what she thought they'd been feeling? The sunlight was killing it, she thought, but he offered to walk her home.

"It's a ways," she said.

"Don't treat me like cripple."

"I don't feel sorry for you."

"So tell me some cripple jokes."

"I don't know any cripple jokes."

"What's the hardest part about eating an Iraq War vet?" he said.

"The wheelchair?"

"So you know some cripple jokes."

"But it's supposed to be 'vegetable.' That doesn't even make sense."

He stopped, so she stopped and looked back. She felt him take her hand. He pulled her down to him. She was bending down to him, and he was kissing her mouth and stroking her head with his hand. The beer on his breath was delicious to her. It was strange to do this in daylight, in plain sight. They moved on again and relief and excitement washed over her. She lost a clear sense of who she was, walking alongside a man in a wheelchair while feeling absolutely like herself. When they reached the house she carried Patrick's chair and helped him up the steps. When they were in her living room she kneeled between his knees to bring her face to the height of his face and they kissed with her elbows resting on his armrests. "Is that OK?" she said. He smiled again. She loved this. It felt like it belonged to her. It made him gorgeous and tender-looking. "This is nice," he said.

"This is nice," she said.

She put on the television and got them beers. "This is my favorite reality show," she said.

"I hate reality shows," he said.

"Soon you won't," she said.

"We'll see," he said.

Making out with him was like both making love and doing a pleasing household chore. They were making out and then making love. There was touching and stripping and also tending and positioning and aiding. Together they got him from the chair to her bed. She had feared the sight of his legs but his legs looked normal. Perhaps they were thin from disuse. She expected a tangled white scar at the base of his spine, but his surfaces were smooth. The only visible trace of the war on his body was the missing pinkie. When she was on top of him she looked down on him and everything was normal. He smelled good and looked lost and happy. Later they lay there.

"This is going to gross you out," he said.

"Nothing will gross me out."

"Do you have some kind of empty bottle? I need to pee."

She laughed.

"It would be easiest," he said.

She brought two beer bottles. "Brown, so you don't have to feel bashful about the color. Two, because I have faith in you."

"Help me sit up. Then go have a smoke."

"I can't watch?"

"You can totally watch."

"I'll go have a smoke."

On the side porch she sat on the top step and stared at the houses across the street. The sophomores were playing video games or out. She felt wonderful. She pictured Patrick in her bed and the wheelchair floating in the middle of the floor. She loved Antoine Greep because his smile was his own and because he was the son of Bobby Greep but most of all because he got beyond the clichés. Patrick would be like that, she knew he would. Reporters interviewed soldiers at airports all the time, and to a one the soldiers spoke in banal pieties. Somewhere behind them, out of view, across the desert, in bloody, smoky, dusky, thundering remoteness, experience lacerated clichés. She knew it did, it had to, it was real. Experience tore apart anything you could say. Even the C-grade horror of her inconsequential life evaded original formulation. She said uncle at a light breeze. The war threatened life. It took life and left behind sad dudes mumbling banal pieties. Heather craved with incorrigible prurience to hear what was not getting spoken. She wanted descriptions of the war as it was. She wanted naked, ugly, violent truth. Was she a voyeur and a pervert? She was a poet, she knew she was, and she could not help her appetites, she had to make the best of them, it's what Neil Dubuque would have done.

She wanted badly to go back inside and ask Patrick about the war. She was dying to. It almost belonged to her now, and as soon as it did she could become a war poet of a kind. He had been in it, and it made him different. He could mean more than any of them ever could because he knew true stakes. He would take his experiences and add his intelligence and move the world beyond clichés. Then she found herself thinking of Emily White and *The Marshall Stang* story and she had to resist with considerable effort the giddiness that threatened to conquer her.

He was waiting for her when she went back in. In the already familiar shapes of her room, amid furniture transplanted from the dorm in South Coke, he looked out of place, tentative and delectable. She had this boy in her bed. "What's the hardest part about eating an Iraq War veteran?" she said dirtily and stayed a while longer.

In the first workshop she frankly almost died. Ahead of time she bolstered her courage by drinking a screwdriver and thinking of Lenny Bruce. OK, two screwdrivers. She entered the seminar room floating on them, bracing for outrage, expecting people to say, "You can't write like this," and "It's slutty and vapid," and "What about Wallace Stevens?" Neil Dubuque rode as a ghost on her shoulder. But once at the table she herself became the ghost. Karla Worth chose whose poems to look at, winnowing quality from mediocrity by ignoring mediocrity, implying it in this way. For an hour they discussed a poem of six lines by a high-strung, pale-skinned boy named Turner Carruth. The girl with the bachelors in English from Yale, Frannie Kingdinger-Dollenmaier, opined that the economy of suppression yielded radical fragments unassimilable to a poetic totality. The girl from Australia with fulvous teeth said that that's what she liked.

Karla Worth in drastic strokes on the backboard showed the alternative line breaks that would enhance the dramatic urgency and double the music. Sworn to silence by workshop etiquette, Turner Carruth kept sighing.

Other poems were critiqued. Fifteen people surrounded the table. One by one their faces glowed then dimmed as their lines were selected and destroyed. Marie went third and everybody loved her oblique kinky pious thrusting mélange. As the three hours passed, each new poem received less time and harsher criticism. Heather stopped being able to focus. She watched light from the descending sun hit the branches of the oak outside the window. Across the way the industrial face of a modern dorm concealed young lives of shit beer and crude sex. Heather missed the act of devastating SJC and South Coke with brilliance and lax morals. She was not devastating Arden. She did not belong at a table with Turner Carruth and Frannie Kingdinger-Dollenmaier and Marie Shea and Karla Worth and all the aliens from Planet Harvard.

Karla was saying Heather's name. The clock on the wall showed the session was over. "'Blowjobs in the Interregnum?'" Karla said. "Comments? Quickly?"

The dirty word in her title hung in the air like a fart. Otherwise the silence in the room and the blood in her eardrums were at war.

"It was awesome," Marie said.

They were out of time.

The shuffle of people getting themselves together and leaving.

"I'm going to the Krieger," Marie murmured. "If ever I needed a drink."

If ever *you* needed a drink! Heather thought.

"Did you *hear* what they *said* about my *poem*?" Marie said over whiskey at the Krieger. "Pretending to praise it? Charity and Frannie pretended to be generous, which is worse than just being harsh. They knew exactly what they were doing to me. Plus everybody totally missed the Virgil stuff. Karla should have gotten it. She doesn't take my work seriously enough to see what's right there in it."

"You must feel terrible," Heather said.

"The whole poem depends on a knowledge of Virgil. I can't pander."

"Have you seen Patrick?" a boy from the program came and asked them.

"Why are you asking us?" Marie said.

"I haven't seen him," Heather said.

"Oh," the boy said to Heather. He stood there for a second looking confused. When he had gone Marie raised her eyebrows. Marie knew nothing about Heather and Patrick. Marie ridiculed the creepy soldier whenever his name came up. Heather decided not to say anything right now about the guy she was falling in love with.

The second date had been better than the first. To avoid eyes they went to the Tipton Inn on the outskirts of Arden. From the parking lot in the evening haze you could see the purple silhouettes of grain elevators above cornfields. Inside a bartender with sprawling peroxide hair called you "hon." Heather and Patrick arrived separately, and she found him in his wheelchair alone in the crisp darkness shooting pool. She watched him unnoticed for a moment. He was focused with something like anger, and she could tell he was accustomed to shooting but unaccustomed to shooting from a wheelchair.

When he saw her he smiled and challenged her to a game. She got beers for them and returned to the table. He finished his first beer and clanked his second against hers. She felt his eyes on her as she bent over the table. When she won, he said, "You were supposed to let me win."

"So I could hustle you later?" she said. "Or are you hustling me?"

She went for shots of Crown Royal and two more beers and met him at a booth. The excitement of familiarity with a strange, handsome boy was more than she thought she deserved. It was bliss. He asked her if she didn't hate the program.

"You hate the program?"

He collected himself. "All my life I've been trying to get where everybody else already is."

"Everybody feels like that," she said. "Wait till I tell you about workshop this week."

"You pride yourself on having caught up. I mean, I do, one does. But you never catch something moving ahead of you and faster than you are. You think you have, and then it does something else. It always stays ahead. There's no fair way to catch it, to close that distance. You play by the rules of a game you've only shown up at the end of. Everybody got started long ago. People got started when they were ten years old. Those *Greater Than X* guys got started when they were seven. They were deciding between Plato and Nietzsche when I was deciding between Daredevil and Spiderman."

"We're babies," she said. "You're twenty-five?"

"Do you know Blaise Pascal?" he said.

"She's in this program?"

"The French mathematician."

She blushed.

"Don't blush. Everything is new to me. I'm reading totally randomly. I want to read everything, but where do you start? It's like trying to build a cathedral out of the half a dozen cinderblocks in your backyard. Pascal was remaindered at the bookstore. I copied out my favorite part. He wrote little observations." Patrick pulled out a sheet of paper and unfolded it. It reminded Heather of junior high. In microscopic and robotic handwriting he had transcribed: *What a great advantage to be of noble birth, since it gives a man of eighteen the standing, recognition, and respect that another man might not earn before he is fifty. That means winning thirty years' start with no effort.*

"That doesn't even mention women," she said. "Plus it's 2005." She paused, and it dawned on her: "Plus it's America. You're missing the whole point!"

"What's the whole point?" he said.

"Invent yourself," she said. "Neil Dubuque's father drove a taxi in Saint Louis. It's the best thing about this country."

"That we pretend there aren't advantages?"

"That you can be whoever you want irregardless of who you were. I love pen names and stage names and rags to riches stories. This is the best nation in the history of the world for rags to riches. My favorite thing ever is Jay Gatsby. And Andy Warhol and Bob Dylan. Nobodies who made themselves heroes."

"Jay Gatsby is fictional."

"Can we really tell the difference? Or do we care?"

They drank from their drinks.

"Am I being totally naïve about how hard it would be for you to use the war as material?" She didn't ask this easily, and he must have been able to tell.

"It would be hard for me," he said.

He stared at the table and worked with his teeth on the side of his thumb. The four-fingered hand lay on the table. She fixed on the strangeness of the empty space above the bone. "What do you read?" he asked.

"My favorite fiction is young adult fiction and also *Of Mice and Men*. I read it every year and always cry. I'm a sucker for that vision of a gentle idiot cupping furry animals in his big dumb hands, I'm sorry, I just am."

Of Mice and Men made her cry, she went on to say, because it made her think of her daddy. Her daddy didn't want anything more than to go to the Upper Peninsula in Michigan. Then her mind skipped to Iraq again. "My favorite thing I read over the summer was *The Marshall Stang Story*. I can't believe those boys know Emily White. OK, so I guess I see what you and Pascal are saying, I hate it too, but for me it's territorial, which is different. I get so excited about Antoine Greep, not even knowing him, just being from the same town."

Suddenly she realized her mouth had been launched. Booze helped. Patrick's eyes did too. Regarding current events Heather cared little about the substantive stories, she told him, the elections and statistics, the mergers and earthquakes and coups. She lived for the murder cases, for images of shattered families whose lives belonged for weeks and months to all America. Whenever the networks broadcast in solemn and urgent and delighted tones the news of a school shooting, she felt moved, horrified, included, transfixed, momentarily free. Such catastrophes justified you and exploded your vitality and relevance. Tragedy and scandal were like falling snow or winds so heavy they brought down trees on houses. She kept an eye open for whatever would next grip the attention of the universe. When it came along she escaped herself by way of it with an ecstasy of dislocation to rival sex. She envied her parents for having learned about Charles Manson in real time.

At the booth at the Tipton Inn Heather told Patrick about these feelings and also, since he'd been living on Mars, about the Babylon Seven. It was the smiling, unsuspecting headshots of the Seven that forced your heart finally to grasp the utter local horror of combat. Henry Fleming was an enigma, missing in action. Antoine Greep, handsome and eloquent, was a national hero. Duckworth and Wilson and Frank and Eccles and Schwartz were dead. The magnetism of the story depended above all on Greep's eloquence and handsomeness and family celebrity and blackness. It mattered to America, and it mattered to Shakopee. Eight soldiers were ambushed by antiquities smugglers near Babylon last May. "You really don't know this?" One soldier died in the ambush. The survivors were taken and held in a nearby village. The Shiite fundamentalists who captured them beheaded five in real time on the Internet. Then the camera spun and fell and went black to the crack of gunshots. Antoine Greep appeared at Babylon to tell the story. He fought his way to freedom against incredible odds. The networks had given hundreds of hours to the story since the moment it broke. They showed the same photographs and aired the same videos and stated the same facts until you forgot what it felt like not to know.

"So five died," Patrick said, "Greep escaped, and the other one—"

"The one you look like was shot by the guards during the escape. The only time Greep cried during the big interview with Spencer Talent was when he talked about it. But when the army went back and raided the compound they found only five bodies. Nobody knows what happened to Fleming's body. The big deal to me is about Greep and Shakopee. He got a parade, and he brought the news crews to town and put us on the map. My daddy started to say, 'I like black people OK.' He never used to say that. It's such a trip, to turn on TEX and see the buildings downtown."

The topics of war and the literature of war did not bring out the conversationalist in Patrick. The topics of parents and hometowns and childhood and childhood friends seemed to, so she turned to those. When he talked about his mother and father and the first ten years of his life, he relaxed at his very essence. He became a different person from the tense, guarded, irritable, beautiful, righteous soldier who surveyed the aristocratic party scene of the Midland writing program with an incredulousness and fascinated distaste so like her own. So, if she was falling in love, she was falling in love with two Patricks.

They went home together that night, and again two nights later, and then lots of nights after that. Both had been longing for companionship that delivered them from the program, and they found it. As they fell in love and got to know each other every trace of summer was leaving the Indiana air. The trees changed; winter drifted in. She discovered that, more than anything, she loved watching TV with Patrick because he was hungry for it and had hardly ever seen any. On her sofa, Patrick drank as she drank, keeping pace with her, bottle for bottle, rivaling her daddy at being good to watch with. She made him watch everything about Antoine Greep. With the TV on they got high and had sex and lazed on the sofa as his wheelchair floated nearby. Her Venetian blinds would be shut and the TV glowing and candles burning in the corner, simulating the atmosphere of a dorm room. The six weeks between mid-September and Halloween were just about the nicest weeks of love she would ever know.

Yet the good always contains the bad, and the bad was this: her poetry languished.

What was she supposed to write? I'm in love with a wonderful boy?

In college the motor of angst propelled the part of her that wrote. Even when she had boyfriends, the motor spun and dissatisfaction wailed like a flange. With Patrick it came to rest. She felt less nervous, the urgency of doing vanished as the happiness of being arose. She tried to recall what should have been easy to recall, fresh in mind— but she could not stay in touch with Heather Kloppenberg the artist. Who had that even been? She allowed herself to regard Patrick as her project. She understood that in this new devotion she was betraying hours and hours of classroom time in women's studies, not to mention some fundamental beliefs.

Word got around that Emily White, the author of *The Marshall Stang Story*, was coming to visit the *Greater Than X* boys, Caleb and Seth, and would be a guest at the Halloween party Marco was throwing. Heather nearly shit. Then she literally cried when Patrick said he wouldn't be going. "You can, but I'm just not." They hadn't until now come close to fighting, but for the three days before the party it was a fight. "You can't hate Marco that much," was Heather's line. "How can you hate him that much? You're not that big of a recluse. I'm a recluse so I get it. But I saw you at Captain Weatherbee's. You were fine. We'll go for an hour."

"No."

She cried and pouted and cried. It felt like a miracle when he finally gave in. It was on Halloween day itself. She was giddy as she drove from her apartment to his to pick him up. For some reason her heart sank when he rolled out onto the porch in a mask. It was a Goofy mask. Perhaps she did not realize until then how much she loved his face, how much she saw in his face, and how little she liked Goofy. "You can take that off until we get there," she said as she drove. "How do I even know it's you?"

"It's me," he said.

"I can't know for sure," she said.

"Who else would it be?" he said.

She was dressed as a fairy. She tried to feel excited about the party as they left the town limits in sullen silence. Or who knows what kind of silence: she couldn't see his face. As soon as they arrived at the farmhouse, Patrick stationed himself in a back room and rolled tightly into a corner. He gripped a can of beer, but she had no idea how he planned to drink it, because he didn't take the mask off.

212

She strolled the rooms wearing a smile she didn't feel and then found herself smoking alone on the front porch. The porch stretched the length of the house before a handsome front door and a huge old glass pane buzzing and rattling with the force of the music from inside. The wind was barely stirring the cornstalks that long ago should have been plowed under. Across the road the corn formed a dry, dark wall, and above it a distant rise formed a darker wall. The telephone wires glinted faintly in light from the house. If she had walked around back she would have been able to see the glow of the nearest suburbs of Arden. The people partying inside had never lived in the Midwest and eighteen months from now would never return. When Heather looked at the soybean fields she thought of the county fair in Shakopee. When the others looked they thought of edamame. She knew this because Marie said so, teaching her what edamame was. She had never heard of it. She wanted Patrick to come find her. But Marie came. "Are you a butterfly?"

"A fairy. You're a flapper? You look so beautiful!"

Marie was Edna St. Vincent Millay. "Come on," she said, "they're getting high."

"Who is?" Heather said.

"The cool kids. Everybody is dressed as potatoes."

In a moment she was following Marie up the old, beautiful stairs. The major crisis in the lives of the farmers who had built these stairs had been the Civil War. The ceilings were high, the molding dark, the doorknobs glass. Marie led her to a bedroom parsed by curtains hung from ropes. Pillows covered most of the polished floorboards. They were joining a group barely aware of the people joining it, a group of stoned potatoes. Baked potatoes, was the joke. Marco, flabby, dressed as Hulk Hogan, puffed his cheeks at Heather and Marie. It was almost impossible to picture his penis. Between Caleb Beck and Seth Rosenberg sat a beautiful woman not in a costume. It was her. She had large green eyes and pale skin and gorgeous brunette hair and a smile that took care of itself. Heather knew this already from the media but delighted to find it true in life. Emily was high but still looked sharp. There were other familiar and unfamiliar faces, ten or so total, but the energy of the room flowed to and from the *Greater Than X* boys, who held forth.

"The possibilities for fiction are shrinking," Caleb said. "It's a corollary to the normative, psychological model for describing human existence. When people consider their lives now, they don't do it in terms of ends. They do it in terms of norms. *Am I normal?"*

"Are you asking?" Seth said.

"I have the strangest feeling I've heard this before," Emily said.

"They don't think about goals, or movements, or causes, or ideals," Caleb said. "They think about health and mental health. Nobody dreams of anything greater than mental health. Nobody dreams of culture or liberation. Cathedrals? No. Revolution? No. Treadmills? Yes. Self-confidence? Yes."

"I have the weirdest feeling I've heard this before," Emily said.

The joint came around. It was even better once the smoke had begun to mingle with Heather's blood. The potato costumes were funnier. She went from sitting against the wall to lying on her back with only her head propped. Marie stretched out next to her and their thighs touched and relaxation snuggled down Heather's limbs.

"The details of your mind can be accounted for," Caleb was saying. "That's the theory. You've got a ledger in your skull. That's the theory. Drugs and therapy keep the balance. It's a precise and introverted notion. It's entirely normative."

"It's his hobbyhorse," somebody said.

She was losing track of who was speaking. She wanted the boys to stop talking or even to go away. They did not stop talking or go away.

"Each emotional state has been assigned a number by the American Psychological Association. The DSM tells you how long you should mourn your dead father."

"How about your living father?"

Marie was laughing.

"They postulate a nonpathological duration for grief. You get three months. After which you're sick. After three months, it's official. Everything can be diagnosed. Every diagnosis has a number. Those numbers describe the ledger in your brain."

"Hence the novel is dead. Never mind video games and Internet porn. Blame the APA."

"The problem for fiction is this. No void. No mystery. No haze of dignified confusion. Everybody has to know *why*. Picture asking Oedipus *why*? It's impossible. The DSM has no numbers for Sophocles. Picture asking Lear. Everybody in *King Lear* is irrational and nuts. They stomp around the heath. The weather matches their guts. What's the DSM number for a thunderstorm on a heath? Give me that number. I claim it. I saw an article about how Michelangelo had autism."

214

"You saw that on the Internet."

"Except that Michelangelo did not have autism. The twenty-first century has autism. What Michelangelo had was genius and the Sistine Chapel. What we have is autism and Walmart."

"We've got ibuprofen," somebody said.

"Ativan," somebody said.

What are they talking about, Heather thought.

"Twinkies," somebody said.

"Pastries and queers."

"Pass the joint," somebody said.

"What we don't have is Lear and Oedipus. What we do have is Dr. Brad and Winnie Wilson."

"We're still wondering about the fiction."

"I'm getting to the fiction."

"Let him get to the fiction."

"You write a novel. Winnie Wilson chooses it and features it. You talk about your novel on Winnie Wilson. You sell five hundred thousand copies. But what does Winnie Wilson ask? When you're on the Winnie Wilson show, what does she ask?"

"Who the hell are you?"

"What I think of the APA?"

"Whether it's true or not. That's what she asks. She wants to know how autobiographical it is. How point A in your life corresponds to point A in the novel. How point B corresponds to point B. Forget tradition. Forget imagination. Forget myth. Forget history. She's like the therapist trying to reduce your unhappiness to childhood factors. She's like the psychiatrist assigning a number to your grief. She discovers the DSM number by the end of her show. It confirms her method for next week. Oedipus is terrifying. King Lear is terrifying. But Holden Caulfield is just a twerp with an attention deficit disorder."

"Twerp. That's good."

"I am so sick of *Catcher in the Rye*," Emily said. "I had to read it four times for school. I liked it until I was clobbered to death by it. It seems so essentially immature."

Immature? Heather loved *Catcher in the Rye*.

"And everybody's relieved," the other voice continued. "It's all explained. Winnie Wilson explained it. She got to the bottom of the mystery."

"Like genitalia."

"Shut up, Mike."

"I'm not fucking around. It's like vaginas."

"Vaginas."

"Vaginas."

The first voice continued, ignoring about vaginas. "Imagine Winnie Wilson asking Thomas Mann how autobiographical *Death in Venice* is. Imagine her asking Proust. Imagine T. S. Eliot having to explain how his poetry relates to his tenure as a cub scout."

"Eliot received tenure as a cub scout?"

"Because vaginas used to have hair on them." This voice was lower than the first voice. "It used to be that you never really knew about the mystery of the woman, because the mystery was hirsute."

"Hirsute?"

"OK, maybe not hirsute."

"Who do you even go out with?"

"I meant hairy, OK?"

The higher voice continued. "And since we live in this climate where people have to account for everything that goes into what they invent, they stop inventing. Invention becomes the territory of idiots. Screenwriters. Stephen King, R. K. Rowling."

"J. K. Rowling."

"Just as a tangled haze used to surround fiction, so a tangled bush used to hide the vagina."

"King Lear was one hairy pussy."

"Don't even get me started on the paradox."

"Nair, Gillette, and the DSM."

"This is just disgusting," a woman said. "There are women in the room."

"Women no longer mysterious."

"Disgusting."

"A novel comes out. Everybody wants to know if it's true. But if a memoir gets fabricated, people go apeshit. Yet in the same nation—in a nation crazed by the hunt for truth, persecuting liars, deploying Winnie Wilson to guard the truth, going apeshit when the truth can't be nailed down—in that same nation—"

"In that same nation the pussies are all bald."

"Just stop!"

"In that same nation the president cobbles together a case for war and nobody asks a thing. Winnie Wilson will plumb the depths of

216

The Gazebos of Jackson Township. Spencer Talent mouths the talking points."

"It is a publishing industry with no tolerance for hairy genitals."

"But a presidency thick with pubic hair."

"Maybe you're just nostalgic for muff."

"And Edward R. Murrow."

"And Edward R. Murrow."

Suddenly it felt as though hours had gone by. Heather thought of Patrick and opened her eyes, and the blitzed faces belonging to bodies lazing in potato costumes touched her with panic. "What?" Marie said, when Heather scrambled up.

"He has no way of getting up the stairs," Heather said. It truly seemed she had made a profound mistake. "He'll have no idea where I am!"

"It's fine," Marie said.

"It's not fine!"

But in the hallway as she tried to hurry down stairs she encountered Emily White. "I just love your curls," Emily said effortlessly, "and your wand!"

"I would die to have your hair," Heather said. Suddenly Patrick no longer struck her as a crisis. "I know who you are. I recognized you from your interviews! I can't believe this! Your book was my favorite one all summer!"

"Thank you so much." Emily had written a great book and was beautiful too. Heather thought of Pascal and the unfairness of noble birth. It was 2005 in America, and there was no such thing as a noble birth. "It must be so exciting to have a best seller," Heather said.

"I just have to share this, I'm totally boasting, but I just learned today that they've greenlighted preproduction on the film version."

"You've got to be flipping out!"

"I don't usually walk around boasting, that's for sure."

"I want you to meet my boyfriend," Heather said. "He's a veteran."

"You're Heather Kloppenberg!" Emily said. "Everybody talks about you and him. Patrick . . . ?"

"Crane," Heather said.

"Like Stephen Crane?" Emily said.

"People talk about us?" Heather said.

"I get the sense it's because nobody ever sees either of you! That's the way to guarantee it. I'd love to meet Patrick. What unit was he in?"

"I don't even know," Heather said. "He was in the army. You must really know Marshall Stang so well! Is he really like that?"

"He's *more* than really like that. Bad news through and through." She smiled.

"Patrick is downstairs," Heather said. "Come meet him! This is amazing."

"Let me give this to Seth." She was holding a baggie. "I'll be down in a minute."

Heather's excitement turned into anxiety as she moved from room to room, failing to find Patrick. She asked everybody; nobody had seen him. She went back upstairs and down again, past trolls and slutty kittens, robots and severed hands, potatoes and more potatoes, checked everywhere three times, and grew self-conscious at the certain spectacle in her own panic. Emily smiled at her as she completed her second lap, and she felt mortified. At last she went outside. The drugs made everything harder. The darkness blinded her at first. She was standing by the cab of her truck already beginning to cry when she heard him call her name. The rubber of the mask still muffled his voice. She turned and saw the rim of his wheels glinting in the shadows. Goofy in the darkness. "I was terrified," she said. "Take that off!"

"Terrified of what?"

"I looked everywhere. How did you get down the steps?"

"Are you ready to go?"

"We can't go!"

"I didn't want to come."

A great heaviness settled through her. "You don't want to meet Emily White?"

"Why would I want to meet Emily White?"

"She wrote *The Marshall Stang Story*."

"People were saying that."

"You don't care?"

"I want to leave," he said. "Let's go."

"She could help you publish your fiction!" Heather said.

The silence that followed was deep and dark. On the drive home he was silent until they reached her driveway. She thought she was angry with Patrick until she realized he thought he was angry with her. "What did you tell her about me?" he said. At last he took off the mask. His eyes were what she loved above all—his eyes.

"Emily? Nothing! I told her I was dating a veteran. She already

218

knew your name—and my name. She was excited to meet you. Patrick!" The tears were overwhelming her. "What's going on? I don't get this! We were just so happy!"

"Nothing, I'm sorry," he said. "We're still happy." It wasn't convincing. "I just didn't want to go to that party."

"You should have said so."

"I said so." He relented a little, felt a need to explain. "I get pains in my hips. Thank you for leaving."

That night the sex seemed better than possible. She was miserable with it, ecstatic, hungry, fed. He was rough, then soft, conflicted, engaged, contrite, and remote. They did it, and it seemed endless, and then it was over. But when she woke from dozing later on she found he was not in bed. This had happened before. But she rolled over and saw his wheelchair still in the room. That had not happened before. How could it? The wheelchair was sitting where they had left it however many hours ago.

Her brain went blank. Fear. She looked at the clock. She listened hard. She thought she heard the sound of someone moving about. Someone had entered and dragged Patrick into the other room and bound him and gagged him and drugged him and skinned him. Could she smell blood? Would you even be able to smell the blood? It smelled like copper. She was always ready to think in terms of austere blond men in pristine clothing breaking into her house and binding her and slowly driving life from her limbs with wires, saws, and dildos. She listened and could hear mechanical noise. She watched the hallway wall and saw the light change. The TV was on. She could hear its silent whine now. The clunk and chunk of the VCR? She rose as silently as possible.

When she peered into the living room she saw him standing. He was on his feet in front of the television. She was dreaming. She was not dreaming. She was perfectly awake. She had told him for the first time during the lovemaking that she loved him. She expected to see the dirty thrashing of limbs on the screen. He had risen to masturbate because he was bored with her body and full of contempt for her weakness for loving him. How could he be standing? She tried to make out the limbs and organs on the screen. She saw instead a fuzzy crowd.

The angle changed and the camera showed the president grinning. A flight suit covered his body. The poor resolution of the video on the VCR made the flight suit look green. His arm clutched a helmet.

Patrick's silhouette, strange on its legs, leaned to the VCR and pressed a button. Heather realized she had not been breathing. She exhaled a breath like a gasp. His head twitched hearingly, but he remained intent on the VCR and television. He let go of the button. The camera followed the jet fighter so that it moved more slowly across the screen than it must have moved across the sky. The angle changed. Against the backdrop of the carrier the plane showed its speed. In a moment the president was standing in the crowd again, grinning again, clutching the helmet. "What a fraud," he said to the TV. Then, turning to her: "What a joke and an imposter." He had heard her but had waited. He was so calm it terrified her. He was the one who would murder her. "You were going to find out anyway," he said.

"Your legs," Heather said. "Patrick—?"

"It's John," he said. "My name's John Townley. I wanted you to see this. It was breaking my heart not to show you this. I want us really to know each other."

Later she would have trouble remembering what happened next. She dressed and gathered her things in such a state of confusion and fear that her memory failed her. Later she was in her apartment, hyperventilating a little, and wondering if she should call the police.

THE WINNIE WILSON SHOW

Heather Kloppenberg did not sit on the couch, perpendicular to John in the chair, looking away from him toward Winnie. She did not. She was not there. John's gaze did not stick miserably on some fanfare of auburn curls at her pretty ear. A thigh in the black fabric from Nordstrom did not sink deep in the cushion of the sofa. The idea that it was beyond all possibility that her body and his body had been naked together did not run through his heartsick brain. He did not get to look at her again, one last time. None of this happened because it was not Heather Kloppenberg who had come at last to bust him on TV. Instead it was Antoine Greep who appeared, the real Antoine Greep, the slandered hero, the until-now vanished man.

Winnie had just asked Greep if John Townley were Henry Fleming. "It's the Henry Fleming you know?" she had asked.

"It sure is," Greep had just said, "it sure is."

Greep claimed before eight million viewers to recognize in the form of a stranger the face and body of a close friend lost in combat. John's eyes searched Greep's face and Winnie's face, then swept the audience. In the three-minute pause, designated for commercials, as technical men did technical things, as Winnie smiled at nothing and as Antoine studied his hands, John's mind ran across the long, bizarre path that had led him here. He was looking for some clue. Every step of it made sense until now. This last step—the real Greep's step—astonished him. It was an outrage against psychology and probability. John almost asked outright, during the break, what it meant. He felt bound by strangeness to silence. It was a moment answerable only by passivity, by waiting. He sat helplessly and searched his memories for a clue. What clue?

From the awful empty grimness of New York after Nerissa, he had fled to an MFA program in Indiana, the famous Midland Program in Writing, which it blew his mind to be admitted to.

In Indiana, sick with himself, he became someone other than himself.

It happened as if accidentally: he found a wheelchair on the curb while moving in. He sat in it on a whim, tired from hauling boxes. Then he wheeled himself down the sidewalk and got a picture in his mind. Still grieving for Emily, still loathing Stang—months after a normal heart would have healed—he wheeled the wheelchair to the army surplus store in downtown Arden and bought clothing to wear to class. He didn't believe he'd actually do it even as the clerk swiped his card. Then he realized he'd do it. But even still he planned to claim nothing. He just had an instinct to present himself this way. He was only extrapolating—and only slightly—the acts of dissimulation that he had already taken pretty far by the time he left New York. He had become a practiced innocuous liar. In Indiana he resigned himself to the total personal isolation he had enforced on himself in New York. After Nerissa he did not wish to kill himself, not physically, but he wished to commit something like a suicide of personality. He was nothing to anybody, not as he was.

Then he met Heather. She loved instantly the person he'd become. And since he had not really become that person, since that person was only a shell protecting his still tender insides from the scrutiny of a dismissive world, she fell in love with a phantom. She fell in love with a shell. And he fell in love with her—with the too real living person he took her to be. Until Halloween he maintained his shell so that she would love it.

He had loved her from the moment he saw her at Captain Weatherbee's, not only because she was pretty but because she didn't make him feel small. She was the anti-Emily: nervous rather than calm, jittery rather than centered, curly and auburn rather than straight and brunette, rural rather than urban, normal rather than wealthy, Midwestern and wild and mild and proper and sweet—excitable, self-conscious, poetic, marvelous. He allowed himself to be loved under false pretenses because he liked her so much. He allowed this until he couldn't stand it any longer. Then, at that point, he revealed himself. When he revealed himself, she fled.

So, under conditions of maximum solitude, he had carved the pages of *Petting the Burning Dog* from nothing—from research, from imagination, from what counted as nothing. In order to appear in the world as a best-selling warrior he had had to vanish as a living person.

It was November when the decision was made, and he drove his few belongings from snowy Arden to barren Apalachicola in one go. He did not call ahead as he left. His plans were vague. When he reached his home county he did not turn down the roads toward his parents' house. He drove the back roads aimlessly, drove obscure roads discovered back during his canvassing days, until he found himself watching for houses for rent. Down a dead end on the north side of town, far enough from the gulf that it seemed like deep Georgia, he found a cabin with a sign. He dialed the number while standing in the driveway looking at the thing. It felt good to be rid of the wheelchair. That was just about the only pleasure. Within an hour he placed the deposit and paid the rent for November. The landlord was a fat man who expected too much of his suspenders.

John had never not planned to tell his parents he was home again. New York and the Midwest lay behind him like dreams dreamed at length, like long spells of sleep that had aged him from a teenage boy but changed nothing fundamental—except for whom he loved. He was back where he began, back here as the same pathetic nobody. He had never not planned to tell his parents he was home. But standing on the gravel driveway of an obscure and dilapidated cabin he couldn't imagine telling them. What would he tell them? Such a revelation would break their hearts. They had been excited about the Midland Program in Writing, would be baffled by the rented property, would implore him to move to the house, to his old room, to their old ways. In the meantime they would wonder what they had done wrong.

He wanted things that did not seem to be of this world, so settled for nothing. Here there was nothing: scrub pine, blank red clay, silent winter forest, crunching gravel. The cabin smelled like newspapers steeped in rainwater and admitted so little sunlight that it could have been half-underground. More moss than paint covered the exterior sills. Wall-to-wall carpeting in the bedroom had absorbed the stink of a dog. He imagined never again knowing anybody.

After he unloaded, he showered, and wires of fur stuck to his feet. The water could have scalded rocks. Mold made fractals where the tiles met the tub. The kitchen faucet had dripped for years so that a dark-yellow boa ran to the drain from the curved white side of the basin. There were two bedrooms, and one became a study. He set a sheet of plywood on half-rotted sawhorses and set the typewriter on that. He stacked some books there and arranged whiskey bottles on the corner. He rinsed out two mugs to have at hand.

For whatever trips he needed to make to Shepard he imagined wearing a beard and changing his hair. He planned on getting fat and wondered if he could. It would be less weird than the wheelchair and glasses he had disguised himself with in Indiana.

Instead of getting a job, he got an Internet connection. Students at the university in Indiana earned money by rewriting business school application essays for people in Korea. This he could do from home.

He called his parents on Thanksgiving. "We'd be happy to hear more from you," his father said. The clarity of the connection was piercing.

"I'll try to be better about it."

"How's the weather?" his father said.

They thought he was in Indiana. John looked out the window at the sky above them both. "A professor offered me his farmhouse outside Arden over the Christmas break." Lying like this felt like licking death's face. "I was thinking of staying here and getting some writing done."

"Sounds lonesome," his father said.

"We'd love to see you," his mother said. She had gotten on the line too. "You wouldn't have to stay long."

"I'll try to come in the New Year," John said.

Your mind got funny when you lived alone in a cabin. That winter, his contact with the world was anonymous and electronic. But he did not hate working for Writing to the Future, the online essay service. The Korean people would send essays in bad English, and he would rewrite them until they sounded native and charming. A year later, these Koreans would enter business school in America. John earned thirty-five dollars an hour. He was paying two hundred dollars a month in rent and a hundred more for food and gas. He ate oatmeal and beans and rice until the campaign to fatten himself began. Then he ate oatmeal and beans and rice and as much fast food as he could stand. He did his own reading and writing in the morning, ate lunch, left the house in the afternoon to walk through the scrub pine or sometimes to drive furtively to town, returned for an early dinner, and spent the evening on the Koreans. Writing to the Future boggled his mind. Who was responsible for these words? To what souls did they correspond? They had nothing to do with his soul. He could not have cared less about business or business school or Korean strangers. But the words came from him. He produced essays spoken in the voices of men and women who did not exist.

Already in the first weeks of that employment, *Petting the Burning Dog* ran in his blood like an illness waiting to become full blown. Almost from the moment he sat in the wheelchair he knew his artistic future centered on a war he had never fought in in a place he would never see. The war compelled the interest of Heather and Emily. It gave Stang the true proportions of heroism. It rocked with mysteries and horrors of conduct and decision, fear and bravery, technology and banality, the themes that could make a piercingly audible thing of the printed page. All the other books in the vanishing bookstores bored him and more: symbolized what he himself suffered from, the nothingness of feeling and the nothingness of action. Emily had grasped four years ago what he only grasped now. Stang, enlisting, grasped it almost five years ago. All the other books peeped pointlessly against the thunder of the media of light and noise. A single mediocre video game could do more to change the consciousness of his generation than the greatest book by the greatest novelist alive.

But what did he have to go on? Almost nothing. He would not enlist. He could only read what others had written. His anger toward Stang, his envy, his jealousy, his feeling of abasement remained so powerful that it took weeks, during his retreat in Florida, to see the obvious. Stang, above all, was what John had to go on.

The thing Debbie Duncan said at the door, when John went over, should not have surprised him, but it did somehow. "Stop loss," she said. "He got called up again." Her eyes were haggard, her arms pendulous, her whole demeanor heavy, almost broken by what things had come to.

Her trials only made John's task easier. Perhaps this was the first of his truly pernicious acts. He would not have to deal with Stang at all, would not have to beg and plead, to give himself away, to hint at his undertaking. "Forever ago I left a box of comic books here," he said.

"It's been forever since I seen you," Debbie said. "I seen your mom at the store, and she didn't say you was home."

"I just pulled in. I'm meaning to surprise them."

"That'll make them right proud. I ain't seen a box, but you can look for it."

He knew Stang and Stang's room too well even to have to search.

Where the *Penthouse* and *Playboy* magazines used to be was a box of photographs and videotapes of the war in Iraq. His heart leaped when he found it, but not with surprise exactly. Some of the photographs John recognized from Emily's book. But the videotapes were a find. They made him think of Heather—Heather who would have loved the stash, would have died to see it. He folded the flaps down and carried the box out and Debbie watched him indifferently and sadly from the door, ashing a cigarette on the porch as he left.

It took two weeks of ten-hour days to watch everything and study all the pictures. Iraqi men scowled at passing Humvees, women cried, children chased vehicles and held aloft closed fists for games of Rock Scissors Paper, rounds cracked, frames shuddered, the screen glowed green with night vision images. Hours of pointless banter in tents and barracks filled many of the tapes. The utter tedium came across. The moral range came across, too: there were noble soldiers and vicious ones. Some scenes from the tapes John recognized, sort of, from *The Marshall Stang Story*, but in Emily's book they differed too much from the originals to be transcriptions or even, fairly, true paraphrases. John got the sense that Emily had never seen this trove of moving images—that the videotapes were Stang's secret stash, that Stang had bent and broken the truth in interviews, that he had given Emily what she wanted to hear instead of what he really experienced, what he actually saw and did.

For a week John watched the tapes without inspiration, with no sense that they solved the crisis of his art. When he thought about transcribing and shaping the material, it was like thinking about trying to make a rainbow-colored collage from an old *Wall Street Journal*. The footage was too flat, tedious, ugly, black and white. As with life itself—as with his own life, in these places, in this century—the surface, for all its visual intensity, bore little relationship to his intuitions of a profound meaning permeating all reality. The war, like his life, had, just had, to be more than this—richer, fuller, heavier, less mediocre and blandly horrific. But only strange murmurings deep inside him, not the evidence of his eyes, suggested this could be so.

On the eighth day of viewing, everything changed. At four in the afternoon, his neck stiff from the vigil, John saw on the screen the image that marked the true beginning of his descent, his ascent. He saw himself—saw what Heather saw when she first saw him—saw Henry Fleming of the Babylon Seven.

A group of six or seven sat in a desolated, dim bunker. One man cackled on and on about sexual exploits. Fleming—it had to be Fleming—draped lose arms across bent knees, his butt on the concrete floor, his lower back against the grimy wall. The camera passed over him, stopping only once or twice, capturing his presence, his wincing guarded indifference, his on-edge-ness.

John could tell from the footage that Fleming belonged to another unit—that his connection to Stang was glancing and accidental. All told, the lieutenant about whom so little even now had been discovered by the press, had been in Stang's viewfinder for twenty minutes. It was only an effect of Stang's obsession to record everything that Fleming showed up at all. He said little, seemed unsure of himself, emotionally pent and awkward, tense and unhappy. The resemblance to John was great enough that John saw it first thing. But it was not so great that it lasted. Within thirty seconds John was watching the expressions and mannerisms of somebody very different from himself. Nobody really very much looks like anybody else—not for long.

But by the time he went to sleep that night he had practiced imitating in the bathroom mirror every frame of the footage of Henry Fleming. That was the first true inspiration. By the end of the next day he could perform it to his own satisfaction—hold his head like that, swallow his words like that, radiate a nearly identical air of being deeply ill at ease. In the following days he researched and wrote with a consuming sense of purpose, knowing almost fully what he was now about. Without even being entirely sure what he had, he knew that he had it.

He adopted the persona merely to get the book written, as he had adopted the wheelchair merely to be able to endure the thought of showing up for class. What would happen with the pages once the pages were written he did not give thought to. He neither planned definitely to push on with it, to publish the imposture, nor not to do that. At times he believed he was only writing fiction. It simply made it possible for him to write—and writing made it possible for him to be.

When the pages were done, he found himself seeking an agent agnostically, just to see what would happen. The anonymity of mail and e-mail was the next accidental blessing. All along he waited for somebody to say, "Are you really who you say you are?" but nobody did. He assumed it was a question so without tact that nobody could bring herself to ask it. When the agent he found sold the manuscript, and he signed a contract with the publisher, he signed it agnostically, just to see what would happen. In the same spirit, he gave the interviews that followed: appeared for the first time on Winnie Wilson. At that point it had gone far further than he ever expected. Then it went further still. All the while he expected it to crumble at any minute. That it never did amazed him. Here was the world's strangeness pertaining overwhelmingly to him.

The three minutes were up. The technical men flashed warning lights. Winnie smiled the same, but in a new direction. Antoine Greep, the real Antoine Greep, was here to make it crumble.

Of all the strange moments that constituted the history of his ruse—adopting personas in New York bars, keeping the wheelchair, mastering the details and mannerisms of a life not his own, becoming first a lover and later a celebrity under pretenses entirely false—this moment on the soundstage was the strangest of all. Antoine Greep—that name—lived in his imagination and on the pages that were its bounty. Antoine Greep, for John, seethed with the vile, winning, sinister, cheerful charisma of Marshall Franklin Stang and of something else—of the evil he felt pulsing in the bowels of this war. Yet Greep was also a man the nation knew, a hero of an episode in a conflict with few heroes. He was handsome and unassuming; and he looked at John, here in the lights of the soundstage, with not a trace of anger. He declined to destroy him. And not only.

"I can't believe this," Greep said. "Give me a hug for Christ's sake."

Winnie sat between them, lips pursed, saying nothing. Her eyes glinted with the genius that turned America's best stories to fat capital. What happened next had to have shocked her. It made John feel like he was losing his mind. Greep rose from his seat, blocked the audience's view of Winnie, and wrapped toned, fine arms around John, who remained seated. "No hard feelings," he said.

"No hard feelings?" Winnie could not help saying.

"Shit happens," Greep said. "Stuff happens. I've got nothing against Hank and his book."

"This is the Henry Fleming you remember?" Winnie said yet again.

"Of course not," Greep said. "He's porked up. And that beard, that be pretty ill advised, you ask me. But you see my Afro. We all got our thing now. But yeah, Hank is Hank."

John studied the eyes of this man. John sensed with full confidence that Greep was pretending. So did Winnie. It flamed in her furious eyes now. Could the audience see it? Inexplicable perversity, something unaccountable, was ruining what should have been the best show of the season, the big reveal.

"Besides the beard and weight gain, this is the Henry Fleming you remember?" For the first time in a twenty-year imperium, panic touched her voice.

"Sure enough," Greep said.

"You will always wonder about this," Greep said to John on the Chicago street two hours later, after the taping. They walked out together, John still on his crutches. As if from the power of the natural light, the mild Greep vanished, replaced by an angry one. What had John expected? Frankly, nothing. He was past all expectations. "You have no idea how I know you. But I know exactly how you've used me. You're truly a sick motherfucker. Some vet might put a bullet through your brain. Fine by me. You have no idea what I did. No idea. But I know exactly what *you* did. Lucky for you I've got my reasons not to care. Lucky for you I've even got my reasons to *thank* you. But that don't mean I'm going to thank you. Because you are truly a sick motherfucker. You deserve to burn in hell. If there was a hell, you'd burn in it. But there's no hell for you to burn in because I've been to hell and am still here. There ain't no hell worse than what I saw."

"You want to get a drink?" John said.

That stopped Greep short. He grinned. "I'll drink a beer," he said. "I'll drink a beer and tell you about fucking the girl I know you're still in love with."

XV.

Cyclical adhans, muezzins with the teetering, delirious pitch of a culture not your own. Meat sizzling against an odor of garbage. Flies, sun, stink, darkness. A room ten by ten. Larger? No. The scream of children happy and unhappy. The groaning and coughing of a car of a vintage predating your birth. A woman laughing with laughter infusing your veins with hatred. Time in a fever. Tremendous pain. What was wrong with me?

Sunnis prefer to behead you.

Shiites drill holes in your knees.

Sunnis prefer to behead you.

Shiites drill holes in your knees.

Unawake and not sleeping I reviewed facts as you make facts of notions in ill sleep: equations, algorithms, chord progressions, minor thoughts transformed by sickness and darkness to urgent revelations. Patterns of light. For some time I worked through the conjugation of *jaceo*. Men in robes moved against me in dream memories. I had a vague sense I would recall some horror in the same way you think you might sneeze. Hours had vanished; horrors.

I came to from what felt like an interval of erased abuse. It could have been days. Had there been electrocution? No. My body was a scar of a body, a wound of one. I hated the woman laughing and the muezzin butchering pitch. His voice buzzed and crackled, and it landed on no notes you accepted as notes. There was no Mozart here, never any Mozart, no clean vegetables, no organic kale, never a crisp diode in a new DON'T WALK sign.

"Are you married?"

His feet at the level of my eyes.

Married. Not married. "Yes."

Two weeks in Berlin: a dreamlike fortnight with Hillary wasting good mornings dozing in sunlight after spending long nights deep in clubs and bars. Last October. When my leave came I flew to Germany, and she flew there. The train to Berlin from Grafenwoehr: the strange ruins of East Germany scrolling by, its Soviet hopes, manifest in modern lines, looking defunct and sadder than old American advertisements for a utopian space-age that never came. Decaying modern buildings offering proof that the future is already almost over. Sixty years ago the world believed it was changing forever. Now it never got that hopeful. Every affluent monument looked forward to ten years of looking good. Nobody was building cathedrals, everybody was hammering together superstores. Would I see the New York Public Library again? Adnan Antoon and the terracotta lion of Shaduppum we plagiarized and smashed? Outside in the air of the adhans stood no superstores. That was democracy's outfit and what you deployed troops to raze mosques for. *You might feel freer than you do in your narrow freedom.* If a man could get his face to flicker once on television sets across the globe then he was scratching the itch that pharaohs scratched with pyramids. Nobody would remember any of this. Cell phones.

Hillary in October in Germany. A time and place as distant from this anguished moment as the seventh grade, the Nativity of Christ, the in-utero beating of my mother's heart. Meeting her on the concourse at the airport in Frankfurt was like immersing myself in the liquid tones of harmonious strings. I was standing in sound, watching the sunlight gild the tarmac, feeling my arms and legs and core course with wonder. She was perfectly herself walking toward me, her curls and insatiable gaze protesting in its seriousness against her good looks—looks so good that people avoided her, made way, what with that look on her face. "We saw Amsterdam from the plane," she said. "It looks so well-behaved."

She would write a poem, "Amsterdam from Above."

Difficult to talk and to absorb the moment at once. Happiness rendered the words irrelevant. In the golden light of the concourse she looked perfect and familiar, I knew her better than anybody, yet it was also true that for months I had overwritten her body with memories and so felt surprised by her living size. It was also true that for months I had made of her a faithless force betraying me, elsewhere, otherwise, secret, umbrageous. Where was that demon now?

231

How stupid! Seeing her again was like returning to your childhood home after spending a decade in a distant city in a building of a different scale. When I hugged her, the small of her back was compact, so compact. We hugged, and I wondered if I had ever, before then, understood the small of her back.

Twelve strange days, not happy ones, the golden tones of the tarmac tarnishing by the time we checked into the hotel. She had had dreams of finding in me the same boy she parted ways with at Fort Bliss a year earlier, presumably somebody sweet and awkward, a perfect partner for her harmless wicked games. I had had dreams of relaxing into my old self and found there was no such thing. My soul was a voice ragged from screaming over the deafening din of metallic cacophony. Now it was trying to speak in a quiet room. I was no longer who she thought I was, not at all. We both wanted this not to be so, so said nothing about it.

Berlin because it was close and because I wanted to see Nefertiti's head before I died and who knew when that would be.

Now I knew when that would be.

I was about to die. Hillary hated to hear me talk like that.

How different the realization of an idea from the conception of one: as a callow fool in Massachusetts, enraged by lust, spurred into love by the very limitlessness of the erotic horizon that made love impossible, I had dreamed of a deathless suicide, of an act whose ultimacy equaled the seeming ultimacy of desire. I had enlisted in the army to subject Hillary to a fear of failing to possess me as overwhelming as my fear of failing to possess her. In the idiotic reaches of pure intellectual space, I believed this gesture would level the ground between us. When I said I wanted to see Nefertiti's head before I died, I found that the sloped ground between us had become, not more level, but a sheer face. My gesture had not equalized anything; it had radicalized everything.

I saw the gorgeous Egyptian relic in its awesome fragile freshness, the queen's deft head in a smeary Plexiglas box in a hall full of German schoolchildren. Then we had eight days left. We got through the days by becoming strangers and fucking like strangers.

Lying in Iraq on a concrete floor dirty with blood and shit, thinking of sex was like thinking of flying. You could not imagine sex from here.

Courting long ago almost as teenagers in Boston we had revolted against the nightlife, holing up alone. We avoided crowded bars and bottomless clubs, contented ourselves with dorm rooms and overheated apartments with thin walls and groaning elevators just out-side. But in Berlin we joined crowds. We became strangers to our-selves and to each other in order simply to be able to cope. We drank coffee late at night, found nightclubs in the old Prenzlauer Berg, let electronic music shake our ribs. The days lasted hours, and the nights lasted days. We drank vodka and Red Bull and danced under strobe lights with people with limbs and hearts full of drugs. We did not do drugs but should have, given how we were feeling anyway. It was comic, my dancing, worth laughing at, but Hillary never even smiled, because I was a stranger and she was one. Eight months had trans-formed her wardrobe, new undergarments replacing old ones, and in moments of drunken sex in the unfamiliar light and scents of our ho-tel in Charlottenberg she became anonymous, I did, we were to each other. Sadness, arousal; lost and terrible. I had dreamed above all of closing a distance, and she became the remotest stranger of my life. I was this same thing to her.

War entails intimacy as horrible or more horrible, far more. Here I was. This torture in the dusty air of a squalid village who knew where outside of Babylon: intimate. Hillary had always directed our lovemaking, welcoming me into a sphere without limits. Now I took that space by force, and the limits arose instantly. "Leave my asshole alone," she said, "I don't even know what this is." But I didn't leave it alone. "Leave my asshole alone," I thought, lying on the concrete floor dirty with blood and shit.

On our final day we visited the Pergamon Museum and saw the Ishtar Gate. The glory of Babylon had been packed up and shipped to Berlin and unpacked to be gaped at by the fair of hair and skin. In my studies I had never even seen photographs of this artifact, never heard of it. So I wandered into the gallery unprepared to be mesmerized, unaware that such a thing, so much color, had risen in splendor above the ancient floodplain. It outshined and rivaled in gasp-factor the pyr-amids, the Parthenon, the ziggurats, the aqueducts. At the behest of Nebuchadnezzar II, six hundred years before Christ, masons glazed bricks of blue and gold and artists fashioned them with bas-relief monstrosities. Light blue ran in one band, dark blue in another, but within each band were blues within blues: turquoises and delfts, co-balts and midnights. Dragons and aurochs, beige against blue, posed on the gate itself around an archway yawning simply but enormously. Abstract daisies and patterns of black and white and gold bordered the lines and curves. Frozen lions paced down this the original Processional Way in stately futility. There was nothing like this in Iraq and nothing like it anywhere. It stood outside of life. The German and foreign patrons, their footsteps and echoes, the flashing cameras, the murmurs—even the skylights casting modern luminescence on the fields of color—everything was transient except the thing itself.

After that hour with the Ishtar Gate, I thought I relaxed into the old Henry Fleming, found him again. I settled down. It was our last day, our last afternoon. The ringing in my ears died, my voice returned, the din of the metallic cacophony thinned from my brain. Hillary acted as though she felt the difference, and we seemed to me to recapture our old selves. After all that dark unsettled fucking we made love to each other as friends. "That was nice," she said. Looking back, I understand that Hillary by then had already decided it was over. She was saying good-bye to somebody no longer himself.

"Are you married?" He kicked me to get an answer, then squatted again.

Had he asked the question twice in a row or once each day since yesterday? I had been making a recovery, was sure of it. The kicking did not advance my recovery. Was I lucid? It came and it went. An American in Iraq could not help but notice this difference between himself and Iraqi men, that they could squat for hours. On the main thoroughfares in Baghdad, in the shade of the alleys of Tikrit, men in their nineties, boys hardly through puberty, they squatted all day. They had a capacity for physical endurance beyond our comprehension. An enemy insane to be at war with. They squatted to piss. They found our pissing posture execrable. There was not an Iraqi alive who had not known war. Our masters in endurance had taken us in the field. He was squatting. "I am married," I said.

"Married," he smiled, tapping his chest. "Children?"

"Three children," I said.

"Three children," he positively grinned, tapping his chest. "Boy? Girl?"

"Two girls," I said. "One boy." I showed this on my fingers as I spoke. He grabbed my hand and studied the absence of the pinkie. "The boy is the youngest," I said.

"Three boys," he positively remained grinning. He held up three fingers.

I tried to take stock of my body by moving it just somewhat. A great strange painful tightness wired my shoulder blades into difference. Had I been strung up? I thought I could smell myself, but everything stank. I smelled the fetid coppery stink of blood spilled amply. The man wore dishdasha and keffiyeh and sandals. In my state, and from how he spoke and the beard he wore, he was at first an old man to me. Later, he grew younger. In America he would still be young, could not have been older than thirty, but here he had three children and a beard and nothing left but for the beard to gray.

Later there was food before me, a plate of rice and lentils, and he watched me wake to it. Sitting up felt like pulling myself from a substance that was also part of me. A painful tearing. He did not change his expression at the sight of my wincing. As soon as I took a bite my insides choked up. It was like a rotten brick had been lodged there.

"Am I the only one?" I did not want to say "alive."

He grinned, tapped his chest, help up three fingers, and said, "Three children."

I felt more lucid when I awoke the next time, and now it was night, and the guard had changed. It was hours later, or days. This guard wore all black and stared down at me with hatred. His hand rested hatefully on the AK-47 hanging from him. He had buck teeth and bad skin and dark eyes that looked not right, coked up, wired, crazed. People said that Mahdi militiamen used American epinephrine, distilled adrenaline, and other lesser uppers. I averted my eyes and acted how you might act toward a dog who might come after you. He greeted my wakefulness by walking over and kicking me.

"Twenty-three years with Saddam. You think we fear you? You stay twenty-three years too?"

I had been stripped down. The flies had at me. In one of the books from the Green Zone there were pictures of an Akkadian victory stela portraying the taking of prisoners in war. The prisoners had been stripped and bound in order to humiliate them. This had been twenty-two hundred years ago. Had Abu Ghraib happened yet? Looking back, I can't remember. It happened later. I did not see the photographs until months later. They brought this back to you.

The third time I woke I thought I was all right. Again, a different guard, this one with intelligence and sobriety in his eyes, and it took me a minute to catch sight of the efficacious cruelty there. All of it went together. "You do not know your enemy, that is your problem," he said.

My shoulders are broken, I wanted to say, that is my problem.

"We are an enigma to you. We are all one evil face, a scowling dark-skinned, black-bearded, keffiyeh-wearing madman. You do not even say keffiyeh. You do not say shmagh or mashadah or shemagh or ghutrah. You say turban. You say towel."

"You have treated me mercifully," I tried.

"I am not some marshland Shiite farmer. You cannot trick me into politeness. Your Jedi mind tricks will not work on me." He studied my face to see what I thought of this allusion. "This is what I mean. It is so easy for us to know our enemy. We know your movies. Your nakedness and foolishness, your vanity and stupidity, you broadcast them to all of us. You make movies bootlegged in every marketplace from Morocco to Mongolia. Your sexual desires fill the hours on MTV, VH1, FX, your paranoid fears on CNN and TEX News." I was dreaming this part? "You think you are a mystery to us? You are nothing. We are a great mystery to you. You know nothing. Am I a Sunni? Am I a Shia? Am I Kurdish? Am I Coptic?"

"You're a Shia," I said.

With leisure he fetched a length of pipe from the floor and beat my thighs.

It had to have been later. I wasn't feeling better.

"You live on peace. Your peace is hungry. You live on fear. We have been fighting for a thousand years. We have been fighting Saddam for fifteen years. All we know is war. We want life to mean. You want *not* life to mean—*not* women to mean—*not* God to mean. That is what your freedom is. Everything mean nothing. You are free."

I spent days and hours in a ten-foot-by-ten-foot room, and from the echoes from beyond the door and from outside the windows I had established in my mind, vaguely but expansively, a picture of the surrounding halls, rooms, and streets. The picture could only be wrong, and I could not be surprised when two large men in black woke me from sleep and dragged me by my tender shoulders through the open door and I saw nothing that I had dreamed. Objective curiosity and hard terror ran parallel. The trauma made it possible. I could not understand this. I was divided, calm in my guts, panicked on my skin, unwell. My mind skipped back and forth over and over between different kinds of awareness, compressing into seconds and minutes the changes in perspective that should span days. It seemed impossible to me that I would die and impossible to me that I would not. I had pictured a square vertical building of which my cell was one of four or so, while in fact I had spent my captivity in a room off a long hallway, a hallway which in a lucid, terrified stupor, I considered too long, objectively too long, architecturally impossible. Halls take on new properties when you're dragged through them on lame, raging joints. The men urged me and dragged me faster than I could walk. Jolts pierced the balls and sockets of the arms they heaved me by. I can be objective only in retrospect. Do I even remember it?

We entered a large, long, low-ceilinged hall, where six men in six chairs sat bound. The piss of fear darkened their laps and fear roiled their eyes. I knew them but did not. They looked so thin. A seventh chair remained empty. Then ropes bound me to it. Slowly I acknowledged I knew them. Their thinness and bruises made strangers of them. I did not want these bodies to be the bodies of men I knew. In the distance a backdrop had been created, a white sheet spray-painted in Arabic words, the fuzzy black lines denoting hatred as a pure abstraction. A camera on a tripod monitored it indifferently. Two men with AK-47s guarded an entrance, standing to either side. We had entered from the back. A tall man in a white robe was binding Schwartz's hands. Schwartz had never looked so much like a hog. A man in black stood before J'Million and whispered while J'Million screamed. Then he struck J'Million on the jaw with the butt of his rifle. J'Million fell silent as blood ran from his mouth.

Greep sat next to me in a silence so adept and so concentrated that I took it for unconsciousness. Then I saw how strong he was even now. The indifferent camera on the tripod in the dimness against the rancorous banner terrified me as we sat like this: me, Greep, J'Million, Schwartz, Kirk Frank, Eccles, and Duckworth.

The guards circled and harrowed Duckworth and Eccles. They were the sweetest, softest men here. Didn't the Shiites know? Couldn't they tell? There were too few Iraqis to make a mob, fifteen total, but they roused in themselves a mob, were mobbing Duckworth, mobbing Eccles.

One held a digital videotape in his hand, a little black rectangular solid. I ruminated on the strange universality of it: that I, too, used tapes like that. Such tapes captured for Hillary and me moments of casual and innocent joy and happiness.

Men are men, everywhere the same.

A man in black took the cartridge and crammed it into Duckworth's howling mouth. Seeing it in his mouth I finally allowed myself to understand that it was mine, that Hillary's face was in Duckworth's mouth—or so I thought.

XVI.

"Santa ain't black." DuBoyd had said it twice already, and it had become rhetorical. Kids found phrases, it was something they did. Heather Kloppenberg, Miss K., held the book so all the kindergartners could see it. Maybe half the eyes were on it. The rest were on each other, or on fingers that had just been up noses or down pants.

"How do you know what Santa looks like?" Heather's infantile voice—Miss K's voice—which she had used on boyfriends for ten years, she now used mostly on small children. It had been two years since her last and most significant boyfriend. "Have you seen him?"

"Santa ain't black," DuBoyd said.

"Santa be white," Darnellya said.

"Santa be white," the class was saying now.

On the pages of the book a dark-skinned Saint Nicholas was piloting reindeer over tenement rooftops. The class united in squeals against this racial heresy. When the squeals finally died it was not because anything decided the issue but because of who appeared in the doorway. The classroom was a private space that Heather owned and the children filled. Even the most obnoxious kids stopped being obnoxious because the man in the doorway was Antoine Greep. Even late in 2007, any black person in Shakopee of whatever age knew exactly who Antoine Greep was.

Was it what Heather had been waiting for? Had she moved home with this in mind?

He walked the town with a kind of immaculate immunity, a religious amnesty from the mundane. The personality no longer beatified by TEX News was still beatified by local bars, diners, strip malls. The fact that Heather had Greep's daughter in kindergarten fortified

Heather's existence against desolation. It was only *mostly* desolate. After she received her MFA she had moved back in with Kathy and Dwight. She was twenty-five and living with her parents and teaching kindergarten.

DuBoyd was only talking to himself now. "Santa ain't black."

"Jaranya?" Greep found his daughter among the faces.

"We're in the middle of a story," Heather said. She was backing Greep out into the hall. Then she stood at the threshold with one eye on the class.

"Her ma don't let me see her much," Greep said. "I had the afternoon."

Heather was electric with the way she was being looked at. The man had romped as a toddler in the living room of Bobby Greep. He had fought his way to freedom against terrorists. His skin was as dark as it got, his eyes gentle and savvy, his mouth smooth and gorgeous. In all the footage from three years ago his hair had been military short. From the *Shakopee Telegram* she knew about the Afro, but her imagination had not done it justice.

"Can you pick her up after school?"

"Remind me when's after school? Ms. . . . ."

"Miss K. Kloppenberg. Heather." She was a fool—a little girl. "Seven after three?" She was self-conscious, overeager, too exact, a moron. "So three-ish?" Why was she laughing nervously?

"I'll be back."

He did not come back. After the building emptied that day she drove home sick in the heart. Happiness glowed like a sun not yet above the horizon. She had lived with her parents for eight months now, getting high when they went out, drinking whether they were out or not, smoking on the deck. She smoked in front of them, it was a fact of life. Asked to choose between having a nonsmoking daughter and no control, or a smoking daughter before their eyes, they'd take a smoking daughter. Not that her daddy didn't sometimes stare at her like a beaten dog. Her mother chirped, chirped at nobody, never remembered anything anybody said (unless you didn't want her to) and pretended not to notice the cigarettes burning in the air of her house.

She had moved back in because what else was she going to do? The MFA in poetry meant nothing—meant nothing but two years of believing that an inescapable life was escapable. In her case it meant not even that, not even two years but three months, from the night in

September when she first saw Patrick in Captain Weatherbee's to the day in December when in the front room of the house that housed the Program in Writing she overheard the gossip that the veteran in the wheelchair had not only dropped out but vanished from the face of the earth.

Halloween night itself, at the time, struck her as an ultimate moment, a breaking point, the end of the affair. The sight of Patrick standing at the VCR slammed her with the terror of the privacy of every mind. It was too painful to think about. Until that moment she had basked in the privacy of her own mind—in the illusion of sexual inaccessibility created by whatever was elusive and intelligent and ambiguous about her, by the way she dressed and moved, by the mysterious figure she presented to the undergraduate boys across the street, by the worlds of unknown pleasures her pretty being conjured in the minds of shy drunken hipster boys, even cute ones, at Midwestern dive bars. Until Halloween, she had delighted in her own mesmerizing opaqueness, or semitransparency, had delighted in it even when insecurity at the same time waged a war on her capacity to believe in it; had believed in it even as she gave little thought to the opaqueness or semitransparency of others.

Her few boyfriends before Patrick had been selected as geeky, tender, cute-enough recipients of her almost pornographic largesse. She loved to be naughty, but also feared as a good girl the slightest public semblance of naughtiness, and also loathed as a feminist the fact of having to fear as a good girl the slightest public semblance of naughtiness; so she visited her most devilish self on boys who would not blab, who would not quickly lose interest or move on. Patrick had appeared to her not only as a fellow outsider, a kindred middle American among snobs from the coasts, a soldier with real stories, a writer with real stakes, but also as the boy, among those she'd ever dated, most deserving of the sexual mysteries that she knew, under certain circumstances, she could convoke devastatingly. His wheelchair offset the stigma of naughtiness; his status as a veteran did; he deserved her, deserved how she could give herself to him, and she would still be safe knowing that hers was the lesser-known mind, hers was the presiding erotic power. So the sight of him standing at the VCR did far more than undermine a relationship. It reversed a differential. Never, since her first awkward giving of herself to an asshole of a boy—a one-time-only experience—had she felt so vulnerable to the despotism of other people's secret minds. Never had she felt so fundamentally and miserably alone; never had she felt so divested of control.

She loved control, lived on it, knew she did, and the desire to make her own world, to have herself be a product only of herself, lay behind how she made love, how she fucked, how she smoked, how she wrote, how she ate. How she often declined to eat. After Patrick left, after she learned that he did not remain in town to be heard from, to be petitioned by, begged by—which she had hoped for and expected—she stopped eating. She ate what she could. For a year and a half at Arden her arms and legs slimmed into perfect versions of their old quivering selves. The boys she went home with from the bar were allowed into her apartment precisely as strangers. They lammed the tender spot in her heart so thoroughly tenderized by Patrick. She let them do it. If she could not control boys by knowing them, if she could not trust the differential between her mystery and their transparency, she would make mutual opaqueness the brutal premise of any sex she had. She would control, at least, that. It was a gesture so contrary to the natural order of things—opening yourself to the meanness of others was—that, like not eating, it could only mean that she had made a choice, that her will was her own, that she would occupy a nightmare of her own making rather than a nightmare not under her control. It was a world so ugly and so imprisoning that only by contradicting such profound aspects of nature as eating and loving could you feel a little free. Only by warping yourself could you prove to yourself that you were yourself, that you controlled yourself in a world you could not control.

"Antoine Greep came to class today." As soon as Heather told her mother this she regretted it but she could not have kept it in.

"They have him talking to kindergartners now!"

"Jaranya's in my class. I told you that like twenty times."

"You have his daughter in your class?"

She had told her mother this like twenty times.

At dinner her mother said, "Heather met Antoine Greep today."

"John Jones don't trust him," her daddy said.

"John Jones is racist," Heather said.

"Heather!" her mother said.

"Nothing against John Jones," Heather said.

"John Jones don't like black people too much," her daddy said. "I'm OK with black people. I like black people."

241

Harrison Elementary sat in the heart of downtown Shakopee. Heather's parents' house was one stop further from Chicago on the Metra, near Bellepont. On days like today when her father had to take the truck downstate she rode the train to work. From the Shakopee station to the school it was a six-block walk through a downtown barely hanging on. She could never make the walk without saying alas to herself at the sight of the decaying buildings that rose above the storefronts. Once upon a time Shakopee had been prosperous and grand, a town with parades and brass bands and straw hats. Today behind counters in shops caged in bars, Pakistani men sold liquor and lotto tickets and cigarettes to bad looking African American people and worse looking white people. At bus kiosks, haggard women with tarnished faces and stuttering gaits watched her with large eyes. Every time her daddy announced that he would need the truck her mother chattered about the danger of the walk from the station to the school. Heather could not have explained why she feared only upper-middle-class white men wearing pristine clothing, serial killers, computer programmers. Black people and sketchy neighborhoods relaxed her, putting before her eyes the content of the fears that invisibly and pointlessly haunted so many white people. Nothing actually ever happened to you if you smoked or fucked or walked from the Metra stop to Harrison Elementary.

Today she basked in the decay and allowed a luscious sadness to overtake her. The decaying city was good for luscious sadness if for nothing else. Even at twenty-five she could still feel bad in a good way. If she wrote a poem about the day, she would, for the day, be something other than a kindergarten teacher.

When she got to school the sadness diminished to depression and anxiety, poetically useless. At the sight of the halls and her classroom she knew that yesterday was yesterday and today today. Antoine Greep had been a shooting star. True, but useless poetically. By eight it was raining and by seven after three she had had to deal with two sets of twenty kindergartners nutty with rain all day. If it were any colder, the rain would have been snow. As she walked through it toward the station after school it soaked her coat and stung her wrists.

But it was not another normal day after all. A car drifted up to the curb and kept drifting, keeping pace with her as she walked. Her instincts said: glue your eyes to the sidewalk and maintain a brisk pace. The hood of the car hovered in the periphery like something just under the surface of the water. It was dark blue and square with the lines of another decade. She heard the whir of the power window. It was fine. She declared her independence from her parents by not sharing their fears. White people had nothing but themselves to get away from.

"Miss K." She looked. The Afro obscured the far window. "Jaranya's dad." She had stopped, and the car stopped. Rain darkened the sidewalk and mulched the trash on the sidewalk and soaked her through. Antoine Greep could see all of her, could probably see her nipples, could see into her thoughts—that was what his smile said. "Antoine," he said. "Ride?"

The car smelled like stale popcorn how a messy TV room in a college apartment smells like it, butter and bodies mingling. The gray cloth seats held crumbs in their stitched furrows. Twenty years ago she had ridden to Chuck E. Cheese in a car like this. A boy named Brian Baxter had pushed in the cigarette lighter in one of the back doors, and when Mr. Baxter returned from paying for the gas he had yelled until veins rose from his forehead. Even so, she missed being a little girl. "Mind if I smoke a cigarette?"

"Actually, I—" he said. "I was in the army."

"You have to know I know who you are."

He averted his eyes, was bashful like a boy. He was even sweeter in person than he seemed on TV. He simply seemed soft and kind. "When I was over there we breathed a lot of nasty stuff."

"You worry about your lungs?"

"My lungs. Everything. There's still the big Gulf War syndrome nut to crack. We just hangin' out waitin'. Plus with the kids. Where to?"

"Just the station." They were nearly there.

"You got to be riding the train somewhere," he said.

"The station's fine," she said.

"You headin' toward the city?"

"Away."

"Me too." He was turning, then, onto the service road that would take them to the interstate. In a moment the suburban fringes of Shakopee were falling away to fields bleak with the season.

"Jaranya's doing great," she said.

"She wasn't even born when I went."

"She's a dreamy little girl."

"You mean she don't pay you any mind."

"Most kindergartners don't pay you any mind."

"You hungry?"

Her mother would be home from school at four, and her father back from downstate at four thirty. If they went straight there, she would be dropped off and safe by a quarter to four. But if they stopped somewhere her mother would watch from the window. Her mother would see the boxy sedan pull into the driveway. She would squint from the kitchen window to make out the form and color of the man in the driver's seat. How old was Heather anyway? What century was she living in? But still she knew her parents would freak. The psychology of black people was a thick forest to her daddy and her mother. Her parents believed that black people had a psychology. "I like black people OK," her daddy said. Heather had learned at college that populations did not have psychologies.

"I should get home." Heather had to say it. She was raised to say it. But she was going crazy inside and wanted this moment to extend for twenty decades. She had already put off until the distant future the work of even making sense of it, was basking in something larger than you could quickly take in.

Ten minutes later she was sitting, in Denny's, across from Antoine Greep, and he was reading the menu carefully, front to back, like a book. Their combination as a pair created energy. The Afro drew stares—or his fame did? He seemed to need glasses because he held the menu close to his eyes. The waitress came by once, but he did not look at her. She looked at Heather, shrugged and left.

"I burned my parents' house down when I was eleven." He set the menu down to say this.

"Your father was Bobby Greep," she said.

"You get how crazy it is to have strangers knowin' your life story?" he said.

"I'm sorry if that was the wrong thing to say."

"You follow baseball?" he said.

"Love love love the Cubs."

"Right on."

"You burned the house down on purpose?"

"They came home, and I was standing on the front lawn surrounded by fire trucks."

"How did it start?"

"You ask me that. They never asked me that. They hugged me and called the insurance company."

"You started the fire?"

"My father was Bobby Greep."

"I don't get it."

"You think *you* don't?"

"It must have been a nice house."

"It was new. It burned down in half an hour. You know I used to play ball?"

"Minor leagues," she said.

"Minor," he said. "Rub it in." He grinned, and it melted her. "Never again will I have a good old-fashioned get-to-know-you talk with anybody." Then: "I started for the minor leagues. I was Bobby Greep's kid. That's all I ever was."

"You must be proud of him."

"He's dead. Loved him and hated being his son. All I wanted to do was study biology, but instead I played minor league baseball."

"Ready?" the waitress said.

Antoine ordered the Home Run Breakfast, and Heather could not tell if he was trying to be funny. Heather ordered tea. When the food came he ate like he had been chopping wood for five hours. When he drove her home, she felt like crying, and did cry in the empty house, it being both more and less than she wanted it to be.

One day not too long after that she arrived home to find her mother sitting in the living room looking at the newspaper. Heather hated it when her mother got home early from work and ruined the silence of the house. You wanted the doorframe to perform a lobotomy when you came home, which it only did if the house was empty. Her mother was the mathematical opposite of a lobotomy. You wanted the air of the house to be filled with pot smoke. Her mother was diametrically opposed, as a thing in the universe, to all drugs. You wanted two six packs in the refrigerator, the flat-screen television tuned to Winnie Wilson, the computer purring, and the Internet connection up. Today her mother was clucking at the paper, then looking at Heather, wearing the traces of huge news on her face. "You said you met Antoine Greep the other day?"

Heather's heart skipped before she realized her mother meant not the meal at Denny's but the encounter in the classroom. "What about it?"

"There's a new book out that attacks him. It says he was a villain!"

"Villain" was a funny word. Heather was on the couch in an instant to see if the reporter used that word. Her mother read the article aloud even with Heather sitting next to her able to see the words. "'*Petting the Burning Dog*, a memoir by Army Lieutenant Henry Fleming, until now the missing member of the group of soldiers known as the Babylon Seven, challenges the accepted version of the events of May 2004, including the fact of Fleming's own death. Antoine Greep, who received a hero's welcome in the U.S. after ten days of captivity and torture, is portrayed by Fleming as a criminal influence.' Where are you going?" Her mother set the paper on her lap in surprise.

Heather broke speed limits on the way to the Borders out past Alfredo's. The clerk smiled when she asked about the title. "Sold out by noon. First book to do that that wasn't *Harry Potter*. Greep's from Shakopee, right? You should have preordered. Would you like to register for our preorder program?"

She drove home again and ordered from Amazon. Down the hall she could hear her mother telling her daddy about it. Her mother had only the content of the article to go on, but she repeated it to her husband three times as if she'd heard it straight from the Pentagon.

"Ain't it something," her daddy finally said. "I heard about it at work, too. John Jones says it just goes to show you."

Long before her copy arrived, Heather knew that Henry Fleming was not Henry Fleming, that there was no Henry Fleming, not as he appeared in the memoir, that Henry Fleming was Patrick Crane and that *Petting the Burning Dog* was not a memoir but instead a heinous fabrication. She knew it in her bones, just because. She confirmed it by the sound of the voice from the interview on the radio. She recognized the vague North Florida accent, the baritone languor, the sardonic warble of her former lover. She also saw easily enough through the author photo. The beard and the fatness and the long hair could not obscure the urgent beauty of the angry eyes she had fallen for beyond all reason. The interview made her shiver, and the picture twisted her insides into a war council of serpents. How had the world been so easily duped? Where were the other men from the platoon? The captain of the company? The fact-checkers at TEX? Didn't they know there was no Corez in that platoon? Who was running the publishing houses? And how had Patrick Crane—John Townley?—who had not even heard of Antoine Greep in 2005, assumed, without obstacle, this voice from the dead?

Until the book arrived in the mail, Heather did little more than tremble. She could not calm down. She had caused this. She had pointed out his resemblance to Henry Fleming, had stoked his demented imagination. Already, before any of this, she had felt violated, profoundly stolen from. The by now half-healed-over misery of being forsaken and deceived appeared, in the light of this news, quaint, mild—yesterday's misery. This news ushered in unhappiness of a new order.

She smoked and drove and paced and looked a thousand times at the Internet. She would have driven to Chicago to find a copy if the truck were hers. At school she taught poorly. A supernatural agent had reduced her emotions to chemicals and flooded her with all of them at once—disbelief, anger, excitement, panic, lust, vindictiveness, and more anger. Until now she had trusted she would get over Patrick—John—as you got over all boys. Now she thought she might never get over him, not because she wanted to be with him, but because she had given him something she could not get back. She could not get it back because she had given it to somebody who had not existed. It was pride, or like pride, what she had given, but to say so diminished it too much. It was essential self. He had entered the arena of love unfairly and escaped it unbound by the laws that by all rights bound everyone. She could not break his heart as he had broken hers. This made what he took from her feel like rape.

She wanted to call Antoine but did not have his number. The sheet in Jaranya's file listed one number, and Antoine and Claire Greep were separated, and it had to be Claire's. To talk to him Heather had to find him, and to find him she had to set out looking. She went to neighborhoods white people didn't go to and got stared at like a crazy white crack whore. The bars in Devon catered to the distant cousins of the gang lords of Chicago, whose nieces and nephews knew, no question, that Santa be white. Danger occurred to her only abstractly. She sat in bars at four o'clock in the afternoon, meaning to be seen, asking around. Down the counter from her, old men tippled, stinking and wheezing and getting cut off. Female tenders eyed her with naked hatred.

In four days she never found him. She felt silly. You would never go to a white neighborhood to find a white person, which left her only to walk the six blocks to the Metra stop each day. It took five more days for this to work. She was halfway through the decimated blocks downtown when the dark-blue sedan drifted to the curb, silent as a shark.

"I've been looking for you," she said as she slid into the car, her heart a ball of nervous bliss.

"You and everybody," he said. "Unlike everybody, you I don't mind." His grin, his Afro, his radical placidity: he seemed to be the opposite of a traumatized vet. His trauma had to be very deep. Or was he taking something?

"Listen," she said, "I know."

"You know?" he said.

"I know it's false," she said.

"What's false? That deodorant don't really cause old timer's disease?"

"Antoine! This memoir!"

"Oh, that." He laughed. "That ain't Hank Fleming. I don't need you to tell me that."

She had been planning this conversation for a week. This was not how it was supposed to go. "I knew you'd know," she said. "But I thought you might be interested in what I know about it, which is a lot."

He raised his eyebrows.

In fact she did not recognize the magnitude of her fantasies until he dashed them with his casualness like this. She had fantasized about falling in love with a real hero after giving herself to the false one. She had fantasized about righting the outstanding wrong. Of course she had fantasized about Antoine Greep long before Patrick Crane. But the recent fantasies had mingled the plausible with the implausible so utterly that it thrilled her with conviction and fear and desire. Events had played out in her mind like a plot. The solution was perfect—perfect personally, perfect nationally. Together with the real hero she would expose the false one.

He drove past the train station and past the interstate and under the overpass toward Medina. She rode in silence, and he rode in silence. The car smelled like popcorn, and his face, dark against the winter light, showed nothing. They sped across fields not yet devoured by the growing sprawl but soon to be, then entered a subdivision as oppressively new as her parents'. He pulled up a steep sloping driveway before a giant new house. The beige brick and egregious windows and flawless driveway and naked yard made you want to get baked and forgot everything. "You're wondering who lives here," he said.

"You don't live here?" Heather said.

"You're wondering who lives here because a nigger in the army with a daughter at Harrison and a Town Car from the stone age don't live here."

"I thought it was your house until you asked me. I didn't think about it."

He pressed the garage door opener, and light slowly illuminated the space before them. Giant plastic toys were massed in the dimness. He got out without saying anything or looking at her and went into the garage. It was just weird. Was anybody around for twenty miles? She had a premonition so intense and violent that she decided to start walking back toward town. This was how women ended up tied up in basements and eviscerated. Then she changed her mind. In the garage the smell of new plastic mixed with the scent of candles or spice. She would have loved to sweep dust from the shiny paved surface. There was no dust. He had entered the house through the garage, and she followed. It was affluent air she breathed in the hallway. The hallway opened on the living room whose furnishings were pristine and coordinated. The sofa and chairs were low and rectangular and covered in cherry leather. Rugs with faint patterns broke up gorgeous hardwood floors. She thought of her parents' pilled, lumpy furniture, the oatmeal shag of the living room carpeting, the ceramic dogs craning their necks as if adorably and staring into dead space. She followed vague noises to the kitchen, where everything was industrial and flawless.

His back was to her, and he was opening two bottles of beer. The bottles looked inconsequential amid the gleaming cleanness and size of the kitchen. The kitchen had been built for something grander than suburban needs. He would kill her here. She did not know what would happen. He turned to her, offering her a bottle, his eyes watering.

"It's all hers," Antoine said.

"What's hers?"

"Claire's." His nod took in the house. Tears fell. They had lives of their own, leaking from his eyes despite his almost blank expression. She took the beer.

"Claire would say that I *want* you not to believe that we live here."

The words confused her. "Your wife knows about me?"

"You're Jaranya's teacher."

"Would you say again what you just said?"

"I want you not to believe it. That's what she'd say."

Heather still didn't get it and said so. Then he was kissing her.

He led her upstairs to the master bedroom where they undressed and had sex on the bed. His tattoos temporarily overwhelmed her. There was a crucifix on one pectoral and a portrait of the face of Christ on the other. She had never been with a black body, and it against her body drew her eyes. She watched everything, and he kept his eyes closed. He was quiet and still when they finished. She asked him what he had been talking about, about Claire, and he lay on his back with his eyes closed. His eyelids looked tense as if he were trying to recall poetry he had failed to commit to memory for class. She studied his features as he answered.

All his life he had never felt that anything that came to him had been rightfully his. He was the son of a famous baseball player, and it opened every door not only that you tried to go through but even that you glanced in the general direction of. He had black skin and white English (unless he used black English) and upper-middle-class affluence and was raised among white people eager not to be racist. He had no need for official or unofficial advantages and compensations, but benefited from them at every turn—suffered from them at every turn. People wanted black people to get ahead and especially the handsome sons of major league baseball stars. He had so much in his favor: his father's name, the wealth, his skin, his looks. Instead of making him feel vain and act entitled, which they could have done, these things placed an intolerable burden of success on him. When he was eleven he burned the house down. "You did it on purpose," she said. She understood now.

In high school (he went on) he had fantasies of becoming an alcoholic and then a reformed alcoholic so that everybody he knew, instead of having high expectations for him, could think to themselves, "Isn't it neat that Bobby Greep's son got his life back together?" He wanted a lower and fairer bar, a normal one. He met Claire at their public high school in Brentwood—her father was a neurosurgeon—and they competed academically and were at the top of their class. They received scholarships to UCLA and got married the summer after high school. "We were sure of ourselves," he said. "We were young, but we couldn't see what could change. Everybody was so convinced she was pregnant that she got self-conscious that they thought she had an abortion when she never got big. One lady even whispered condolences for the miscarriage."

He deferred the scholarship and played a year in the minor leagues. Then during the first semester at UCLA, he took a course in sociology that explained to him the sociology of his race. "It was a breaking point," he said. "There was no traction. Nobody was judging me for me. I wanted to find myself in a challenge. I couldn't understand how to live according to sociology. I took lit that semester too and thought Faulkner was better than Toni Morrison. I thought Toni Morrison was crap. The class embarrassed me. I didn't want to be Toni Morrison."

"So you joined the army."

So he dropped out and joined the army. The decision placed a great strain on his marriage, but Claire endured it. She stood by him, but could never bring herself to see it his way. She naturally and comfortably accepted how things went. She, like he, had been born into circumstantial privilege weirdly against the grain of racial disadvantage. She had a sociological as well as a personal understanding of her existence. But she didn't chafe at this. She accepted it as a responsibility, an obligation, an office, as if she had been elected to a solemn position. But Antoine wanted something different and found it in the army. In boot camp his father's name didn't matter, nor his race nor his looks. Black meant delinquent, meant a dealer or a repo man on the run from doing time, and he found the lower expectations he had been looking for. His accomplishments suddenly belonged to him entirely. "I loved using my college vocabulary on the drill sergeants," he said.

For Heather, the sex and the monologue transported her, so a slight sound from downstairs failed to register. It could have been the ice-maker or a cat leaping from a table to a hutch. But it was the sound of a door. Then a worried woman's voice called from downstairs. "Antoine?" And already he was scrambling up from the bed and pulling his clothes on. He held a finger to his lips and looked ready for a stealth attack.

"Antoine?"

Buckling his belt he whispered, "I'll get her to follow me out to the car. We'll argue for a while. When we're out there, go out the door in the kitchen and cut across the yard. There's a BP station across the field. I'll be there in twenty minutes."

The plan worked fine, except for the part about his being there in twenty minutes.

After an hour at the gas station, with mud to her ankles from the field, her heartbeat slowly slowing, Heather walked an hour to the Metra, which took an hour and a half to get her home.

She smoked up the next afternoon, shivering on the deck, savoring the drug. Her mom had still been out when she got home from work. The light on the dirt looked blue. She was bundled in four layers. Dirt rose and fell in shallow hills of damp clods where lawns would grow next summer. The flapping Tyvek and the distant whoosh of cars on the freeway was all you heard except for when trains thundered through the backyard on tracks that had run there for the last hundred years. A train came every six hours and lasted for twenty minutes. Across the field on the far side of the tracks, in the wintry distance, a baby-blue water tower stood twice as tall as the tallest trees. Beyond the trees you could see the tops of the grain elevator. She went inside through the garage, smelling the newness. Across the suburb, everything was large and taupe or dun or beige or olive. She missed the ranch house on Watercrest Drive, which was yellow, and which she had always hated. They had moved for no reason. Her father was retiring, and she and her sisters had left the house.

She was still shivering when she turned on the television. On the screen Winnie Wilson was smiling at and for and with and by America. Heather slumped into the sofa, and felt the cushions mold to her body. The winter sunlight, more depressing than no sunlight, was making a pale square of dying color, not even quite light, on the wall. On the television the commercials were blaring and bodies were moving frantically and happily against each other, bumping and smiling, through a new kitchen, lunging for salad dressing. Then the Winnie Wilson logo undulated across the screen, a nautilus stretching flat to a flattened rainbow. Then Patrick Crane was sitting on the soundstage. Or John. He had called himself John that night.

A pair of crutches was leaned against the table next to Winnie's plush chair, and the two of them were talking, private and cheerful, as the music and the applause died. He wore a beard and his hair was long and he was fat but it was him.

She made it to the bathroom in time to puke in the toilet.

Petting the Burning Dog arrived the next night. She tore open the box and was stunned by the object in her hands. At the sight of it she hated Patrick Crane and realized she had not known real hatred until now. Her hatred threw into relief her love for a man named Antoine Greep whom she could barely picture or appraise because of the garish echoes of celebrity that even now rang in her brain from the sound of that name. Who was the man she had made love to yesterday? Staring at the cover of the memoir quote unquote she regarded Patrick with a murderous intensity that would drive her insane if she didn't do something with it, but there was nothing to do with it.

Then she started reading. As she read she discovered herself on the pages almost instantly: in the book a woman named Hillary Dollenmaier looked and dressed and acted and thought as somebody might suppose Heather looked and dressed and acted and thought. The parallels were closer than close, the heartbreak realer than real, the misery of the narrator, in a strange way, like her own, nearly identical to what she had been enduring. As the pages progressed and the parallels escalated her hatred for Patrick did not disappear but forked into a simultaneous countervailing feeling, inimical to it, irreconcilable with it, but intermingled with it. Somewhere along the line he, like she, had had to endure the sudden understanding of the total privacy of every mind. He, like she, longed impossibly for beauty and control amidst ugliness and loneliness and chaos. Beneath the shameful fabrication lay a true feeling whose analogue rotted her own guts. So she not only hated him but came into an understanding of him fully and at once. The double feeling was intolerable. It was awful to understand him and hate him at the same time. Understanding resuscitated love, made love seem possible again; and it was intolerable to feel that possibility at one and the same time with disgust. She resented him for making her the beloved one in a book so evil. And giving her that name? Hillary Dollenmaier?

As she read she wanted to stop reading and wanted it to last and last. She wanted to destroy the book or him or herself. And the solution that occurred to her, in the wake of these feelings, the only solution, was Antoine Greep.

The hardest day of her teaching career was the next day, which she fumbled through, sleep-deprived, wired on ambiguous intentions, searching, groping, and sick with the need to see him. Hardest of all was watching Jaranya work the crayons—was squaring the existence of this little girl against Heather's own. This was the hardest day, but the next day, and the next, and the next were all also the hardest— every day until she saw him again. Because still she had no way to contact him, and he did not come to her. He did not belong in the house she had visited; she could not call the house; she could not ask Jaranya, "Where's your dad today?"

After the longest week of her life, of walking the six blocks to the station, of doing so at a pace comically slow, he finally came.

"Getting cold to be walking," he said through the open window. Inside, the heater smelled old and cozy. She told him she had missed him. It was the understatement of the geological era. "Do you have an apartment?" she said.

253

"Do you feel like Denny's? I love that Home Run Breakfast."

"Do you know what that book says about you?" she said as she bucked her seatbelt. She couldn't wait.

"I've been hearing things. Claire read it."

"You talk to Claire?"

"She's my wife."

"I thought that wasn't so true anymore."

He was not going to sleep with Heather again. The air between them conveyed the fact starkly. There would be no lovemaking to electrify what had to be for her an electric conversation. This was an exit interview. There was heartbreak, and there was logistical exasperation. He seemed to be staring at his knuckles on the wheel instead of the road. In a second they were in the Denny's parking lot. Again at the table he read the menu like a book, holding it close to his eyes, and ordered the Home Run Breakfast. As they waited for the food, Heather ignored his coldness and told him everything—about Patrick Crane and *Petting the Burning Dog*. She wished they had been making love, preparing through that phase of transport to talk about these things, which came out too blandly now, heavily, tediously. The whole thing should feel as epic as it was. When she was finished, he grinned and said, "You liked me even then. That's sweet."

"What is wrong with you? This creep who never met you is getting rich and famous by destroying your name. We can prove he's a fraud with a single phone call. Either of us could do it, and both of us can do it for sure."

"We got interrupted," he said. "You remember that?"

"Interrupted?" She had not followed the step.

"At my house?"

"So?"

"So I was telling you stuff."

His food came, and in the most haunting way he stared at her as he ate. He groped with the fork and kept his eyes on her, this for seven or eight minutes. She got out her cigarettes and smoked two. They were in no-smoking, but the place was empty, and the waitress never came back, and she flicked the ash in her water glass. Finally, he was ready to let it out.

"I never told Claire this. I thought I'd never tell anybody. They assumed I'd never tell. It's psychology, they weren't stupid, why would I tell?"

"Who's they? Tell what?" She understood from the look in his eye and his tone of voice that nothing she knew already would compare to what she was about to learn.

"You think I even know who *they* is? It could be anybody from anywhere on the ladder. You get the feeling things like this go all the way up. I like to pretend it was Rummy himself. Sometimes I doubt I'm pretending."

There was a price to hear whatever she was about to hear. He was working up to it and expected her to wait. He treated himself to the gesture of mystification. He finally said, "What do you know about what I did?"

"You killed your captors and fought your way out. Your squad members got beheaded, five of them you can see on YouTube, but also Henry Fleming."

"Right. OK. Perfect. So let's think about this. A good lookin' son of a major league baseball star kills ruthless terrorists with his bare hands. Could they ask for a better press release? Could they? Could you imagine a better headline?"

"You're saying it's not true?" The question was futile in her mouth even as she formed it. Then her face was showing him everything he was after, the stunned comprehension, the simplicity of it. Her heart had dropped into her knees. "It never happened," she said. "It never happened."

"Oh, we were taken captive all right," he said. "And everybody but me was killed. And the CIA guys found me with a broomstick up my ass and four hours left until I died of sepsis and dehydration."

"So the escape? You told America about your escape!"

"If you look, I never did."

"You did too!"

"If you look, your story that you love so much came from implications. Undenied hints. Crazy anchors. Spencer Talent and all them. You won't find me or anybody official saying, 'He killed them with his bare hands.'"

"In your interviews—"

"In my interviews I smiled a lot and let TEX go to town. You think I liked it? The people who came with me said certain things. The men in suits. I had orders not to contradict them. Not orders. It was weirder than orders. It was dark. Call them recommendations. From who? Don't ask me. I was confused and exhausted and broken, and I took the recommendations."

Minutes passed until she was ready to speak. "But still," she said finally. "But—we can talk about this later—or never—but you should set the record straight. You might not have been a hero. But you weren't this bizarre monster he's saying you were."

"Claire wants me to be quiet. She's tired. The deployment didn't fuck our marriage up. The broomstick didn't. It was the stuff afterwards. TEX News. Interviews everywhere. Morning shows and newspapers."

"I don't believe that's your reason." Had she been so bold as to say this?

He made a show of finishing what was left on his plate. There was nothing left on it. He studied it. "You're right, that's not my reason."

She let him take a long time to say what he said next, and he took it.

"I told you before. I joined the army because I was tired of having everything handed to me. I wanted to succeed because of who I was, not who my father was, or what I looked like, or because I was an upper-middle-class black kid in an elite world hungry for my type. It worked. The army did what I wanted it to. I made friends who didn't love me because I was Bobby Greep's son. They loved me because I was who I was. I loved them. I felt like I was *me*. It was the best feeling in the world, and it touched the whole thing. I loved them with all my heart. I loved Hank Fleming more than I'll ever love anybody again. I loved him because he knew me, knew *me*. He knew and judged and loved the real Antoine Greep. I knew and judged and loved the real Hank Fleming. We'd been to hell together. But in the end only I came back. And when I came back I betrayed him. I betrayed all of them."

This was the second time she had seen him crying, and now he was really crying.

"You'll have to put that out or leave." The waitress had appeared at the table, ignoring Antoine and holding a coffeepot like a mace to hit Heather with. Heather dropped the butt in the water glass. Otherwise Heather ignored the waitress. "So by swallowing this—by letting a stranger destroy your name—you're being true to them. You betrayed them by accepting credit for being a hero when you weren't one. And you make it right by becoming a public villain."

"I'll never make it right. But yes, you get it. I guess that's right. But it wasn't ever a plan, it was only a thing that happened to me. Both things were. First, the men in suits who made me a hero, then the women on the phone who made me a villain. That's a funny word, villain."

"The women on the phone—?"

"The editor, their lawyer."

"They called you?"

"They sent me the pages before that thing came out."

"Patrick's book? And you said they were true?"

"I didn't read them. But I said they were true enough. They *are* true enough."

"They aren't either!"

"They're as true as what you want to be true is true. I said it to the women on the phone, and I'll say it to that dude himself on TV."

"You're going to be on TV?"

Antoine didn't answer and signaled for the check.

She was in the kitchen. She packed the one-hitter carefully. She considered getting tweezers from the bathroom for the spare flakes. She was down to the last of the pot she had bought from Dave Steberski, who was living in Chicago, deluded in the conviction that fame as a rock star was waiting to suck his cock. She had taken him seriously four years ago. She felt ancient now, thinking about that. A car rushed past, and her stomach dropped as she pictured her mother pulling in. It was boys from down the block, barely old enough to drive, skipping school. She could tell by peeping out the window, squinting how her mother squinted. She had to pretend to take Dave seriously to get the pot. She tried to imagine calling him and spending a night out with him and his friends and then having to ask. She tried to imagine not having any more pot. She left the baggy on the counter and went to the garage. It had warmed, and the frozen waves of mud across the street had thawed. She tried to imagine the neighborhood with grass and then with trees. The old neighborhood, the one now filled with black people, had seemed so lived in. It was ten degrees colder in the garage than out on the driveway. From a distance the one-hitter looked like a cigarette. The lady who had just moved in across the street would think the Kloppenberg girl smoked cigarettes, which was true. In a moment the smoke slowed and softened everything. She felt the truest, purest anguish flood into her almost deliciously.

Shivering, she went back into the house. She packed the rest of the pot into the one-hitter and rinsed out the baggy and threw it away. She put the one-hitter in its case and took it to her bedroom and hid it in the space under the bottom desk drawer. She returned to the living room and settled onto the couch. When the television flashed on, it showed Mr. Rogers arriving at the beginning of his show. The color had seeped out of his world. His house looked like an apartment nobody had ever rented or lived in. It looked Soviet. The color of the camera was not black or white or color but a third condition, of a puke-like, pale, etiolated palate, like the image on a videotape that had been copied and copied again. Mr. Rogers warred against his wretchedness with his cheerfulness. Her kids at school were too real ever to cause her immediate sadness. But now she pictured them in empty houses staring at this man. It killed her to think of that, the little black kids watching this white man. Everything on TV was fake. The world got its feelings from things that did not exist. Things that did not exist mattered more than things that did. This had always been the case. Churches used to invent things. But now nobody believed in churches unless they believed in churches too much. Everybody had feelings that meant nothing. She wanted to believe that poetry redeemed this. She believed in Neil Dubuque and believed in herself. But poetry and Neil Dubuque and even Heather the poet occurred to her as antique remnants from a life that had died.

The only number she could get her hands on was the number for tickets. She dialed it a few times, and hung up when the voice answered. There was no talking to Winnie Wilson. There was only talking to people who talked to people who talked to Winnie Wilson. If that. But she had no doubt she could get through if she went about it intelligently. She was intelligent. She held in her exclusive possession the details surrounding a truth that had to come out. The truth lay between two accepted and irreconcilable extremes. There were no heroes, and there were no villains. There were half-truths, tragedy, and chaos. She got the cordless phone and called. She stayed on the line until she was speaking with somebody who seemed to care. Apparently a New York bartender had also called in. As Heather prepared herself to say what she knew, she felt the maddening pressure of all the complications. If she went on the show she could only claim so much. Who was *she*? What would her word be worth? "I know things that Ms. Wilson might wish to share with America," Heather said. I sound like a librarian, she thought. "You can call her Winnie," the man said. "What do you know?"

XVII.

Their fixation with Duckworth and Eccles added the crowning touch of strangeness to the horror. Even in this state of fear I was capable of feeling amazed in perplexity. With knives and execrations and the collective anonymity of men assaulting in a pack, with the inventiveness in torture that no room of torturing humans ever appeared short on, they used Duckworth's and Eccles's bodies against Duckworth and Eccles. I can't write what I saw. If you watched the clips on YouTube you should know that this was worse than those. Worst of all was the change in their faces. Eccles's moody, skittish, loving, craven, slender features twisted into animal misery. Duckworth's jowlish, heavy, slabby, stupid, loving, craven features twisted into animal misery. Before they were made dead they were made beasts, and we watched it while tied to our chairs. Schwartz heaved and hyperventilated, his pants fouled, his body a spasm of fear. J'Million cried and stared at the floor as if willing a deafening noise to cease. Kirk Frank turned inward. Only Greep, in the chair next to me, the two of us furthest from the scene of torture—only Greep retained in his countenance all that he had ever been. He did not grin, but even in these moments of the highest pitch of terror I could perceive his capacity to grin.

Why Duckworth and why Eccles? In the moment I had no idea, so speculated. They were our butts. They were the ones we bullied too. Eccles had never been allowed to love Pat Mapp in peace, his trials of heart forming the substance of a third of our jokes. Duckworth had drunk crotch water only once but figuratively speaking had been doing it all his life. He brought up the dog-pack rear. He demonstrated to us, day after day, the kind of man we were not. We needed him for this. I couldn't deny that I myself had relaxed in the knowledge that

259

at least one from the platoon would never stake a real claim, never enter the elbowing fray of derision and roughhousing, rapaciousness and despotic self-assertion, would always be less than me.

So in the shuddering uncertainty of what I thought for certain were my final moments, I wondered whether it was written by a malicious God on their very faces and bodies, whether Duckworth and Eccles had been marked from birth as weak. Did this gang of thugs see their vulnerability as clearly as we did? Did it foster in them the same aggression? Perhaps as much as the spectacle of the torture itself this question rose from the scene with a morally paralytic stench. The worst of our impulses were the most universal. They ran through all our hearts. If Saddam Hussein had been the legitimate heir to an Enlightenment experiment in representative democracy; if Iraq had emerged into prosperity in the eighteenth century; if the United States of America had been formed in the twentieth century as the tide of European colonialism ebbed; if George W. Bush had come to power as the renegade pawn of an empire fighting a cold war; if the Iraqi forces of democracy had invaded Akron and Ashtabula to stop Bush from getting a nuclear weapon, to loosen his grip on the peasants he terrorized; then would the Iraqi forces of freedom have thrown bags of their own shit to our children asking for food? Would they have grazed the corner of our houses and crushed our bicycles and handed us bogus orange index cards for restitution? Would they have passed out Mesopotamian pornography to our eight-year-old sons and laughed at the anger of our fathers? And would they have moved across our country in platoons of weaklings and wimps and sadists? Would we have sniffed out their Duckworths and Eccleses as they sniffed out ours?

None of this ran through my brain so articulately as I sat bound in that chair watching what I watched. But arbitrariness did run through it, a sense of the universality of the strong destroying the weak. Later, as I escaped, and after I escaped, these thoughts swirled miasmically until they assumed solid form.

The rope that bound me to the chair had been tied sloppily and quickly by a man throbbing with excitement. The men had weapons, epinephrine, and Allah. We had bodies frail with dehydration and sleep deprivation and souls frail with apostasy. Lucidity and fear alternated in my bloodstream. I was floating toward my own death like a man toward a waterfall, not even flailing.

For Greep it was otherwise; Greep did not want to die. He was alert, almost smirking with a refusal to acknowledge the reality of these currents, the truth of this fatal progression. He had managed to free his hands. They were free and working on the ropes that bound him to the chair.

Ten yards away the crowd of a dozen circled Duckworth now, what was left of him, plenty was left of him, the Arabic shouts of the crowd becoming a kind of black noise of vitriol, raw hatred, incomprehensible but more precise in meaning than if we had understood the words. The two armed guards at the door glanced our way less often with each passing minute as the frenzy mounted around Duckworth.

Greep worked on the ropes. I strove to appear captive and passive. So I was not dead yet, I was thinking. I was at least in this way striving. I knew Greep understood what I was doing, because as soon as he was free he slumped in his chair as if beyond struggling and waited for me to catch up. I was to undo my own ropes. The man with the greatest paunch and the whitest beard stood in the fracas, watching with calm, damning eyes. He was the one I feared most. It was hard to watch him without drawing his notice. It was harder yet to free myself in the unobserved instants. I managed. I got the ropes off my hands. Then, as the crowd roared, Greep tossed me what seemed to be a shard of a blade from a lawnmower. Why would they have lawnmowers here? It was a shard of a fan from a car engine. It was random metal. It cut my hand when I grabbed it from the floor. I was bleeding as I cut the ropes. We were free. We could leap from our chairs into a space filled with fifteen armed men mad with epinephrine and faith and anger. I could hear Eccles whining and screaming but could not see anything but the violent mobbing of the angry men.

Before the scene advanced to the final disaster, before my men began to die, my premonition of the universality of cruelty transformed into something like its opposite: peace. The flailing, raging, yearning, hating, wailing, fearing, avenging horde of souls in the room, including my own, became impersonal. We were a single force, as if in a tide pool, distributed equally among parts. We were the breath of God circling back on itself. Our movements formed unlikely currents in the unexpected architecture of a far corner of the universe. The particularity I saw before me appeared as accidental and transient and wondrous as icicles on eaves. The patterns of ruby on Schwartz's forehead, his shadow of stubble and his masses of heft; the lank lines of Eccles's form, the Roman nose and mild stevedore tawniness; the

261

loving, brutal, homely face of J'Million, its splayedness down a center line, the spread of his eyes and teeth; the seaweed hair and bullfrog eyes of Kirk Frank, his expression of wry, silent competence of which something was left even now, even in this ultimate moment of fear; the glorious irreverence of Greep's whole being, his handsome blackness, his teeth like amoral knives; and the infantile tenderness, the hog-farmer jowls of Duckworth, now glistening with tears of immeasurable pain. Around these six men seethed fifteen Iraqis just as particular, just as singular. I could perceive for a moment a soul in each, a soul in all.

"Flem," Greep hissed.

It is strange for me to describe images that have become clichés of the war, as meaninglessly iconic as the smoke billowing from the Twin Towers or the shuddering and shadowy and triumphant and unnerving footage of Saddam Hussein getting hanged. I have never gone to the Internet to see firsthand what I saw that day but can say that the living sight of Duckworth refusing to die was beyond belief. They set him in the chair before the tripod, and all of it looked like a joke of scale, the chair, the tripod, and the men who jostled like orcs around him in a frenzy of wrath. They took turns standing behind him and making statements to the camera. They fed him words he refused to speak or simply was beyond understanding. Then they drew the blade across his throat, and he howled like a rutting lion. Then they drew it across again; and again. The blood left his body, but the life did not, and he rose from the chair and wielded it, the chair, still tied to him, from behind his body like a club, or like four clubs. In combat Duckworth always fired his weapon diligently but never once showed true aggression. Even in the starkest moments of conflict he shied from it and stared around with eyes wide with grief and apology. But for a brief moment, after his throat was cut, his essence took possession of itself, his soul fired, his DNA freaked, he balked in death's face. Amid this final and only gesture of immense defiance, the life drained out of him. He crumpled to the floor, and fifteen Iraqis cheered and fell on him.

Eccles died more easily. I glimpsed the soles of his boots in the darkness of Duckworth's blood and thought, "That blood is Duckworth's life," still alive with him. When his time came, Schwartz's mouth dropped wide in stupid outrage. Kirk Frank went uncomplainingly. J'Million put up a fight, then was tied down and destroyed. But our captors were pausing and panting.

262

What Greep did should have failed. J'Million was still twitching, and Greep was up from his chair and had pulled the sidearm from the holster on the hip of a man examining the dying body. He pressed the barrel to the head of the man with the paunch and the white beard and spun to shield himself with the man's body and backed to the corner. The guards turned toward Greep, who raised the weapon and shot one dead. I was forgotten. In that slim instant I hugged the other guard from behind and laid my hands on his AK-47 and was spraying the crowd. Greep took a chance—risked shooting me—and shot him, too, in the head. Then he shot the old Shiite. I freed the AK-47 from my dead guard; Greep got the other AK-47 into his hands.

Long ago playing soccer in high school, I experienced moments of complicated and tenuous action before the goal, when ten players' feet and chests and heads jerked and vied as the ball bounced and hung and hovered between being sunk in the net and booted out and down the field. The ball defied both teams and bounced in mad suspense in a static width of air. Time slowed. A scored goal felt infinitely close and infinitely improbable. This was like that. Their bodies and our bodies ceased being free agents and became sources of motion controlled by chances unrelated to will. The change in the trajectory of a single limb of a single body would have ended our lives. So in a moment when Greep and I had backed into the hallway, having killed or maimed each Iraqi, I felt a sporting euphoria that was almost infinite. It was an abrupt and fleeting change in mood. I felt pure love for Greep. He had swum against the fatal current and delivered us from death. Then he turned to run.

"We need to get their bodies," I yelled after him. "We have control. J'Million might be OK."

"We'll get backup." He was halfway down the hallway.

"He'll be dead," I yelled.

"He's dead," he called.

I could not follow him. I went back and checked on J'Million as Greep fled. It was reflex and nothing at all like heroism. I shot my way back into the room. I could have saved the rounds. I found two Iraqis wounded and whimpering and everybody else dead or good as. I checked each of my men, trying to put everything out of mind. If I had regarded them as my men, it would have shattered me. So I let them be the mere things they now resembled.

Before I left the room I found the videotape that had been crammed in Duckworth's mouth and pocketed it.

Now came the hardest moments of my life, as I stood alone in a Mahdi Army complex, surrounded by the bodies of friends who had just been living, listening to the sound of a street shocked into silence by the popcorn thunder of a massive discharge, wondering how many seconds or minutes remained until militiamen arrived in packs and killed me. After mere minutes of reprieve my death again was a given. So I moved with the purpose and the calmness of the doomed. I had my senses about me. In an office I found a missile-guidance system, some computers from the late 1980s, and manuals on Apache helicopters. I found hundreds of thousands of Iraqi dinars and thousands of American dollars. Perhaps I only fully grasped the irrelevance of money to life, its abstract uselessness, when I held that cash in my hands. Of course later the cash would save my life. I also found Polaroids of myself and others being tortured.

For a moment I froze, standing in the center of that office, taking stock, trying to think. I could hole up or flee. Those were the options. Greep had fled, and I doubted he would live. He was dead already. He had to be. His grin had no currency here. Were we in a village? If so, then others would arrive in seconds, and there would be no place to hide. If not, then I might stand a chance. So I decided to try. I collected sidearms and ammunition, bundled the cash so I could carry it, and donned a black uniform and mask stripped from a body.

When I stepped onto the street it was with no destination in mind. I assumed I would try for Babylon. But as I walked through the streets, nobody stopped me. They looked at me, saluted me, scowled at me, but did not try to kill me. I experienced what I know in retrospect, and even knew at the time, was a naïve and specious epiphany. I thought, "The problem isn't them. The problem is us." I had placed myself in the garb of another, and that costume and that epiphany caused my desertion. I no longer was a lieutenant in the United States Army. I was a guy who almost got killed by two very different sets of lunatics.

On the streets of a large village there was the flimsy protection of a temporary anonymity. But it would have been a short escape if I had not happened to see Westerners. They were two men with cameras who addressed me in French when I addressed them in English from under my mask. In English I asked them if they could take me to Hilla. It was the nearest city I knew of. "We will drive to Nasiriyah," they said. "We can take you there." They probably thought I was a CIA agent gone off the deep end. Who knows what they thought.

On the drive to Nasiriyah I confessed what I was. They were indifferent. "You should have done this a year ago," one said and laughed. I became afraid they were French intelligence. Then I stopped being afraid of that.

In Nasiriyah they placed me with an Iraqi family who agreed to feed me and lodge me until Adnan Antoon appeared. Sooner or later he would return to his office at the Bureau of Antiquities. Each day the father sent his son to look for Antoon. On the third day Antoon was there, so I went. For the first time he smiled at me. Without the anger he looked like a smaller man. "You have returned, like Enkidu, from the underworld." His pristine Oxbridge accent clashed with everything around us. "But it was not a dream. We thought you were dead."

"I was dead," I said. "I have been dead. I wish to remain dead."

"But you wished so badly to help!"

"Mosul, the Kurdish regions to the north, they are relatively safe?"

"Everything is relatively safe." He laughed. "Relatively. Your Detroit is relatively safe."

"Do you have friends in the north?"

"A professor has friends everywhere, and twice as many enemies."

"Could I get to Turkey? There are excavations up there."

"You wish to walk away from your army."

"To them, I am dead," I said.

"And to you, they are dead," he finished. "I wish to us they were dead. You will need a dishdasha, and a gun, and a driver, and a willingness to die."

"I have the gun at least."

"So American!"

"I will need a passport."

"That is your business. But I have a friend in Istanbul."

Before I deployed to Iraq I had searched on Google for everything I could find. One of the things I found was a website full of photographs posted by a family. The father had worked in the British diplomatic service in Baghdad in the 1970s and taken his wife and children along. The oil was flowing, and Saddam Hussein had not yet staged his coup. Westerners moved freely on the same streets I would drive down in mortal terror. Kids swam happily at poolsides as oil revenue transformed the city from a dusty and idiosyncratic slum to a homogeneous and ugly metropolis.

At the end of the father's assignment, the family drove to London from Baghdad, using ferries along the way. Half the photos on the site were from that trip. I contemplated in a possibly adolescent and facile way the violence and arbitrariness of borders, how, in the age of visas, passports, terrorism, capitalism, police states, and welfare, the social became the geographical. All of it looked innocent: the resolution of the photographs, the make and model of the car, the pools in Baghdad, the optimistic highways of Eurasia in the mid-1970s, the Alps arrived at from that eastern starting point. During my year in Iraq, I thought a lot about those photographs. It was an arbitrary memory, the accidental fruit of an afternoon of browsing the web, but it stayed with me. The war set us down in a foreign and disorienting place, as you might set down roosters in a circle or pit bulls in a cage. You only ever came and went by flying great distances and landing suddenly. There was no continuity, and without continuity it seemed impossible for there to be sympathy, and without sympathy it seemed impossible for there to be peace. I cringe at the sight of these sentences even as they emerge on the screen. I'm not a hippie: I don't think permanent peace is possible and I don't underestimate the difficulty of even tentative and tenuous peace. But there was a great cynicism in the method of our deployment. I was dead to the army, which meant I was free to go, and I decided to take my leave as if human life occurred in one world, not two or three or the hundred and ninety-two national spheres of interest reporting to the United Nations. I took a drive Donald Rumsfeld's never taken, that's for sure.

When you're living in your suburb in Atlanta or Columbus, your mind forms barriers and obstacles, threats and menaces, roadblocks that are social and geographical, technological and microbial, bureaucratic and political. These roadblocks, mostly mental, would prevent an American from traveling from Hilla to Mosul, Mosul to Diyarbakir, Diyarbakir to Ankara, Ankara to Istanbul, Istanbul to Athens, Athens to London, and London to New York. These roadblocks exist, but all of them, after what I had been through, seemed as formidable as a game of cribbage. Antoon's good name solved one set of problems, the cash from the Mahdi headquarters solved another, and my wits, believe it or not, solved the rest.

XVIII.

Desire has no ceiling. That was all that he had learned for certain. Desire never attains its object. He had longed against longing to be Marshall Franklin Stang, but only Marshall Franklin Stang would ever be Marshall Franklin Stang. He had loved Emily White with a passion deeper than God. But the women you loved with a passion deeper than God were projections of God, were projections of Satan, were the froth of a disturbed heart. He had conceived *Petting the Burning Dog* as a novel of thwarted passion and despairing revenge. In the weeks and months preceding its conception—as he wound down his time in New York and moved to Arden and found a wheelchair in a parking ally and purchased clothing at the army surplus store and impersonated a crippled veteran—it murmured below the surface of consciousness, inchoate and undiscovered, as a plot of revenge. He would outdo *The Marshall Stang Story* and eclipse their celebrity. He would outsmart the *Greater Than X* boys and embarrass the publishing houses. He would transcend his own futility. For a time his desire also took as its object some vision of justice. He would lay bare somehow the public falsity of the war itself.

By the time he retreated from Indiana to Florida, these motives had run like sand through the fingers of his brain, to be replaced by thoughts of Heather—constant, crazy ones. He knew she revered above all things the self-made man. She wanted to make herself anew, and she might love John again if he pushed through the far side of the deception into the realm of art. America was America because you could be Jay Gatsby or Andy Warhol or Bob Dylan or Neil Dubuque. You could tear yourself from the skein of mediocrity and weave a personality of silk. He had gone halfway with her, had diminished himself in a wheelchair and claimed a heroic status not his due, but even in this failure, in this paltry half-success, he had demonstrated to himself his powers of self-transformation.

In the autumn weeks of their love affair he had loathed the founding misconception. He understood she'd fallen in love with the shell, the ruse. On Halloween night, standing before the VCR, he had tried to crack the shell. He had revealed himself, and she had fled. So he would not try again to be himself, because that was either meaningless or repulsive. He would make himself so perfectly another person as a kind of last bid.

Yet John also knew on some level that Heather was not the only woman to be courted and satisfied. For Heather even to hear of his fabrication, Winnie Wilson would have to pick up the story. The New York editors would, the journalists and bloggers. And what did they want, all of them? They wanted nobodies who became somebodies and somebodies who fell tragically. Done and done. Every other story that made the soft headlines, if you panned out far enough, was stagecraft and exaggeration, hype and deception, entertainment and halfway hoax. John could play that game.

Even as he undertook the plan, its dubiousness haunted him. When Antoine Greep appeared on Winnie Wilson, filling the chair that was rightfully Heather's, John's failure massed on the horizon, even as Greep declined to precipitate it publicly. What Greep said about Heather over beers that same afternoon at a bar in Chicago blew the dark clouds overhead. And the appearance, a few weeks later, of Heather herself on national media, unraveling the story, revealing all she knew about both Greep and John, and promoting in advance the memoir that she had begun work on, released the torrent of black rain on his head. *Petting the Burning Dog* had not only not brought him the things he wished. It had obliterated the very prospect of them—of their ever again entering his life.

Only at the end of an affair can a person perceive with clarity all the moral turpitude, narcissistic extravagance, and solipsistic excess that surrounds it. Love truly does make us blind. Only after John had been drenched by heartbreak, only as he stood sopping and shivering in the chilly aftermath, did he begin to perceive as the final point of misery in a miserable season the enormity of what he had done. The wickedness. Antoine Greep was a real soldier, the war was a real war, and the prerogatives of the creative imagination meant nothing alongside it. He wondered if he were not the most magnificent abomination ever to be produced by a writing workshop. But even wondering this seemed to make him all the more abominable.

In the dozen years since he met Emily White, he had become a novelist. He knew this was true. He had published only a memoir, and a bogus one, but his mind, through long discipline and deep thought, had been tuned acutely to the awful coincidences of tragic plots. So even as he languished in misery, even as he licked wounds too deep for licking, he beheld, but could not bring himself to admire, the symmetry of the events. Emily had chosen Stang; Heather had chosen Antoine; and the man who had never fired a shot, braved a battle, or done anything more than write, suffered a defeat beyond all humiliation. Whatever he had accomplished he had not accomplished in the realm of real bodies and lives.

After his second appearance on the Winnie Wilson Show, John returned to his parents' house. His mother met him at the door and shook her head and hugged him. She was crying. She was the only woman who would ever face his brokenness and see it charitably.

John moved his belongings back from the cabin and declined to answer questions about where he had been. "Your mother said Debbie Duncan said you've been around," his father said. John let this pass without answering.

He considered his options, but not rigorously. Money remained from the handsome advance for the memoir—almost all of it did— but the lawyers from the publishing house would begin to send letters. It would be a long year. He felt no desire ever to write again, felt something like the opposite, but also felt ruined for normal jobs.

His father's hospitality was thin, cool, but steady. His mother forgave him everything almost immediately. They resumed the old habits and patterns that they had developed in those years after high school. He took a shift at the cat litter factory where Stang had worked, took it out of curiosity, and quit four days later. He recalled with wonder that Stang had worked there for two years.

Each morning, as his father went off to the church and his mother worked in the yard, John tried to read. But words disgusted him. He watched more television than ever before, watched it as a high school football star watches professional football in middle age. And, one day, not long after moving home, he heard, before he saw, a familiar presence on the Winnie Wilson Show. It was Stang, and with him was

Emily, and together they were there to draw out the scandal, to make more money for themselves and for whomever made money from it, to talk about John Townley's fall. John turned off the TV and stood at the window staring at the yard for who knows how many minutes, hours, days, weeks, or private millennia.

Part Three

XIX.

I waited until after it was clear Hillary would have nothing to do with me to watch the tape. Losing her was like losing a foot. In the time it took me to get from rural Iraq to Providence, Rhode Island, and call Hillary from a payphone she had reinvented herself as somebody else's wife. In Berlin she discovered just how utterly I had ceased to be myself, which allowed her to cease to be herself as soon as the world presumed me dead. So when I listened to her voice on the phone I realized I had lost all sense of who I was. She was the only person who could keep the war from taking that from me. But it was too hard. "I was so, in a way, relieved," she said. "I didn't want you to die. But who you were in Germany upset me more than I can say. You weren't at all who I thought you were. I'm sorry, Henry. I think I was engaged to a man who no longer exists. The fact that you've done what you've done proves what you've been through has changed you. I can't give you what you'll need now." And so on.

It wasn't really a breakup, since I was dead. So I stayed dead. I moved down the road and rented an apartment in Pawtucket from an African American man named Booker Washington. The main room was immense, of the same square footage as the house upstairs, and unfurnished. A fuse box broke the drab uniformity of the far wall and pipes braced the ceiling. Thin blue carpeting, smelling like wet couch, covered but did not soften the concrete floor. Swinging half-doors divided the tiny kitchen from the tiny bathroom, the kitchen and the bathroom having been built under the stairs that rose to a padlocked door and drew the eye from anywhere you might stand in the main room. From above came the sound of the barking dog in the apartment upstairs and the whisk of its claws on the linoleum and the pregnant silence between barks. I placed a sleeping bag in the corner and left the rest of my few belongings to be unpacked later. I made a pile like a cairn in the center of the room.

The only furnishing the apartment came with was an enormous old television set, a big screen from the first days of big screens. But some drug dealer or toddler or tormented girlfriend had cracked the screen from the upper-left-hand corner down to the center. The crack skewed the image and cast skittering ghost lines. Brisk, facile anchormen warped across it. Spencer Talent resembled Frankenstein.

The tape. I turned it over in my fingers. It had been in Duckworth's mouth. Greep had told me he'd been making a little something for Breitbart. A last prank. I hooked the camera to the television, inserted the cartridge, and pressed play. Greep's voice warped into audibility. Abstract geometry filled the screen until I recognized it as an accidental shot of his thigh. You could also make out the surface he was sitting on and shadows across a concrete floor. Despite the gash in screen, I recognized it: it was that bunker we lived in. The light and vague shapes gave it away. The sound distorted whenever Greep's voice rose. He spoke against a constant background of humming electromagnetism.

". . . so I didn't want to see her, you know what I mean? She was visiting friends upstate I hated. Never realized how much I hated them until I thought about joining her and them getting high, drinking, sitting on the lawn, bitching about kids they didn't even have to watch."

"How many rich girls you date in your life?" It was Schwartz.

"We're talking grade-A lawn, too. This was Nerissa. It took that invitation to upstate to make me realize just how much I hated her. Hated her until the fifteen minutes before I was boning her, then boned her, then hated her again."

Casual silence. An image only somebody who had squatted in that bunker ever could have recognized.

"Ten years older than me. I was twenty-one. She saw thirty-five in the rearview mirror. That pussy was slack. Half the time it was sour."

"Just so wrong." It was J'Million.

"I was a punk kid, living in Queens. I was unemployed and boning a rich mom. J-Mo who worked for William Shatner was putting me up."

"Fuck you, William Shatner," J'Million said.

"Why didn't you just break up with her?" It was Eccles.

Still no faces, only voices.

"Bingo," Greep said. "Why? Because her dad was hooking me up. Owned twelve TV stations in New York and New Jersey, had a buddy owned a record label I was going to work as a promoter for. So I had to keep it friendly, you know what I'm saying?"

"Just fuck the bitch," Schwartz said.

"Her dad liked you?" Eccles said.

"You doubt it?" Greep said. "Because I'm black?"

"Racist," Schwartz said to Eccles.

"Shut up Schwartz," Greep said.

Laughter.

"I was crashing with J-Mo and eating raw garlic."

"For health?" Eccles said.

"To gross her out," J'Million said.

"Bingo," Greep said. "Also stopped shaving."

"Shit, bro, didn't know you started!" J'Million said.

Laughter.

"Shit," Greep said.

"Ate garlic and stopped shaving just to gross her out?" Eccles said.

"J-Mo?" Schwartz asked. "What the hell kind of name?"

"J-Mo," Greep explained. "I was eating raw garlic. I was also eating canned food. People lived there before us stockpiled cans for Y2K. Shit you wouldn't touch until the end of the world. A billion cans of canned yams. I hate yams. So that weekend she wanted me to come up. She paid for the ticket, I wouldn't of gone otherwise."

Outside an ambulance howled down the rutted Pawtucket street. The stench of dog lifted from somewhere.

"The only bus went at six thirty. Either that or one at nine at night and I'd get there after everybody's passed out. So I aim for six thirty. But then I oversleep."

"You never oversleep," Eccles said.

"He's right," Schwartz said.

"You never plain sleep," J'Million said.

"I oversleep. I practically bust a nut to get to Port Authority. A taxi driver gets my last eighteen dollars. Nick of time type of thing. I'm in the station, running like Bo. I just make it. I feel like puking. My lungs are gone. But I'm in my seat. Then the bus goes. Suddenly I've got six hours just to sit there. Chinks are yapping on their cell phones to other chinks."

"Racist motherfucker," J'Million said.

"You know how they do? The chinks? I watch the trees. I'm a poet. I watch the Hudson. I fall asleep. I wake up bus sick."

"You never get motion sickness," Eccles said.

"He's right," Schwartz said.

"You never get plain sick," J'Million said.

"Finally, we get to my stop, way upstate, and I'm the only one getting off. I'm expecting a town, but it's an intersection. It's not even an intersection. It's a bulge in the blacktop. The bus pulls away and crosses a girder bridge painted blue and short enough and narrow enough to look stupid."

"Like a stubby dick," Schwartz said.

"You'd know," J'Million said.

"There's a river down there, you can hear it. Plus, the sun. Good air, all that shit. So I don't feel so bad all of a sudden. Woody Guthrie kind of stuff. Beats Queens."

"Woody who what?" J'Million said.

"But then you remember about the pussy," Schwartz said.

"But then I remember about the pussy. And suddenly I know one thing for sure."

"You're not in Kansas anymore?" Eccles said.

Silence.

Schwartz: "You are so fucking stupid."

Greep: "I know I got to shave."

"Done change your mind," J'Million said.

"The heart is a dark forest," Greep said.

Narrative pause.

"There's a barbershop and a drugstore. But it's not a town. It's ten percent of a town. I look at my watch. Noon. On Saturday. Perfect time for a barbershop. So I go to the barbershop. It's got two parts connected up front, ladies and gents. Place says open, so I walk in, but there's no men. One side has metal chairs, cracked cushions, clippers, a shaving cream machine, *Soldier of Fortune*, *Playboys*. But it's dark. Other side, lighted up, is ladies. 'Can I get a shave?' I say. Could of been bleeding Cheez Whiz how they stared back at me."

"'Cuz you're black," J'Million said.

"'Men's is closed,' they say. 'What,' I say, 'because I'm black?' 'You'd better get out of here,' they say. So I get out of there. I stand in the parking lot and stare at the bridge."

"The stubby dick bridge," Schwartz said.

"What the fuck you talkin' about?" J'Million said.

"Then I see the drugstore and get my brainstorm," Greep said. "In the drugstore there's an old man working. By old I mean everything in the casket except his eyes. He got these cloudy, hungry diamonds eyes in a shriveled-up face. His skin, bones, fingers, and toes—all fucked for this world. Everything's sagging, slumping, creaking, or stinking. Must of stopped grooming during Watergate. He's thin as fuck. His eyes are glowing in his skull, like a cloud with the sun behind it. The shirt he's wearing's huge and new, four sizes too big, fresh out of the wrapper. You can still see the folds. Collar's sharp, sleeves're flat, front and back all starched looking. Why would he wear such a huge shirt? A little fucker like him? Then I realize it's the size he remembers wearing. It was his size thirty years ago. He's been shrinking for thirty years. He turned ninety eighteen years ago."

"What you're saying is is he was old," J'Million said.

"There's also a girl. We're talking eleven, maybe twelve."

"Hot," Schwartz said.

"So wrong," J'Million said.

"Not so hot," Greep said. "She's the granddaughter. She's the great-granddaughter. She's the great-great-granddaughter. Tits so new you can tell she doesn't know they're there. Fat with kid fat. Stringy hair. So it's the three of us. I stand there. She stares at me like a little cow. The codger is trying to pull a receipt off a stake. His hands are shaking. He ends up tearing the receipt in half. Then he holds the halves in his shaking hands, trying to put them back together. The girl stares at me and doesn't care what she's staring at. Her body's twelve, and her brain's about seven. She's sipping from a straw in a plastic bottle of Pepsi. She's chewing on the straw. There's no Pepsi in the straw. Her tits are waiting to become tits."

"Enough with the tits," J'Million said. "Girl's a baby."

"Codger is working a full-time job dealing with his hands. The yellow paper flutters. I look around. I walk the width of the store how you do, looking down the aisles. The razors are against the wall, way down by the pharmacy. I find three kinds of razors and one kind of shaving cream."

"Barbasol?" J'Million said.

"Barbasol," Greep said.

"Fuckin' hate Barbasol," J'Million said.

"Me too. All I want is gel. I decide to ask about gel. The codger is still holding the yellow paper in his hands. Fluttering like an autumn gale."

"Nice."

"But he's not facing me now. He's squinting at the nicotine gum on the shelf behind the counter. You could spray-paint the Gettysburg Address on the back of that shirt. The girl has not moved an inch. Her tits have not moved an inch."

"Fucking quit it," J'Million said seriously.

"I ask for gel, and what does the kid with the tits say? Nothing. The straw stays in her mouth. Nothing is happening. Finally, I notice the codger is turning around. He fixes them cloudy diamonds on me. Then he aims his body toward the end of the counter and starts walking. It takes time."

"Like this story," J'Million said.

"The girl could probably run an eight-minute mile, even with the tits. But following the old man involves standing in one place and waiting. Twenty minutes later we've gone four yards. At which point a bitch on wheels comes in. She's standing at the counter glaring at the girl. She glares at the girl, and then at me, and then at the old man. She asks the girl about nicotine gum. The girl chews her straw. Three days later we get to the Barbasol. The codger picks up a can in his hand."

"Shaking hand," J'Million said.

"Shaking hand," Greep said. "'Gel,' I say. 'Toothpaste?' he says. 'This is fine,' I say. 'What?' he says. 'This is fine,' I yell."

"Barbasol," J'Million said. "Shit."

"With the Barbasol and a bag of razors I walk out of the store and over to the bridge. There's a gorge. There's a bed of rubble on either side about as steep as bleachers. I almost break my leg getting down to the river. But the river is gorgeous, so I feel OK. I'll shave, and I'll deal with the pussy when I come to it."

"The heart is a forest," J'Million said.

"Under the bridge there's a concrete ledge along the water. I take my shoes off and sit on the ledge and the water's halfway up my calves. I lean down, cup water, splash my face, load up with foam. My legs are spread, my feet dangling. I open the bag of razors. I take a razor, dip it in the river, and draw the blade across my jaw. Then it dawns on me. I've got to piss like a horse. Great. But then it dawns on me. I've got a bridge over my head. The middle of friggin' nowhere. I'll be discrete. I'll just stay sitting. So I unzip and piss. Sitting on the ledge. I piss and piss."

"You feel like a million dollars," Schwartz said.

"Except for the Barbasol," J'Million said.

"Except now it happens," Greep said.

"Now what happens?" Eccles said.

"My hand is still holding the razor. I go to tuck and zip and I'm not even thinking about it."

"Thinking about what?" Eccles said.

"Not even thinking about it," Greep said.

"About what?" Eccles said.

"Slicing his dick," Schwartz said, trying to ruin it.

"I slice the head of my dick."

The men erupted. They howled and moaned and expressed disbelief in moans. Their noises came in three waves.

"It slices that distance. From my pee hole to the edge." Greep's fingers appeared before the camera, framed by the dark window. They measured a gap the length of a razor blade. "The perfect size. And let me tell you. Your dick don't wait around to bleed. I was standing up in a major fucking panic. This river is suddenly looking like an African sewer. My dick is swimming with sewage. It's trickling blood like it's got its own mind. I put my dick in my pants. My white boxers become red ones. There's this carnation of blood spreading everywhere. I zip up my jeans and try to forget about it. I scramble up the rocks. I almost break my leg. Then I'm back in the drugstore."

Laughter.

"The old man is a hundred and thirteen. The kid with the tits is ignoring her Pepsi. Then I realize there's still foam all over my face."

"Barbasol," J'Million said.

"I'm half shaved, there's no sign of blood, and I'm shouting 'Band-Aids.' Look like a total crazy person. The old man is holding a box of nicotine gum. The bitch on wheels is watching. They look at me and see no blood. But the codger sets down the box. I'm a regular now. The old man is tottering toward the aisles. I could find what I need myself. But I done forgot and set the codger in motion again. Relative term: motion. I decide I can't wait. I probably break his heart. I find the Band-Aids. I find a tube of Neosporin. I run to the front of the store. The old man serves me before the bitch on wheels. In a minute I tumble down the gorge again. I almost break my leg. Under the bridge I rip open my jeans. My shorts look like the Canadian flag. I look like a clubbed seal. I want to wash my dick off but not in the river. I wipe my dick with the pocket lining. I spread on the Neosporin. The blood and the Neosporin don't mix. Trying to put on the

Band-Aid is like trying to Scotch-tape pudding to the nose of a dog. I do my best. Then I finish shaving."

"Not with the Barbasol."

Static washed across the screen and the audio crackled into silence. An even field of snow filled the screen and then squeezed into snowy lines and what next materialized from them hit my sternum like a hard pitch. You might feel betrayed that I have constructed the memoir to depend for its climax on the revelation that as Eccles stood by grinning and watching, Duckworth had laid his massive frame atop the squirming and miserable body of the Iraqi girl Shamhat. You might want fifty-thousand words to culminate in more than the unsurprising moral putrefaction of an idiot and a wimp. By this point in history, good men corrupted by a bad war is not the freshest story in the repertoire. Would it help to know that it gets worse? That Eccles did more than stand by and watch? That the Cabbage Patch Kid lay on the floor within view? Since it happened not in a story but to me in the one life I've lived, and since I had carried with me throughout the year in Baghdad and even until then a kind of tenderness and hope and sympathy, a willingness to find love and decency even in men in their darkest hours, I was nauseated and transformed. On the tape Duckworth is bellowing in the intolerable ecstasy of an animal violating another in order to find brute relief. You see his bland face tense in orgasm above the flattened, childish, immaculate body. You see the crying eyes of the girl. You see the red yarn of the hair of the doll. After that moment Eccles ceases to be merely passive and spectatorial. It's more than I'm willing to describe.

Only now did I finally understand things that had remained unclear to me. The videotape clarified decisively the strangeness of the events of our captivity. Shiite militias were not in the habit of taking prisoners nor of executing them nor putting them up for ransom. They did not behead people. Those were the delights of al-Qaeda in Iraq and of Sunni henchmen who ravaged like stray dogs a country not so long ago run by a despotic master holding the leashes. Shiites on the other hand had principles and procedures and a dedication to something more than grisly effect. They certainly had a dedication to sexual purity. So of course the videotape drove them insane. They lost their senses. We had raped their girls, filmed it, and watched it. What did it matter that Shamhat was Sunni? That she had mingled with the soldiers under the sanction of her father? That money changed hands? The gang that tortured us tortured Eccles and Duckworth with especial madness because Eccles and Duckworth appeared on this tape.

"We're making a little something special for Breitbart to watch," Greep had said. Breitbart would know exactly who held the camera, but he would not be able to catch him. That was the point. Duckworth and Eccles would hang for Greep, and to Greep it did not matter. It was a trophy of his impunity, the impermeable armor of his cleverness. On the tape, what surrounded the pornography incriminated Greep, which was why he had not let me take the camera. There had been editing to do. Yet for the sake of the Shiites, for the ears of militiamen who did not know our voices, the editing did not matter. They had no way of connecting the voice from the monologue with the hand that filmed the sex with the face of the soldier who sat among the seven. So Eccles and Duckworth did not hang for Greep in the figurative way he had intended. They lost their heads for him in fact.

He had patronized them during their hours of great duress, as Eccles was losing Pat Mapp and Duckworth's puppies were getting nailed to walls, as tours were getting extended. Greep had bought tricks for them with a teenaged Iraqi prostitute, a girl all of three years older than a boy we played Rock Scissors Paper with, a winsome cherisher of a Cabbage Patch Kid. Greep had filmed what he filmed and condemned us to death. It explained J'Million's outrage on the drive to Babylon—he had seen it and known. He could have told me, would have told me if I had asked or even simply stopped refusing to listen. But I had been longing for something transcendent and meaningful in the ruins of Babylon. I had folded as a commander. I had traded the camera for Greep's cooperation. "I don't understood why you would let them hang," I yelled at him in my brain.

"They got off," he answered back. "They were into it."

"You don't feel bad about any of it."

"I feel terrible. I'm going to throw myself on my sword."

"You really were going to let Breitbart see this?"

"Why shoot it, otherwise? You think I like watching ugly dudes screw? When Breitbart saw that he would of blown fuses over his coleslaw for a century. He'd of seen it was me, but he couldn't of proved it. It was the point from the start. Whoever's behind the camera is invisible. And whoever's invisible is innocent. Unless he opens his stupid mouth."

A second time snow washed over the cracked screen. The old scene warped back into resolution, the abstract shapes and shadows of the bunker, Greep's monologue winding down. "So what happened?" Eccles was saying.

"I called Nerissa. She picked me up in front of the drugstore."

"You get the job?" J'Million said.

"The job was crap," Greep said.

"What about the pussy?" Schwartz said.

"Never again," Greep said. "It was the best lie I ever told."

"What lie?!" a chorus said.

"Idiots," Greep said. "You really think I'd cut my own dick?"

"You never cut your dick?" Schwartz said.

"So did you even date Nerissa?" Eccles said.

"Of course I dated Nerissa. Except her name was Tina. But that was what the lie was for. I wanted that job. And I couldn't stand her. So I came up with a good lie. A great lie. A story about cutting my dick. Tina picked me up at the drugstore. I said, 'We can't make love, baby, listen to what happened, you won't believe it.' And she believed it. With all those details? Nothing like a little fictional self-mutilation to get out of a sticky situation."

"So you didn't even get the job?" Schwartz said.

"So there wasn't even no Barbasol?" J'Million said.

THE WINNIE WILSON SHOW

It was not hard in the way Heather thought it'd be hard—she felt the words coming and knew she'd be OK. She didn't know this until this moment. Ten minutes ago in the greenroom, staring at donuts, avoiding the mirror, her brain went blank like a whiteboard fresh from the box. Perspiration had made a disaster of her lower back, soaking through the clothes from Nordstrom that an intern named Vanessa had helped her pick out yesterday. The sweat was a solution leaching every last word from her brain.

All her life, in the wrong situations, so in most situations, the cat got her tongue. "Cat got your tongue!" her grandmother used to say, and Heather always pictured the proverb graphically. She hated cats. Maybe she wrote poems just to rescue herself from the stupidity of flustered silences. But now, here, ten minutes after a horricular panic attack, in view of all America, all the anxiety was gone. She was sitting on the soundstage, glowing in angelic light, breathing weird air, and chatting with Winnie Wilson. She was not writing a poem in order to be heard. She had not written a poem and had written, instead, for the first time in her life, prose. Would Neil Dubuque forgive her from the hereafter? Television screens across America would soon be broadcasting her wisdom about prose. It was too outrageous to believe: so many eyes on her—her! The opening chitchat chilled her out, easy as anything. Then the real questions came.

"I understand you've decided to experiment with the form," Winnie said. "It would have been natural to write it in the first person, no? To tell your own story? Use your own voice? But you're not doing that, are you?"

"Five years ago I would have done that," Heather said. "Five years ago all I wrote was poetry, and it was only ever me me me."

"So now you're treating real people as fictional characters, including yourself. What changed?"

Was that how Heather would describe it? Was she treating herself as fictional? It didn't matter. Seth Rosenberg and Caleb Beck, as much as she hated to admit it, were right at least about this much: Winnie Wilson could think of things only in a certain narrow way. If you got this far, you had to go with it. You get famous with the talk-show host you have, not the talk-show host you might want or wish to have at a later time. "Everything changed," Heather said. The camera showed her in profile; she could tell by the blinking lights. She paused steadily, thought deeply—was at the height of her beauty, she knew she was!—more comfortable in her body than ever before in her life.

"Is this your story," Winnie said, "or John Townley's, or Antoine Greep's?"

"Yes," Heather said, "and yes and yes."

"In the excerpt we saw, you're quite hard on yourself," Winnie said. "Or hard on the character named Heather Kloppenberg."

"You call *that* being hard on myself?" Heather almost said. "I wouldn't say hard on myself," she said. "I'd say honest with myself."

"Does writing in the third person make it easier to be honest in that way?"

"I'm not sure."

"But you knew you had to do it?"

Heather studied her lap. After sleeplessness, after excitement, after panic, after relief, her mood changed yet again. She felt a little annoyed. She wanted to make herself clear to Winnie and the universe at large. She thought she knew what to say. She tried this: "At first I was writing out of anger. But I wasn't getting anywhere. And I knew I felt love for both of them. So I had to find a way to show it. But I couldn't have shown it if I wrote me me me page after page after page. That's how I began. When I was younger I thought that love was about putting myself in the right position in relation to somebody else."

"You're still young, honey."

"Now I see that love is about getting outside of myself."

"Do you have a title?"

"I have a working title."

"Will you share it with us?"

"No," Heather said. "It'd give too much away. Do you mind if I say hi to my mom and dad?"

"Not at all!"

Heather glanced at Winnie, then at the camera again. She listened to herself say hello to her parents. Her father, she had no doubt, would be in that living room in Shakopee, holding a glass of Crown Royal and grinning to the moon. John Jones would be there, and Beverly Henningfeld, cackling as though she'd shit. Shakopee was going nuts. Her mother would be clucking and nervous as a prairie dog. Heather wondered if John and Antoine were watching too—they had to be watching! She hadn't asked Winnie for permission to say hi to Tyler, but she heard herself saying hi to Tyler, too.

"Tyler?" Winnie asked, with raised eyebrows.

Heather blushed and smiled and turned her head happily away from the sightlines of the audience. "My editor," she said, which was true enough. Then an ad for trash bags came on.